WARNING SIGNS

SAFETY became elusive. Looming catastrophes could easily be seen. With big planes came big problems. With the world's biggest plane, problems grew to the size of Everest. Even so, in the midst of the chaos, what choice did the workers have other than; "Carry on." So they did.

Down in Flames

by

Neil Prior

ISBN-13: 978-0692384886
ISBN-10: 069238488X

For Irene: who liked the first revision and the twentieth

Chapter *1*

"HOW CAN WE HELP them if we're all dead?" Kylee McKenna asked, but no one replied.

The pushed-to-the-limit Bell jet helicopter skimmed the windswept mountains near Lake Tahoe, California. It was an hour after sunrise, but the sun was nowhere near. It was the third day of spring, but the winter storms were far from over. With every mile they flew, the clouds dipped a little lower, the temperature—a little colder. Kylee cranked up the heat, but it didn't help. She still shivered. She tried to pour coffee from her Thermos to her travel mug, but that didn't work. She spilled some onto her lap and most onto the floor. The turbulence would not let up.

The noise was aggravating; on the verge of intolerable. Overhead, the rotor pounded a steady rhythm. From behind, the 1400-hundred-horse turbine engine screamed like a 747. The cheap headset made every word a chore.

Kylee's husband, Evan, leaned back from the copilot seat and pushed the intercom mic to his lips. "We've got one storm coming and two more lined up. If we don't get them now, we never will."

"Slow down," Kylee told him. "We'll still get there."

"You're the nurse; you know that time is critical."

"It's been eight hours since the crash. If we're ten minutes late, it won't make a difference."

Evan flashed his 'whatever' look. He went back to studying the direction finder on his knees. He lifted the device to show Kylee but kept his eyes on the monitor. "This gave us a head start. The feds don't have it. Civil Air Patrol doesn't have it. In this weather, every minute counts." He faced right, tapped twice on Daz Donahue's shoulder, and pointed at a snow-capped ridge. "Keep your eyes sharp. We're closing in fast."

Daz nodded while listening to the radio chatter in the background. He turned down the volume then faced Evan. "Flight Service wants to know if we have survivors."

He winced slightly as last year's throat operation turned his frustrated voice into a growl. He massaged his chin and turned his face into a scowl. For Daz, the rough flight was literally a pain in the neck.

"Stand by," he called on the radio. "We're on the approach." He swiveled his head toward Kylee and aimed his thumb at her bag. "Grab your gear, hon. We got nothing but rocks and ice below."

"And three survivors, God willing." Kylee tightened the strap on her helmet, adjusted the visor, and tucked in strands of her shoulder length, honey blond hair. She ran a quick inventory of her custom-designed emergency pack; a flashlight, burn kit, trauma kit, frostbite kit, rock climbing kit, and three injectors for fentanyl. Satisfied with the contents, she closed her pack and zipped up the top of her sage green flight suit. She crammed her wedding ring into her purse, pushed her purse beneath the seat, and slipped on a pair of all-weather gloves.

"I've got the phone numbers," she told Daz.

"Phone numbers?"

"For the families. The media's going to be crawling over this. I want the families to find out first."

"Agreed," Daz said.

"Crossover; straight-ahead!" Evan pointed at the hills. "Look for anything orange."

"Orange?" Kylee raised an eyebrow.

"Mojave Air has a desert theme inside and out."

"The tail's orange and terracotta," Daz said. "The rest of the plane is—and I'm not kidding—snow white. Yeah, their planes look great on the tarmac, but in the mountains …"

Kylee gazed out the window. The queasy stomach and tingling spine were not just from the turbulent ride. Below them was a barren landscape of granite spires and glacial rocks that comprised a deadly trap—below the tree line and sixty miles from the nearest sign of civilization.

"We have crossover," Evan said.

Daz flew the chopper in a tight circle. "We got nothing. Not even close. Your machine's busted."

"We're directly above it." Evan shoved his monitor to the floor. "Open your eyes. They're down there somewhere."

"If they are, they got trouble." Daz slowed the speed to a hover.

"Circle the ridge. That storm dumped three feet of snow, but I guarantee we got 'em."

Daz zoomed in on the storm scope. "Better hope so. That squall line's closing in fast. We have thirty minutes—if we're lucky."

"Daz, you're the best pilot in the company. Wind and snow; that's all it is."

"I'm the oldest, you mean. And I didn't get this way by buttin' heads with God." He rapped his finger on the clock. "Twenty-nine and counting."

Blinding clouds of white powder swirled among the rotor downwash as Daz guided the helicopter to the windward side of the summit.

Kylee quickly became oblivious to the buffeting. She fixed her gaze on a blue gray monolith that resembled Half Dome of Yosemite. It was much smaller, of course, but in its own way, it was equally beautiful and challenging—especially in the midst of a storm. In the back of her mind, out of habit, she pictured a route from the base to the summit. With ten-point crampons and a good pair of boots, it would be a walk in the park. A shame she grabbed the flight suit instead of her down jacket. Too bad she left her climbing helmet at home. Another day perhaps.

She looked away, trying to keep her mind on the search. Then she looked up. Near the summit, a flash of orange caught her eye.

"There it is!" she said. "I see the tail."

"That wasn't there on the last pass," Evan said.

"Orange tail on a white bird," Daz said. "You nailed it. That's Mojave Air."

"Our downwash must've blown away the snow," Evan said. "It looks like they're in a drift. I'm guessing six, seven feet deep."

Daz kept the helicopter level with the aircraft but several lengths back. "Let's dust off another layer." He eased forward and up. The helicopter rumbled like an old Ford and crept closer to the fuselage of the downed plane. Flying snow cut the visibility to near zero, and turbulence pushed the rotor close to the granite.

"Back off." Evan tapped Daz's arm. He gestured at the ground behind them. "We're stirring up an avalanche. If that top layer cuts loose, we'll send them down the ravine."

Daz pulled back on the stick and put distance between them and the victims.

The downed single-engine, 1000-horsepower, Gibraltar-model plane rested precariously on an ice covered field that sloped downward at a gentle angle. Far behind, the hill became a ramp, then a steep downgrade, then a cliff. In every sense, it defined the classic slippery slope.

"Be careful," Kylee said. "One crash was bad enough for these guys. If we have to hike up, we'll do it. Whatever it takes."

Evan shook his head. "We can land *above* them and work our way down."

"All I meant was—"

"Hold on, you two. Would you look at that." Daz jockeyed the stick with one hand and pushed the mic to his lips with the other. He gazed at the mountainside in front. The clouds of swirling snow parted, revealing the incomplete outline of the downed Mojave plane. He began an itemized list; "Fuselage; totally intact. Right side; clean from this angle. Left; not a scratch or dent."

Evan went on. "The cowling is buried and likewise the cockpit."

Daz pointed at the wings. "Flaps extended, what, ten degrees? Even if they slowed for a crash, you're talking ninety at impact."

"But you have powder and soft pack; that's an airbag for what it's worth."

Kylee touched Evan's shoulder and aimed him slightly back. "There's a good sign."

"What?"

"The cabin door's open. That means you have survivors; someone strong enough to push the steps to the ground and walk out."

"But not strong enough to close it. In the middle of a blizzard, body heat is one personal effect you do not want to lose."

"Part of the door is buried," Kylee said. "Maybe it got jammed on a rock or froze to the ice."

"Anyway, you're spot-on; someone alive had to push open the door. That's encouraging." Evan scanned left and right. "Daz, how close can you land?"

"The only flat ground is the top of the ridge. I can't risk a touchdown, but I'll drop you low enough for a jump."

Evan looked back. "Watch out, Kylee; you've got five feet of powder." He gently touched the tip of her nose. "Try not to sink too deep."

"I ski this every winter. You're the one who hates the snow." Kylee grabbed the handle of the aft door and slid it to the rear stops. The wind scattered the loose papers and charts beside her. She ignored it and told Evan, "First me, then my pack. Then you and your pack."

"Roger." Evan yanked out the intercom wires to their helmets and waved a go-ahead.

Kylee took a deep breath and prepared to sink to her chin in the white powder of the Sierra Nevada. She let go of the door post and nervously rode the downdraft to the expected soft landing, spreading her arms as she dropped. But then came the ankle-twisting surprise as she hit solid ice, barely three feet below the skid. What little snow pack there was, was blown away by the force of the rotor. Kylee fell to her butt and threw a nasty look at her teammates. She massaged her ankle and regained her composure.

Evan grinned and tossed the equipment to her side. He followed it down.

After Daz flew the helicopter to a neighboring valley and landed, Kylee and Evan were at last able to speak without an intercom.

Kylee scanned the horizon and took in a deep Sierra breath. "Except for the cold, this would be an awesome hike."

Evan strapped the crampons onto his boots. "Yeah, well, I'll take sea level and a sailboat; no hills. And no ice—except in a rum and Coke."

For temporary distraction, Kylee averted the crashed plane. Instead, she gazed at a stand of white pine that was heavily laden with snow. She looked closer and spotted a sole Jeffrey pine poking out from the fresh powder. Four hundred years old, she guessed. A real survivor. She sighed, looking at her warm breath clouding up in front of her.

"Unfortunately, this wind's not going to help." Kylee shivered and knelt beside Evan to realign his crampons.

"I know what you're thinking, but this plane's VIP. That means you got hot coffee by the gallon and quilts that are heavy and thick."

"Then hypothermia is not our biggest problem. There's a good chance we'll find survivors."

"Maybe so," Evan said. "But where's the welcome wagon? You've got three souls on board; a pilot, co-pilot, and Fred. They must've heard us by now."

"One passenger and two crew." Kylee took cautious steps toward the wreckage. "I was going to ask before, but with the noise and us being rushed—"

"Ask what?"

She lowered her voice. "Daz said your father was supposed to be on the flight."

"Not quite." Evan stabbed his crampons into the ice and bypassed a rock. "He canceled like he was supposed to. You see, Dove Air has a policy; you can't have two executives on the same flight, especially the two founders. If the plane goes down and you lose 'em both, the company's crippled. It's bad news, for sure. But if you lose just one ... well, let's not talk about it."

"Except for Fred. You said it yourself; if you lose him, you lose the company."

"Perhaps." Evan wiped the pelting snow from his visor and studied the aircraft below. "But right now, don't think of it. For the next twenty-three minutes, that's our mission. That's where our minds have to be. Cross your fingers; we're looking for three alive."

"That's all I want."

Kylee shifted her pack. She carefully made her way across along a long, broken slab of ice that was brushed clear by the helicopter. She grumbled to herself about the irony of the whole situation. Today was supposed to be her day to confront Evan about their lack of time together. This afternoon was supposed to include a discussion of their recent—and misguided— priorities. Regrettably, Evan's sixty hours a week at work was a great way to build a company but a lousy way to build a marriage.

A few hours together was what Kylee wanted; a few hours at a restaurant, movie, ball game, or the Apple Valley mall. A walk in the woods, holding hands, or watching the sun set over the Victor Valley; Kylee was not a high-maintenance woman, but she did have some standards as to what a marriage should be. For the past year of their seven-year marriage, those modest standards had not been met.

A pity the only reason they were here was for the plane crash. A weekend or two like this—without the stress—would go a long way to easing her mind. A nice hike in the Sierras—without the pressure of a search and rescue—would be a nice route to happiness.

The wind picked up, and suddenly, her mind was back on the mission. She pushed aside her daydream and focused on aircraft in front of her. She eased across a last patch of snow and went to the right wing.

Evan, following behind, stumbled once but quickly caught up and moved ahead. As he circled the tail, he ran his hand along the rudder. "The front of the plane is buried, but this half is not bad. I've seen worse."

"I'll take your word on that." Kylee nodded. "I've never seen a plane crash before."

Walking side by side, they neared the open door. Then Evan held up his arm. "I'll look inside."

"You're the engineer, Evan. You check out the airframe. *I'll* look inside."

Kylee pushed, but Evan was faster. He scrambled to the stairway, propped his foot on the top step, and rested his hand on the door frame. He leaned in.

Kylee clambered for better position behind him, but despite her best efforts, Evan got the first impression.

As he raised his visor and looked forward, he immediately dropped his arm. His body wavered and his knees buckled. He spun unsteadily and plopped down on the ledge of the exit. His face turned an ashen white and only half-due to the Sierra snow that pummeled his cheeks.

"What is it?" Kylee frantically peered over his shoulder. She yanked a flashlight from her pack and squeezed in for a better view. She aimed the beam at the cockpit but quickly snapped off the light when it became clear that this was not a comforting sight. Retreating to the outside, she rested her hand on Evan's shoulder and took shallow breaths to stay on her feet.

"I worked in ER, but I never went to an accident. My heart goes out to the paramedics."

She slipped off her helmet and let it fall to the snow. Her hair fell across her hazel eyes like a veil, softening the image—the reality—of a crashed plane in the Sierras. The hope of a rescue suddenly faded, replaced by crushing waves of despair.

She removed her pack and set it inside. If not for the clock, Kylee would have sat on the steps and cried. Sobbing would have been so much easier. Instead, she checked her watch and slowly gathered her nerves. She eased into the cabin and raised her light to take in the worst of a bad situation.

"As bad as it looks, we still have a job; make the assessment and report back."

Kylee gazed at the pilot. He was flat on his back, but his body seemed frozen and tortured beyond recognition. His face and hands were burned to the third degree by searing, super-heated oil from the turbo engine. His left arm was severely outstretched, seemingly reaching for the exit. On his ring finger was the outline of a wedding band.

The body of the co-pilot had fared only slightly better, although most of his remains were hidden by his seat and the pushed-back engine. His face was also burned by spattering oil. Kylee cringed at the obtuse kink at the sixth vertebra.

"Broken neck," she said as she sat on the armrest. "At least he didn't suffer."

"Poor Fred; God help him if he's under that." Evan gawked at the engine that poked into the cockpit. He shook his head and exhaled a frosty cloud. He set his pack of tools on the floor with a dull clang. "Okay, I have to do this fast or I'll pass out. As long as I stay moving, I'll be fine. I'll get them out before you know it."

"Not our job, Evan. We're done here. You know what they said."

"The Safety Board? Find survivors, but leave the plane and bodies intact."

"Yes; for the report."

"In good weather, yeah, I might agree. But with these storms coming in, our next break is mid-April. For once, do what your gut tells you. Let's get these guys home while we still have a chance."

Kylee shrugged. In her heart, she agreed. A small violation with the National Transportation and Safety Board—the NTSB—seemed a mere technicality. In this situation, the Board would surely understand. Getting the victims home was a simple extension of Kylee's job; an effort to be welcomed by the victims' families.

For now, she set aside her toe-the-line instincts. She helped Evan spread apart his tool assortment; bolt cutters, pliers, hand jack, and hand axe. She tossed her now-useless pack to the snow beyond the cabin door and then plopped onto a seat. Already, she felt exhausted.

"For a while, I thought—I hoped—we had something. I mean, you can't tell from the outside; the plane looks fine."

"Question is," Evan said, "what were they doing here in the first place?"

"That last storm must've hit them hard."

"Can't see how." Evan pointed at different sections of the plane. "You have no ice on the wings. Probably no ice on the prop. The wheels are up, and the flaps are down, but ..."

"But what?"

"That's not the strange part." He motioned at the neighboring mountain. "They should've been coming in from that direction.

It's possible that the plane could've spun around at impact. But if it didn't, then for sure they were off course."

"Or circling to land."

"A mountain landing at night? No way." Evan continued to sort his tools.

"So what happened?"

He shrugged. "Who knows. But five feet to the left or right, and they might've survived. One rock in the middle of nowhere and they had to find it."

Kylee stared at the aircraft engine, slowly moving her light across pockets of oil-spattered wreckage. She paused when the realization struck her. "Darling, I think the fumes are getting to us."

"It's not the fumes that are making me ill." Evan slid off his helmet and set it by the door. He ran his fingers through his sandy blond hair.

"Where's Fred?"

"What do you mean?"

"You know—Fred Mott—the third victim, the CTO of the company you work for. He was supposed to be on the plane. Where is he?"

"I hate to say it, but he's under that." Evan waved at the huge engine. He grabbed the flashlight from Kylee's hand and swung the beam forward. He slowly scanned it.

With a closer look, Kylee saw no sign of a third victim; no foot, no hand, no hint of someone trapped beneath the engine. Then she focused on the midsection and rear. The damage in that part of the plane was much less severe, and there was no chance of overlooking a body there.

"He's not here and not at home," Evan said. "I don't know where he is."

"Then who opened the door?"

"Good point."

They poked their heads out the exit and carefully surveyed the ground for footprints and the landscape for a survivor. The only noise came from the wind whistling through the fuselage and the low rumble of the helicopter beyond the next ridge. The only visible sign of humanity existed within the confines of the aircraft.

"Fred was never on the plane." Evan grabbed his pack and eased down the steps. To prove his point, he took a pry bar and forced open the baggage compartment. "You see; no luggage and no briefcase *anywhere* on the plane."

"Something doesn't add up."

Evan slammed the baggage door closed and jammed his helmet back onto his head. He pushed the hair out of his eyes and pushed down on the visor. He stared at a darkening gray sky. "The front's moving in, and we have to move out. I'll work on the pilot, and you talk to Daz."

"Yeah, thanks."

While Evan squeezed himself and his tools up to the cockpit to begin the extrication, Kylee yanked off her gloves and pulled a handie talkie from her Velcro pocket. She arranged for a discouraging pickup.

"Bad news, Daz," she softly called over the radio. "We couldn't see it for the snow, but the damage was total."

"What are you saying?"

"Regrettably, no survivors. Evan's working to get them out. But we'll need two sleeping bags."

"Understood."

"Even if we got here last night, it would've been too late."

"Sorry to hear it," Daz said. "And sorry to say it, but don't you need *three* body bags?"

"No, we only found two victims. Apparently, Fred was not on the plane."

"Better double-check that, hon. I got confirmation that Fred was definitely on board."

"We'll get back to you."

This was not a complicated recovery mission. There were simply too few places to hide a victim. So far, the body count remained a solid two. With time running out, Kylee was not in the mood for a debate. She returned to help Evan.

With both strength and finesse, Evan—after a few scraped knuckles and bumps on his elbow—was able to extract the pilot without seriously disrespecting the integrity of the body. He and Kylee easily moved the victim down the steps and onto the snow.

Kylee carefully rearranged the pilot's separated shoulder and arm. "This part of the job, I hate."

"We all volunteered," Evan said. "Not that it makes a difference. Let's just get it over with. Let's get them and us back home."

The pounding noise and blinding snow returned as Daz dropped off the improvised body bags.

Kylee slipped on her helmet then counted the supplies. "I said *two* bags!" she yelled over the radio.

"You'll need three. And I had to lean halfway to Sunday to get the third. How about a little thanks?"

Kylee grumbled her appreciation and set upon her task. While Daz hovered overhead, whipping up more snow and ice, she and Evan enclosed the pilot in the nylon bag. She snapped the hoist cable to the bag and sent Daz off to his parking spot on the neighboring ridge. Daz would load the deceased pilot on board.

As Evan searched his pack for a hack saw, Kylee picked up the pliers that had fallen by the wing. She glanced at the snow by her boot. "Okay, who's bleeding?" She checked her hands and jacket.

Evan picked up his gloves. He walked over and kicked at the nickel-sized, red spots that dotted a group of footprints. "Not mine."

"Are you sure?" Kylee checked his face and hands. "You could've cut yourself on a cable."

Evan shrugged then disappeared inside. "It was probably the pilot's. But listen, we got a situation here." His voice became muffled as he crawled up the fuselage and banged the pry bar against loose metal.

Kylee slipped on her gloves. She studied the ground. "I'll tell you this; dead bodies don't bleed. At least not this way."

She kicked around the snowpack and uncovered more red spots. A few more kicks, and her heart began to race. Fumbling her gloved fingers, she pressed the button on her radio mic. "Daz, I think I found Fred."

"Alive?"

"I hope so." She uncovered enough of the spots to define a straight line. Then she grabbed her climbing gear and medical supplies. As she looked down at the blood, she realized that it was not a life threatening condition; minimal bleeding from someone able to walk. Hopefully, the survivor was still healthy and still able to walk.

Her fleeting optimism immediately passed. Kylee looked ahead and shuddered. The intensely cold weather was still a concern, especially in this Siberia of the West. To be thorough with her assignment, she picked up a body bag then moved ahead.

Quickly, the trail led to a snow blown ridge. Kylee eased her way around large slabs of bluish pink granite. Visibility dropped, but she continued forward. She distanced herself from the edge of the cliff and began a systematic search of the ragged boulders, looking for anything that hinted of shelter.

"Fred!" she called in a loud and clear voice. No response. She climbed a rock and yelled again, her voice to the point of straining. She stepped behind a rock, out of the wind, and listened for any sign of humanity other than the incessant pounding of Evan's makeshift hammer. She called again, listened again, but heard nothing. Only then—when she was certain that her cries would not be answered—she stepped to the ledge.

A harsh wind blew across her visor and burned her eyes. Her ski goggles would've been so much nicer, but she saved her complaints for later. Kylee blinked until she could see clearly enough to move ahead. Then she carefully peeked over the ledge toward the rock-strewn floor. Now her curiosity took hold.

There it was, halfway to the floor; a shiny metal object protruding from, or stuck between, a large crack in the granite wall. Whatever it was, it was definitely man-made and not a fragment of the wrecked plane.

"I got something," she called over the radio.

"You found Fred!" Daz gave a raspy cheer.

"Not quite. But I'll check it out."

"Be more specific. Exactly what do you have?"

"I'll let you know when I get there. Give me five minutes to rappel, another ten to climb out."

"I need you here," Evan said. "This seat's not gonna budge unless we're both behind it."

"Just let me do this."

"Look around. You think this storm's gonna wait? You said it yourself; we don't need three more victims."

Kylee ignored her husband. Instead, she set down her pack and withdrew her climbing rope. She looked around and found a rock to secure her cam. With a smooth motion, she tossed the doubled-up length over the side. She checked her hooks and harness for a quick descent to the mysterious object. Technically, it was a straightforward operation—much easier than her climb up The Nose of El Capitan last October. Before long, she was at the object's side.

She immediately recognized it as an aluminum carrying case about the size of carry-on luggage. Kylee didn't know how it got there or why, but she knew that it was somehow important, somehow related to the crash. She had to retrieve it. She tugged on the handle, but the case didn't budge. Undeterred, she tied a clove hitch around the handle. She braced her feet against the granite then tugged with all her strength. To her surprise, the case jumped free with a sharp metallic squeal.

She swung to mid-air, losing her grip on the handle. The case flew around her body like an out-of-control missile. She squirmed to avoid the entangling rope and watched as the case flew by her feet and smashed onto the rocks. Suddenly, the entire contents spilled to the wind and snow.

Like bats from a cavern, out flew a steady stream of bills—and not those end of the month power and gas bills, but fifty- and hundred-dollar notes. At least that was what Kylee guessed because she couldn't recall which was Grant and which was Franklin. Loose cash and packets of bills; she couldn't believe her eyes. She had never seen anything like it.

She hung in place, transfixed by the sheer magnitude of cash that sailed past her face and into oblivion. One way or another, that much money meant a whole lot of trouble for anyone involved.

"You wouldn't believe what I just saw," she called on the radio.

"Kylee, you know you don't climb without a partner," Daz said as he flew overhead.

"Once in a while we improvise. Every rule has the exception."

"Let me tell you another rule. This storm's dropping the ceiling. If that pass gets covered, we spend the night in a white-out. My rule is; I don't risk my life for any deceased. Now, unless you got Fred sipping tea right next to you, I suggest you climb out and get on board. Bus leaves in five minutes!"

"Roger," she told him on mic, still dazed. "No patience," she muttered after keying out.

She took a long look at the bills that fluttered down the cliffside. She wondered what it meant. But it was too cold, and there was too much stress to think about it now. Perhaps Daz had a point. Perhaps the only rational choice was to call it the end of a sad day and fly home to the warm weather.

She wiped the snow from her visor and looked down. She squinted then stared at the sobering outline of what appeared to be a black leather shoe in the rubble below. It was easy to spot for Kylee; a manmade object isolated by the stark wilderness. Was it litter or something more ominous? Her gut told her that beneath the snow, there was a body attached to the shoe.

She released the knot that held the metal case then let it fall to the ground. Her mission now; confirm or deny the existence of a third victim. After a quick rappel to the granite floor, she stood with plenty of rope at her feet.

Her pounding heart slowed to a whisper. There was no need to push away the drift of snow that had formed near a fine, Italian loafer. The shape was all too clear. In a single breath, Kylee became oblivious to the bone-chilling cold. Instinctively and compassionately, she knelt beside the form. She removed her gloves and gently brushed the icy veil from a terrified face of Fred Mott.

Death by trauma, she surmised. But how horrible it must have been to have survived the first impact—the plane crash—and not only survive but come out with barely a cut and bruise. Then he was taken down by one hapless misstep in the middle of the night.

Kylee stared at his ice spattered face, but something about it frightened her. She faced away, but that didn't help. Fred's eyes—still open, now haunting—seemed to stare at her no matter how she turned. She closed her eyes, but like a widescreen disaster movie, she couldn't help but see one terror after another.

In a jumble of images, she pictured the faces of Fred, the pilot, and co-pilot; first as the crisis struck them, then as they and their plane descended to a dark, icy wasteland. She saw the plane hit the mountain, and she saw a burning, crushing engine slice through the cockpit. She saw the pilot as he reached in vain for Kylee's help. She saw Fred, stumbling out the door, clutching his case—for whatever reason—then staggering across the snow and ice. Her mind burned with the image of Fred's horrified face as he took that final fall to a sudden death.

Kylee became terrified herself; motionless, nearly freezing in fear. But as a bone chilling gust of wind jarred her, she shivered and slowly opened her eyes to the rocks and snow around her. Her visions dissolved.

"Two for pickup," she called in a subdued voice. "One DOA."

"Roger … On my way."

Despite the intense cold and her numb fingers, Kylee shortly had Fred wrapped in a body bag. From then on, it was a straightforward task to coordinate with Daz and raise Fred to the chopper. Daz flew to the next ridge to load the body.

Shortly, he returned to raise Kylee with the same hoist and cable. Once on board, Kylee managed the details. She shuffled backboards and oxygen tanks in the rear of the chopper then struggled to stow Fred. Her mission was nearly accomplished.

"It's never routine." She plopped on the rear seat and buckled up. "My only solace is a soft bed at home. After this, that's the one comfort I want."

"Hey guys, how about some help down here?" Evan's voice crackled over the receiver.

"Sorry, bud. Your meter's expired. The main pass just shut down, and I barely got fuel for the alternate. I'm dropping a line and pulling you out. We're plum out of choices."

"What, and leave the co-pilot? It's bad enough to die here. I am not going to leave him to rot."

Kylee clicked on her mic. "At nine thousand feet, that's not going to happen."

"I've got a plan!" Evan shot back.

"You've been banging for a half-hour. You're no closer now than—"

"This engine didn't keep anyone warm. He's all stiff like the pilot but doubled over. There's no way I can get him over the seat. But ..."

Kylee stared at the downed plane for any sign of Evan or the co-pilot. Suddenly, Evan's head popped through the packed snow about where the engine used to be.

"We're going through the front window." Evan used his hands to articulate his plan, but Kylee didn't understand his wild gestures.

Evan smashed the acrylic window with his axe. "I cut his harness and wrapped it around his chest. All you gotta do is lower the hook through the windshield and pull us out."

Kylee lowered her head. "Evan's gone mad. I swear; he's lost it."

"Let's go! Let's go!" He waved them in.

Daz reluctantly obliged. He hovered the helicopter above the wreckage. Visibility dropped as the blowing snow picked up.

Kylee slid the rear door open and took hold of the hoist controls. "Can't see the ground," she said as she continued to lower the cable. "Can't see the plane."

Daz struggled but kept a near-steady hover. He nodded at the floor. "They're right below us. Keep watching."

"It's starting to clear." Kylee had to blink twice to believe what she was seeing.

But there it was on the hard-packed snow; the stark white outline of a perfectly formed Gibraltar airplane. Everything seemed intact except for the missing engine. And technically, that section wasn't missing at all. The entire cowling was simply pushed back to the cockpit, much like a turtle hiding its head in the shell. It was a fatal outcome to an odd situation. Kylee felt her sadness return. Then a turn for the worse.

"I see flames," Evan said in a much too calm voice. "Behind the compressor."

"Say again?"

"Whatever you do, don't back away. The rotor's beating down the flames, but not for long. We better move fast."

Kylee saw black smoke pour from the exit. "Don't do it, Evan!" She frantically beckoned him up. "Don't risk your life for a dead body. Save yourself. The whole plane's gonna blow!"

"I got the harness latched!" Evan said. "Small problem with the foot."

"What happened?" Kylee turned to Daz.

"Static charge," he said. "With this dry air, you gotta drag the cable first. Otherwise, you get sparks where you don't want them."

"Sorry."

"My fault. I should've warned you."

Kylee leaned out the door and yelled, "For the love of God, Evan, get out before you kill us all!"

No reply, but something odd was happening below.

"What was that?" Daz said when the helicopter took a precarious dip.

"Can't tell for sure." Kylee squinted at the taut rescue cable. "Oh no, don't tell me."

"What is it?"

"The plane's slipping, and we're tied to them! Evan, get out of there now!"

Daz swung his head and glared at Kylee. "That plane slides over the edge and we're still latched …"

"Evan, cut him loose. We're all going down!"

Finally, Evan seemed to listen. He called back, "Crank up the hoist. Get me out!"

The helicopter jerked back as the plane slipped under the force of the rotor. There was another snag, billowing smoke, and a nerve-wracking shudder. Then, miraculously, Evan and the co-pilot popped through the cowling like a cork from a wine bottle. They were finally free.

The wrecked plane gathered speed and momentum as it slid backward along the steepening ravine. Daz swung the helicopter, and Kylee got the full view of the action.

The plane slid along the snow until the wings sheared off on a boulder. Then fuel fed the flames into a huge orange fireball that lit up the overcast sky with an eerie glow. Kylee felt the heat on her face. The snow on her visor melted in large drops. She watched the explosion quickly destroy the remaining fragments of the plane.

As soon as she could, she cranked the winch cable until the high-risk cargo was aboard. That included Evan and one deceased Mojave Air co-pilot.

Daz flew a final circle around the burning plane. Then as quickly as they had arrived, he guided the helicopter through the alternate pass and set a track to the South Tahoe airport.

Kylee stowed the last victim in the rear of the helicopter. Then she collapsed onto her seat, totally spent; physically and emotionally. With a sad shake of her head, she stared at the distant black smoke. "And how do we explain this?"

Chapter *2*

"THIS ONLY ADDS to the rumors." Russell Torello cornered Evan in the Cottonwood Building break room. He gazed out the window at the 1200-acre Dove Air facility in Apple Valley, California. He grabbed a Styrofoam cup and poured himself a Kona.

Evan did the same. He slipped a dollar into the vending machine and selected a package of powdered donuts. "What rumors?"

"Everyone knows it. They're just afraid to ask." Russell sipped his coffee, burned his tongue, and wiped his chin. "Except me, the only one with a backbone." He swung his gaze inwards toward the wide expanse of cubicles. Like prairie dogs on the plain, the other engineers ducked out of sight.

It was hard to believe that this round-about-the-belly, hairline-to-the-summit man was their self-appointed leader, but Evan, on this dismal Monday morning, was glad to hear an honest, working man's opinion. Two days since the recovery, and he was all talked out about Fred, and the Mojave Air crew, and the Sierra crash. A change of pace would suit him fine.

"What rumors?" he asked again.

Russell, a fast and close talker, seemed excessively—and perhaps reasonably—agitated this morning. He spoke faster, stood closer, and waved his free hand. "The usual," he said, lisping from his burnt tongue. "Small layoff to start. Total shutdown later."

"Really?"

"We've had no sales for two years, and we're dripping with red ink." Russell tugged at his belt and tucked in his striped, blue shirt. "On Friday, the company founder dies. Today, the stock price drops. We're prime for a takeover. Don't get me wrong; we all liked Fred. What happened was horrible. But regardless, we know what happens next; reorganization, consolidation, unemployment."

Evan calmly stirred his coffee. He backed off a step, but Russell followed. "You know my father. You know his motto; no layoff, sellout, or shutting down. Treat Dove Air like you treat your family. It'll be rough, but hey, we'll make it."

"Last year, we might have believed it. But look on the floor; those guys, I'll tell ya, they're scared. Fred's death is going to kill the company. That's what they're saying. And your father ..."

"What about him?"

"Two heart attacks, then his wife—your mother—died. Bad enough, I understand. But to run this place you gotta be healthy. We thought that maybe you would ..."

"What, take over the asylum?" Evan grinned. "Yeah, someday, when we're desperate. But now, we're not close to desperate. We're going to miss Fred; that's a given. But we have ten thousand workers to finish what he started. The one advantage we have is momentum. In the long run; one man—including Fred—will not make a difference. That's straight from the management handbook."

Russell shifted his eyes and shuffled his feet. He popped open his sticky bun package and bit into the pastry. "Question is; do we have enough momentum to last a year and a half? Because there's your dad's schedule," he set his pastry on the counter and moved his hands close together, "and there's reality." He spread his hands far apart.

Evan motioned with his half-full cup of coffee. "You haven't been to Hanger 63 for a while, have you?"

"The hanger?"

Evan tapped him on the shoulder. "Come on, let's walk."

Russell seemed confused but nevertheless held onto his sticky bun. He picked up his coffee and followed Evan to a company golf cart. They drove through a maze of back alleys and cactus lined paths, ultimately stopping at an access door of the main assembly hanger.

They entered a dusty, musty hallway that was lined with photographs of old and new company aircraft. Evan straightened a frame as he walked by. "These pictures belong in the main lobby. Not back here. People lose track of where we came from."

He ran his hand across a fading color photo of his father—Paul McKenna—and Fred in Air Force uniforms. He stepped down the hallway and tapped his finger on key photos; a Dove Air business jet over Mount Whitney, a cargo jet over Denali National Park, and single-engine plane flying low over the coast of Spain.

"This is where you came in, right?" he asked Russell.

"Gibraltar—my first real job, five years ago. I designed the black box and aileron servo." Russell moved to the next photo and jabbed his finger on a photo of a sleek 200-passenger jet skimming the mountains of Northern California. "Shasta—my second job."

Evan nodded. "We proved that we could do it—despite the rumors of layoffs and shutdowns. Eight hundred shipments, and we're on par with the big boys. That's part of our momentum." He prodded Russell along the hallway. "But that was then, and this is now."

He pushed on a set of double-doors that opened to the five-acre final assembly hanger. Like walking into a nighttime World Series game, the bright lights and loud noise seemed to overwhelm Russell. Of course, in this case, the noise was the piercing shrill of a dozen air wrenches and powerful, lifting hydraulics. Dozens of kilowatt lights beamed down on a white composite skin of a huge, four-engine, wide-body jet.

Evan wrapped his arm around Russell's shoulder and nudged him closer to the frenetic—but well orchestrated—choreography of men, women, and machines.

"That banner only tells half the story." Evan aimed him at the display that hung over the fuselage; Everest—The World's Biggest Airliner Making the World Smaller.

"This jet is going to put Dove on top."

"It's been a while," Russell said. "All I saw was a shell."

"I thought so." Evan grabbed a tan hard hat that matched the color of his hair. He passed a black hat to Russell. "Look around, Russell. There's no layoff here. No way."

He led him to a chained-off area four stories beneath the tail antenna of the mammoth jet then waited for a break in the near-constant noise. He told Russell, "When you get back to your cube, drag your friends here. Show them what I'm showing you. You tell them they should have one thing on their minds; build this plane! Forget NASDAQ. Forget the news. Just get Everest off the ground. Got it?"

Evan leaned closer when a forklift passed by. "Tell me your first impressions."

Russell's jaw automatically dropped as he stared up. "Big."

Evan slapped him on the back. "That's why you're engineering. Marketing, though—we'll cover the highlights … And here's what we got … We've got two decks for six hundred passengers; coach to First Class. Of course, in my opinion, it's all First Class. We don't make anything else.

"Now, if you're military, you can take out the seats and put in three army tanks … plus the crew … plus the fuel. Or if you want to party, we can deliver a half-million Chicago pizzas; anywhere in the world. Fresh or frozen; we'll get it there fast."

Evan continued to walk, wave, and point. "At forty thousand, we'll be above the weather. That means a smooth ride. Regrettably, we took out the casino and bar, but the airlines told us they want seats. More seats, more passengers, more tickets."

"More profit," Russell said.

"That's what the buyers want. Personally, I see the technology. And I'll tell you this; when we do take over the market, it'll be the engineering that drives us there."

"That's where I can help." Russell held his hat and pointed at the cockpit window. "We've got no-distortion radios, no-glitch computers, and navigation that never gets lost."

"Leave the marketing hype to me, Russell. You and I both know that we have issues ahead. This is only step one of a twelve-step program."

"First recognize you have a problem."

Evan turned his head. "Yeah, and wouldn't you know, here comes step two."

"John Waterman," Russell said. "I haven't seen him in ages. He looks pretty good with a few more pounds."

Evan gave a second glance at Waterman, trying to see him from a working man's point of view. At six foot two, John was slightly taller than Evan. At thirty-six years, slightly older. In a Bill Blass suit, he was better dressed. With graying hair and a mustache, he seemed more distinguished.

Waterman had the appearance of an executive. Maybe that was why he was VP of sales and marketing. Of course, appearances could only carry someone so far. With sales thin and Waterman not, Evan wondered; what exactly did he do beyond shuffling papers and snacking on *pâté maison*?

As Waterman neared, Evan extended his hand.

Waterman took it, shook it, and released his grip. He also apparently failed to notice Russell's own extended hand or Russell himself for that matter.

"You know Russell Torello?" Evan asked.

"Of course." Waterman kept his gaze on Evan. "I must've been the last to speak to Fred. Friday night by the battery station. Fred sat me down for a lecture on risk analysis. We disagreed, but you have to give him credit; despite his age, he was still sharp."

"Risk analysis, yeah; I did that in Vegas. But Fred knew what he was doing. He said that building Everest—or any plane—is a balancing act."

"How so?" Russell asked.

"If we move too slowly, we lose orders; that's competition. Move too fast, and the plane's unsafe; there's a good chance of a crash."

Waterman cringed. "With over a million pounds of metal and fuel, that's one nasty crash."

"Not to mention six hundred passengers," Russell said.

"One hint of trouble," Evan said, "we shut down the plant. No one in his right mind will buy an unsafe airplane."

"So the balance," Russell said, motioning with his hands, "is between crashing and delivering late."

"Now you're thinking like a manager."

Waterman rolled his eyes and tugged at his red Fendi tie. He abruptly turned and called out to some mutt of a dog scrounging in the corner by an acetylene torch. "Coco!" he yelled. "Get away from that tank."

With barely a nod to excuse himself, Waterman chased the dog. He corralled him and disappeared to his previous assignment, whatever it was.

Russell and Evan plopped onto a cabinet for a clear, out of the way view of the technicians, fabricators, and engineers who crawled over the wings and fuselage.

"Coco," Russell said. "What's a dog doing here?"

"Waterman's little joke. Officially, he's the company mascot; named Coco after his big brown ears."

"His ears are pitch black." Russell laughed.

"You're not the first to notice. Unofficially, he's Coco; short for 'co-pilot.' It seems your new computer makes the co-pilot about as useful as a lap dog. That little white mutt, according to Waterman, can sit in the right seat and Everest will fly just fine."

"So much for the pilots' union."

"If I had my way—" Evan paused when his phone beeped with a text message. He looked at it and moaned. "Round one; the feds. I now have a three o'clock meeting."

"Friday's crash," Russell said.

"The first interrogation."

"Well, good luck."

"Yeah, they got the song. I've got the dance."

***

It was mid-afternoon when Evan met up again with Daz and Kylee. They hastily prepared a strategy for their first official meeting with the National Transportation and Safety Board.

As they walked to the conference room, Evan told Kylee, "Be truthful. Answer their questions. But don't speculate and don't volunteer more than what they ask. And whatever you do; do not talk about the money."

"Evan, I saw a half-million dollars fly out of that case. I can't believe there's no connection to the crash. Honestly, what was Fred doing with that money in the first place?"

"Well, we believe you saw something," Daz mumbled.

"What's that supposed to mean?" Kylee poked his ribs.

"It was windy. It was cold. Your eyes were tearing up."

"I did not make a mistake. I know what I saw."

Evan looked at her. "You said the guy on the bills looked like Davy Crockett."

"How would I know who's on a hundred-dollar bill? I've never seen a bill over fifty."

"You could've picked one up."

"Excuse me if I had a job to do."

"Besides that, no one deals in cash anymore. Everything's online or wire transfer."

Kylee nodded. "I know. I've seen you pay for a candy bar with your debit card. Nevertheless, I am telling you what I saw. A case this big," she used her hands to show the dimensions, "should hold a half-million. I checked it out."

Evan checked his watch. "Nevertheless, stay calm and follow my lead. If we stay cool, this will be over before we know it."

Kylee sighed.

Evan saw one of his father's admins by a conference room door and assumed she was the escort for the Safety Board visitors. "Is this the place?" he asked her.

"They're ready," the admin replied. "I'll wait here until you finish."

Evan glanced through the room window. Two young, heavy set government agents in well-worn suits were already set up with an aeronautical map. They motioned for the Dove group to enter.

After the polite greetings, Investigators Chapp and Ward offered coffee and comfortable chairs. Daz, Evan, and Kylee declined the coffee, but Ward picked a paper cup from a stack and helped himself.

"Let's get started." Chapp settled in his chair at the conference table. No smiles, barely a warm handshake. They also had a job to do and moved the agenda quickly.

"Tight quarters," Ward said as he squeezed his way to the table. He set down his coffee, ripped open a packet of sweetener, and poured it in. He remained standing. "So far, we don't know a lot. We met with ATC—"

"Air Traffic Control," Evan said to Kylee.

"Yes," Ward said. "We received their report this morning. And I'll summarize." He stirred the sweetener, leaned over his map, and smoothed the folds. He jabbed his finger and carefully slid it. "From here to here, the flight's on track. They start dropping here … radar loses it … and this is where they impact. About thirty miles difference."

"At their speed," Evan said, "that would be about fifteen minutes."

"Correct. And for fifteen minutes, there was no communication with Center."

"Okay."

Chapp lifted an operating handbook and flipped to a page. "I understand Gibraltar has a black box."

"Not required," Evan said. "But on the early models, we made it standard. It's old Euro style."

Chapp closed the book. "That means you lose data after a crash."

"After a few hours, yes; we lose some data. But for *every* flight—crash or not—we capture data and analyze it. We see trends develop before it escalates to a crisis."

"It's a safer way to design a plane," Daz said.

"So you say," Ward said.

Evan raised his voice. "The Gibraltar has an excellent safety record. No other plane comes close."

"Nowadays perhaps. However, when you first started—"

"We had one minor fault with the engine, and that was it. Production was never an issue. That's been established. Now, if you really want to check out Friday's crash, check out the crew. They flew eight hours a day for the past two weeks. If that's not pilot fatigue, I don't know what is."

"It's on our list," Chapp said, "but that's not why we're here."

"Go on," Evan said.

"I read your prelim, but we're shy a few numbers."

"Such as …?"

Chapp put the handbook into his briefcase and brought out a notebook. He went to the third page. He appeared to be refreshing his memory.

"I fail to comprehend." He closed the notebook and leaned forward in his chair. "How is it that you were first on the scene? We had Mountain Rescue and the Civil Air Patrol; five planes and helicopters. Yet somehow you got there first. What kind of luck is that?"

"You read the report," Evan said. "I thought I was clear."

"I prefer face to face. It's been a couple days; it might be easier to fill in the gaps."

"As far as I'm concerned, the report stands as written." Evan took a deep breath and spoke his mind. "On Friday night, we got the news; the charter was late and may have gone down. So I called Daz and went over a plan. We got ready. Actually, Daz, Kylee, and I got ready for a fast trip.

"As it turned out, we got a break in the weather and got moving. It was red line the whole way. Sure enough, we got there before the clouds moved in and boxed you guys out. Point is; we knew exactly where to go. Remember; our job is to build planes. We've got the equipment to find a locator—even if it's buried in a cave. If you don't believe it, I'll get Russell with his schematics. He'll be glad to show you how."

"No need," Ward said. "But this is a high-profile case, and we will be watched. If we don't follow the book—"

"It's too late for that." Chapp fumbled through his briefcase. He stood and placed a Gibraltar aircraft photo at the center of the table. "Allow me to summarize … Here we have the top-selling Dove plane, not including jets. It's your one bright light in a dismal market."

"The market is rebounding," Evan said.

"May I finish?" Chapp picked up his photo and waved it. "We have this high-performance, complex aircraft go down in the middle of nowhere. The same company that makes the plane also arrives first at the site. Oh, and by the way, during the rescue attempt, the entire plane is burned and destroyed. Did I miss anything?"

"That's exactly what happened," Evan said.

"And the reason for the crash?"

Daz spoke up. "Crew fatigue; like Evan said. They simply dogged themselves into a crash. They set the autopilot wrong or fell asleep at the wheel."

"Carbon monoxide?" Ward asked.

"Can't happen." Evan shook his head.

Chapp collected his charts and photos. "I've never seen a perfect system. Sooner or later it's bound to break." He looked over his glasses at Evan. "Sooner or later every plane falls from the sky."

"What will the official report say?" Daz asked.

"We may not know for months," Chapp replied.

"What will you tell the press tonight?" Evan asked.

"Same story; the accident remains under investigation. Cause unknown. We are looking into all possibilities."

"Including crew fatigue," Daz said.

"Including crew fatigue."

Kylee never did find the right moment to share her discovery of the money. "Those guys were sharks," she whispered when they were far down the hallway.

"Just doing their job," Evan replied. "Can't say I'd do it much different."

"At least we got the bodies out for them. That'll help."

"How's that?"

"The autopsy will tell us if carbon monoxide was the cause."

"I suppose, figuratively, we'll hold our breath on that."

"So is it true?" she asked, tugging at Evan's sleeve.

"Is what true?"

"What Chapp said; every plane crashes."

Evan took a deep breath. "Yeah, it's true; even for Everest. But if losing three men is a tragedy, what do you call it when six hundred passengers head for the ground?"

Chapter *3*

"YOU WANTED to see me?" Evan leaned his head through the open door of his father's office.

Paul McKenna looked up from a stack of papers. He made a small motion with his hand and leaned back in his chair. "Come in, shut the door."

"First tell me; good news or bad?" Evan shuddered. All it took was a glance, and he had answered his own question.

The drawn blinds leaked streaks of harsh light across Paul's creased and tired face. His red eyes glowed from too many numbers or not enough sleep. His body slumped. He had dropped nearly a hundred pounds after his last heart attack, and the skin hung on his chin like a pelican's pouch. He seemed twenty pounds on the lighter side of gaunt. His thinning, gray hair begged for a decent combing. No man who looked like that ever had good news.

"We got problems," Paul said. "Fred's dying only made it worse."

"That's understandable, and everyone on the floor knows that. From what I've seen, they're half-sad, half-scared. They appreciate what you're going through, but crisis or not, you gotta talk to 'em. Two days and we haven't seen you. That's not healthy—for you or the company."

"Sit."

Evan closed the door behind and sat.

Paul glanced through the office window to the sea of cubicles that spread out before him. Then he slipped on his reading glasses and pushed a spreadsheet toward Evan. He lowered his voice to a hush. "Cash flow. We have no sales, but we do have a marching army. At this burn rate, we're out of money before Everest flies."

Evan picked up the paper and tried to calculate the bottom line numbers. "How close are we?"

"It's conditional."

"On what?"

"If we have a layoff, we'll make payroll and our deadlines. But—"

"You gave your word; no layoff, no shutting down."

"That was when Fred was alive. He was working the issue. Now however, we are in a serious bind." Paul tapped his fingers on his desk, rummaged his drawer for a pen then tapped the pen on his desk. He barely looked at Evan. "I'll make the announcement at three and follow up with a press release."

"Announcement?"

"For the Chief Technical Officer. I've made my choice."

Evan felt a twinge. Finally, his sixty-hour work weeks were paying off. His long years of dedicated service, not to mention his technical achievements, were finally being recognized.

"John Waterman," Paul said, averting his eyes from Evan's. "I've already told him. I didn't want you to be surprised."

"Too late for that."

"John has contacts in the Pacific Rim. He'll get us the launch customers and deposits, which, hopefully, will keep us going." Paul looked at Evan. "I know what you're thinking."

"Then share it."

"In the long term, the job's yours. My job too when you get down to it. I've told you before, and everyone knows it; Dove Air is a McKenna company. That's you, me, and no one else. Waterman has one job; make sure we stay in business long enough for you to take over. We shook hands on that, but I'll write it down if you want."

"I can do the job; you do realize that. Whatever you want—cash flow, early demo, early shipment—you name it, I will make it happen."

"Now that's what I expected," Paul said.

"What?"

"It's your work that counts. You wouldn't believe how many guys want you in that job, regardless of your last name."

"Now I'm confused."

"Like I said; Waterman is a short-term fix to a long-term problem. Work with him. Tell him your ideas. Just get that plane off the ground!" Paul picked up the phone as if to terminate the meeting. He swiveled his chair to face the office window. He held his phone tightly. "Give me the distribution on the press release."

Evan raised his hand to his forehead and tried to calm his nerves. He groaned, but Paul never heard. Paul simply lowered his voice and prattled on about the evening news. Evan realized that the meeting was officially over, so he slid his chair and abruptly retreated to the exit.

The outcome of the painfully short meeting seemed abundantly clear; John Waterman—Dove employee for two and a half years, former university professor, former competitor who once vowed to put Dove out of business—was now a leading executive and possibly the one person who would determine the fate of the entire company.

In no mood for a twelve-hour work marathon, Evan cut his schedule short and headed home to his uncomfortably small, two-bed, two-bath house in Apple Valley.

"I can't believe him anymore," he said to Kylee while he yanked a beer from the fridge. "One day it's one story, the next day—who knows what."

"He wants you to be patient." She casually poured herself a cup of chamomile and blew over the top. "What's wrong with that?"

"I'm convinced that we'll be out of business before Everest flies. It makes no sense. Customers aren't going to buy a plane looking at the specs. I don't care what Waterman says. You need engineers to get it off the ground; not some professor who drinks sake with a plastic *o-choko*."

"Whatever," Kylee said. "It could be your father has other motives."

"Like what?"

"You said it yourself; Paul worked long hours, and he had the blood pressure to prove it. He's already had two heart attacks. Maybe he's worried about the same happening to you."

Evan gulped his beer and set the can onto the countertop. "Except for that thirty-year head start he has."

"You know what I mean."

"And I meant what I said. We're on the verge of shutting down the business. Unless we're smart about who does what, we might as well close the doors and head on home. We are that desperate."

Kylee stirred in a spoon of low cal sweetener into her tea. "What's the worst that could happen? Dove shuts down and you spend two weeks finding a new job. You told me yourself you could do it."

"You don't understand. If we make Everest fly, we'll change the way the airlines do business. Fifty years from now, they'll still be talking about us—if we do it right."

"Now, there's one difference between you and me."

"How's that?" he asked.

"You're thinking fifty years from now. I'm stuck on last Saturday."

"Pardon?"

"Am I the only one who sees it?"

Evan shrugged. "Sees what?"

"A plane crash in the middle of the mountains, a ton of cash, Fred lying dead at the base of the cliff. And no one but me wonders what happened."

Evan gave a blank stare. "I thought we closed that issue."

"I didn't close anything." Kylee put her tea cup onto the counter with a sharp rattle. "You weren't there. You didn't see Fred's face. He was begging me to help, pleading with me."

Evan took in another swallow of beer. "Now there's one distraction I don't need."

"Excuse me?"

"I came home to tell you I might be out of a job in four months. But somehow we wind up talking about you."

"No, I was talking about Fred; how he died and why. That shouldn't be a distraction. You worked for him, true?"

"What's that got to do with it?" Evan said. "If my prediction comes true; in four months, I won't be working for anyone."

"My hunch tells me that Fred had something to do with that."

Evan slowly crossed his arms. He said nothing.

Kylee picked up her tea cup. She held it lightly with both hands. "But okay, let's talk about you. Worst case, you take time off—a couple weeks, a couple months—and then start again. Is that so bad? I know you hate the long hours. And I can tell you, I don't care about fifty years from now. All I see is today and what your job is doing to the both of us. You're hardly home. And when you are home, we always argue. That's not healthy—for you or for us."

Evan paced to the breakfast nook then spun around. He raised his eyes and his hands. "You married into a family that makes planes. And yeah, once in a while, we have deadlines. Why does that surprise you?"

"Once in a while? Evan, it's one deadline after another. It never stops. And Everest—that's the worst of all. Every week you have problems; one crisis then another. Everest almost killed your father. And now Fred. I don't know if he died for the company or not. All I'm saying is; be careful and slow down. Take time off if you have to. It's not the end of the world."

Evan shuddered when his cell phone chimed. He yanked the phone from his pocket, slid it on, and spoke. "Yeah, Daz." He turned his back.

"You got five minutes to get here," Daz told him. "And no guarantees at that."

"Where and why?"

"The Oasis. Next door actually. The parking lot and one fine piece of engineering."

"Fine, I'll grab the bait. Order me a cold one."

Kylee slowly set her hands on her hips.

"Emergency downtown," Evan told her. He slid his beer into the fridge.

"Yeah, right." She leaned her head toward the fridge. "When you get back, that's where your dinner is."

Evan acknowledged by snatching his jacket from the dining room chair and hustling to the garage. In no mood for an argument—or as Kylee called it, a discussion—he slipped his still-warm MGB into gear and raced the five miles of city streets to the small restaurant and tavern next to the mini mall. He was glad to have any excuse to leave the house.

Five minutes were long gone, but it turned out it didn't matter. Most of his frustrations had slipped away as he downshifted and snagged a parking spot across from the quick-ship store.

Immediately, he understood what Daz had meant. He jammed his keys to his pocket, dodged an SUV on his walk over, and then held onto Daz's Harley for support. He struggled for the words. "This kind of art you don't find in a museum."

"What did I say?"

"Tell me it's real … Six cylinders. Two-sixty horse. One-thirty-five top speed. Numbers suck, but without a doubt, this is the best shape to come out of Britain; the Jaguar E-Type. XKE, as it were. And it's showroom, Daz. Not a blemish anywhere. Whoever owns her, treats her with a fair respect." He fell to his knees by the front tire and slipped on his reading glasses. "Wire wheels and not a speck of dust. How on earth—"

Evan heard footsteps approaching and assumed Daz was coming for a closer look. Not quite. He peeked left and saw the unmistakable shape of a lady's foot in what appeared to be an expensive open toe shoe. Evan didn't know one shoemaker from the next, but he did have an appreciation for the timeless beauty of a woman's leg; especially one that extended past a knee-high slit in a red wool skirt. Red as in the color of the signal red Jaguar that he knelt beside. Red as in the matching tunic and scarf that he gazed at. Evan struggled to his feet and gathered the words that would somehow shield his embarrassment.

Daz, moving in from the background, offered his version of an introduction. "Ma'am, you'll have to excuse the boy. He's got a calendar at work; classic cars. Stuck in August. This model seems to be his favorite."

"Sixty-four Jaguar," Evan stammered, "if I'm not mistaken." He jammed his glasses into his pocket.

The woman gracefully removed her sunglasses, and during that awkward moment between glance and stare, Evan took in the image of a beauty more dazzling than the machine. With those heels, she stood nearly eye to eye; her emerald green eyes in contrast to his cerulean blue. Her pencil thin eyebrows matched the color of her shoulder length auburn hair. No curls in her hair; just a slight curve inward to properly frame her oval face. If Evan were to hazard a guess, he would place her age comfortably at the mid-twenties, no higher than twenty-seven.

"Sixty-three," she said.

"Excuse me?" Evan raised an eyebrow, hopelessly misplacing his train of thought.

"You can't tell from the outside, but Jaguar installed a bigger engine in '64. It still had issues, but not as many. They made some other changes, but I wouldn't call them improvements. Of course, when you get down to it, the year doesn't matter. It remains a beautiful car."

"No argument." Evan forced his gaze to the headlight assemblies.

"So, you understand horsepower." The woman unlocked the car. "How about carburetors?"

Evan perked up with a broad smile. "That's my MGB at the corner. Not the same carb, but I bet it's got the same problems."

"You mind if I open up the, uh, hood?"

"Let's see what she has." Evan wiped his palms on his shirttail while she unlatched and raised the hood.

"It was fine yesterday, but now it drops out around a hundred and ten."

Evan detected the slight hint of a foreign accent, but he couldn't pinpoint a region. "You mean kilometers an hour?"

"No. Miles an hour. As you said, it is good for one-thirty-five."

"So I said ... Well, here's your culprit." Evan gingerly retrieved the remnants of an old oak leaf and held it high. "It must've blown in from your Sunday drive in the country. You can't open the throttle with this blocking the cable."

"All that without dirtying your hands. I'm impressed." She smiled then abruptly asked, "What's your name?"

"Evan," he replied, no hesitation.

"Thank you, Evan. Lucky for me, you drove by."

"A car like this, I'd be a fool not to stop. Oh, and by the way, what's your name?"

"My name?" The woman returned with her easy smile. "Mireille."

Evan immediately extended his hand. "Pleased to meet you," he carefully enunciated each syllable, "Mere-ay." He wasn't sure if he pronounced her name properly, but when she nodded, he knew he was close.

The clearing of a throat in the background reminded Evan he was not alone with Mireille. "Oh, yeah, right. My good friend, Daz—Daz Donahue."

Daz stepped from the shadows and tapped his baseball cap. "Ma'am."

"Mr. Donahue," Mireille replied. She faced Evan again. "Now this may be impulsive, and I don't make it a habit of asking strangers, but I need a car—a reliable car—for the next week. And this Jaguar; I cannot depend on it one day to the next. You, Evan; you seem like an honest man."

"Seem like it, and actually, I am."

"Then, if you please, ride with me and tell me; should I keep this car or buy something more sedate." She glanced at Daz's Harley. "How do you say; we will make it a test drive."

Evan lit up like a boy with a new bike. Then he curled his lip when his hand slid across the cold chrome of the elegant machine.

"Problem?" Mireille asked.

Daz held up his left hand and discreetly slid an imaginary ring up and down the length of his ring finger.

"I understand." She opened the driver-side door and set a packet of papers behind the seat. "Your wife does not allow you to ride with strangers."

"No, that's not it," Evan pouted. "I am wondering though; how safe are you at a hundred and ten?"

She laughed a delicate laugh. "Safe enough. I have been driving British cars since I was sixteen."

"That would make it, what, eight years?"

"Wouldn't you like to know. But if you prefer, I will drive slower than fifty-five."

"Miles an hour?"

Mireille smiled.

With that tacit assurance, Evan slid onto the passenger seat and settled in to enjoy the thrill of a fine British touring car rolling down the California countryside. And Mireille did keep her promise; speed was no more than fifty-five. But on those winding San Bernardino mountain roads, it sure felt like a hundred and ten.

Squealing tires, wind through the open windows, plenty of horsepower to pull them through the curves. Evan's pulse doubled the speedometer reading. Any thought of his original mission—should she keep the car or sell it—disappeared like the passing landscape. Obviously, both the car and the woman were high-performance and prone to distract him.

Mireille slid the Jaguar to a stop at a vista point that overlooked the Victor Valley. She turned off the ignition as a gentle cloud of dust settled on the roof and hood. Suddenly, the silence was nearly as intense as the roar of the engine. Mireille stepped from the Jaguar, and with total disregard for the classic car finish, she sat on the headlight fender assembly. She gazed at the landscape below.

"You did fine," she said when Evan stepped from the car.

"How so?"

"A few twists and turns, close to the edge. I've had men cry before."

"I can't imagine."

"Take a seat." Mireille patted the opposite fender.

Evan declined but moved to her side. He carefully avoided the sparkling red finish. He glanced at her face. Despite the harsh, late-afternoon sun that baked down on them, she seemed cool and calm with no hint of imperfection. But with Evan's reading glasses in his pocket, he couldn't tell for sure.

"You see, Evan; clear head." Mireille lifted a finger to her temple.

"How's that?"

"A fast drive through the hills. No distractions, no clutter. You have to focus. You have to clear your mind of everything but the drive. Now we stop—like a reset button."

"Problems at work?" Evan asked, hoping for more background.

"Not anymore." She motioned at her papers. "I just signed the biggest deal of my life. Now that I think of it—with my clear head—it was a good choice."

"Well, this clear head is envious."

"Problems at home?"

"Possibly." He glanced at the packet and then faced Mireille. "Family or work; it's hard to say which is the biggest pain in my life."

"I know something about men and problems. Perhaps I can help."

"How so?" he asked.

"With two questions. It worked for me, and it might work for you."

"Okay, I'll bite."

"Pardon?" Mireille said.

"Go ahead, ask."

Mireille paused, shifted her hips on the fender, and faced Evan. She touched her lip then waved her hand. She looked at his eyes.

"First; an easy question. I'll admit it is somewhat cliché, but I will ask. Where do you want to be ten years from now?"

Odd question and certainly an abrupt change of topic, but she seemed genuine. Evan encouraged her. "By where, you mean …?"

"Goals, ambitions, dreams; whatever you call it. Personal or professional. In ten years, how do you see yourself?"

Evan held back a grin. "That is a basic interview question."

"Yes and no. I acknowledge that you may have asked it of others. But have you ever answered it yourself, honestly? You seem like a passionate man, so I am curious; what excites you? What is your reason for being?"

"What excites me, huh?" Evan walked along the gravel. He tried, as Mireille suggested, to reset his mind to a clean page, as it were. When he returned to her side, he tried to be sincere. "A week ago, I agree; that would have been an easy question. Now, I'm not so sure."

"It still is. Dreams don't change overnight. How we get there—perhaps. Now, clear your head, and say the first thought." She pressed her finger to his temple.

"You really want to know." Evan grinned and let it grow to a smile. Here was a total stranger, willing and almost eager to hear a man's frustrations. Again, he paced the gravel shoulder. Asking him about his true passion was asking what he would do if he won the California Lottery—same odds of coming true. He returned to Mireille and stood face to face. He lowered his gaze slightly to meet her eyes.

"For starters, I can tell you I'm an engineer." He waved his hand from heel to hair. "If you haven't guessed already."

"It was that, or a pilot or," she laughed, "a marketing director."

"Please." Evan shuddered. "But pilot; that's close. I design planes for a living. I enjoy it more often than not. But thinking back, I've had better years."

"Not back," Mireille said. "Forward. Your perfect job would be what?"

He glanced at Mireille as a cool breeze brushed strands of hair from her face. "I still want to make planes, but—and please don't laugh—but ever since I was a kid, I wanted to fly like the Jetsons."

"Who?"

"You really don't know, do you?" Evan raised an eyebrow.

"Does it matter?"

"I suppose not. But this is one dream that almost got off the ground."

"Almost?"

"Back when the company had money, we could build anything. My father, bless his heart, tossed me a few million. I took it, made a prototype, and actually flew it. An aircraft like you wouldn't believe. A flying car is what they called it. Small, fast, computers for everything but the cup holder. I knew we had a hit on our hands, but ..."

"What happened?"

"The usual; the money ran out and priorities changed." He flipped up his palm. "Now yeah, I have the same dream, I suppose. The plane's just a little bigger, and someone else is in charge. But if we get it out—"

"You will have a hit."

"If you believe our marketing."

"You see," Mireille said, "you proved my point."

Evan raised his brow.

"Your work," she said. "It's more than a job. You have passion. In the long term, that's all that matters."

"Long term; funny you should say that."

"Funny?"

"Never mind; long story." Evan knelt beside the front wheel and checked for dust on the brakes. He stood again and told her, "So it seems you know something about cars and men."

"More of one, less of the other."

"So far, I know nothing about you."

Mireille slid off the fender and rested her fingers on the door handle. She looked over the rooftop at Evan. "I can tell you this; as of this moment, I am late. If I don't get these papers recorded and sent, *my* dreams are going poof." She waited for Evan to settle himself on the passenger seat. Then she switched on the ignition.

Although Evan had his own list of personal and professional questions, he never found the chance to ask them. The back to town drive mirrored the wild ride up the mountain. He was sure that any distraction would send them over the edge.

Besides, Mireille seemed preoccupied or suddenly shy, saying little more than; "Hold on tight … Dotted line—okay to pass … I can't believe they gave him a license."

No radio, no music, no favorite movie or book. No hint of her own passions. Their conversation had flowed in one direction; from him to her.

Before Evan realized it, Mireille was dropping him off where he started. His only comment; "Keep the Jaguar. No way should you sell it."

Between the double kiss on the cheeks, the swirling scent of rose petal perfume, and the light touch of her hand on his elbow, Evan's face flushed to the same color as Mireille's scarf. There was something vaguely uncomfortable about the whole meeting. But as she drove down the highway, Evan slapped himself for getting no more than a first name and a pleasant memory. Then he ran his thumb across his wedding ring and cursed himself for wanting more.

Chapter *4*

KYLEE WOKE to the scent of slightly burnt Colombian coffee. She squinted as Evan made his way to their bed.

"Today, it's whatever you want." He lowered a breakfast tray and showed her coffee, a tomato-and-cheese omelet, wheat toast, and fresh squeezed orange juice.

Kylee raised her head from her feather pillow and rubbed the sleep from her eyes. "Guilt gift or bribe?" she asked with her rough wakeup voice.

"You're welcome."

"Let's see; middle of the week, you're late for work, and breakfast in bed. Shall I go on?"

"It's Waterman's show now. Let *him* deal with the problems." Evan set down the tray as Kylee sat up. "I've got two months vacation. One day will not make a difference."

"I thought you said—"

"Forget what I said. Today is totally yours." He placed a pillow behind her head. "If you want us to go shopping, that's fine. If you want to check out Fred, we'll do it. Autopsy, financial history, travel history; we'll uncover what we can. I'll drive you around, make calls, talk to HR. Anything to make you happy."

Kylee picked up a slice of toast and bit off a corner. "There was one idea I had." She wiped her lips and looked out her north facing window. "Now that you mention it."

"If we can do it in one day, let's get moving."

"I think so." She sprinkled more salt on her omelet and munched. She casually waved her fork. "If we call him now."

"Him?"

"Daz."

"Daz?" Evan said. "What, you and I can't do it? Why—"

"I want to go back to the site of the crash. I told you I called Marlene."

"Your friend."

"At San Bernardino General. That's where they took Fred and the others." She set her fork down and looked at Evan. "The autopsy came back clean; no carbon monoxide, no sharp lacerations, no nothing. The cause of death was something else. There's got to be a detail I missed; papers, receipts, notebook. Some hint of what Fred was up to."

"The Sierras." Evan shuddered. "You want to spend the afternoon in a blizzard."

"Actually, all the storms moved north. The weather's clear now, and we won't be rushed. There and back in one day. You meant what you said, right?"

"I've got no problem," he said. "But Daz; he's a busy guy."

"Start with a call." Kylee lifted her nightstand phone and passed it to Evan. "Make sure you mention my name."

"Yes, ma'am."

Evan made the call, and before Kylee had finished her omelet, he got the final okay. "For you," Evan said, "Daz would fly us to Hawaii. All you have to do is ask."

Kylee smiled.

***

By noon, Kylee, Evan, and Daz were once again airborne and approaching the High Sierra site of the Mojave Air crash. Compared to last weekend, this two-hour flight was a tourist's delight; clear skies, no wind, and T-shirt temperatures. If not for the plane wreck, this outing with Evan would have been a fond memory in the making. Kylee felt determined to make the most of it.

In a short while, Daz landed the helicopter within hiking distance of the wreckage. When the whine of the engine came to a merciful halt, the silence of the landscape returned. Kylee tightened the laces of her Scarpa boots and scouted a vista point that overlooked the neighboring valley.

The bright sun and awesome view reminded her of her year-ago hike near Tuolumne Meadows in Yosemite. A clear head, she had always said, comes from clean air and quiet. She stretched her arms high over her head and rolled her neck to release the last of her tension.

"Hey, the crash is in the other direction!" Evan yelled. He hustled close and tugged at her sleeve. "Daz is halfway down the ridge. He's going check out the engine."

Kylee let out a heavy sigh. She pulled a yellow headband from her pocket and slipped it over her head and ears. "You know where I'm headed."

"Treasure hunt, I assume."

"Call it what you want. But if I find one fifty-dollar bill—"

"Then I'll find the others." He gave her a quick salute and then disappeared to consult with Daz.

Kylee headed to the site of Fred's fall, but for this venture, she chose a somewhat longer, more level route. She kept her climbing ropes in reserve at the helicopter. All she needed was a good pair of boots, good lungs, warm gloves, and a bag of chalk for those slippery rocks.

As she neared the point of Fred's impact, she slowed her pace and moved her gaze to the melting snow by her feet. She expected to see loose cash; a Franklin note half-buried in the snow, a wad of bills stuck in the mud. But not a penny showed; no evidence of anything manmade except for Fred's busted aluminum case. She picked up a handful of dirt and snow, studied it, and dropped it. All she had now was a dirty glove. As Evan hurried to her side, she prepared herself for his "I told you so."

"Daz was fine by himself," Evan said as he caught his breath. "I thought you could use another pair of eyes."

"You may have better luck dealing with Daz. At least he can take a picture and have something to show. All I got is mud and ice." She stepped around a rock, grabbed Fred's case, and showed the empty inside.

"This is where he fell?"

Kylee rolled her eyes then looked across the ravine. "I don't get it. The wind blew out most of the money, but some of it, I swear, dropped at my feet."

"Could be a rockslide buried it." Evan motioned at the gravel that had covered the cliff base.

"What, and leave my footprints on top of the snow? Not a chance. I'm just sorry I dragged you to the high country."

He gave her a hug. "Hey, I promised a day together. Down south or in the hills; it makes no difference to me."

"I was so sure I saw it. I thought we'd come here, find cash all over, and I'd prove you wrong. Once again, I have no clue what I'm talking about."

"Not quite." Evan grinned. He reached into his pack and pulled out a muddy, half-torn wad of paper. He picked away loose snow and mud then held it near her face. "Here's your cash. The field's full of these. Only difference; it's not really money."

He spread open the wad and shook off specks of gravel. "It looks like a stock certificate from Dove Air; preprinted but with no name and no share amount. Essentially a blank page. But it does have a green logo, and it might be worth something ... someday."

"You think so?" Kylee slumped her shoulders when she took hold of the remnant. Somehow the image of worthless green pages flying out of Fred's case was less than interesting. She curled her lip and tossed the paper onto the ground.

"Best leave it where you found it," Daz called out as he scrambled down the hill.

"How's that?" Kylee asked.

"The Safety Board's coming tomorrow," he said, drawing near. "If you got evidence, leave it for them."

"Right now, it's litter." She looked down at the ground and up at the forty-foot cliff. She paused. "But that; that is definitely not."

"What's not?" Evan asked.

"You guys worry about the NTSB. Leave the evidence to me." She slipped off her gloves and dipped into her bag of chalk. She rubbed her hands together then nonchalantly scaled the near-vertical granite slab. Her hands searched for the narrow cracks and her feet followed with a tenuous hold.

Daz called up to her, "You know, there's an easier way. The chopper's—"

"Evan is not the only one with sharp eyes," Kylee said from the rock. She stretched her shoulder to the limit and groaned. "There, just about got it."

"You be careful," Daz said, raising his voice to the point of hoarseness.

"Don't worry," Evan said to Daz. "She's done it before."

"I knew it!" Kylee waved a leather bound phone with her free hand. She motioned to Evan and then tossed it down to him. She quickly retraced her path down the wall.

"Fred left the plane for one reason only," she said. "That's to call for help. He had to get high up the hill to get a signal. He had to walk and talk to have any chance of a rescue. Unfortunately, he took one step too far."

Evan, half-listening, poked the On button. He smiled as the phone lit up the screen. "I swear, Daz, I got to get myself one of these. A four-story fall and it works like a champ. And sorry, Fred; I am curious about your last call."

"Smart phone with built-in satellite," Daz said. "I didn't think Fred was into gadgets."

Evan fumbled his way through the applications to the phone directory. "Sorry, Kylee. Looks like the last number was not 911."

"Then what was it?"

Evan hit Redial. He listened intently to the voice at the other end for barely a phrase or two. Then the battery died and the display went blank. He passed the phone to Kylee and told her with a faltering voice, "His last call was not for a rescue. Nope, no way. Poor Fred; his last words were about NASDAQ. It seems he called his stockbroker, made some kind of deal, and then slipped over the edge."

Chapter **5**

AS EVAN STOOD in line at the Dove cafeteria chalupa stand, he saw Kylee at the nearby salad bar. She piled her plate with a mound of baby spinach, tomatoes, chopped eggs, and cheddar cheese, topping it with vinaigrette dressing. Evan moved to her side, set his chalupa on her tray, and paid for both meals.

"Who's your escort?" He tapped the red Dove visitor badge on her black pullover sweater.

"It was supposed to be you, but Claire—over there—offered to help." Kylee swung her head toward the cafeteria table that was near the patio window. "Curly brown hair, about my age, white top."

"Sure, I know Claire from HR. Two months on the job and she's still smiling. I'm impressed."

"She seems nice enough."

"She is," Evan said. He walked over and sat opposite of Claire. "Claire ... always a pleasure."

"Evan." Claire moved her plate of lasagna and cleared a space for Kylee. "We were talking about your father."

"What about him?"

"Paul hired me—more or less on the spot—when we met at a conference in New York. I told him what I did. He told me what he did. Of course, after he told me about the company and the people here, how could I resist?"

Kylee nodded. "He can be sweet when he wants."

"When he wants; no argument there." Evan grabbed his chalupa and let the grease drip onto the plate.

"I mean it," Claire said. "Paul has a way of twisting your arm while kissing your behind."

"Pain or pleasure; you never know which." Evan glanced to his right. "And speaking of sweetness, here comes the king of diplomacy."

Daz stormed through the cafeteria aisles like a shark through a kelp forest. He pushed vinyl chairs aside and squeezed by crowded tables until he came chest to face with Evan.

Evan continued to eat.

"We're setting up for major blow-out." Daz loomed over Evan and growled just loud enough for workers at the surrounding tables to hear. "Waterman's test; you know about it, I assume."

Evan took another bite.

"We're not close to being ready," Daz said. "We got twenty seals from the bulkhead to the tail, and they all need inspecting. Give us three weeks, and we *might* have a chance."

"What's John got to say?"

"I'd just as soon talk to that mutt dog of his. You know I'll get the same response; a bunch of lip flappin' and tail waggin'. "

Evan sipped his Coke. "Tell you what; I'll stop by after lunch. This could be a safety issue. And wouldn't you know; I'm still in charge of that. I'll compromise with John; how about two weeks?"

"They're all idiots, you know. Every single one."

"By the way, Daz, this is Claire. She works in HR, and she's probably taking notes."

"Sorry about that, hon," Daz said sweetly. "Let me rephrase that; they're all *clowns*." He gave Claire a creased grin and abruptly exited the cafeteria on the same path as he entered.

"What was Daz yelling about?" Kylee whispered.

"The usual ranting."

"Give me the layman's version, Evan. I can understand."

"High altitude test for cabin pressurization. Basically, we pump up the inside of the cabin to normal times two. Then we poke around the outside, checking for holes and leaks. At eight miles up, air is precious. We can't afford a single leak."

Russell, listening to the chatter, pulled up a chair next to Kylee and set down his tray. He said, "You know, Daz has plenty of hot air. If you get him on board, you don't have to worry about decompression."

Claire laughed.

After Evan had managed the introductions, he looked at Claire and said, "... and once you get to know Daz and Russell, you'll understand how this company works."

"Now that's a scary thought," Russell said, smiling at Claire. He nibbled his beef enchilada. "Working here is like watching TV; it's both educational and entertaining."

"If you get bored," Evan said, "change channels or get another job."

"Of course, around here," Russell said, "you'll never get bored."

"So, you're a scientist?" Kylee asked Russell.

"You could say that."

"Then perhaps you could explain this." She reached deep into her purse, retrieved a balled up napkin, and dropped it onto the table in front of Russell. The napkin unraveled, spilling out dirt, twigs, and a muddy, crumpled sheet of paper.

Russell grimaced but managed a quick response. "Yesterday's lunch, if I'm not mistaken."

"I found it at the crash site. I think it means something."

"I can't believe you brought that back." Evan scowled. "We already told you what it is."

"I want a second opinion."

Russell poked at the bundle with the handle of his knife. "Looks like a stock certificate. From Dove Air, judging from the corners."

"You see." Evan leaned back and dropped his napkin to his plate.

"But ..." Russell mumbled.

"But what?" Kylee asked.

"It's not the standard size or color. Besides, I thought Dove was going online with their shares. Why would they print something like this?"

"I knew there was something funny."

"I wouldn't go that far." Russell slid the packet closer to Kylee. "It is unusual though."

"I'll keep it." She grabbed the napkin, balled it, and then crammed it into her purse. She took out Fred's phone and placed it by Russell. "What do you know about satellite phones?"

"What else do you have in there?" Evan asked.

"Now you're talking my field," Russell said. "I did my masters on sat' comm."

"Great," Kylee said, cutting her salad. "I'm hoping to find the phone directory, calendar, or any kind of memo. But the battery's dead. I thought that maybe somehow, you could, you know, recharge it."

Russell fingered the phone. "Maybe, maybe not. I hope you're not in a rush."

"No, tomorrow would be fine."

"I was thinking more like two weeks from Tuesday."

"Oh."

"And that's pushing it," Russell said. "Honestly, I've got a dozen servos to test, and we are so far behind."

"I see." Kylee puckered her pouting lips and lowered her hazel eyes.

Russell gulped his enchilada and finally told her, "However, I will do what I can."

"Thanks, I appreciate it."

"Is this legal?" Russell asked as he lifted the phone and examined it.

"Of course, it is. Well, I'm pretty sure."

"I guess it doesn't matter." Russell shrugged. "Fred's gone; technically, it's your phone now. I'd say it's legal." He stashed it into his pants pocket and went back to his lunch.

Like a bodybuilder on a challenge to build calories or like an engineer with his head in his avionics, Russell scarfed down the rest of the enchiladas, Spanish rice, and black beans. His sporadic small talk abruptly ended with a quick, "Glad to meet you, and I'll see you later."

With a slight grin, he knocked off a clump of rice from his shirt, picked up his tray, and hustled to the bus racks. Moments later, Russell disappeared to the neighboring building.

Kylee turned to Claire. "He's kind of sweet; don't you think?"

"I suppose, in some kind of engineering way." Claire's face began to flush.

"He is single. Isn't he, Evan?"

"And available."

"Well, there you go. My work is complete." Kylee winked at Claire and told her, "Have a nice day." Then she got up to leave and asked Evan to escort her back to the visitors' entrance.

"Thank you for lunch," she told him by the guard's desk.

"Lunch with you is never a simple meal, is it?"

"That's what makes me interesting," she kissed him on the cheek, "and entertaining." She dropped off her badge, started her Jeep, and drove to her job at the Apple Valley Community Clinic.

Evan sighed. He hoped that Kylee was correct and that the most interesting part of his day was the lunch he had just had. Too many problems. Too many deadlines. Always running to keep from falling behind. To go two days without trouble was an anomaly. He checked his watch and shuddered; his two-day limit was coming up fast.

He walked the garden paths between buildings and finally made his way to the main assembly hanger. As he passed through the connecting door to the production area, it was more than intuition that told him he had another crisis on his hands.

Yellow lights flashed, and caution tape surrounded the perimeter of Everest. Posted signs said Keep Out, but Evan figured that didn't apply to him. Safety-critical tests still required his blessing.

Waterman and his dog stood center stage and orchestrated the whole affair. He waved his arms and barked orders to the dozens of workers. Coco, like a first-rate assistant, wagged his tail in unison.

Evan, more curious than concerned, approached the first technician he saw. "What's with the light show?"

"Cabin pressure test; we're pumping up to forty on the inside."

"Forty? No way. That's twice the test limit."

"Hey, I just turn the knobs and crank up the pressure. You got a beef, speak to the safety manager." The technician nodded toward a balding, painfully gaunt, gray-haired man. He stood at the top of the metal stairs that led to the Everest raised floor.

"Listen, I am the safety manager!"

"Not anymore. Waterman told us at break; he's hired back old man Harris." The technician laughed. "Surprised, huh? Me too. I thought Harris died after he quit. Who knows, maybe he did. The man's a walking corpse."

Evan bounded up the metal stairs, two steps at a leap. As he neared the top landing, he slowed to give the once-over to the man who apparently now held a critical job at Dove.

Len Harris leaned against the scaffolding railing and gazed down the length of the stark white fuselage. He carried a logbook in his left hand, an inhaler in his right. Below them, the air compressor roared, making any normal conversation nearly impossible.

"Len!" Evan shouted as he tapped his elbow.

"Evan McKenna!" Harris turned and grinned. He moved his inhaler to his pocket and offered a trembling handshake. "It's good to see you again. We can use your help."

"That guy says you took my job." Evan aimed his thumb at the technician.

"John told you about this, right?"

"No."

"This is awkward." Harris tightened his neck muscles. "Yeah, starting today. I'm surprised he—"

Suddenly, the compressor shut off, and Evan, taking advantage of the relative quiet, got straight to his point. "I'll talk to him later. But I'm telling you; you got to stop the test. Shut it down cold!"

"Too late." Harris snagged his inhaler and took a whiff. "We're already probing."

Evan scanned the length of the fuselage. He counted a half-dozen technicians working on the near side. No doubt, there was an equal number on the other. Each carried shreds of toilet paper or an electronic stethoscope to detect leaks in the aircraft skin.

"It's not too late," Evan said. "Twist the handle to Vent."

"I checked the log books, and I signed 'em off. Don't worry, it's procedure."

Evan frowned when he saw technicians huddling near an emergency exit. A lot of pointing and note taking was going on. He was immediately suspicious. Finger pointing was never a good sign.

"Give me the log book." Evan shoved out his hand, and Harris obliged. He thumbed through the assembly reports, searching for safety hazards. He shook his head and jabbed his finger at a recent entry.

"We got problems." He handed the book to Harris. Then, like a captain on a sinking ship, Evan shouted orders to everyone in sight. He screamed and waved as he raced across the decking. "Get away from that window! Hit the emergency vent!"

But nobody moved. The one technician who turned his head merely looked at Harris. Harris did nothing more than lean against the railing and fondle his inhaler.

Evan scrambled across the raised deck in a last attempt to plead face to face with the men on the platform. Seconds counted, but Evan, regrettably, was a second too late. He heard the loud whistling of air escaping from the aircraft seals. He saw the men leaning close. He felt his heart pound because he knew what it meant.

With an ear-shattering bang, the acrylic window exploded from the fuselage like a cork from a champagne bottle. It hit one technician squarely in the chest, sending him flying across the deck to the railing behind. He smashed his back then crumpled to a heap. Whether he was alive or not, it was anyone's guess. The same force knocked two more technicians to the deck; they were shaken but not seriously hurt.

"Call First Aid!" Evan shouted to the workers below. "And 911!" Evan knelt beside the fallen worker and checked for vital signs. The technician was breathing and had a faint pulse, but he also bled from his mouth and aimlessly rolled his eyes. At least he was alive, if barely.

"911!" Evan shouted, but that was all he could do. The worker needed professional medical help, and Kylee was long gone.

Evan read the man's badge. "Help's on the way, Bill. Until then, don't try to move." He stretched out Bill's legs and yanked off his own chalupa-stained shirt to keep Bill's head off the cold steel decking. "Take easy breaths. We'll get you to the hospital. Kylee's there, and she's the best nurse in California."

He felt sick in his stomach; half with empathy for Bill, half with the knowledge that this accident was nothing short of preventable. Evan did the best with the little he had. Slowly—after the First Aid team arrived, after the paramedics arrived, after Evan followed Bill to the waiting ambulance—Evan's heart began to beat with a calmer pulse.

He returned to the accident scene and put on his shirt. He picked up the assembly logbooks and then compiled a list of names. His list of accountable parties grew with each page turned. Everyone from the window assembler to the president himself had some blame to share. Conveniently, Waterman and the managers had disappeared to a meeting. It was left to the window assembly foreman, Cullin Black, to explain the debacle.

Evan met him near the three-foot tires of the main landing gear. "I checked the records," he began as calmly as he could, considering his mind was still with Bill. "And wouldn't you know, that window was put together on a Friday morning."

"Okay." Black shrugged.

"On Friday afternoon, the inspector finds a crack in the corner. He writes it up."

"Great, you can read the logs."

"And then, 'BB,' whoever that is, never followed up on Monday. He never replaced the window."

"You gotta a gripe; write it down and submit it. That's procedure."

"So we had a sloppy job installing the window and workers who can't remember one day to the next. Now, I got a foreman with the wrong answers. And I got this mess to clean up." Evan raised his head toward the blown-out window.

"Maybe you haven't heard; you're not in charge. Except for the dog. Yeah, that's it; you're in charge of the dog. You want a mess to clean up, there you go. Get busy." Black aimed at the corner of the hanger where Coco was relieving himself.

Evan's blood pressure soared. "One last question." He took a deep breath and looked directly at Black's eyes. "Who's your boss and where can I find him?"

"That's two questions, and like I said, I ain't got time for this." Black's eyes narrowed to slits, and his neck muscles began to bulge.

Evan knew a lost cause when he saw it. He shook his head and turned to walk away. Then from the corner of his eye, he caught the glimpse of a fist coming in fast. Instinctively, he spun, missing a shattering blow by a whisker. In most cases, he'd let the assault go with a warning, but now, with his pulse racing and frustration building, he fought back. In a two-step move, he pounded Black's kidney and then slammed him with an arm lock into the side of the Everest tire.

He snarled at Black, "Not the same as a window flying in your chest. But remember this when you cut corners; we got people up there, not machines. You make a mistake; someone's gonna bleed."

Evan released Black and stormed off to his office. He closed the door and plopped down hard on his chair. He grabbed handfuls of papers on his desk and randomly shuffled them to keep from pounding his fist. He was beginning to hate this place.

For the first time in his career, Evan typed out his résumé. His head throbbed with regrets and misgivings, but his mind was made up. Despite Paul, despite the now-worthless stock options, despite Kylee's family in the area, he figured it was time to explore new job opportunities with his friends up north. He finished a rough draft, ran a spell check, sat back, and saved his file. Then his phone rang.

It was Claire. "To let you know, Evan, we walked him out."

"What do you mean?"

"Just that; we walked him out. You know; we fired Cullin Black."

"Wow, I didn't see that coming. I thought we'd put him on ice for a while and let him cool down."

"Zero tolerance. We had no choice in the matter. Any hint of violence and the employee has to go. Of course, with the long hours here and problems at home, Cullin was going to break sooner or later. And the boss's son—what better way to vent. Sorry, Evan."

"How about my response on the floor?"

"Response, as in pushing Cullin into the wheel?"

"Urging, is how I would phrase it."

"That was self-defense," Claire said, "and your witness backs you up."

"Witness?"

"Harris saw it all. Actually, he said you were rather restrained. He said he understood the frustration, but it was Cullin's fault from start to finish."

"Harris said that?"

"I guess you found a new friend."

"New friend." Evan chuckled. "Just what I need."

"One more thing," Claire said. "There's an all-hands meeting at four."

"What about?"

"Another reorganization."

"The ink's not dry on the last one," Evan said.

"Your father asked that you stop by his office; he wants to give you a heads-up."

"We'll see."

Despite the second-hand invitation, Evan skipped the meeting with Paul. Instead, he worked on the final draft of his résumé. It seemed a much better use of his time. He finished it around four o'clock, put it in his ready-to-send folder, and walked off to the company meeting.

With the standard company-wide meeting format, some twelve hundred workers gathered in and around the main assembly hanger. Rumors were again flying, but no one in the audience, including Evan, had confirmation of any plan beyond 'changes ahead.'

Paul stood at a raised podium and looked across the sea of employees. A smile quickly spread across his face. He waved, and immediately a round of applause broke out. He waited for calm then spoke into the wireless mic.

"There's not a single place on earth I'd rather be than right here with my friends and family of Dove Air."

Slowly, his smile faded. He lowered his gaze and lowered his voice. "As you know, this company, or any company for that matter, survives on sales. That's the nature of business. We are not the government. And contrary to what some of you believe, we are not a non-profit organization. At least not by design.

"Since the birth of Dove, fifteen years ago, we've had a great run. Gibraltar, Whitney, Shasta; those aircraft made this company and made us a leader in the industry. For that, we can be proud.

"But this downturn, I'll be honest; it's a nightmare. The economy, the market, the consolidation of airlines. We've got three strikes against us. Now with Everest late; how long can we survive with no sales coming in? Sooner or later, the money runs out."

Paul seemed to choose his words as though he was giving a eulogy for a good friend. With the poor wireless link, some of the words faded, but he held the mic close and continued.

"I've prided myself on the way we've run this company. We don't take government handouts. We don't cater to some corporate giant. We set our own destiny. We're independent, but we are also a part of a worldwide effort to produce the world's greatest plane.

"Here is my dilemma; how do we avoid layoffs and stay in business long enough to fly Everest? There's no easy answer. But we do have friends in the industry; other people who believe in what we do, who believe that Everest can and will be the plane for the next generation."

Paul wiped his brow then motioned at a hallway near the podium. "To that end, I'd like to announce our partnership with Trudeau Industries." He waited until a projector displayed a ten-foot-tall image of the Trudeau logo—a streaking 'T' covering a small font 'rudeau.' He held his wireless mic low, waiting for the murmurs to die down.

After a long pause and with sporadic workers still chattering, Paul continued. "Most of you know Trudeau. You know their French design. You know their products. They're experts in software and robotics. And that, as it turns out, is exactly what we need to get this plane off the ground."

Before the echo of that bombshell subsided, Paul launched into a series of Trudeau publicity photos that highlighted their operation in Grenoble and some of their worldwide divisions. He displayed top-level accounting numbers then quickly got to the bottom line.

With what seemed to be a carefully edited script, Paul introduced the vice-president of Trudeau—Pierre Simon.

Pierre walked out, and immediately, everyone—including Dove workers a hundred yards back—leaned forward for a closer look. Tall, heavy, day-old beard, mid-fifties body; Pierre, with his Armani suit and red tie, seemed vice-presidential material. He spoke a few words and showed a good grasp of heavily accented English. He talked about partnership and teamwork. He stuck to standard corporate phrases and highlighted—in a hundred words or fewer—the historic mission of Trudeau.

Some workers seemed elated; others dejected. It was either, "Great, we need the money," or "There goes the company." Not much in-between.

After Evan heard that Pierre would be Waterman's new boss, he said, "Let's wait and see. This might be worthwhile."

That wait-and-see lasted for about two minutes. Then Pierre introduced the VP of marketing for the new Dove-Trudeau partnership. Everyone turned and stared at the hallway next to the podium. Evan's eyes widened, and his jaw dropped when she stepped from the darkness.

There she was; decked out in a tailored business jacket and matching knee-length red skirt. Poised, professional, enthusiastically confident, a definite icon of success; her name was Mireille Prudhomme.

Evan immediately recognized her as the woman with the signal red Jaguar, the woman with the hard to place accent, and the woman who could make a man dream of tomorrow. Beautiful and alluring as before, but apparently now, with the reorganization, she was Evan's new boss.

After the meeting, Evan ran after her. But with the tide of workers heading home, he found it an upstream battle. When he finally caught up to her, she was driving to the nearest exit in her now-familiar Jaguar and with Pierre as a passenger.

Evan sighed. At least he had a last name.

Chapter *6*

KYLEE CALLED in sick for the first time in her life, yet she had never felt better. She had a good breakfast of yogurt and strawberries. She downloaded a Mariah Carey song. She slipped into her favorite black pants and burgundy top. She put aside the keys to her Jeep and caught a last-minute ride with Evan.

"We're commuting together," she said as Evan grabbed the keys to the MGB. "Would you like to know why?"

"I assume it's Claire. Coffee, shopping, or some girl thing. You have one lunch together, and now you're best friends."

"Not quite, but I agree that we do have a lot in common."

"Tell me; why are we commuting?"

"I had a call from Russell," Kylee said as Evan opened the garage door. "It seems he can help us."

"Russell, huh? By us, you mean you."

"For now, yes. Later on you, Paul, and the police may get involved."

"Good luck with that." Evan pulled on the car door. "You want to find out about Fred. I want to figure out my father."

"What does Paul have to say?"

"Like he tells me what's going on. I'm his son. I'm supposed to take over someday. But I'm bettin' that Russell knows more than me. Officially, I am on nobody's need-to-know list. And that bothers me no end."

"You think that there might be a layoff coming?"

"Two days ago, I would've said 'no, definitely not.' I thought Dad still ran the place. But now, I'm not sure who's in charge." He looked at Kylee. "Whatever you do, do not lose *your* job."

"Don't worry. I have plenty of sick days and plenty of time to investigate Fred."

"I was afraid you'd say that."

"This week or this year," she said, "I don't care how long it takes—I'll uncover what happened."

"Well, this week or this year, I might figure out my father. Sometimes, he just doesn't make sense."

Kylee fixed her hair, fixed her makeup, and set the radio for smooth jazz. She had a one-day plan and help with her investigation. For her, that was all that made sense.

They arrived at the Dove plant and parked. Evan kissed her goodbye then took off to his office in the Juniper Building.

Kylee headed to the visitor lobby and found Russell. He signed her in and escorted her down a winding lavender path to the Cottonwood Building. Kylee picked a small blue blossom and sniffed it. It reminded her of spring.

She felt confident and eager to start her investigation, but as soon as she stepped into Russell's lab, she felt like a child on a first visit to an ER. To someone who preferred sand over silicon, outdoors to indoors, Russell's environment of meters, scopes, cables, and flashing lights caught her off guard.

"I've worked with EKG monitors," she said, "but it doesn't come close to what you have here."

"What, these toys?" Russell laughed.

"Now, this; I understand." She flipped through a sporting-dog calendar. "You know, Claire has a Bernese Mountain Dog. Ever talk to her about that?"

"Claire, from HR?"

"Yeah, you remember—the pretty one. She knows all about dogs and engineers."

"Same difference, huh?"

"You know what I mean. She seems nice."

"I'm sure she is." Russell rolled a vinyl chair to Kylee and grabbed one for himself. He swiveled his monitor and displayed rows of data. Like a trained Springer Spaniel, he kept his mind on his work.

"Let me tell you, this is one beautiful sat' phone. It took me half the night to tap into it, but once you get by the password, the rest is cake."

The rear cover of the phone was removed, and a dozen blue wires dangled from Russell's equipment to the phone like IV tubes to a critical patient.

Kylee moved in for a look. "Why do you need a password? Evan had it working on the mountain top."

"Apparently, Fred turned it on and left it on. Evan was using Fred's password until the battery died."

"I see." She tried to keep up with Russell's logic, but Russell was talking pretty fast.

"You say this fell on the rocks?"

Kylee nodded.

"I wish we could build our stuff like this. It's solid as a rock and light as a chicken sandwich. But here's what you came to see." He tapped the keyboard. "You have a hundred features. So far, I have six up and running. Look at this."

With a few more clicks, the numbers scrolled. "Here's Fred's directory. You've got your usual favorites; his wife, Paul McKenna, Fred's admin, his mechanic, some medical group, and this guy— Pierre Simon."

"Who?"

"A week ago, I would've asked the same question. But now it makes sense. Pierre is one of the Frenchmen taking over this place. Obviously, Fred was part of the pre-merger inspection. Due diligence and such."

Kylee wrote down names and numbers as fast as she could.

"I'll get you a printout."

"Interesting, but not unusual." She let her gaze roam the lab.

"Not that. Then maybe this." Russell pointed at the top lines. "Six calls a day for the last week. Each one was ten or fifteen minutes. Likewise, the last call Fred ever made. You're probably wondering; who's at the other end?"

"Evan said a stockbroker."

"Close." Russell pressed a key, and his monitor jumped alive with the logo of a Texas longhorn and a name; Bullman Stock Investing.

"It's a data link," Russell said. "Not a real person."

"And not too informative," Kylee said.

"Kylee, please, you don't have to be an engineer to add two and two."

"Well, sum it up for me."

"It's obvious; with inside info and a simple text, Fred could make millions. And he could do it from it office or from a mountain in the Sierras. I'm sorry; that's what it boils down to."

Kylee softened her voice. "Just doing it for the money."

"Apparently so." Russell leaned back in his chair. "Easy money, I guess."

"No such thing. Especially with Fred being dead."

Chapter 7

EVAN KNEW her face, and he had her name. Now, he had a chance to understand her intentions. The morning after the announcement, Evan was summoned to Mireille's hastily arranged, corner office in the Juniper Building. Despite his earlier apprehensions, he vowed to keep an open mind.

Mireille hung up her phone and stood close to Evan. With her white blouse, gray jacket, and matching skirt, she seemed as stunning as on the day they met.

"I'm sorry that Paul never showed a picture of you," Mireille said. "Or talked about you. I would've introduced myself. You remember; that day you poked under my Jag."

"I was not poking." Evan scowled. "Which reminds me; we drove up and down those hills for an hour. At some point, you knew I worked at Dove, but you never said a word."

"I wanted to, especially after I realized how much you loved your job. But legally, I was not allowed."

"Not a hint."

"Fortunately, the situation has changed. That's why I asked you here. Please, have a seat." She motioned at a small conference table.

"Dove and Trudeau are partners now," she said. "And the way we work is straightforward. Dove has the hardware. Trudeau has the cash flow and the software. The challenge is; how do we work together and build Everest? That's where you come in, Evan. I asked around, and it seems you're the one expert everyone trusts. You know what you're doing, and you go the extra kilometer."

Evan grinned. "How can I help?"

"I need someone to run the operations group."

"You have Waterman for that."

Mireille rolled her eyes. "You'll be the director. You'll meet the milestones, plan the resources, budget, and so on. Naturally, your salary will be commensurate. By the way, you'll get a company car and one of these." She slid him a familiar satellite phone.

"Yeah, I've seen it." Evan fondled the smooth leather case.

"You have?" Mireille raised an eyebrow. "It's still a prototype."

"Fred Mott."

"Yes, I almost forgot. At Trudeau, it's standard policy; key people must stay in touch wherever they are."

Evan set the phone aside. "Company car, you said."

"I thought you would like that." Mireille stood, adjusted the blinds on the window, and pointed. "If you look between those trees."

Evan stood then squinted. "Great, what is it; a Lexus?"

Mireille held her face close to Evan's to see what caught his eye. "No, the car next to it."

"You're not serious."

"I wouldn't lie to you, Evan. It's a brand new Jaguar XKE."

Evan's heart began to pound, and he took a deep breath. He inhaled the lilac scent of Mireille's delicate perfume. Beautiful car, beautiful woman; there had to be a connection. Then he moved away, trying to keep focused on his work. "By the way, what happens to Waterman?"

"That's our next assignment. Let's walk."

Mireille's matter-of-fact tone hinted that Waterman's pleasant morning—if he was having one—was soon to be derailed. Evan held back a satisfied grin.

The beautiful morning suddenly seemed sunnier as Evan followed Mireille along the rosemary-lined garden path that led to the main assembly hanger. The fresh air eased his normally tense neck, and he couldn't help smiling at the workers who walked by.

As Mireille picked up the pace, she pulled keys from her purse. She jingled them and passed them to Evan. "First John, then the Jag."

"Okay."

"Then the Everest schedule," she said.

"I saw that coming."

"Nothing is free. We all pay, in one respect or another. But not to worry; I checked out Dove and Everest. I believe that you are both in good shape."

Despite the temptation, Evan carefully avoided denigrating his own company. It would've been bad form, especially during his first official meeting with his new boss. He looked to his side and saw Waterman.

"There's John," he softly said. "And he's got that mutt dog with him. Hard to say who's more useful."

"Mutt?" Mireille laughed. "I don't think so."

When they approached, Mireille suddenly dropped to her heels, her knees almost hitting the sidewalk. She spread her arms and called out, "*C'est joli! Viens ici, mon petit chiot.*"

Coco raised his already-upright ears. Like a dog running home, he wagged his tail, shot out his tongue, and dashed to Mireille. She lifted him as she stood then hugged him tightly.

"You must have liver bits in your pocket," Waterman said. "He never does that for me."

"I have a way with animals."

Waterman raised his brow. "Two-legged or four?"

Mireille held Coco face to face. "John, I thought we could talk in your office," she said, keeping her eyes on Coco.

Waterman winced. He moved to get within her view. "This looks private enough."

Mireille surveyed the courtyard. A few workers wandered in the distance, but otherwise, it seemed clear.

"Fine." She set Coco to the ground then drew a long, deep breath. "We have a special project. Starting now and for the next four months, you can help us with the Pacific Rim. I understand that you have contacts, and the Rim is our weak area—especially the Japanese. It is well established that the Japanese are a demanding group."

Waterman began to fidget. "Special projects; around here, that's the kiss of death."

"Not at all. The Japanese are our second-biggest market. We need them, and they need us."

"And the operations group?" Waterman looked at Evan.

"I'll work myself in," Evan replied.

Waterman's voice fell to a growl. "You can't get rid of me that easily."

"John, no one is trying to get rid of you. You will spend half your time in the field. The other half—in Apple Valley with our sales team."

"The old man won't go for it," Waterman said, turning away.

"Already a done deal. But if you wish, you may confirm it with the CEO."

"Around here, it's never a done deal." Waterman walked a few steps and snapped his fingers. "Coco, come!"

Coco circled Mireille's ankles, started a run to John but suddenly returned to Mireille. He wagged his tail faster.

"Coco!" Waterman raised his voice, but Coco stood fast. He beckoned with his arms to no avail. He narrowed his eyes. "What good is a dog if I spend half my life in Japan? Go ahead, you keep the mutt!" He stormed off, flailing his arms and mumbling something about "Paul this" or "Paul that."

Mireille picked up the dog and cuddled. "I know a purebred when I see one. My little Papillion. I guess now you're mine."

Evan smirked. "You're making friends left and right." He stood close and patted Coco's head.

"So it seems. However, I believe that my new friend deserves a new name." Mireille hesitated then smiled at the dog. "From now on, you're Jean-Petit."

"I'm sorry. You said that way too fast. Did you just call him 'John Pretty'?"

"No, Jean-Petit. It means 'Little John.' "

"Now, that makes sense."

Chapter *8*

"JUST GETTING HOME?" Kylee sat up in bed and spun the clock radio for a clearer view. It was ten-thirty, and she was tired.

"We had to get the nose gear cycled." Evan placed his keys and phone onto the nightstand then rubbed his hand against his fourteen-hour chin stubble. "It's an all-night test. If we delayed it, we set back the whole schedule. Waterman left us in a bind; that's for sure."

Kylee tried to keep her voice calm. "It's been that way for weeks. I hardly see you, and we never talk. It's like you live at the plant. And when you're home, you shut down; TV, beer, and microwave nachos. That's not my idea of a marriage."

"Listen, Kylee, I'm tired. How about we—"

"Just tell me when."

Evan unbuttoned the top of his shirt and took in a deep breath. "When we get Everest sold, we might have a chance to slow down. We might afford a break. Until then, it's more of the same."

"That's not what I asked."

"I'm sorry. You lost me."

"I want to know," she said, "when do I meet her?"

"Her?"

"You know who. Mireille; your boss of the month. High-strung, demanding, okay-looking Mireille. I'd like to meet her."

"Why?"

Kylee laughed. "What do you mean, why? I heard she's wealthy, single, and French. If *any* of that's true—"

"You don't believe I've been working? How about this?" He lifted his scraped knuckles. "Ten hours in a wheel well; does that sound romantic?"

Kylee grimaced. "I also heard she's taking over Fred's job."

"How do you know that?"

"I spent ten hours on the Internet. I know the story of Trudeau. I know how they acquire companies. I know they're aggressive."

Evan laughed. He shuffled to the bathroom and flipped on the lights. "It could be you wasted ten hours. If anyone got the short stick on this deal, it's Trudeau."

"And Fred; did he feel the same way? What was he doing with Mireille?"

Evan firmly shut the medicine cabinet. "I don't want to hear about Fred. I don't want to hear about Mireille. For some reason, you just don't believe me. There's nothing between Mireille and me. There was nothing between Mireille and Fred. There was nothing between anybody and Fred. What you have is one paranoid obsession."

Kylee swung her feet over the edge of the bed. "What I have is nightmares every night. I see Fred's face. I see the plane going down. I see flames. I wake up screaming. Evan, you know that. You know something's wrong. All I want is a little understanding. All I want is the nightmares to stop."

"How is meeting Mireille going to help?"

Kylee went face to face with Evan. "You might be right; I might be totally wrong. Mireille and Fred; it could be nothing. But I do have intuition. I'm hoping that if I meet her—or Pierre—I can start to move on. I'm hoping for once, I'll be able to sleep the whole night."

She softly stroked Evan's wrist and hoped her hazel eyes would compensate for her lack of makeup and her flannel pajamas. "Come on, five minutes to say hello. A handshake and a 'Welcome to California.' I'll keep it to small talk. I won't mention Fred, or the money, or stockbrokers. I'll share a coffee with the boss, and then I'll leave you alone … for a while."

Evan squirmed. He tossed his shirt onto a chair. He stepped to the bathroom mirror, stared at himself, and ran his fingers through his hair. He splashed water on his face, dried it with a towel, and then turned to Kylee. "All right. You want to meet her; we'll do it. I'll give you two hours Saturday night."

Kylee narrowed her eyes, suspecting a trap.

"No, really. It's already set up. Part business, part social."

"Go on."

"We have customers coming in from Korea, and we have one day—one night—to dazzle them. We show them the plant, the plane, and the schedule. We top it off with cocktails at seven. Mireille's going to the party. Employees can bring a spouse—if they want. There's your chance; yes or no?"

Kylee hesitated. She didn't like hasty decisions no matter what they were. She moved Evan's shirt from the chair to the hamper. Then she looked at him and asked, "What should I wear?"

***

On Saturday night, Evan and Kylee drove to the Marriott. When they arrived, the party was well underway with the cocktails flowing faster than the Sierra runoff. Claire had organized the entire event, and from first appearances, it seemed First Class through and through.

In the corner, a jazz band played; any request from Beëthoven to Bon Jovi. Wandering from group to group, an LA magician impressed them all; card tricks, slight of hand, and a whole lot of fire for his final disappearance. Everywhere Kylee turned, servers pushed endless carts of caviar, champagne, foie gras, autumn rolls, and bulgogi. Not bad for what she paid.

She looked across the room as a young woman escaped a circle of smiling men. Probably Mireille, Kylee surmised, but possibly not. She was much younger and prettier than Evan's description. But who else would head straight for Evan, enticing grin on her face?

Evan managed the introductions.

"Finally we meet." Mireille extended her hand. "I must say, Kylee, you are very brave."

"How so?"

"To be young and beautiful in a room full of engineers and pilots. You will be, oh, what's that word—a magnet for attention."

"Call me crazy, I married an engineer." She wrapped her arm around Evan's waist, squeezed him, and smiled at him.

"Then congratulations."

"Or condolences," Evan said.

Kylee organized her first impressions. Mireille obviously had a lot of money and power. Naturally, either attribute was a red flag. She couldn't help but notice that Mireille's complexion seemed as flawless as a Parisian model. Her hair was a delicate shade of auburn—no hint of roots. Her Louboutin shoes seemed a perfect complement to her size seven feet. Mireille was beautiful by most anyone's standards. She was set apart from the average boss.

Kylee cringed, feeling a bit intimidated. But then she thought; one on one, woman to woman, with no groveling man around, this California woman could hold her own. It was just a matter of looking beyond the face and dealing with the words. French accent aside, Mireille's words—her voice—were simply average. But then, the night was young, and more conversation and more words were sure to follow.

Unfortunately, Kylee turned her back for barely a moment, and Mireille was gone—leaving her with nothing more than echoes of a token hello. Kylee had asked for five minutes, and that was all she got. And Evan, to her dismay, seemed to have the same business model. He latched onto the Korean chief pilot and hustled him off to enjoy *banchan*, cocktails, and old stories of the 747.

"Thanks a lot," Kylee grumbled. She tried to mingle the best she could, but soon, she found it a wasted effort. Korean customers with accents, Frenchmen with accents, engineers with their own jargon, and Guatemalan busboys who only knew Spanish; no way did she fit in. All she could talk about was dogs and the weather. Even then, she could only hope they understood.

Finally, at the sit-down dinner, she realized that there was at least one other topic that she and the others shared. On her right was Evan; on her left, Pierre. Across the table sat the CEO of Korean Air.

She leaned close to Pierre and casually asked him, "Tell me, Pierre, how did you know Fred Mott?" She waited for his response. When she heard none, she blamed the background noise or some language barrier. She reached into her purse and pulled out a printout. She placed it in front of Pierre.

"Does this look familiar?" She lightly nudged Pierre and tapped the image of the Bullman Stock logo.

Pierre's wandering gaze finally settled on the paper. He took it and checked the front and back. "What is it?"

"Fred Mott's stockbroker, I think. At least he made a lot of calls to this place." She poked at the Longhorn cattle image. "I need a broker myself. I'm wondering if he's any good."

Pierre passed it back. "Sorry."

"Are you sure?"

With a firm nudge, Evan told her, "Not the time or place." He narrowed his eyes then abruptly stood. He turned his back on Kylee and faced the neighboring table. "Mireille," he said. "Showtime."

Kylee let out a deep breath, exasperated. Her personal agenda had just been shut down, hard. It seemed clear that Mireille's highly anticipated sales pitch would dominate the rest of the night. Any dialogue about Fred would be lost among the noise. She folded her hands on her lap. It was time to become a corporate citizen. So she kept silent and carefully watched.

Mireille walked like a Hollywood actress and took her place at a podium. Claire swung a spotlight to highlight the Trudeau logo as, once again, the boss took center stage. Mireille held a wireless microphone and immediately launched into her opening remarks.

"Gentlemen ... ladies, I ask that you look around this room. Take a careful look at this group of scientists, engineers, pilots, financiers, and managers. These are the people who will make Everest fly. I have no doubt in my mind; we will be successful. With our combined efforts, we will build the next-generation aircraft. We will allow more people to fly more places. We will change the face of world economics. Remember this day as a part of history."

Kylee watched and listened to Mireille as she used flawless English, a hint of French, great enthusiasm, and the perfect amount of hand waving. Just how scripted was the episode? It didn't matter. Mireille had the spotlight, and she was stunning. Every eye in the room was transfixed on her as a leader and motivator. Kylee slumped in her seat. The woman who had it all was now tugging at Evan's hand, encouraging him to be at her side.

It took a blinding spotlight for Kylee to open her eyes. Visually, they were a perfectly matched set. Mireille had dressed in her black skirt and white blouse, accented with a red scarf. Evan had worn a gray blazer and sunset red tie. His new hair color seemed to be a shade closer to auburn.

Kylee wasn't sure—did his tie clasp match her earrings? Evan had mentioned that Mireille often used a personal shopper and stylist. Obviously, that stylist had spent much of the morning with Evan and didn't stop with what Evan had described as a "new haircut and tie."

Evan followed with his own ad-lib speech—equally elegant, articulate, and enthusiastic. With Mireille at his side, they became a perfectly tuned set of stereo speakers. With Mireille at his side, they seemed the perfect ambassadors for a new partnership. The way they smiled and waved at the crowd, it seemed clear that this couple couldn't be happier.

Dessert came, but it didn't matter. By now, Kylee had a pain in her stomach and a headache that wouldn't quit.

Chapter 9

"IF WE WERE in France, this would already be fixed." Pierre slapped his hand on Russell's flight control computer. He grabbed a pen and tapped it on the monitor. The screen flashed; Error Code 999—shutdown complete. "We are in the middle of final integration. If you cannot outsource the software, this will happen again."

Pierre abruptly stepped away and raised his hand. He waited for Mireille, Evan, and Russell to follow his aim as he gestured to Everest. "Most of your plane you outsource; wings, landing gear, hydraulics. Why not software?"

Russell frowned. "Any more outsourcing, we'd be out of a job."

"Another crash like this," Pierre jabbed his finger at the monitor, "and you will lose your job anyway."

Russell popped open his eyes then quickly narrowed them. He glared at Pierre.

Mireille set Jean-Petit onto the concrete floor. She gently coaxed Pierre's hand away from the monitor. "What Pierre means is; we'll all be out of a job. Your module is a key part of the plane. If it doesn't work—hardware or software—we don't have a plane, and we don't have a product."

Evan stood shoulder to shoulder to Mireille. He pointed at the frozen screen. "What Mireille means is; we'll get you the help you need. Make a list of the issues and what we have to do to fix them."

Russell pressed the reset button. "Okay, so far we have about twenty problems. We have the flap hydraulic blowout at full extension; we need a software limit as a workaround. We have the actuator temperature problem—"

"Not now," Evan said. "Send me a PowerPoint."

Pierre tugged at the sleeve of his suit. Like a referee at a boxing match, he slid himself between Evan and Mireille. "For our planes, we already have the software. We already have the tests and the results. You should simply merge the two and run it."

Russell opened his mouth as if to speak, but the words failed to follow.

"Put it on your list," Evan told Russell. "Get their software and test it out."

Mireille nodded her agreement.

Evan yanked out his new phone and made a note. He checked the time; 7:12 p.m. He had three more engineers to meet, six more problems to solve, and then home to a frustrated wife. It was only Monday.

**

"Tell me, what's the big surprise?" Evan asked Kylee when he finally arrived home. "Your text said it's something good."

"I don't know why you got a phone," she said. "When I call, you never answer."

"Yeah, well, Mireille wants them off during meetings. Etiquette, she says."

Kylee stood in front of Evan, held his fingertips, and gave him a big grin. "Anyway, what would you say if you and I started commuting together?"

"I'd say what's wrong with your Jeep now?"

"Nope, try again."

Evan freed his hand and pointed to the far corners. "I'd say the clinic is that direction, and Dove is over there."

"I got a job at Dove!" Kylee squealed.

"You did what?"

"Starting tomorrow. I'm the new admin for Human Resources. Claire got me the job. Actually, I got the job, but Claire put in a good word. She said that I have great listening skills. Empathy; that's what it takes to get ahead."

"You're serious."

"She called this morning. She said to come in for an interview. I said, 'what interview?' She said HR, new position, lots of responsibility. She said if I want the job, I'd have to move fast. So I did."

Kylee bounced to the living room desk and retrieved her Dove employee handbook and badge. "They hired me on the spot. I'll report to Audrie, who reports to Mireille. And Audrie, Claire says, is nothing like Mireille. I think I'm going to like this job."

Evan fingered the badge and peered at the Dove book with a photo of Paul and Fred on the cover. "More money?"

"No."

"Shorter week?"

"Hardly," she said.

"Company car?"

"Yours, if you let me."

"And you took this job because …?"

"I thought you'd be proud," she said. "You know I was burned out at the clinic. I had the same job for five years with ten different managers. This year's been the worst. One day to the next, I never know what's coming. I mean, I like the work. I just hate surprises. Dove Air should be good for me—for us."

Evan loosened the top buttons of his shirt. He ran his finger across the day-old stubble on his chin then shook his head. "I guess you caught me off guard. I've been so busy at work; it never occurred to me that we had the same problem. Well, almost the same problem. You know, with my promotion, you don't have to work."

"I didn't have to work before, when you get down to it. We've always had money. That's not why I took the job. Claire says I'm psychic. You need people like me at Dove. I can sniff out who's doing what to who. She said if I can avoid one wrongful termination lawsuit, I will have paid for myself. So there."

"Psychic powers, huh? What good is that when you spend all your time at a computer? That's what they do, you know. Fill out forms and file 'em."

"Claire says there's a lot of stress from the merger. Not to mention noise from the union."

"You mean because I got Cullin fired."

"He's still upset. Well, him and others. Trust me; it won't take much to push these guys over the edge. But I can help. I can talk to them and discover what the real issues are. If we do it right, we won't see them in court. You might know engineering, Evan, but people—human beings—are my talent."

"The great negotiator." Evan grinned then nodded. "You think you can do it?"

"It's body language. I don't care what someone says; I look at their eyes."

"Well, these eyes are bloodshot and tired. We'll talk tomorrow." Evan undid the last of his shirt buttons and headed for the bedroom door. "I can't wait to hear what Mireille has to say."

"I won't be working for Mireille."

"Darling, I'm beginning to think that everyone at Dove and Trudeau works for Mireille. The woman takes over wherever she goes."

"I can tell you this; my intuition says Mireille is not the honey boss you think she is."

"Come again?"

"You don't see it, do you?"

"See what?"

"Of course not, you're a man." She followed Evan to the bedroom. "The woman flirts her way to the top."

Evan set his keys and phone onto the nightstand. He raised his voice. "I can tell you for a fact, Mireille does not sleep around."

"I said 'flirts.' And with her looks, she doesn't have to sleep around. I see how men act around her. Disgusting."

"She's got degrees in aeronautics and accounting. She speaks four languages. I'd say Mireille is smart enough to get to the top— with or without her looks."

"A little defensive, are we?" Kylee smirked. "Maybe it's good I work at Dove. Someone should keep an eye on you two."

Evan blinked. "Sounds like a hidden agenda. Tell me again how you got the job? You said it was Claire's idea?"

"At this point, it doesn't matter. My desk is between you and Mireille. I guess we'll meet at the cappuccino machine." She gave a loving smile and a pat on the behind as she passed by Evan. She said good night and went to bed.

***

The next day, Evan got ready for his first 'I told you so.' As he approached Kylee's cubicle, he found her chin-high in files and folders. The top file was labeled 'Years of Service.' He saw page after page of Date of Hire spreadsheets on her computer.

All he got from Kylee was, "Don't say a word."

Evan obliged with a sympathetic tap on her shoulder. "We'll have lunch. I'll stop by around noon." He felt a tapping on his own shoulder that was anything but sympathetic. He spun around and came eye to eye with Daz.

Daz glanced at Kylee. "Excuse me, I need the old man." He jerked his head and aimed his thumb at a nearby conference room. "Two minutes, if you have it."

Before Evan could answer, Daz was halfway there, eyes straight ahead, feet nearly stomping. As Evan caught up and stepped inside the empty room, Daz closed the door behind. He immediately waved an accident report.

"You got your copy?" Daz asked, voice booming and his vocal chords straining.

"While it was warm."

"They're desk pilots. Each and every one." Daz paced the room and randomly waved his papers. "They spend two hours at the crash site for what? Junk science. Half-truths and innuendoes. I can't believe they want to release this."

"They already did. It's supposed to be prelim, but you know the routine."

"Yeah, rubber stamp and move on to the next crash."

Daz tossed the report onto a table as Kylee came through the door with a handful of her own papers. "What's going on?" she asked, quietly. She closed the door behind her. "I can hear you halfway down the hall."

"Your federal government at work." Evan picked up the crash report and flashed it by Kylee. "The official story of Mojave Flight Seven."

"I take it you don't agree."

"They got the flight number straight," Daz grumbled. "From then on, it's a matter of opinion."

"Let me explain." Evan grabbed Kylee's papers then placed them on the table. He pulled up a chair for her to sit and learn. He took a seat next to her, set down the report, and tapped the cover. "Normally they put together a team. The 'party system' or 'go-team' is what they call it. One or two guys from the Board, a union pilot, a manufacturer rep. That way, all sides give an input. In theory, it's balanced."

"In theory," Daz said.

"It's a whole lot better than it used to be," Evan said. "Normally it works. But now—"

"Now I'm confused," Kylee said. "Dove built and designed the plane. And Daz is the best pilot I know. Why—"

"Why weren't we on the team? No, you are not confused. That was our question. Apparently, our rescue got them a little perturbed."

Daz sat opposite Kylee. "One misstep and suddenly we're blackballed."

"All you did was push the plane over a cliff and burn it to a crisp. Why would they get upset over that?"

Daz wagged his finger. "Sarcasm, Kylee. That's not your style."

"Hey, I agree with you guys. What happened on the hill was unavoidable. We had bad weather, bad terrain, and no time to mess around. Accidents happen. They can't blame us for that."

"Actually, they can," Evan said. "They said we should've left the bodies alone. It was their job to investigate—bodies and wreckage intact—unless we had permission."

"What, and leave them there for days or weeks? No way. You did exactly what you should've done, Evan. You got them home as soon as you could."

"*Now* you agree."

"I was under pressure back then." Kylee turned to Daz. "Sorry, Daz, you know I hate turbulence. I wanted to get home and get my feet where they belong."

"No offense, but sooner or later, we'll make you a pilot."

"Funny," Kylee said. Then she picked up the accident report, read through the top-page synopsis, and frowned.

Accident Report: Preliminary

Nonscheduled 14 CFR Part 135: Air Taxi and Commuter

Accident occurred: Friday, March 21, Alpine County, CA
Aircraft: Dove-Gibraltar

Injuries: 3 Fatal

On March 21, at approximately 22:45 pacific daylight time, a Dove Gibraltar aircraft was substantially damaged with a collision with terrain in the mountains south of Highway 4. The commercial pilot, commercial co-pilot, and passenger were fatally injured. During subsequent recovery attempts, the aircraft was destroyed. An instrument flight rules (IFR) plan was filed for a flight from Los Angeles (LAX) to South Lake Tahoe (KTVL). Reported weather at the airport was clear, temperature 28 degrees Fahrenheit, wind from the southeast at 15 knots …

"CFIT," Daz muttered as he grabbed the report and thumbed through the pages.

"What's that?" Kylee asked.

"Controlled flight into terrain. One way of saying they never saw it coming."

"Like I saw in my nightmares."

"What they don't talk about is wind shear." Daz flipped to page six. "You get standing waves set up in those mountains, and, goodbye; you're on your back and headed for the ground."

"Can't be, Daz," Evan said. "Look at the weather report; the storm was an hour behind them. Yeah, there was turbulence, but compared to us, it was smooth and clear. Everything was fine then they cut the power and headed straight for the mountain. They were lost or confused. Possibly both."

Daz threw up his palms. "I knew the pilot. He made that run a hundred times. He could've done it half-asleep."

"Bad choice of words. Now you're talking complacency. Think of it this way; we put in so much automation, he could've been half-asleep. And look at this …" Evan slid his finger to the critical paragraph. "Eight hours a night for two weeks straight. Like I said, what kind of schedule is that? They were pushing the limit. They were flying zombies if you ask me."

"The easy way," Daz said, "is to blame pilot error. It doesn't matter if a meteor falls from the sky and knocks off a wing. You're the pilot; you should be able to land. At least that's what they tell ya."

"Bottom line," Evan leaned back in his chair, "we won't be sued. According to the Safety Board, Dove was not at fault. With the plane and the engine destroyed, they couldn't tell one way or the other. Pilot error is what it comes down to—and no lawsuit for us."

Daz scowled as he pushed open the door and stepped into the hallway. "Do not get me started on lawyers. My blood pressure is pushing its own limit. I got work to do. Call me when you get the Mojave Air response. I'm sure they got something to say about this."

"No doubt," Evan said. "I'd love to listen in right about now."

Daz disappeared while Evan summed up the Mojave Air situation. "Closed case, if you ask me."

Kylee folded her arms. "You believe the government?"

"We got the FAA monkey off our back; for now, at least. Believe me; that's one distraction we don't need. But …"

"But what?"

"The crash was a wake-up call. This report; it's got me worried. I mean, sure, the Gibraltar got a clean bill of health. What more could we ask? It's bad enough to have one of our planes go down—"

"And lose three men."

"But if they blame our design," Evan took a deep breath, "everyone would point at us. Suddenly, my career's in a tailspin. Who knows, I might wind up selling bagels on the corner."

"Career—that's what you think about? What about the passengers? The surviving families? What about the people who fly the same kind of plane? Don't you worry about them?"

"In this business, you can't worry about the passengers; it would drive you nuts. No plane would ever be safe enough. No design would ever be done. Once in a while, yeah, you consider it. But every hour, every day? No, no way."

"Then how do you know your plane is safe? Especially Everest; that plane's a hundred times bigger than Gibraltar. It carries six hundred passengers and two hundred tons of fuel; that's got to keep you awake at night."

Evan nodded. "I agree. By the time we look at every nut and bolt on that plane—every actuator, valve, switch, hose, wire, computer chip—there are a million ways to make a plane crash."

"That's comforting."

"Yeah, well, you know we check every bolt. We check everything. We do what we can to make sure it never fails. But still …"

"Engineers are not perfect." Kylee finished the thought.

"Where have I heard that before?"

Kylee shrugged.

"I've got to double-up on our tests," Evan said. "I've got to make sure we don't overlook any fault with the hardware or software. We were lucky. We weren't blamed for the crash in the hills. But Everest is so big, I'd be out of my mind if I wasn't scared. We have one chance to get it right. We don't say it publicly, but everyone knows it; if Everest goes down, so does the company."

***

The next morning, two coffees before dawn, Evan ushered Daz and Russell to a five-seat conference room in a quiet corner of the Cottonwood Building. Russell arrived in his usual tennis shoes, jeans, and Great White Shark T-shirt. Daz, more conservatively, found his gray slacks and striped cotton shirt, but he neglected to iron or shave.

Evan twisted the handle of the window blinds to privacy mode. "Now we're set."

"Set for what?" Daz cleared his throat, plopped onto a swivel chair, and crossed his arms.

"I need your opinion, guys. But first; a couple comments and a couple questions."

Daz reached across the table to Evan's take out bag of coffee and bagels. He ripped the bag apart to find a Kona and some packets of raw sugar. He made some odd, half-awake motion with his hand, and Evan took that as a cue to start the meeting.

Evan stepped to a flip chart that was propped on an easel. "In my opinion, Everest is nothing more than a big version of Shasta. We sold over eight hundred Shasta, and you won't find a more reliable jet. The first question is; how can we make Everest top that record?"

Evan turned to a clean page and listed the major aircraft systems. "Here's what we're up against. Okay, start with the stabilizer. We've got triple-redundant controls. Same as Shasta. Aileron actuators, same as Shasta."

"Except for the low-speed servo." Russell pointed at the list.

"Okay. Almost the same."

Daz squirmed in his seat and peeled off the ends of his Styrofoam cup. "Great, we have ten systems and two hundred modules. Is there a—"

"Point to all of this?" Evan asked.

"I just want to know if I'm missing lunch or dinner."

"Neither," Evan said, "if you can finish the next list."

"And that would be?"

"Tell me in twenty-five words or fewer, what's different?"

"Between Everest and Shasta," Daz said.

"Correct. And that's what, about four words."

"Okay, wise guy; here's the list." Daz tapped a pen to his chin. "We've got software, navigation computer, modified cockpit, and software, of course."

"You said, 'software,' twice."

"I'll say it again—software! I'll say it four more times if you give me thirty words."

"I'm glad I'm not alone." Evan wrote on the flip chart and twice underlined the word. "We have two problems with software; most of it's new, and a lot of it's going to be French."

Russell leaned forward. "With fly-by-wire, software controls the plane."

"But we already know that."

"Tell us something new," Daz said.

"Let me put it this way," Evan said. "Mireille's sharp. She knows her code and gets the job done. I trust her. But this Pierre fellow; he's a wild card. He's too arrogant for my taste and too quiet."

"Agreed." Daz stepped to the easel and flipped to a clean page. "What's your plan?"

"I want to test Trudeau. I want to see how good they really are. And I don't want to wait until Everest flies. That's way too late. I want to test them now; this week if we can. Our plane and their software. Actually, the Shasta simulator and Pierre's software."

Russell swiveled a full circle in his chair. He threw up his hands and grinned. "Finally, someone listened. I've been asking everyone for this. *Now* you're talking sense."

"Okay, another email I missed. But give me the gist of it. It's the CAS, right? The Command Augmentation System."

"Exactly. It's the one module that controls the whole plane. They've had it for weeks now. I've warned them about the glitch and spin at twenty thousand, but Pierre and the others—they don't listen. This is one place where you don't mess around. You either find and fix all the bugs, or—let me quote Mireille—" Russell puckered his mouth for his French accent, "you don't have a plane."

Daz grinned then pounded his fist on the table. "Let's get 'em. Let's nail their hides to the wall."

"We'll make it a fair test," Evan said. "Step by step, by the books, and with the simulator. Like we found it ourselves."

"One suggestion." Daz pressed his finger to his lips and waited for the dramatic silence.

"Yes, Daz?"

"If you want to show your father what these guys are made of, don't do it in some back-corner lab. Visibility—that's what you want. Put the CAS in Shasta with Pierre's software. I'll take it to twenty thousand. When that baby fails, the nose drops and we head straight for the ground. I'll hit the recover button and level off. Of course, by then your father will be reaching for his pants. And I don't mean for his wallet."

"I like it," Evan said. "We have the aircraft. We have the computer. All we need is Pierre's software. Let's do it."

Daz looked at Russell. "You will install the recover software, yes?"

"I'll make a note," Russell mumbled.

Later that day, Evan passed a draft copy of the new test to Mireille. To his amazement, she agreed to his conditions.

"No problem," Mireille said. "With Pierre's help, we'll be ready."

"You sound pretty sure of yourself."

"You sound doubtful."

"Let's say I'm impressed," Evan said. "And that hardly ever happens."

Mireille brushed back the hair from her face and showed a mysterious, Mona Lisa smile. "It's a matter of knowing what you want and having a plan to get it. No magic."

Evan lowered his eyes. "Unless you're Dove. It seems our five-year plan changes daily."

"Don't worry. Trudeau is like the government; we're here to help."

Evan shuddered.

Mireille gently held his elbow and grinned. "Sometimes, Evan, you are too serious. Trudeau is not at all like the government. We have a saying: *L'argent; c'est le maître absolu.* Cash is queen. We move fast, make money, then find the next opportunity. We're a team now. You, me. Dove, Trudeau. I assure you that we will succeed; if we believe in each other. I have confidence in you, *mon cher.*"

She let her hand drift to his hand. "If you need this test to have confidence in us, then very well, I will do whatever it takes."

Evan kept his hand in place. He looked into her eyes and hoped that he didn't appear as someone who doubted her abilities. "I thought the expression was, 'cash is king'."

"Not anymore. There's a new girl in town." She flaunted her American Slang app. "Let's get with the program."

***

Two weeks later, Kylee formally apologized for accepting her job at Dove Air. As Evan passed her cubicle, she shoved aside a stack of folders and her morning coffee. She spun her chair and stared at Evan with her red, tired eyes.

"This was not what I expected," she said, keeping her voice low. "I was trained for people, not paper. I mean, look at this …Vacation hours, sick leave reports. I'm working overtime for what? Accounting and paperwork? I can't believe I gave up my nursing job."

"What's Claire got to say?"

"I've seen her once. All she said was; 'Hang in there. It's almost over.' "

"What's almost over?"

Kylee shrugged. "I don't know. But it's been two weeks, and I haven't thought of Fred. I haven't had one nightmare. That's promising, I guess. Even so, I thought once I was here—"

"You'd have more time and more help—for Fred, that is."

"Maybe," she said.

"You're surprised we're actually busy."

"I didn't say that."

"You didn't have to." Evan looked over Kylee's shoulder and scanned her desk. "I thought Mireille gave you a sat' phone."

"Yeah."

"Where is it? I called twice this morning. No answer."

"It's in my desk."

"That's a good place for it."

"I told Mireille I didn't need a cell phone." Kylee grabbed her coffee and sipped it. "She gave me one anyway."

"She's not going to like this."

"Yeah, so?"

Evan widened his eyes. "Anyway, the reason I called you; Daz is taking up Shasta. We got an Everest mod in, and you can see the whole test on the monitors. Grab your bagel and let's go. If you're interested."

"You really want me there?" Kylee flashed a bright smile.

"Let me put it this way, there's a reason for the midnight shift. If you can see what we do here …"

"Then I might complain less. Is that your plan?"

"Cynical, are we?"

"I know you, Evan. It's always one scheme or another."

"Sorry, but today is a freebie. If I can educate one former nurse ..."

"Save that for your gullible engineers. It turns out; I'd love to go, hidden agenda or not. And if Daz is the pilot, so much the better. I haven't seen him fly since we went to the mountains."

Evan tore off a chunk of Kylee's bagel and shoved it into his mouth. "Then it's a date. When you see the test, try to look impressed. These guys have been pulling sixteen-hour shifts. They're tired; real tired. Give them some praise or a smile. That helps ... Shall we?"

They linked arms along the winding acacia- and cactus-lined path that led to the lobby of the demo lab. On a day like this, the cactus was thriving. Eighty-eight degrees and barely enough wind to nudge the American flag. The air conditioned lobby was a welcome oasis in an otherwise-stifling Dove industrial park. Evan swung open a set of double doors and led Kylee to a darkened amphitheater. Dove and Trudeau workers sat among rows of color monitors.

"This is where we dazzle the airlines." Evan led her up one row and down another. "From here, we can show everything from fuel flow to the video playing in seat 7-A. We can monitor noise levels and—"

"What's this screen for?" Kylee stood in front of a nine-foot TV.

Evan turned on the full-motion display. "This puts you in the pilot's seat."

Kylee jumped back as a jagged mountain came crashing forward.

"Wait a second, let me zoom out ... That's better. And perfectly on schedule; Daz and Shasta are airborne." Evan snapped on a set of wireless headphones and adjusted the mic. "How do you read, Captain Daz?"

"Five by five," Daz replied.

Evan turned to Kylee. "Today we're testing the CAS. The Command Augmentation System. The goal today is to take Shasta up to twenty thousand with maximum power and minimum fuel. Basically, it's our computer and their software."

Russell gave a quick, acknowledging wave. He grinned.

"With a small modification," Evan said, beckoning Mireille. "With your permission, Mireille, I'd like do an engine-out at twenty thousand. Recovery, climb, then back to normal."

"Fine," she said. "Whatever you think we need. Let us know when you're ready." Mireille excused herself to Pierre's monitor.

Stepping away from the background, Paul went to her side. He kept silent but wrote a few notes. Like most of the workers in the room, Paul had no clue what was coming next. Certainly more drama that way. Evan had no issue dealing up a surprise of his own for his father.

"Let the show begin." He leaned close to Kylee and whispered, "With Pierre's software, it's pass or fail. If he passes, great. If he fails, he's back to France. And oh, what a shame. But don't worry; either way, it's safe."

Evan picked up the flight test sequence and called out the procedures. Daz acknowledged and took the aircraft up to the assigned altitude.

"Increase power," Evan said calmly.

"Increasing power," Daz replied, equally calm. "Oil pressure on number two is running high but okay. Outside air temp—zero. Hey, I'll bring the cold air back for ya." He laughed and followed with a cough.

Evan turned to Kylee and explained. "So far, the module's passing. A dozen tests and not a single issue. Looks like an 'A plus.'" He gave a thumbs-up to Mireille. "And now the improv ... Okay, Daz, let's run the modified test."

"Shutting down number one."

"Turn right, heading zero-niner-zero. Climb and maintain two-two thousand."

Evan leaned to Kylee. "This is normally where we see a glitch and spin."

"What does that mean?"

Evan lifted a finger for Kylee to stand by. He slowly lowered it as Daz continued to climb.

"Passing two-one thousand," Daz said. "All okay. Adding more rudder."

"Strange, it should've happened by now."

"What's strange?" Kylee tugged on Evan's sleeve.

Evan looked at Russell. Russell shrugged.

"Passing two-five thousand," Daz said. "Increasing power."

"I'm stunned." Evan shook his head as he grabbed his clipboard. "Their software works. It's another passing grade."

"Two-eight-thousand," Daz said. "Increasing to full power, number two."

"Let's move on to the cruise cooling test," Evan said.

Daz refused to acknowledge. "I felt a shudder. Continuing to climb."

"We got nothing on the monitors. Let's move on."

"Almost there."

"Save it for later, Daz."

"Adding elevator."

"Stick to the cards," Evan said, raising his voice. "Abort the climb. Abort the test. Half-power number one and two. Descend immediately!"

Evan stared at the huge monitor. The screen showed a telescope image of the Shasta in a wild, nose-up attitude.

"This can't be good," Kylee said.

Mireille left her post and stood shoulder to shoulder with Evan. She stared at the monitor. "This was not part of the test. What is he doing?"

"He felt a surge. It might be a problem with the CAS."

"We are not cleared for that airspace."

"I know. He's almost done." Evan switched on his mic. "I've got Kylee here, Daz. And she can tell ya; we got no problems."

"Passing three-zero thousand."

Mireille stared at Evan's monitor. She pressed her finger onto the screen. "Actually, you do have a problem. Temperature is off scale."

Evan pounded on the keyboard and pulled up a new set of numbers. He opened his mic again. "Daz, looks like you got a fire on number two."

Silence for an eternal moment, then Daz came back. "Confirmed. Emergency procedure on screen. Shutting down number two."

"Halon release, fire extinguisher on number two," Evan said.

"No pressure," Daz said. "Canister empty."

"Okay, plan B."

"What's that?" Kylee asked.

Evan ignored her as he continued to bark out a long string of numbers and commands. "Never Exceed is six hundred knots. But you're fine; we tested it to six-fifty. Get the nose down and you should reach it and recover at …" Evan yanked out his calculator and tapped on the small keypad. "Okay, that's cutting it close."

"What altitude?" Daz asked.

"Looks like a house skimmer—five to eight thousand feet."

"Not a problem." Daz lowered the nose. "Four hundred knots and accelerating. Fire progressing."

All eyes were on the big screen as the aircraft trailed ominous, black smoke. It seemed to head straight for the ground.

"Five-fifty knots. Fire progressing. Barber pole approaching."

"Cutting it too close," Evan said. "Drop back to plan C."

"What's that?" Kylee asked, forcibly.

Evan kept his eyes on the monitors but quickly explained, "Raise the nose, slow the speed, pop the window, and bail out while he has a chance."

Kylee staggered away from the screen and closed her eyes.

Mireille leaned closer to Kylee. "The Dove plane is experimental. Daz has a parachute and he knows how to use it. All he has to do is release the cockpit window and squeeze out. I've seen it done—on the ground."

"Please, Mireille. I'm busy." Kylee closed her eyes tighter. She started a hushed prayer.

Mireille moved next to Evan. "Slow down and aim the plane over the desert!" she shouted into Evan's mic.

"I can do this!" Daz shouted back. "Six hundred knots. Altitude; you don't want to know."

"Pull up! Pull up!" The automated voice blared at Daz.

"Pull up! Pull up!" Evan and Mireille shouted.

"I can do this," Daz said with a strained voice. "Fire is—"

Suddenly, and despite all the twisting of knobs and pounding of keyboards, the video turned to a blue screen. The voice transmission became indecipherable static. All eyes in the dark room, save Kylee's, were glued to the monitors in front. No image, no voice, no sign of the man who had pushed Dove to forefront of aviation. No one moved. No one breathed. Then, like the hand of God striking down and shattering all hopes and prayers, the entire building shook with a pounding boom. It echoed from the mountains to the south desert floor. The hand of God had just violently slammed the door.

Chapter *10*

THE TELEMETRY monitors in the demo lab flashed red then flatlined. With them, faded any real hope of seeing Daz alive again. Yet everyone in the lab kept their eyes on the screens in front, as though willpower itself would bring the video and Daz back to life. But unfortunately, the room full of equipment remained shut down. The entire team of professionals—Evan, Mireille, Pierre, Russell, and Paul, and others—remained silent as the equipment in front of them.

Everyone remained silent and staring—except Kylee. She prayed despite the rumbling outside. Despite the wide-eyed looks of those around her, her eyes remained closed.

Evan placed his hand on her shoulder; partly to ease her apprehension and partly for his own support.

"He had a parachute?" Kylee asked, trying to stay hopeful.

Evan didn't—couldn't—answer. He hoped his silence would say enough.

Mircille eased her way to Kylee's side. "He was going too fast. It wouldn't have helped," she softly said.

Kylee winced. Her entire body shivered. She staggered to the amphitheater exit and stumbled outside, splashing the dark room with rays of sunlight.

Evan glanced at Mireille but avoided her eyes. When the lobby door slammed shut, Evan also shivered. He slid his headset down to his neck. He moved slowly but steadily to the door, squinting and shielding his eyes as he passed through.

He found Kylee at the end of the sage garden path. They stood next to the long-range tracking telescopes and stared up. Evan scanned the San Bernardino foothills. His heart sank with the image that ominously appeared in the cloudless sky. Overhead, a straight line of serrated black smoke pointed like a finger of death to the mountain ridge. There was no other sign of Daz or the plane he flew.

Overhead speakers crackled with a tell-tale static. Where was the deep, self-assured voice of the test pilot who knew the Dove planes better than the people who designed them? To Evan, the whole situation made no sense. The day was simply too beautiful for any harm to come to a good friend and a well respected man. His heart was not ready for anything but a "welcome back and a job well done."

He rested his hand against the tracking camera but pulled back when the heat of the sun-baked enamel burned his fingers. The hot, dry sandy soil of the garden path filled his senses with a dusty memory that would surely stay with him for the rest of his life.

As Kylee continued to gaze silently into the distance, the bright sun fell onto her face and forced the first of what was sure to be a million tears.

Footsteps sounded from behind as the demo lab began to empty. Evan ignored them. His eyes, his mind, jumped from Kylee to the sky, to nowhere in particular. He preferred to close his eyes, but the memories of Daz were as haunting as the sights around him.

It took the high-pitched whir of the tracking camera to snap him from his aimless gaze. The black tube cranked up and pushed him aside. The blinking red and yellow lights pulsated with a new urgency. Evan wondered; what was that camera searching for? What was so important? In a heartbeat, he understood.

Between the mountain peaks of the Cajon Pass, he caught the glimmer of sunlight from a desert mirage. Not smoke or flames, but some kind of moving spot. He squinted as the object grew larger and well defined. *Could it be?* Evan wondered. Could it be Kylee's prayers were mercifully answered?

The static from the loudspeakers suddenly vanished, replaced with an eerie silence that froze the workers behind him. Evan stared at the horizon for any sign of humanity. Then he heard a faint voice. He turned and listened.

"Daz to base," was what he heard—or wanted to hear. "Daz to base." Louder this time.

Evan stared at the hills. The telescope swung up to follow the image of a Shasta jet screaming his way. Before Evan could hug Kylee for each of her prayers, the jet roared overhead and blew up enough dust and sand to blind the telescopes. Those instruments fell silent, but the unabated roar of the Dove engineering team took over. They filled the air with an overwhelming round of applause. Now there was no doubt; Daz was alive.

Evan slipped on his wireless headset. He clicked on the mic and called up to the man of the hour. "Talk to me, Daz. You got folks down here just waiting to breathe."

From the sound of his voice, Daz was happier than the others—but for a different reason. "This one's for the record books!" he shouted, pushing his hoarse voice to the limit. "We've got the first Shasta to break the sound barrier."

"The sonic boom." Evan bobbed his head at the obvious. "I'm amazed you still got wings."

"Yeah, I got one engine, no flaps, a hand-held transmitter, and plenty of wings. This bird knows how to fly!"

"Do me a favor; get that bird on the ground. As of now, the flight test is over. What do you say, we call it a day."

"Roger that, my friend. Make it a cold one. I'm coming home."

It took a Sam Adams lunch at the Oasis lounge and a lot of re-living the past flight for Evan and Daz to settle down. They slowly got to the point of the morning's exercise.

"What went wrong?" Evan asked as he snacked on a pretzel. "We we're supposed to nail Pierre to the wall. All we got was major egg on the face."

"I did my part," Daz said. "It didn't quite work out as planned."

"Work out? It wasn't close to our plan. Between the engine-out and the fire, we almost lost another pilot."

"Hardly," Daz said. "Start to finish, I never lost control."

"You were halfway to LA before you dropped the flaps and nearly ripped 'em off."

"I had to slow down somehow. Speed brakes were inoperative."

Evan popped a pretzel into his mouth. "A lot more than speed brakes were inop on that plane. I can't figure out; why a fire on number two?"

"You don't remember, do you?"

"Remember what?" Evan said.

"Five years ago. Thrust reverser. Big problem with the hose fittings."

Evan shrugged. "It must've been my week off."

"It was more likely your first week on Gibraltar. After five years, you're still playing catch-up."

"I know every service bulletin on that plane. The thrust reverser was never a problem."

"Not quite," Daz said. "We had an issue with the prototype. Hydraulics—well, they leaked into the burn chamber. Talk about your flame thrower."

"How come I never heard about it?"

"Found and fixed. No big deal. Production was never an issue."

"Apparently, no one fixed the prototype," Evan said.

"That's my guess. And you can guess who the safety manager was back then."

"That's gotta be Len Harris."

"Your good friend," Daz said. "You think he's a joke now, you should've seen him then. It's a wonder we got any plane off the ground."

"Now, he's back for Everest."

"In more ways than one, it seems." Daz stared through the Oasis window. "Turn around and check it out. Ain't that your ol' buddy?"

Evan leaned over the back of the chair. He saw Harris circle the Jaguar and make a beeline for the Oasis door.

"Now what does he want?" Evan moaned. He motioned for the check.

"And he brought two of his friends."

The uninvited trio stumbled through the door and scanned the dimly lit bar. Harris stood in front. The two men behind him could have been outcast bikers, but Evan recognized them as cronies of Harris—old members of his Stress Analysis Group. Evan sensed the stress of this meeting would rise to new heights.

Harris zeroed in on Evan's table, followed by his two men.

"Len," Evan said, slowly looking up. "I take it you're not here for the Buffalo wings."

Harris frowned. "I understand you had a problem with engine two."

Daz looked cross-ways at him. "By problem, you mean that fireball?"

Harris backed off, pulled his inhaler from his pocket, and allowed his friends to advance. "You know Markus and Madison?"

"Mister Sullivan. Mister Grier." Evan barely lifted his head to acknowledge. "Always a pleasure."

Sullivan stroked his gray beard, shook his head, and spoke. "I don't care what you say; hydraulics aren't the problem."

"I haven't said anything yet," Evan said. "The plane's sitting in Hanger-2. The cowling's not off. It might be the hydraulics. It might be something else."

"You can't pin it on me," Sullivan snapped. "I did my job, and I got the paper to show it."

"What are you talking about?" Daz stood and squared his shoulders with Sullivan. "That was five years ago. You can't remember every hose, every fitting you worked on."

"You bet I can. I got lives depending on me. Five years ago or yesterday, I do my job and I do it proper."

"Great," Evan told him. "Then don't worry. The logbooks will tell us the full story."

"One more thing." Grier pushed his way forward, relaxed his crossed arms, and pointed at his oil-stained T-shirt. "Local 231."

"Of course, the union. Where would we be without them?"

Grier looked at Sullivan then back at Evan. "Not without the union—with us."

"Come again?"

"Listen, I know how you guys work. And I don't trust ya. That's why we got a union rep." Grier pointed at himself again.

"I'll be there when you get the logbooks and when you open the cowling. And you guessed it; I'll be there every step."

"Reasonable request," Evan said, trying to catch him off guard.

"No request. I'm stating a fact."

"Then let me tell you this. There's no 'you guys', 'us guys' or 'anybody guys.' Whether you like it or not, we're on the same team. If anyone trips, we all fall. Believe it or not, we are not out to get you. I got a plane to build, and you, Markus, and Len; I'm counting on you to get it done."

The three visitors looked at each other. Grier reached over and grabbed a handful of pretzels. Harris puffed on his inhaler and glanced at his watch.

Sullivan said, "Good. We understand each other."

Harris flicked his hand toward the front door. Immediately, Grier and Sullivan took off. Harris lowered his voice and said to Evan, "Sorry, guys. I'm the middle man here. I'm trying my best to work both sides. Nothing personal; don't let the boys get to you."

"What I don't need is trouble with the union. Aerodynamics—that's trouble enough."

Harris patted Evan's shoulder then went out to join his friends.

Evan pushed aside his beer. He asked Daz, "Where can I hide to get some peace and quiet?"

"Criminy, you picked the wrong job for that." Daz took his seat and grumbled. "Those union boys are going to nag you every step of the way."

"Thanks for the reminder. I get one of their guys fired, and suddenly, I get a reputation."

"Cullin Black."

Evan grimaced. "Yeah, and now they're paranoid. One mistake and I'll have their job—that's what they believe. I mean, how do you deal with guys like that?"

"Watch your back, I'd say. Trust no one. Given the chance, they'll take you down."

"Now, who's paranoid? If they really want my job, they can have it. I'll tell ya, this stress; I don't need."

Daz picked up the check, glanced at it, and then passed it to Evan. "Only half-paranoid," he said.

"Excuse me?"

"We're here, but who's watching the Shasta?"

Evan took on a blank stare but leaned forward to listen.

"Harris made it clear; he's to be there when we poke around. Him or his boy, Grier. No tampering with the hydraulics, books, or anything."

"Obviously, we're not to be trusted."

"And who's watching Harris?"

Evan returned with his blank stare. Then suddenly, when the connection was made, he popped open his eyes. He dropped a twenty on the table and slid his chair. "I got a bad feeling about this. Can't leave those kids alone for a minute. Let's ride."

Evan pushed his Jaguar to new speeds back to the plant. He drove to screeching halt in front of the bay doors of Hanger-2.

Daz swung the passenger-side door open before the engine came to a rest. He had his foot on the ground before Evan pulled the key from the ignition. "Trust no one," he kept saying to himself. "Never turn your back."

Daz and Evan raced through the hanger door, nearly bowling over the mechanic, Tom Hernandez.

"Tom." Evan steadied the man. "I'm sure glad to see you."

Hernandez shifted his wrench and wiped his brow on his sleeve. "I barely got started. Can you believe it; half of my tools are missing."

"What do you mean, 'barely got started?' "

Daz stared at the Shasta aircraft and told Evan, "Cowling's off."

"I thought we fixed that issue years ago," Hernandez said.

"You mean the chance of fire," Evan said.

"Looks like more than a chance."

"Looks like we got no investigation," Daz said. "Exactly how long were you out?"

"Ten minutes to borrow a wrench," Hernandez said.

Daz stepped to the engine and peeked inside. "Unfortunately, we are one beer too late. In ten minutes, anything could've been swapped." He told Hernandez, "Go ahead, tear it apart. We'll need it for the report."

Evan beckoned Daz to retreat. When they were comfortably out of ear-shot, he said, "Okay, we have no evidence of tampering and no record of what really happened. But Harris, I'm guessing, is a weak link. What do you say; we get him alone and have a little heart to heart."

Daz grabbed a crowbar and slapped it across his open palm. "I know exactly what you mean."

"Put that away. We'll be subtle, but I will mention San Quentin. At his age, any jail is capital punishment."

Daz dropped the crowbar onto the cement, and the loud clang echoed across the hanger. He scowled. "No joy. But if Harris is behind this—"

Evan held up a couple fingers. "What is that?" He listened then turned to an approaching shadow by the hanger door. "Kylee?" he said as she rounded the corner.

Kylee walked forward, pounding her feet. "Russell said you'd be here," she mumbled beneath her breath.

Evan blinked. He felt totally dumbstruck. He saw Kylee's darting eyes and trembling lips. Her breathing was short and labored. She waved her hands then suddenly crossed her arms. She jerked her head and finished with a quiver.

"What's wrong?" Evan asked.

Kylee scowled and stared into the distance. She raised her voice and spoke fast. "I found out why I was hired. There's going to be a layoff, and this time, it's no rumor. I know for sure. Claire told me; she said it's official. And she told me my part; exit interviews."

"What?"

"They hired me to listen, they said. They hired me because I'm good with people. I don't want any part of this. People are coming to me on the worst day of theirs lives, and I'm supposed to listen? Make sure I have sympathy, they said. Give them a kind word. Maybe they won't sue. What kind of company is this anyway?"

"No one told me about a layoff."

"Evan, you're always the last to hear."

"When?" Daz asked.

"Starting Thursday. That's why I got stuck with paperwork. I thought it was benefit reports. It turns out to be severance packages."

"It's not your fault," Evan said. "You were just doing your job."

"How many?" Daz asked, a little bit louder.

"I'm not sure, but I processed about three hundred reports."

"Jesus," Daz muttered, "That's a fourth of the whole company."

Evan frowned. "At this site, yeah. How many overseas?"

Kylee turned up her palms. "All I know is what they told me. And that's not a whole lot."

"There's got to be a mistake."

"No mistake. They said your father signed off on it."

"I don't believe it. My father said there would never be a layoff. We're like family, he said."

"That was before he met Mireille. If you ask me, she's the push behind this."

"Mireille does not run the company," Evan said. "Trudeau is a partner, yes. But they're in no position to tell us what to do. No way. Not even close. Mireille stepped over the line. If my father's going to wimp out, then stand back; I have a few words of my own."

"Looks like the rumors were true," Daz said. "First a takeover then a layoff."

"Trudeau is *not* taking over Dove. They have shares of our stock, but that's far from a takeover. Mireille will learn that lesson if it's the last thing I do." Evan pulled the Jaguar keys from his pocket. "You guys sit tight and let me handle this. I'll get back with the real story."

Evan quickly drove cross-campus, parked by the Juniper Building, and went straight to executive wing. He fumed, on the verge of a fire himself. When he found Mireille at her office, it took his remaining strength to keep from flaring up. He walked in and tried to stay calm.

She had a spreadsheet on her screen and a calculator in front. Pierre sat by her side, keeping notes. Mireille paused to acknowledge the intrusion. She closed her spreadsheet and hit Clear on her calculator. She asked Evan to close the office door.

"This confirms it," Evan said. "I'm always the last to find out."

"Confirms what?"

"I thought I was doing you a favor. I heard the rumors, but I said my father—and Mireille—would never do it. A layoff is not in the cards, and it never has been. If we lose a single worker, there's no way we can get Everest out."

Pierre looked at Mireille. He tapped a face-down paper. "May I?"

Mireille nodded.

"Look at this," Pierre said with his heavy and—by now, annoying—accent. "The balance sheet for Dove Air. You know it and I know it; Dove has not sold a plane for two years. Honestly, the first Everest sale *might* come in December. Dove has cash reserves. But with this burn rate, you're out of money in four months. You're out of business before you sell the first plane."

"Maybe so, but you lay off workers, guess what; the schedule is now ten months out and we lose anyway."

"So, what do we do?" Pierre stared at Evan.

"There has to be another way."

"We have a plan," Mireille said. She grabbed Pierre's accounting sheet and placed it face down. "After all, there's a reason Dove and Trudeau are partners. We take the best of both companies, put them together, and make the best plane possible. We proved it today. We took Trudeau software, put it in a Dove plane, and it worked. Except for that discrepancy at the end, we proved that we're a team."

"If you combine two companies," Pierre said, "there is always overlap. Our plan is to cut the overlap and tighten the team. We will keep the schedule *and* the cash flow."

Evan searched his head for a strong, cohesive argument. All he came up with were reminders of how Trudeau passed his last-minute, surprise flight test, and how Dove Air failed with the last-minute, near fatal crash. And that beer at lunch didn't help.

"I agree that we have a mess."

"I would've told you before," Mireille said, "but your group is pretty much intact."

"What do you mean; pretty much intact?"

"You have the airframe and power plant," Pierre said. "That remains on the critical path. We need your help."

"Except …" Mireille said.

"Except what?"

Pierre glared at Mireille and shook his head to silence her.

"He has to know," Mireille said. "Better to find out now."

"Find out what?" Evan asked.

"Daz Donahue has to go," Pierre said. "The one man from your group."

"Daz? What? No way!"

"We have no choice," Mireille said. "You saw him today. The man is a cowboy. He doesn't take orders, and he breaks the rules. He's rude. Donahue, and men like him, put the entire effort at risk. And what you pay him is obscene."

"Dove wouldn't be here today if not for Daz. He's the backbone of the company—the one pilot who can fly any plane we make. Don't think of cutting him loose!"

"I'm sorry, Evan." Mireille tapped the paperwork. "He's on this list."

"Forget the list. If you want to save money, I'm telling you; Daz is not the way to do it. He's worth a dozen Trudeau workers."

"You exaggerate." Pierre frowned. "But is he worth three Dove workers?"

"Easily. You don't know what he's done for this company."

"Fair enough," Mireille said. "Then I'll give you three more names. If you agree; Daz will stay, the others will go"

Evan sensed a trap as Mireille angled her monitor and clicked a tab. She scrolled down to 'TERMINATION NOTICE: Len Harris, Markus Sullivan, Madison Grier.'

Evan's stomach twisted in a gut-wrenching knot.

"Three more troublemakers from what I hear," Mireille said. "It doesn't matter who goes; we save money either way."

"When can I decide?"

"Before you leave this room," Mireille told him. "We have to move fast."

"Then I have no choice." Evan sighed. "Daz stays, the other men go. I'll deal with the consequences."

Chapter *11*

"IF YOU HAVE a layoff, a lot of people are going to die."

Kylee shivered. She nearly dropped the phone from her hand. Her head still pounded from her ranting session with Evan. She stood, knees shaking, and peered over the top of her cubicle. The threat seemed so personal and powerful, the caller had to be nearby. She saw Claire—busy on her computer—but no one else. Kylee sank to her seat.

"Who is this?" she hissed. Her only reply was a disconnect. She checked the caller ID, but it showed 'unidentified.' It could've been an inside call, could've been outside. It probably didn't matter; the caller would've been smart enough to stay away from his own phone.

She walked unsteadily to the break room. She tried to pour coffee into her Yosemite mug, but her hands shook and the caffeine, she realized, would only make her nerves worse. She also realized she had to talk to someone—the police, Dove security, or Evan. She paced the room, trying to decide whom to call first. Then Mireille—the last person on her list—popped in.

"Hello, Kylee," Mireille said. She reached for a Styrofoam cup and poured herself coffee. "Claire said you looked upset. I understand. The event is stressful for each of us."

"Event?"

"The layoff," Mireille said with a hushed voice. "It's a management word."

"The *event* is only part of it. The call I just got—that's why I'm upset. I can't believe anyone would say that."

"Say what?"

" 'If there's a layoff, a lot of people are going to die.' I mean, how do you respond to a threat?"

"Oh."

"That's it? Oh?"

Mireille shook a packet of sweetener, ripped it, and poured in her coffee. "If that's all they said, it's not really a threat."

"Pardon?"

"This happens often in France. 'If you lay me off, my family will starve. The entire village will starve.' It never happens. They all get new jobs."

"But this was an American voice."

"Are you sure?"

"Of course, it was. Well, I believe it was."

"You see," Mireille said. "You're not sure what you heard. It could be American. It could be anyone. It could be you misunderstood what they said. I'm sorry, we have plenty of security. There is no need to change plans. The event goes ahead."

She gave Kylee an assuring tap on the shoulder. She dumped the coffee, set the cup next to the sink, and disappeared to the hallway as quickly as she came.

Kylee shrugged and tossed out the Styrofoam cup.

On Thursday, the event went ahead as planned. Over three hundred workers at the Apple Valley campus—one by one—got their notice, their boxes for personal belongings, and one last chance to speak their minds. Then they would turn in their badge and depart. There were too many long faces and sad goodbyes. After two days of nonstop interviews, Kylee drove home and collapsed on the living room sofa.

Evan sat beside her. "Did you recognize the voice?"

"From the crank call?" Kylee dug into her pint of almond mocha ice cream. She hoped a brain freeze and a few hundred sweet calories would knock away her tension headache. "No, and believe me; I was listening. If I had talked to him, I would've known. But Claire did half the interviews, and some of the guys didn't talk to us at all. Those are the ones I'm worried about."

"Well, security has a list. Unless something comes up …"

"Yeah, get back to work—that's what Mireille would say."

"By the way, you know John Waterman's voice, right?"

"Of course. Why?"

"He's gone too. Thank you, Mireille. That's one less bureaucrat, if you ask me."

Kylee groaned. "You know what they say; take away one bureaucrat, and another moves in."

***

One week made all the difference. The layoff was over, the motivational memos were emailed, and Kylee cleared her desk of her most pressing work. After one week, Kylee felt close to human again.

Then slowly, like an unshakable curse, her Fred Mott visions returned. At first, it was a flash here and there—a fleeting memory. But after a while, one vision triggered another. Night after night, she would wake in a cold sweat, seeing Fred's face and a fire-and-ice background. She saw planes falling from the sky. She saw faceless men who burned in the wilderness and reached for her hand.

Evan was no help. With his long hours and deep sleep, more often than not, he slept through the episodes. When he did wake up, his only assurance was; "Get some rest. Sooner or later, you'll get over it."

Kylee didn't get over it. If anything, her visions became worse. Finally, after terrifying nights and drowsy days, she went looking for professional help.

"I've always relied on the kindness of engineers." She smiled sweetly at Russell while he sat at his bench in the Cottonwood Building. "And you're one of the smartest I know."

"Well, you just paid for the first hour." He smiled. "How can I help?"

"Evan calls it an obsession. I call it therapy. I can't rest until I figure it out."

"Figure what out?"

"Fred and his satellite phone. Fred and Bullman Stock. Fred and a plane crash in the middle of the Sierras. I say there's a connection, but Evan says the whole thing is a red earring."

"It's red herring."

"I know." Kylee rolled her eyes.

"But regardless, I'm not going to judge." Russell grabbed his can of Pepsi and took in the last ounces. "Grab a seat. Let's talk."

"It's this stupid website." Kylee plopped onto a rolling chair, nudged Russell aside, and typed in Fred's stock link to the computer. The familiar Texas Longhorn appeared. "No matter what I do, I can't get another window."

She clicked all over the screen and typed random numbers into the log-in.

Russell reached over and gently slid the keyboard his way. "First off; it's not a traditional website. It's more like a direct link to somebody's server. Not that it matters; but you need a password to get beyond the log-in."

"I know, but can't you, you know …"

"What, type in the backdoor password and skirt the firewall protection?"

"Okay."

"That's not how it works. Without a password, what you see is what you get." Russell popped a candy in his mouth.

"You're saying my hour is up already?"

"I'm afraid so."

Kylee frowned. "No, it can't be. Come on, Russell, this is my only chance. You gotta help me. I mean, there's no listing for Bullman; here or nationwide. I checked the Internet; absolutely nothing came up."

"That's not unusual. It could be a new company or a private thing. You know; members only."

"This is so frustrating. We are this close to finding out."

"Finding out what?"

Kylee lowered her voice. "Evan told me not to say it, but really, I never agreed."

"Say what?"

"The reason I need this; Fred had a half-million dollars on him when he died. I want to know why."

Russell froze in his chair as a gummy bear rolled to the floor. His mouth slowly gaped.

"If there was a crime," Kylee said, "this company may be involved."

Russell faded his blank stare. "You said a half-million dollars?"

"Roughly."

"Cash?" he asked.

"I saw it myself."

"Why on earth would Fred have that?"

"Okay." Kylee nodded. "Now you're caught up."

"I mean, no one deals in cash."

"So I've heard."

"Except drugs," Russell said. "You think—"

"Not Fred. The crew—I can't vouch for."

"Someone's gotta be missing it."

"Maybe not," Kylee said. "When we went back to the mountain, the cash was gone."

"Are you sure?"

"Yeah, I'm sure. I'm sure there was cash, and I'm sure it had something to do with Fred. You and me—we can figure it out." Kylee tapped her finger on the Bullman logo and looked at Russell. "So, what do we do?"

Russell reached across his bench for another Pepsi. He wrapped it in bubble wrap. He snapped open the can, pushed in a straw then stretched across his bench for a sticky note. "Well, this could be a lead ... Orion-Sat is the provider for the sat' phone."

"Go on."

"It took some doing, but I found the name of the real customer."

"Not Fred?" Kylee asked.

"A Mr. Noname," Russell said. "He has a P.O. Box for an address."

"No name," Kylee said. "I get it. And where's the box?"

"Somewhere in Hesperia. Midtown."

"It's a start," Kylee said. "Finally we're getting somewhere."

"What do you mean, *we?*"

"My partner and me," she said. "My partner who is going to help me with the plan."

Russell grinned but let it quickly dissolve. "What plan?"

Chapter *12*

"I'M TELLING YOU, Kylee; we should've picked Hawaii." Russell squinted through the windshield of his minivan. He stared at the steady stream of people who passed through the glass doors of the Hesperia Post Office lobby. He finished a bag of nuts and tossed the wrapper onto the back seat. It had been five days since Russell and Kylee had formed their new team, and Russell was hungry for some excitement.

"Trust me," Kylee said. "This is a Las Vegas crowd. You send them to Maui, they'll be dreaming of the Bellagio. You got your beach crowd, and you got your gamblers. I'll bet you lunch; our guy's a gambler."

"Lunch, huh?" Russell grabbed a powdered donut and tapped it. "You're not exactly a high-stakes woman."

"I'm trying to keep your losses low. Although I know you could afford it."

"Oh, really?"

"You forget; I work in HR. I know your salary. I know your stock options. I know you have six weeks vacation."

Russell narrowed his eyes. "Do you know what I'm thinking now?"

"Russell, you don't have an evil bone in your body." She grabbed a straw and poked it into her iced tea. "But you could tell me what you think of Mireille."

"Mireille? How did we get onto her?"

"Come on, you don't see the connection?"

"What connection?"

"Fred dies and three weeks later, Mireille shows up. Coincidence? I don't think so."

"There's no coincidence about it," Russell said. "It was inevitable that Trudeau would take over. Three weeks, three months—it was long overdue. You don't hear me complaining. Without Trudeau—without Mireille—I'd be standing in the unemployment line."

"Okay." Kylee calmed her voice. "But personally, what do you think of her?"

"Mireille?" He grinned. "God, she's gorgeous. I mean for a woman boss, that is. You should see her in a black—"

"I thought so. Typical male response."

"You asked and I answered."

"Great, Mr. Got-to-be-honest. Then you tell me; what do you think of Claire?"

"Claire?" Russell ran his fingers through the graying hairs by his temple. "She's a nice-enough girl. Cute too, I suppose. But ..."

"But what?"

Russell halted in mid-sentence as he gawked at the post office door. "But we have our mark."

"Our what?"

"Gray pants, purple shirt. Male Caucasian, what, about twenty-eight, twenty-nine." He aimed his finger below the dashboard. "That's our packet."

The man stopped by a newspaper box and ripped open a large, bright red envelope. He tossed the envelope by the box and casually read the contents. He kept his grin as he walked to his car.

"How do you pass up a registered letter?" Kylee nodded. "Las Vegas Sweepstakes; how greedy is this guy?"

"Looks like I owe you lunch."

"Start the car. He's got the Camaro."

"Yes, ma'am." Russell eased forward on the gas. "Keep your eyes open if he pulls too far away. I've never done this before."

Kylee gulped her iced tea and let the warm summer air blow across her face and hair. The chill of anticipation raced up her spine. As she had predicted five days earlier; this was turning out to be a simple assignment. Good news was bound to follow.

Russell tracked the Camaro across town like a pro. The driver seemed in no rush. Kylee guessed that he was heading home, or to his office, or perhaps to the headquarters of Bullman Stock, as it were.

Russell kept pace, but after a couple of unexpected turns, they drove through a part of the county that Kylee had never seen before. She checked the street signs and checked her map. Discreetly—without Russell noticing—she capped her iced tea bottle, put her wedding ring into her purse, and shoved her purse beneath the seat. She unfolded her map and noted; nearest police station, nearest fire station, nearest hospital, nearest way out.

"I hate to say it," she said. "But our man's stopping. It could be those apartments."

As Russell slowed his minivan and looked for parking, Kylee studied the two-story, gray building that had seen better days. Bars on the lower windows; window sills on the verge of collapse; trash cans begging to be emptied; graffiti tags from the neighborhood gangs.

"This has to be a mistake," Russell said. "There's no stock trading company here."

"He took the packet. Who else could it be?"

"Unless Orion-Sat gave us the wrong P.O. Box."

Kylee shivered. This was a long way for a case of mistaken identity. This was one red herring that already smelled bad.

Nevertheless, she said, "Let's see how it plays out. We paid for the show. There's no harm in getting our money's worth."

Her hand bounced from the door handle to her lap and to the door again. She glanced at the building, half-hoping for a street tough to wander by, half-hoping for any excuse to cancel. When she saw no one but the man in the Camaro, she mumbled, "Okay, Russell, let's do it."

"Hold on, not so fast." Russell squirmed and swung his head left.

"What?"

"I was afraid this would happen; it's the super-sized root beer."

"You mean …?"

"Straight to the bladder," Russell said. "I swear my kidneys are shot."

"Now you tell me?"

He stared at the side view mirror. "I saw a gas station a while back."

"Forget it. We are this close. We are not giving up." Kylee stared out the front window. "Look, the guy's sitting in his car, reading the letter. He can't see us or that alley. You're a man—get busy."

"You're serious."

"You've got two minutes; starting now."

"Okay, okay. Don't do anything rash." He slipped out the door, trotted to the alley, and disappeared.

Regrettably, the two-minute schedule was optimistic. The Camaro man jumped from his car and hustled to the front lobby of the building. He slapped the letter in his hand.

Something about the situation didn't make sense. Kylee didn't expect to tail some young guy in a fast car to a trashed neighborhood. She had planned to follow a middle-aged stockbroker to a luxury business park. Despite the obvious disconnect, Kylee chose to follow her instincts and follow the man inside.

She walked into the lobby and closed the door behind. First impressions were harsh; damp air, water-stained carpet, the strong odor of cigarettes. Kylee took shallow breaths and kept her mind on her mission. She quickly scanned the dark hallways that led from the common area. She looked for more strangers or familiar faces but saw no one. The street noise settled to the rumble of passing trucks and the echoes of barking dogs.

She carefully listened to the building sounds; a blaring TV from 1-C, a man and woman arguing over money in 1-F, a fire door slamming shut. She paced along the first floor hallway, but with no other hint of life, she went to the second floor. At each apartment, she paused and listened. At 2-B, she heard a sniffing dog. At 2-F, a baby cried. At 2-H, she heard a creaking floor. Kylee placed her ear against the door.

Suddenly two voices.

"It's a come-on," a man said.

"It's legit," the other said. "I've seen 'em before."

"Yeah, like your timeshare in Arkansas."

"That's different."

"Do I have to explain the meaning of 'scam?' "

Kylee had heard enough. This was definitely her man, but Bullman Stock Investing—definitely not. Regardless, she got the address and if, for some reason, she had to return with reinforcements, she knew exactly where to go. She eased herself to the stairwell and tiptoed to the lobby. When she passed the front door, she took off running. A quick look to the side and she caught Russell hustling her way; shirt tail out, glasses bouncing on his nose, two hundred and forty pounds of shaking, sweating flesh.

As Kylee dashed by the Camaro, she glanced at the front window and saw a familiar shape. Barely slowing her pace, she dipped her head by the rear license plate and burned the numbers to her memory. "Five, Papa, Sally."

"Sorry." Russell panted when he met her mid street. He stood close and exhaled hot root beer breath as he waved his arms. "There were a couple kids—"

"I knew it." She pushed him toward the minivan. "I knew we were on the right path."

"Bullman Investing at this place?"

"Better." Kylee slid into the minivan and rummaged through her purse for a pad and pen. "Five, Papa, Sally." She wrote as fast as she could. "Got it."

"Got what?" Russell climbed to the driver's seat.

"The Camaro—it has a Dove sticker."

Russell shrugged.

Kylee poked his arm. "Don't you see it? Our connection is that man. This place and Fred *are* related."

"All I see is that you wasted three hundred bucks to send a bum to Vegas."

"Russell, dear, what we found was worth a million bucks."

"Just tell me when to cash out," Russell said. "Or in."

"I will."

***

That afternoon at the Dove plant, Kylee called Russell with the next step of her plan. "We have buy-in from Bob," she said. "He's with me at the computer graveyard."

"That was fast," Russell said.

"It would be faster if you were here—with your special apps."

"On my way."

Kylee hung up the phone. While waiting for Russell, she found Fred Mott's computer and set it aside. She pulled a keyboard and monitor from a shelf and asked Bob to connect it. Then she pulled a cold Pepsi from her handbag and slapped it with Bubble Wrap. Now she was set.

In a few minutes, she heard a faint rapping at the door. She opened it and smiled. "Russell, you know Bob Aukram from accounting?"

"Sure." Russell extended his hand. "Welcome aboard."

In front of Kylee stood her new recruits; her investigative team as it were. And this team had a nice balance, she believed. Compared to Russell, Bob was much older. He had a full head of hair on the lighter side of gray. He was a few pounds lighter and a few inches taller. With a gray suit and yellow tie, Bob seemed professional; a true accountant.

Of course, Russell—with his tennis shoes and khaki plaid shirt—seemed like a professional engineer. Kylee was happy no matter how they dressed. She offered Russell a rolling seat, a Pepsi, and a straw.

"Thank you," Russell said, opening the can. He sat down and got focused. He pushed a memory drive into the PC and quickly went through a dozen windows. With every click, he smiled and gained confidence. In a short while, he offered his seat to Bob. "Okay, Bob, this will give you access. The rest is up to you."

"What exactly are you looking for?" Bob glanced at Kylee as he installed his app.

"Six months ago, a contractor came in. He had one job; install software on Fred's computer."

"Randy Fosse," Russell said. "You know him? He worked for IT and drove a Camaro."

Bob shook his head.

"Anyway," Kylee said, "just after Fred died, Randy was back. According to security, his 'purpose of visit' was to remove software."

"From this computer?"

"Yes," she said. "It must've been related to the merger. However, we don't believe that Randy had the authority to install or remove software. As a follow-up, we would like to see what he was up to."

"Randy or Fred?"

"Both."

"Well, Randy may have taken the program, but the data's still here." Bob scrolled through pages of files and stopped on a long list of random numbers. "That's interesting," he said, mostly to himself.

"What is?" Kylee stared at the numbers.

"I'm just a junior accountant. But some of these guys; they're pretty creative."

"Trudeau, you mean?"

"I mean Dove." He looked at Russell. "Can I get a copy of this?"

"Coming up."

"It looks like Fred had two apps." Bob angled the screen. "One gives him Trudeau financials. The other app lets Trudeau see our stuff."

"Strange, would you say?"

"It's pretty common for a merger. Routine almost." Bob clicked on another spreadsheet. "Let's see the burn rates for March … Jesus, would you look at that?" He shook his head with a nervous laugh.

Russell grabbed the printout and slapped it on the bench. "Bob, you're the expert. Give us the bottom line; do we have a revelation or not?"

"Depends on what you're looking for."

"Something illegal," Kylee said.

"Legal, illegal; that's so black and white. Believe it or not, accounting is often shades of gray. Now, exactly what Fred was doing—that will take a while to sort out. He was a smart man, and I don't want to second guess."

Kylee aimed her finger at the screen. "Okay, what do you have on Mireille?"

"Mireille?"

"I mean Trudeau."

"Those files; the numbers are English, but the headings are French. I'll need a translator." Bob looked over his nose at Russell.

"Don't look at me. I barely make sense of the English."

"Good stuff, huh?" Kylee poked at Bob's ribs.

"You're a sweetheart." He clicked the exit tab and spun his chair. "Send me a copy, and I'll get to work. But if you want two English words to summarize … it's big."

"I knew it!" she yelped. "Evan McKenna, I told you so."

Chapter *13*

IT WAS seven o'clock, and dinner was on the table. Kylee greeted Evan with a wide smile and a playful kiss. "You'll never guess who I saw today."

"Your mother."

"Nope."

"Your Aunt Amy," Evan said.

"Nope, Bob Aukram from accounting."

"Yeah, sure, I should've known. Bob from accounting." Evan loosened the top button of his shirt and headed for the bedroom. He placed his phone and keys on the nightstand.

Kylee followed him in. "Don't you want to know why?"

"It's about work, I assume."

"Kind of."

"Sorry, love, I spent fourteen hours on the vertical stabilizer, and work is not on this man's agenda."

"You might put Fred's secret files on your agenda. According to Bob, there was some strange accounting with Trudeau. Unethical at best; or criminal. 'Watch out for the feds,' Bob said. 'They'll come and shut us down.' How about that?"

"Go on," Evan said.

"Bob's going to report back. But I could tell; he got excited. We talked about payoffs, bribes, lies, and creative accounting.

Someone's going to jail; that's for sure. He said there might be a link."

"Link?"

"To Fred's death," Kylee said.

"Really."

"You should learn to trust my instincts," Kylee said. "My hunches can trump your numbers almost any day."

"Well, tonight I'm tired. I'm heading for bed. *My* hunch is that you'll leave me alone so I can rest." Evan dropped his shoes and plopped into bed. He barely said a word.

First is denial, Kylee told herself, *then recognition. He'll come around.*

Friday at Dove Air. Once again, Kylee was back on the job; filing and emailing from her desk in HR. It was tedious and repetitive work, but she didn't mind. She now had a team to find the truth about Fred Mott. She had friends and a worthwhile cause. In a few more weeks, her nightmares would end. In a few more weeks, her marriage would return to normal. All things considered, her life was going well.

She stretched her legs and put her palms behind her neck. She relaxed for a deep breath then heard the voice that made her shiver.

"Kylee, you're working too hard." Mireille leaned on the cubicle wall and rested her elbow on the edge.

"Come again?"

"I can see it in your face. The stress must be hard on you. Especially with the, you know, layoff."

Kylee hesitated. "I manage."

"You deserve a break."

"I'm doing fine, believe me."

"I have a surprise."

Kylee cringed. "Surprises and me; we don't get along."

"I think you'll like this one. Besides, I already signed you up." Mireille showed a brochure. "Two days at the Summer Springs Inn."

"Keep talking."

"That's a spa."

"I know," Kylee said.

"You've been there?"

"No."

"Then this will be a weekend you'll never forget." Mireille slipped the brochure onto the desk. "Mud baths, massages, wine tasting, horseback riding; whatever you want."

Kylee flipped through the color pages. "I thought we just had a layoff."

"We did."

"I'm not complaining, mind you. But why are we spending the money? We let go three hundred people. It doesn't make sense."

"It was booked well before the layoff. If we cancel now, we lose the deposit. Cindy's gone, so it's you, me, and a couple others."

Kylee fingered the brochure; smiling people, guilty pleasures, a trip already paid for. Cynicism only went so far. "Very well," she said, growing a smile. "When do I leave?"

"Get there around six tonight. Here's the map." Mireille flipped over the brochure.

"What about Evan?"

Mireille showed the putting green photo. "He'll meet you later. I thought golf for him. Dinner for you both. How's that?"

"I suppose."

"Great. I'll see you there."

Mireille left the building, but Kylee's head continued to spin. She couldn't imagine Mireille as a spa buddy; sharing a mud bath and sipping chardonnay. She couldn't imagine a vacation with Mireille anywhere near. But a fancy dinner with Evan was a surefire agenda to fix a teetering marriage.

By her third cup of Colombian, her mind was half on work and three-fourths out the door. It made her wonder why every Friday couldn't be like this.

Claire poked her head over the cubicle wall. "Take a long lunch," she said.

"I wish." Kylee tapped a stack of papers.

"You'll love the spa. So why wait? Go to lunch and don't come back."

"I've got six of these." Kylee scowled. She clicked on an insurance form. "And each one has a problem."

"Problems are for Monday. Believe me, if I had a Summer Springs reservation, I'd already be gone."

"You think so?"

"Listen, I'll cover any calls. You and Evan; go out and have fun. Like Mireille said; you deserve it. Besides; next weekend, I get the spa." Claire glanced at a wall clock. "And like I said; by noon, I'll be gone."

Kylee nodded. "I have been working hard, haven't I?"

She crammed the Summer Springs packet into her purse. She squirmed just long enough to make it appear doubtful. Then with a quick, "See you on Monday," she tucked her handbag between her arm and chest. She scooted out and didn't look back.

She hurried home, stopping only long enough to pack a bag and leave a note for Evan. The weather was gorgeous and getting better—no need to waste it at home. Slowly, as she drove the scenic miles to the resort near Palm Springs, she felt the tension leave her body. She craved a Shiatsu massage and a glass of Riesling. She hoped for a quiet night with Evan.

She cranked up the volume to her jazz album and let out a satisfied sigh. For one afternoon, she could easily forget about Fred. She could easily forget about work.

Summer Springs Spa and Resort, when she finally arrived, looked a whole lot better than the brochure; lush gardens, perfectly manicured roses, lily ponds and fountains, stone walkways leading to elegant patios. Kylee pulled up to the valet parking, and like Cinderella's story, her old Jeep vanished into the illusion of a grand limousine. She was immediately greeted by a young man with the spa uniform; green shorts and a yellow T-shirt with a palm-tree emblem.

He opened the Jeep door and fetched her bag. "Welcome to Summer Springs, ma'am. May I have your name?"

"Kylee McKenna."

He checked his tablet and smiled. "Ah, Mrs. McKenna, your room is sixty-one. You can follow me, if you like."

"Don't I need to—"

"Register? It's been done."

"My bag?"

"I'll have it sent to your room."

Kylee threw back her shoulders and straightened the waistline of her top. She brushed back her hair and slipped on a pair of Ray-Ban sunglasses—her one extravagant accessory. "Then let's go."

As they walked random paths along the gardens, the greeter pointed out the lap pool and steam rooms. He showed the tennis courts and putting greens. As they passed the night club, he mentioned the jazz bar, wine tasting, and nationally known entertainment.

"Entertainment?" Kylee glimpsed a Callaway golf bag at room sixteen. "I think I found my opening act." She stopped at the room and pointed at the monogram on the leather flap. "E-M," she said to the escort. "That's my husband's. You got the room number wrong."

"I don't think so, ma'am."

"Oh, I think so." She slipped him a five-dollar bill. "This is definitely Evan's. See, the door's open; that means he's waiting for me *or* his clubs. I'll take it from here." She pushed the door fully open.

The escort shrugged but promptly disappeared.

Kylee patted the head of the blade putter. She stepped into the suite and closed the door behind. "Nice," she said, looking around. She became suitably impressed with the stereo speakers, the Queen Ann desk, wine cooler, and a widescreen TV.

"Well, no TV tonight. That's for sure."

She walked to the bedroom, expecting to see Evan and the rest of the luggage. She saw a bag and shirt on the bed but no Evan. She did hear water running. No doubt, Evan was in the shower.

"Won't this be a nice surprise," she said to herself. She tiptoed to the bathroom as the water stopped and the shower door swung open.

Evan was there all right; stripped to the waist and standing next to the shower like a Roman statue. He stared, mouth-agape and eyes wide open. He stared at a totally naked, totally unsurprised Mireille. Actually, with the red towel wrapped around her hair, she was not totally nude. Even so, her well tanned body glistened with sensuous drops of warm water. And those breasts, hips, and soft shoulders—there was not a tan line to be seen. The steam of the shower filled the air, and with the backdrop of Italian marble, Mireille appeared as a goddess; comfortable and proud of her human form.

Kylee shivered as though a cold wind had blown straight to her heart. "I was too blind to see it," she softly said.

Evan blinked then turned to face her. "Kylee?"

"Too tired last night, were you? Now I get it!" Kylee nearly screamed. "You and that woman! How long, Evan? How long?"

"Kylee?"

"Don't bother to tell me. You know what? I don't care anymore! If you want her, go for it! She's all yours!"

"It's not what—"

"Oh God, I'm going to be sick." Trying to keep from screaming, she ran. Kylee ran for the front door and slammed it against the wall. She grabbed the golf bag and tossed it to the sitting room floor. The clubs spilled out like a random pile of sticks.

Evan raced from the bathroom, nearly catching her. But he stumbled on the clubs and fell to his knees. He looked up, more in shock than pain.

Kylee scowled at him. She grabbed the front door and slammed it closed. She yelled through the solid oak core. "It's over, Evan. I don't want to see *her*. I don't want to see *you* ever again!"

Chapter *14*

EVAN SAT on the dusty floor of a small, isolated hanger that housed old and abandoned Dove Air prototypes. A rolling toolbox braced his back. An oscilloscope warmed his lap. Cables draped from the cockpit of his fan-jet to his scope. He twisted a knob, made a note, and then reached for a wrench.

When he heard a door open, he spun around, accidentally knocking the wrench to the floor. The sharp echo snapped him from his technical focus.

"Daz said I might find you here." Mireille closed the door behind and let Jean-Petit sniff the nose wheels of the fan-jet.

"My one hiding spot." Evan stood and brushed the back of his pants.

"You don't have to hide—at least not from me."

"Funny, you could say we've been seeing too much of each other." Evan glanced at Mireille. "If you know what I mean."

"Americans." She shook her head. "What happened at the spa means nothing. In Europe, it's natural. No one cares."

"Tell that to my wife."

"The human body—clothes or not—is a gift. It is good you can admire a woman."

"You're not helping matters."

"Surely, Kylee understands. When you said you were confused, and you couldn't help yourself—"

"Mireille, you have a way of twisting the facts. *Your story* would get me killed. What she saw was bad enough. Don't make it worse by telling her I was confused."

"But you were."

Evan raised his voice. "Yes—about the room number. Not about sleeping around. I still can't believe I did it; sixty-one, sixteen. Okay, I got it backward; it happens. I saw Kylee's bag. That's what caught my eye. And the door was half-open."

"That was *my* bag. I had more on the way."

"Now I know." Evan leaned against the fan-jet and crossed his arms. "So I walked in and looked around. My room, my wife; that's what I'm thinking. Then I hear the shower, then the guy outside with my clubs. Now, I got a choice; yell at the wife for leaving the door unlocked. Or I could pick up my clubs. Or I could—"

"Surprise her."

"Yeah, door number three. Boy, did I pick wrong."

"You explained this, yes?"

"Not a chance," he said. "Kylee hates confrontation. She took off and kept on driving."

"Where is she?"

"She didn't say. But then, she didn't have to. She runs to the same old place; her cabin in the woods. Her sanctuary; that's what she calls it. *Her* hiding place."

"Call her and apologize."

"No phone," Evan said.

"Go visit."

"I'll give her a couple days to cool off. That usually works. I mean, she can't really believe that you and me; we'd … you know …"

"And why not? We work together. We eat together. As a couple, we look superb." Mireille paused then gazed at his eyes. "At least that's what Kylee believes."

"Yeah, well, I've given up on women." Evan rapped on the composite cowling and rubbed his hand along the smooth finish of his aircraft. "Lift, thrust, drag, and gravity; technology, I understand."

"Love, trust, and respect. You'll need that for Kylee."

"I'll try it." Evan twisted a knob on his equipment. "When I see her."

"Of course, meanwhile, I have my top engineer hiding in this cave like a runaway child."

"You could've called." He tapped the phone in his pocket.

Mireille stepped between Evan and his equipment. She glared at him. "Allow me to rephrase myself. If *you* have personal problems, then *we* have problems. At work, specifically. Everest is not going to build itself. I need you on the floor, thinking straight. This thing between you and your wife, it makes your head twisted. *Tu comprends?*"

"Not quite that simple."

"Then explain."

Evan poked at the instrument panel. "I can keep my personal life separate. For me, that's not the issue."

"Then what is the issue?"

"Frustration," Evan said. "I have plenty of it, mostly from the schedule."

Mireille nodded.

"Believe it or not, we have a complete set of Everest software." Evan tapped his finger on the fan-jet. "It's installed here and ready to use."

"Okay."

"We can trim three weeks from the schedule if—"

"If you drag engineers here; if they learn your code; if they make it useful. In other words; if you disobey your father and steal his people."

"You've talked to him," Evan said. "You know he's stubborn. He doesn't believe this plane is anywhere close to a jumbo; software, hardware, prestige, anything. That's my frustration. An hour here is an hour wasted; that's what he believes."

Mireille peeked at the cockpit. "What do you call this?"

"Officially, it's the Mac-1."

"I see."

"Unofficially, it's the flying car, Evan's folly or, good money after bad. Stop me anytime."

"Stay with the Mac-1."

"Anyhow, it's got twice the technology of Everest, half the risk, and most of my passion."

"Yet, your father killed the project."

"Because he couldn't understand." Evan stepped around the aircraft and pointed at the features. "Six fan engines, vertical takeoff, parachute recovery system. It can do three hundred knots at thirty thousand feet. And it flies with no wings except for these." He rapped on a stubby slat. "The whole thing is fast and cheap. But because software runs it, no way can it fly—according to my father."

"Of course, software runs all of Everest."

"But Everest has wings. It looks like a plane. This thing—from what he said—is an airborne washing machine. Totally unsafe; except for washing clothes." Evan slumped his shoulders. He glanced Mireille's way and caught her smiling.

"Safe is good," she said. "And I have to agree with Paul on one point; it is different. There are no gauges, only a few controls, and someone left out the yoke."

"There's no yoke, no steering wheel, no nothing. One joystick does it all; left, right, forward, back, up, and down."

"Does it fly?"

"I've had it up a few times. It has a few bugs, but nothing major."

"Bugs?"

"It leans to the left on takeoff." Evan ran his hand along the side. "Ignore the door dings."

"Software, huh?" Mireille fingered a three-inch binder labeled; System Control. "Mind if I take a look?"

"We had a consultant check it out, and he was stumped. Yet another reason for my father to pull the plug."

"It can't be that hard; I did this in what you would call high school. Differential equations; yes, I am familiar."

Evan looked at her face but couldn't tell if she was serious or not. Nevertheless, he tossed another binder onto the pile. "Okay, then let's do it."

Mireille rolled a chair next to a work station, grabbed a binder, and kicked off her shoes. She sat down and went to work. She immersed herself in her own special world. Hour after hour she tapped at the keyboard. She checked the Mac-1 code and wrote obscure French notes in the margins of the binder.

Evan couldn't tell if she was helping or not. He couldn't tell if she had the vaguest notion about mechanics. Once in a while, he would lean close and take in the fragrance of orange blossom perfume or her sweet breath of La Vie mints.

More often than not, Evan would drift from his issues and let his mind wander. He took in visions of a California beach, or a drive in the San Bernardino Mountains, or a shower at a Palm Springs resort. Hour after hour, Mireille stayed focused, and Evan remained preoccupied. Neither was working on Everest.

Suddenly, Mireille spun her chair and pushed herself from Evan. "We're finished!" she said.

"What? What do you mean, we're finished?"

"The code." She pointed. "It's fixed."

"Oh."

"I think it's time for a real test."

"You mean, go on a flight?" he asked.

"Of course." Mireille yanked out the last of the connecting cables. "Anyone can make a plane that sits on the ground. Let's fly."

"Feeling brave?"

"I have confidence in you and your machine."

"With your software," Evan said.

"*Mais oui.*"

Evan cranked up the hanger door and rolled the fan-jet into the sunlight. "I have to warn you; I haven't flown this in ages." He pulled up on the gull-wing door and let Mireille strap Jean-Petit onto the rear seat. While Mireille settled in, Evan took the pilot's seat.

He snapped on the power and scanned the panel. "I made it simple, like a Buick."

Mireille ran her hand along the instruments and stopped at the joystick. "Simple is good. But some pilots like knobs."

"What you see is what you get. Remember, this is fly-by-wire. The computer has total control." He pointed at the screen displays. "You've got speed, altitude, fuel, radios, and a navigation map. The other stuff—oil pressure, electrical, check engine light—that doesn't appear unless there's a problem. Of course, that'll never happen." He winked.

"Then please explain." She pointed at a warning light.

Evan winced. Without comment, he jumped out and disappeared around the building. He returned with his Jaguar and a sheepish grin. He popped open the hood and strung a set of jumper cables to his fan-jet. "I told you; it's been a while."

Despite the momentary lapse, Evan quickly regained his confidence. He powered up the panel and powered up the engines. He grinned as, one by one, the fan engines sprung to life.

"Sweet, we have six green." He checked the gauges, and everything appeared good. "Looks like we're safe to go."

"No surprise, yes?"

"Of course not." Evan replied, avoiding her eyes. "Let's see if your image scan works."

Mireille pointed at the parking lot stripes beneath the cowling. "As long as you have a line or a cross reference, we can't go wrong."

With a sweating palm, Evan eased up on the Up-Down button. The engine purred as they hovered in place. "You see, quiet like a Jaguar."

Another nudge, and suddenly, they gazed over the tops of the Dove-campus buildings.

"You see," Mireille said. "Stable. Like a statue."

Evan eased forward on the joystick and accelerated to the neighboring hills. When they were clear of civilization, he ran through the standard flight test; high-speed banks, hover on a mountain top, reverse thrust, and fast dives. Everything worked as advertised. He saw nothing but green lights and smiling faces. For thoroughness, he took the fan-jet screaming along Pacifico

Mountain and down to Devil's Playground in the Mojave Desert. He could not have paid for a smoother ride.

It was at the dry Soda Lake where Evan and Mireille swapped seats and the real flying began. Mireille had loosened Jean-Petit's harness so he could peek out the window, but the next flight was sure to make him soil the plush leather seats.

"How do you call it—nap of the earth." Mireille slammed the joystick forward, and they took off like a falcon, straight for the Calico Mountains. She punched the Avoid-Terrain button and relaxed her hand from the controls.

"I never tested that feature!" Evan nearly screamed as they passed the 300 MPH mark on their way to the hills.

"Don't worry," Mireille said. "I tested it while you were looking at my breasts."

Evan closed his eyes; half-embarrassed, half-scared, totally lost for words. With a deep pressure in his stomach and a quick change from shadow to light, Evan looked out again. He saw the fan-jet soar through the desert canyons. They skimmed the dry Mojave River and headed to the lush mountain forests south of Apple Valley. Again, Mireille pushed the aircraft to the limits, diving between Ponderosa pines and punching through clouds.

"Better than sex. Isn't it, Evan?"

"I just saw my life pass by. Sex is not quite the same."

"Someday it will be."

Evan didn't know what she meant by that, but he settled in to enjoy the ride. They landed at sunset exactly where they began.

Mireille pried herself from the cockpit, grabbed Jean-Petit, and then hurried to Evan's side.

Evan shook his legs to steady his feet on the tarmac. He grinned. "What a flight."

"We call it making a memory." Mireille stood in front of him and held his hand. Then she raised herself on her toes and kissed him on the lips.

Evan simply stood there and took it in.

"I'll see you at work." She beamed a flashy smile. She made a hasty retreat around the corner and out of sight.

Evan's heart still raced at the red line.

Chapter *15*

FRIDAY MORNING. Evan checked his calendar at work. It had been nearly a week since Kylee had disappeared, nearly seven days since she had stormed off with a horrendous misunderstanding of an honest mix-up.

She had often taken vacations without him—skiing, SCUBA diving, rock climbing. And while on vacation, she rarely sent emails or made phone calls. That was Kylee. More often than not, the change of pace set her straight and made her a much happier worker and wife.

Time to herself was one thing, but stubbornness was no substitute for common sense. Evan had always hated her cabin; the isolation, the lack of comfort, the danger of the wilderness. It was no place for a woman—or man—alone.

In the back of his mind, he sensed that everything was fine. But still, the doubts lingered and slowly grew. He called her at home, but no one answered. He walked to her desk, but she wasn't there. He saw Claire, but she was no help.

"Don't worry," she said. "She's fine by herself."

Evan was not so sure. He checked the clock and counted the hours since she had left. Kylee and her 'sanity breaks' never did make sense—whether they lasted an hour or a week. Evan expanded his search. He went to the parking lot but saw no Jeep. He called her friends, but no one knew where she went or why.

Her new boss, Audrie, said little more than, "Family emergency—according to her text. And nothing since Friday."

Mireille, understandably, had no issue with her absence. "Let her take as much time as she needs."

Evan agreed but also believed that her time was up. And by now, his second cup of cup of coffee—or adrenaline—was kicking in hard. He blamed himself for not putting an end to her nonsense long ago. For one night, she might have been safe. One week was out of the question. He clicked on a map and frowned. He despised being so far from the cabin. He cursed the slow mountain roads and a car that low on gas. Now, with his patience running low, every moment counted.

He glanced down the long row of hangers and flashed on a plan. He realized that there was only one rational way to deal with the situation, only one path that made sense. Evan jogged to his hanger and double-checked the directions on his map. Then he climbed into the fan-jet, spooled up the engines, and took off for the San Bernardino hills. As soon as he could, he pushed forward on the joystick and made Mireille's flying look like a casual country drive.

Soon, he hovered above the cabin. Dust swirled and pine trees swayed, but Kylee was nowhere to be seen. The front door of the cabin was open, and surely the noise—subdued as it was—would draw her to her feet for a look. He circled before landing and squinted hard, but there was no sign of activity, no sign of anyone home. He set the fan-jet down on the dirt that comprised the side yard. He threw open the cockpit door and jumped to the ground before the engines had wound down.

He bounded up the steps of the cabin deck and pushed aside the screen door, calling her name. No reply. A sinking, burning feeling took hold of his heart. His cursory scan told him the cabin was empty, but still, he searched every corner twice.

He hustled to the front deck and yelled. Again, no answer. His stomach churned when he scanned the shore of the distant lake and saw a hawk circling above the rocks. Frustration easily took hold. With a thousand acres of forest, he had no clue where to go. He grabbed his satellite phone, ready to call the Forest Service, when a dark silhouette caught his eye.

There, in the shade of a front yard pine, a figure slowly rose. That had to be her, he told himself. He ran toward the person, and sure enough, it was Kylee—apparently healthy and uncomfortably silent.

"Are you all right?" He gently grabbed her shoulders and stared.

Kylee dusted the back of her denim Capris and straightened the front of her floral T-shirt. "Of course, I am. Why wouldn't I be?"

"I haven't seen you for a week. I thought for sure you were—"

"Lost?" She gave a small grin. "Up here? No, I never get lost."

"Didn't you hear me?" Evan pointed at his fan-jet. "And I yelled from the cabin."

"I was resting. I knew you would find me sooner or later."

Evan shook his head. He expected anger, fear, or a hint of loneliness. Her calmness caught him off guard. He took a deep breath to settle himself. "I'm sorry I didn't come sooner."

"It was best you didn't. I needed time; much more than before. If things come too fast, I have trouble sorting them out."

"I know the feeling."

"Do you mind?" Kylee sat on the dry grass and motioned for Evan to join her. She poured herself cold lemonade and offered Evan a sip. He declined.

She stared at the lakeshore and sipped from her plastic Yosemite mug. "I feel better," she said. "It took a while, but here I am. Calm. Settled. I know where I'm going."

"Listen, Kylee, what you saw at Summer Springs, I can explain."

She lifted her fingers to his lips then placed her hands on her lap. "There's no need to explain. I understand what happened."

"You do?"

"Of course. And I understand that it was not your fault."

Evan let out a long sigh. It seemed a week alone and the fresh mountain air was all she needed to clear up the confusion. "I am so glad to hear that," he said. "I was afraid. Afraid that you wouldn't believe a word I said. But it's true, you know; it was not my fault."

Kylee curled her bottom lip and kept her gaze on the lake. "I try not to think about it. But Mireille is truly evil. I blame her every inch of the way. She enticed you. People say she's beautiful. I don't see it, but apparently, men do. You're a man; what can I say?"

She took another sip, curled her lip again, and went on. "I blame myself. I mean, here I took the job to keep an eye on you two. I know that was wrong. I should've trusted you. Well, up to a point. Mireille—I don't trust for a moment. Then I got distracted by the layoff and the Fred Mott thing. I kept my eyes closed. It was like a beacon in front of my face—you and Mireille. I just wish you would've told me yourself."

Evan arched his eyebrows. "Listen, Mireille and me, we're not what you think."

"It was only by the hand of God I got there when I did—before it happened." She turned to Evan. "Nothing did happen, true?"

"I swear. Not even close."

"Good. I have a plan to keep it that way."

"I'm listening," Evan said.

"That's part of the plan," she said.

"Pardon?"

"Our number one problem."

Evan folded his hands on his lap.

"We don't talk. Rather, we talk, but nobody listens. And that's a far cry from college. Remember then? However, nowadays ..." She shook her head. "No time is no excuse anymore. So, my plan is this; we'll make time. Starting this weekend, and every weekend until I say otherwise."

Evan leaned forward.

"Here at the cabin," Kylee said. "No TV, no apps, no iPads, no games, and no phones." She pointed at his pocket. "Satellite or normal. Just you and me—that's it."

"You're serious."

"I'm serious about our marriage."

"And my job? How do I work that in?"

"Delegate. That's why you're the boss." She widened her eyes and glared at him. "If you don't work on your marriage, bottom line is; you won't have one."

Evan ran his fingers through his hair and leaned his head skyward. He tried to find an argument, but all he saw was the image of Mireille; red towel on her head, drops of water glistening from her soft, curvy, sensuous body. His throat went dry and he coughed, trying to force the image from his head.

"Fair enough. We'll try it. I mean, we'll *do* it. I'll make arrangements at work. So yes, Kylee, yes. I'll sign up for whatever it takes."

"Good, you'll thank me."

Despite his skepticism, Evan—after forty-eight hours of home cooking, walks in the woods, and easy conversations about the early years—put Mireille and work far into the background.

Kylee's face—smooth, tanned, and wholesome—was the only face he saw with his eyes and his mind. It was a good feeling. His problems at work faded to small issues for someone else to deal with. For forty-eight hours, he was close to feeling unconditionally happy. Kylee's calmness in the middle of a crisis was exactly the reason he married her. Like an honest day at the spa, he felt his tensions slowly disappear.

Kylee had dropped his phone into the bottom of a cookie tin and pushed the lid securely shut. Despite her action—or perhaps because of it—Evan was headache-free for the first time in a long time. Despite his initial reluctance, he looked forward to their next wilderness retreat. Only one thing could top off a perfect weekend, and as a special treat, Kylee obliged.

"It's got six engines and four seats." He gave her a tour of the fan-jet and wiped away the dust with an old bath towel. The setting sun enhanced the bright red finish, and he wished he had brought a camera. With the pine trees in the background, this seemed the perfect setting for a brochure.

"This is what you had before Everest?" Kylee shook her head. "It's so small."

"George Jetson had one. So can I." Evan laughed. He popped open the pilot-side door and helped Kylee onto the seat.

"Where are the gauges?" She kept one hand on the door handle but scanned the cockpit.

"Coming up." Evan snapped on the power switch and pointed at the console screen.

"Wow!"

"That's the best compliment I've heard."

"These I recognize—altimeter, speedometer, fuel gauge." She moved her finger to a pale red display. "Radio, right?"

"Very good. That's all you need; and this …" He moved her hand to the control stick.

"Whatever you do," Kylee said, "do not turn on the engine."

"Not for Lesson One. But how about this?" He pulled out the Coldplay CD from the player and slipped in the Dave Matthews Band. He turned up the volume until Kylee began to sway with the music. Some technology she didn't seem to mind.

Since she was in a good mood, Evan went on with the lesson. He showed her everything from the autopilot to the air conditioner. He demonstrated the combination lock and the seat recliner. He wasn't sure if it was the music or his skill as a flight instructor, but whatever it was, Kylee, after years of avoiding Evan's passion, finally took an interest.

She pushed the buttons, twisted the knobs, and memorized what she could. With the engines off, she seemed eager to try it all.

Evan smiled. The trip to the mountain was suddenly a good idea. He caressed the back of her neck, leaned close, and kissed her on the lips. He had one last request to top off the night.

"How about we swap seats and I'll fly us home?" He tapped the ignition button. "You work the music, and I'll do the plane."

Kylee smiled and tapped his hand. She flipped off the music and shut down the console. "How about a rain check? It's dark, it's windy, and this is still experimental." She pushed open the door, stepped out, and leaned her head back in. "It's not safe for either of us."

Evan slowly lowered his jaw, hearing echoes of his father's unsafe-at-any-altitude voice. He tried to stutter at least one word of disappointment, one phrase that would somehow encourage her; but she slammed the door closed and returned to her cabin.

"Come on, Kylee." He threw up his hands as he followed her. "It's a short flight. You can almost see the airport from here."

She dragged a moldy tarp from her log pile and draped it over the fan-jet. "Next weekend, we'll give it a whirl. Tonight, let's keep our heels on the ground." Loose bark and dirt fell across the cowling, and she made no attempt to brush it off.

Evan cringed, grinding his teeth and tightening his neck muscles. He lowered his eyes. When Kylee dropped rocks to secure the tarp to the ground, each thud was like a hammer to his heart.

Kylee gently lifted his chin with her finger. "Sooner or later, we'll flip on the engine."

His perfect night shattered, Evan lost his appetite for any conversation or argument. When Kylee finally drove them home to Apple Valley, Evan could do little more than sit quietly with his hands folded on his lap. After an hour of winding roads, all he said was, "Can we have some different music?"

Kylee probably didn't hear him, so she played Tim McGraw again, slightly louder.

They pulled into their driveway around nine. As Evan dragged himself from the garage to the kitchen, he said, "It's been a long drive. Wake me at six."

Kylee followed close behind. "Next weekend, I'll take your steaks and your Green Day. Rest assured, we'll make this marriage work despite your taste in music."

Evan grumbled while he glanced at the phone on the counter. "Seventeen messages," he said. "Not a good way to end the weekend."

He pressed Play and pulled off his jacket. Kylee headed for the fridge and pulled out a cherry yogurt.

Mireille's voice boomed through the kitchen as if she was there herself.

First message; "Evan, call me."

Next message; "Evan, where are you? I tried your phone, no answer. I tried text, you never got back."

Next message; "Evan, it's really important. Drop whatever you're doing. Call me now."

Kylee peeled back the top of the yogurt container and smirked.

Next message, Mireille went on; "Okay, I don't know where you are, and I hate to leave a message. But you have to know; we're taking Paul to the hospital. Call me."

Chapter *16*

EVAN FELT a cold shiver run up his spine. He pressed the Time Received button.

"Sunday, four-thirty-one p.m."

He pressed Next Message.

"Sorry, Evan," Mireille said. "Paul is being airlifted to San Bernardino Memorial with a heart attack. I'm—"

Evan listened closely, but the background noise cut off the rest of the call. He didn't bother with the next twelve messages. He tucked his jacket beneath his arm and swapped keys on the counter. He scowled at Kylee and raced to the garage.

All he heard was, "Evan, I'm sorry." Then he slammed the kitchen door shut. He jumped into Kylee's Jeep and cursed that he left the Jaguar at the Dove hanger. Before the garage door was fully closed, he was halfway down the street and headed for I-15.

"Voice dial, Mireille," he said into his phone.

Seconds later, she answered. "Evan, where are you?"

"Never mind. How's my father?"

"I left a message."

"I know," Evan said, "but tell me how he is."

"Okay, well, he's out of surgery. We think we got here in time."

"What do you mean, you think?"

Mireille hesitated. "It's too early to say. Where are you?"

"About a half-hour out."

"Is Kylee with you?"

"Don't get me started." Evan gripped the steering wheel. "My father's dying and I'm playing cards at the cabin."

"He's unconscious now. The doctor said fifty-fifty. I'm here. Claire's here. You're the only family he has."

"My phone's on now. If there's any change, let me know." Evan pressed harder on the accelerator and snaked his way through the interstate traffic. If only he had kept his phone on; if only he had flown home; if only he had his fan-jet to fly to San Bernardino. A dozen if-only cases and most of them, he concluded, were due to Kylee.

When he arrived at the hospital lobby, Mireille was waiting. She had casually dressed in blue slacks and a flowered blouse. In the midst of a crisis, she seemed calm, poised, and distractingly beautiful.

They hugged. The scent of her lavender and the warmth of her embrace settled Evan's heart and cleared his mind of frustration. For a moment, he didn't want to leave. Her touch seemed soothing, compassionate, and understanding. He felt safe.

Mireille gently tugged his arm and coaxed him along hallways to the first floor ICU. As they stepped around the last corner, he saw Claire in the visitor waiting area. She looked as concerned as any family member.

Claire stood, lightly touched Evan's elbow, and gave him an update. "There's been no change. Dr. Kuni has him on beta-blockers. He said the angioplasty went well. So far, his condition's critical, and, uh, he'll probably stay that way for a while. I wish I could tell you more." She released her touch and retreated to her chair.

Mireille said, "Thanks," to Claire and then led Evan to Paul's private room. As they passed the on-duty nurses, one of them looked up but said nothing. The other three talked among themselves.

Evan faltered at the doorway and gazed inward. The hospital smell, the flashing blood pressure monitors, the oxygen and IV tubes poking at Paul's pale and limp body; Evan hated hospitals and this was exactly why.

Mireille held his hand and guided him to the side of the bed. There, she gently squeezed Evan's hand and released it. She smoothed the folds of a sheet around Paul's chest, turned to Evan and told him, "I'll be with Claire."

Evan watched Mireille leave and resisted the temptation to call her back. He reluctantly looked at Paul. He shivered as the anxieties flowed back in full force. His gaze jumped from Paul's face to the monitors, then to the door and to the ceiling. His mind flashed from the monitors, to Everest, to Fred Mott, and to everyone at the company.

He couldn't help but recall old family memories; home in Apple Valley, vacations to Scotland, a first flight in an old Cessna. He couldn't help but recall memories from first grade to college graduation. A hundred cherished thoughts and Evan wondered if he would ever have the chance to say thanks.

He leaned over, touched Paul's head, and smoothed the disheveled gray hairs. He tucked in the loose blanket around his feet and turned off an overhead light. That was all he could do. Eighteen years of education and he felt helpless as a child. He carefully lifted a chair from a corner to the bedside. He sat down, and for the first time in his life, he lowered his head and prayed.

Moments seemed like hours, and Evan could only sit, wait, and wonder what would happen next. He kept looking at Paul's face, hoping to see open eyes, hoping to hear at least a "Where am I?" But all he saw was a pale old man; frail and motionless. Any hint of a strong, passionate father seemed forever gone.

Mireille slipped quietly into the room and took her place by Evan. She placed the back of her fingers against Paul's cheek as if to check his temperature. She pressed her finger to a pulse monitor and straightened the IV tube that pumped solution to Paul's veins.

"Kylee's here," she said, setting her purse on the guest chair.

"I know. I saw her walk by."

"She wants to see you."

"Tell her it's not a good time," Evan said.

"You must tell her yourself. She also wants to see Paul."

Evan groaned. He knew that Kylee deserved to see her father-in-law. After all, Paul had always treated her like the daughter he never had. It wouldn't be fair to Kylee—or Paul—to deny her a visit. He looked at the clock and double-checked his watch.

"I need a break," he told Mireille. "Let her in. I'll be back in ten ... Coffee?" He checked for change in his pocket and dollar bills in his wallet.

Mireille shook her head.

Evan wandered the hallways and finally found the vending machines. He chose decaffeinated coffee, hoping that a nap during the night would help him ease him into the morning. He sipped his coffee as long as he could, appreciating a respite away from the stress. When he finished the coffee, he trudged to Paul's room. To his dismay, Kylee was there. That sight jarred his nerves more than a double-shot espresso.

"Dr. Kuni is good," she said, scanning the chart at the foot of the bed. "Actually, he's very good. And fortunately, he was on call. Sunday is not his normal shift."

"So I heard."

"Dr. Herdu will be here in the morning. He's also good." Kylee glanced at Evan but mostly looked at Paul.

Evan didn't respond.

Kylee fingered the IV bag and then ran her hand across the EKG monitors. "I talked to the floor supervisor. She said to stay all night if you want to."

"I planned on it."

She eased closer to Evan. "I brought your car."

"The Jag?"

"I took a cab to work then drove it here." She dangled the keys in front of her.

Evan took them, reached into his pocket, and pulled out the Jeep keys.

"I'm sorry," she said, dropping the keys into her purse. "If I had known—"

"Hey, it happens." Evan took his place by Paul's bed. "Late is better than too late. I suppose I should be happy for that."

"Is there anything you want?"

"Time to sit with my father. In the morning, Daz will get the fan-jet. Mireille will get my things."

"Your things?"

"Yeah, I'll be overnight here. Maybe a hotel tomorrow. When he wakes up, I want to be close."

"And me?"

"Go home, get some sleep. I'll call if there's any news." Evan, recalling that she rarely used a smart phone, glared at her. "Check the machine when you get there."

Kylee's eyes turned glassy and watery. She opened her mouth as if to say more. With a slight shudder, she exhaled deeply and turned away. She hesitated, adjusting the purse strap on her shoulder. She looked down and then walked off to the hallway that led to the nearest exit.

Evan moved to the doorway and watched her until she disappeared. Then he looked for Mireille, but she was also gone. As he walked to the break room for another coffee, he saw Claire. This seemed a good chance for an update.

"Claire," Evan said as he approached.

Claire set her magazine aside and looked up. "Actually, I don't read magazines ... Especially this." She tapped the cover of *Sports Illustrated.*

"Yeah, this is not a favorite place."

Claire stood and looked at the clock on the wall. "Dr. Kuni should be back by one. I don't expect anything new."

"Listen, Claire, you don't have to stick around. Mireille and me—we're fine. I appreciate your help."

"So far, I haven't done much; cancel Mireille's appointments, cancel Paul's appointments. I'll cancel yours if you want."

"Please." Evan checked his pockets. "I left the phone in the Jeep. I'll get Mireille to pick it up tomorrow ... So, what happened?"

"You mean at the office?"

Evan nodded.

"I can tell you, but it's all hear-say."

"That's fine."

Claire set her purse on a chair. She looked toward Paul's room then at Evan. "It was the usual Sunday afternoon. Paul was there, catching up. Mireille was there, trying to find Paul. Last-minute purchase order or something; she needed a signature. So she walked into his office. Straight away, she knew that something was wrong. She said he kept rubbing his arm like he was distracted. His face looked all sweaty. Paul blamed his heartburn.

"Mireille—she wasn't convinced. She asked him about his meds, but he refused to answer. His stubbornness—that was part of the problem. Anyway, she went to her office, got some big-dose aspirin, and just about moved his jaw to chew it. When she stepped out again to call 911, Paul followed. He got two steps then collapsed; out cold on the floor."

Claire gently touched Evan's elbow. "The paramedics said he was lucky that Mireille was there."

"She saved his life?"

Claire nodded. "I'm hoping she did."

"Remind me to thank her."

***

Two days later, with Evan and Dr. Kuni by his side, Paul slowly awoke. He gently rolled his head on his pillow. As if rousing from a deep sleep, he opened his eyes and blinked. He breathed in through his nose; the oxygen tubes making it more of a snort. He coughed, gripped his chest, and licked his dry lips. He spoke with a gruff faltering voice.

"What are you doing here?" He looked at Evan and squinted. "Sweet Jesus, who's running the plant?"

Evan grinned. Paul, it seemed, was very much alive and apparently in good spirits—if not totally ignorant of his critical situation. Evan leaned over the bed, carefully moved in, and hugged his father. Then he backed off and laughed. He fought back a tear.

"I left Mireille in charge. And she's doing fine."

"Dear God!" Paul bellowed with half a voice. "You left that woman to run the company? What was going through your head?"

"I thought you liked her."

Paul swiveled his head and gazed at the heart monitors. He looked at the tubes sticking in his arm and at Dr. Kuni in his white coat. It seemed he understood where he was, but nevertheless, he asked the doctor, "Do you mind? I need five minutes alone with my son."

Dr. Kuni narrowed his eyes.

"I'm not going anywhere," Paul said.

"Three minutes," Dr. Kuni replied. "I'll be outside." He stepped out but kept the door open.

Paul took a shallow breath and coughed. As he settled himself, the harsh lines of his forehead disappeared, and he took on the face of a frail old man.

"My mistake," he softly said. "I should have trusted you from the start. I should've trusted you long before this mess. October was all I wanted."

Evan shrugged. "Wanted? For what?"

"I had to save the company. Without Trudeau, we'd be on the streets."

"Yeah, well, everyone knows that," Evan said. "And no one blames you; if that's what you're worried about."

"You don't understand." Paul squirmed and grimaced. "And don't make me repeat this. My head's pounding. You gotta listen close."

"Take your time. *I'm* not going anywhere."

"They have twenty-five percent stock in Dove," Paul said between shallow, sporadic breaths. "You know that. And you know that they want fifty-one percent."

"I assumed that, yes."

"You can also assume that I'm doing my best to avoid it."

"Go on."

"I have an agreement with Pierre." Paul sat up the best he could and went on. "It's covered with a hundred pages of legal documents, but …"

"But what?" Evan asked.

"It's the second round of financing. In October, that is. They give us funding—two hundred million to ramp up assembly. We give them shares of Dove. How many we give; that depends on the price. Bottom line; if our stock is strong, we keep the company. If not, we lose control."

"What?"

"Talk to the lawyers," Paul said with a gasp. "It's all about money, shares, and control. Simple—when you get down to it."

"You bet the company?" Evan shook his head. "That's not simple by any means."

"It's a moot point now. You're in charge. I'll call it a safe bet."

"Me?"

"You don't expect me to run the company. Not with these tubes; not from a bed. From this moment on, you're the president. I expect you to act that way."

"God, I hate surprises. This is about the worst way to take over—you know that."

Evan grimaced. He felt on the verge of a tension headache. Then he looked at Paul's sad—but hopeful—eyes. Suddenly, a headache seemed the least of his concerns. He gave his father a pat on the shoulder.

"But if it keeps you alive, I'm not going to argue. I'll work it out with the attorneys later … much later."

Paul closed his eyes and let his mouth droop. He sat still, struggling for breath and looking as though he needed more sleep. He jerked his head and gave the last words for the night; "Keep us strong."

Evan stood still, struggling for words.

Dr. Kuni returned and broke the silence. He motioned for the ICU nurse to come in with her tray full of drugs. "Gentlemen, this meeting is closed."

***

At home, later that night, Evan found Kylee at her desk; a stack of internet printouts in front of her, scotch tape and a stapler beside her. From the looks of it, she had compiled a complete history of Fred Mott and Trudeau. She held scissors in one hand, a scrapbook in the other.

"Well, I'm not going to move out," Evan told her as he put his phone on the charger.

Kylee put down her scissors and folded her arms. "And why would you?"

"You don't get it, do you?"

"Get what?"

"The cabin. Going there was bad enough, but you made me sit there with no phone, no nothing. Dad could've been dead and buried before I found out. That doesn't bother you one bit."

"That's not true." Kylee raised her voice. "What if you were in France and you found out? Phone or not, you're twelve hours away at best. Don't blame me for what happened. That's how it worked out. Be glad you saw him when you did."

"This whole thing you got going; spying on me at work, your obsession with Fred, that cabin. I can only take so much."

"What are you going to do?"

"For now, I'll live in the guest room. I'll do my own clothes and buy my own food. If I see you at work, I'll say, 'Hi.' Beyond that, I can't guarantee what's going to happen."

"A separation?" Kylee dropped her crossed arms as her eyes began to water.

"It's the same house; nobody's going to know."

"I'm going to know." Her voice wavered.

"The way I see it; we have no choice. We're both stubborn, and we're not going to change. At least I know my limits. I know what I can take and what I can't."

"What do you want me to do? I can't change what happened. Paul's getting better now. You should be grateful."

"He's not better! Why would you say that?" Evan searched the closet for a spare clock. "And don't play dumb. You know exactly what you can do to fix this."

"Like what?"

"For starters; two things." He glared at Kylee as he fumbled for his clock. "Forget the cabin. Forget Fred."

"I know what you think, but there's nothing wrong with the cabin. I did that to bring us closer. Two days a week would not be the end of the world."

"It's as simple as this; if you want me back, forget the cabin and forget about Fred."

Kylee stared at her printouts and fingered the scrapbook she had compiled.

"Be glad," Evan said. "Two days ago, I had a different plan. This one—at least you have a choice."

Kylee kept her gaze on her papers. She lowered her voice to a whisper. "I'm sorry. I can't."

"What was that?"

"I said I'm sorry."

Evan went to his dresser and picked up enough clothes for the next day. He quietly walked down the hall, dropping a sock halfway there. He never looked back. As he closed the guest room door behind him, he softly said, "Then I'm sorry too."

Chapter *17*

THURSDAY, a few rays after sunrise, Evan met Mireille at the Dove executive lobby. His first day back, her first day with a new partner.

"I heard about your father." She kissed Evan on both cheeks. Her hands rested gently on his elbows. "That's encouraging. And I'm glad you can make our seven o'clock."

When the guard buzzed the security door open, Mireille urged Evan down the hall.

"It's our first conference—worldwide, that is." Evan quickened his pace to keep up with Mireille's long legs. "This should be interesting."

"You're in charge now, *mon cher*. We have ten executives waiting for your words."

"Is it true?" Evan tugged at her elbow.

"Is what true?"

"Trudeau might get fifty-one percent—especially with our stock in the toilet like it is."

Mireille held her elbow close and coaxed Evan to move faster. "That's the deal your father and Pierre worked out. Personally, I'd rather have a third of a company that's booming than a hundred percent of one that's failing. Of course, with you and me at the top, there's no way we can fail."

"You and me?"

"Pierre's in New York. I'm here. You're here. It's up to us now." As they passed Mireille's office, she snapped her fingers. Jean-Petit raced to her heels.

"And all I need is a good night's sleep," Evan said.

"I thought you were home."

"In the guest room; in a hard bed, next to a loud furnace. We've got a few issues to sort out. The guest room was a compromise."

"If I can help—"

"You can help me survive the meeting."

Mireille pulled her phone from her purse and checked a few notes. "Okay, we've made the official announcement. They know you're in charge, and they have a rough agenda."

"With one day to get ready, the entire meeting might be rough."

Mireille shook her head. "They want to see a face and hear some assurances. They—and the media—want to know that Dove is still under control."

"The face, I have. Control, I'm not so sure."

"For this meeting, we can outline the rollout. Do not say anything fancy." She laughed. "Introduce yourself, and cover the agenda. You know; the media, the flight, the captain."

"Yeah." Evan nodded. "I thought I'd have Daz with us. He'll be the captain and—"

Mireille frowned. "I know how you feel, but that's going to be a tough sell."

"How do you mean?"

"Trust me on this, Mr. President. Ken Nakamura should be your pick."

"What?"

"He has Everest experience. He photographs well, and he's known on the Rim."

"Everest experience? He sat in the simulator."

"He's flown everything but Everest. He's a good pilot." Mireille slowed her pace and faced Evan. "First impressions, *mon cher*. If I'm wrong, you come back with *Monsieur* Daz."

Evan didn't want to start his first day back with an argument, and that one hour sleep didn't sharpen his wits. He looked at Mireille's sparkling green eyes and couldn't help but share her enthusiasm. He acquiesced to her years of experience. Details like pilots, unions, stock price, and office space could be worked out later. This morning, they had a major company to run.

To the surprise of no one but Evan, his leading of the video conference was met with a near-standing ovation. The worldwide management pulled together in the face of the latest crisis and threw Evan their full support. Milan and Devonshire signed up for an aggressive delivery schedule. Kansas City and Norfolk agreed to a hiring and salary freeze. The Taipei, Seoul, and Tokyo delegations especially applauded Evan's choice of an Asian pilot for the first flight of America's premier jet.

As they left the meeting, Mireille leaned close to Evan and said, "We're a good team, yes? Next step; move your office next to mine."

***

Four weeks later, the Dove stock rebounded. Both Paul and the public now had confidence in Evan's leadership. Of course, Mireille never doubted. And because of her unwavering support and steadfast belief, Evan vowed to stay on her good side. He vowed to keep her trust.

Now, he got ready for his first major milestone; the rollout of a freshly painted, completely assembled, hanger tested aircraft with the code name Everest.

And to witness the rollout, the media had arrived in full force on a perfectly calm, perfectly clear day. The Dove PR team passed out the media kits and poured enough mimosas to fill a wading pool. Hundreds of workers headed for the tarmac to witness their part in history.

Between buildings and away from the crowd, Evan and Mireille hurriedly walked a garden path and sorted out last-minute details. As Mireille spoke on the phone with the FAA, Evan heard footsteps from behind. He spun around and saw Daz.

"Last chance to do it right," Daz told them.

"What's that?" Evan stopped and motioned for Mireille to do the same.

Daz eased himself between the two. Out of breath and aggravating his voice, he said, "I see you got a nice show lined up; Ken Nakamura on the left seat, some Korean on the right."

"Jee Sang-Ki," Mireille said, clicking off her phone.

"So we look good on the Pacific Rim. So they see what; Nakamura walk and wave, take off and land. Then he stands on the jetway with a big smile." Daz held up his hand and grinned. "Great, maybe you'll get an order, maybe not. Short-term, we're happy. But when you get down to it, safety is our bottom line. Unless you got a plane that stays in the air, unless you got Everest totally safe, you got no product. One crash or one incident; we shut down the plant."

Mireille looked at her watch. "Is there a point?"

Daz curled his lip and turned to Evan. "You need a pilot to find the bugs. You need a pilot to push and twist Everest to the max. What you don't need is some pretty boy for the camera."

"We need you; that's what you're saying."

"Keep Nakamura for the follow-on flights. He'll get the press. Don't worry."

Mireille encouraged Daz and Evan to walk and talk. "*Écoutez, Monsieur* Donahue. No one expects a fault-free plane. That is the purpose of the flights. We will find bugs, fix them, and make Everest safe before we deliver. Nakamura San—he has flown Shasta. He can certainly fly Everest. As for the press, you are mistaken. We have many, many cameras installed. We will follow Everest from the ground, from the cockpit, and from row forty-four of the cabin. We will see the entire flight, start to finish."

"Big mistake, I'm telling you," Daz muttered as he veered off. He flailed his arms as he disappeared around a corner.

For now, Evan didn't have the time or willingness to argue the already-released plan. Instead, he and Mireille kept a steady pace to the rolling doors of the main assembly hanger as the photo op commenced. Once there, Evan felt his heart race and his pride surge.

Some eight hundred workers had gathered in a haphazard "V" formation. Most of them sported a Dove T-shirt for the comfortably warm summer day. The media—local, national, international—stood in front. An impressive sight from any angle.

Evan took his position at the front podium and grabbed a wireless mic. While waiting for the crowd to settle down, he beamed a broad smile. He took a deep breath, held the mic close, and eased into his semi-prepared script.

"Not long ago, my father stood on this spot and predicted that we would make aviation history. He said we would design and build the world's largest, most prestigious, most luxurious …" He turned to Mireille. "Offer us another superlative."

Mireille moved in cheek to cheek. "Most profitable," she said, grinning. "For our customers and us."

Evan went on. "My father said we would make the best jet the world has ever seen. By God, we've done it. You, me. Dove, Trudeau. We're a different group than two years ago. But here we are; a new team with new challenges. We're ready to show anyone—everyone—that we can take on any challenge, meet it head on, and succeed … So, what do you say, team; let's show the world what we've made." He extended his arm upward to the huge bay doors.

While the cameras focused and recorded, Mireille picked up Jean-Petit and stood close to Evan. She motioned to Kylee, who had agreed to relay the event to Paul via video.

The hanger doors parted, and the gold-stripes-on-white Everest jumbo was towed from the assembly area to the full sun of the tarmac. For perspective, the marketing department had lined up six full-sized passenger buses to show both the size and capacity of Everest. A maintenance worker stood, without crouching, in each the four wing-mounted, 100,000-horsepower engine air scoops.

Mireille motioned for those workers to climb down. She prompted Ken Nakamura to walk the red carpet that led to the stairway. Ken climbed to the main cabin door and waited for First Officer Jee Sang-Ki. As both men waved at the top of the stairs, Mireille urged the crowd to the viewing bleachers for Act II of the main event.

What followed was a near-flawless set of maneuvers. From a thunderous takeoff, Everest rocketed across the isolated desert toward to the San Bernardino Mountains. Ken circled at low altitude to give the audience—and those near the outskirts of Hesperia and Apple Valley—the show of their lives.

Ken then applied full power and took Everest into a climb. He tested each of the fly-by-wire control functions in critical low- and high-altitude tests. He capped it off an hour later by executing a perfect sixteen-tire landing.

According to Mireille, the entire event went exactly to plan; the flight took off as scheduled, landed on schedule, and no bags were lost.

According to the media, the flight signaled the start of an airline revolution.

According to Evan, he was on top of the world.

Chapter *18*

"ONE OF OUR planes went down," Daz said quietly, leaning into Kylee's cubicle.

"What?" Kylee lifted her hand to her mouth.

"A Gibraltar—the same type that Fred flew in. No word on survivors."

"God." Kylee hesitated to catch her breath. "How many souls on board?"

"Three. Three men on board. To let you know; Bob Aukram was one of them."

Kylee shivered then quietly asked, "Where?"

"The desert; up north. Grab your stuff and let's go."

Kylee left her computer in mid-sentence. She grabbed her purse and a box of tissue and ran to her Jeep. There, she picked up her climbing gear and medical supplies. On her way to Daz's helicopter, she stopped in the locker room. She changed into her outdoor sportswear; nylon shorts, a black top, and a well-worn pair of Scarpa climbing shoes. She had a hunch that a rough road lay ahead.

After last-minute preparations, Kylee, Daz, Russell, and Evan boarded the helicopter and set a course for the northeast. It was mid-day, and both the sun and temperature were climbing fast.

Kylee adjusted the air conditioner for maximum cooling and her headset for minimum noise. She dug into her purse for her sunglasses and then stared outside at no place in particular. Between the sun, the heat, and three sweating men, she knew a headache was bound to follow. She found her aspirin and doubled-up the dose.

It was early September; weeks since she had spoken with Bob. She blamed herself for not keeping in touch. But her nightmares had vanished, and Bob was making headway with his investigation. Pushing harder would have jinxed the progress already made. But with a plane down in the middle of the desert; the progress had come to a sudden halt. The jinx had moved ahead.

Kylee leaned forward and tapped Daz on his shoulder. "Why does this flight seem so familiar?"

Daz pushed the control to full speed. "Fortunately," he said, "we have no turbulence and no storms coming in. We'll make it a good rescue."

Kylee nodded.

As they approached the accident site, Russell leaned forward and tapped Daz on the shoulder. "I got a weak signal. Looks like twenty miles, heading one-one-zero."

Evan stared outside. "Mountains, valleys, and a whole lot of rocks; this is a bad place for a landing."

"If there are survivors, we'll get to them first." Russell patted his newly designed, super-sensitive direction finder. "They could be on the moon, and I'd still find 'em. All we need is their ELT."

"ELT?" Kylee asked.

"Emergency locator—"

"Transmitter," Kylee said. "Got it."

"As long as we can keep one step ahead." Daz gestured to the back. "You got the sheriff's department, the FAA, and Civil Air. Each one is looking for the same crash. Of course, thanks to Russell, we got a head start."

"Hey, we offered to help," Russell said.

"They're still sore about what happened before," Kylee said.

"What happened up north was not our fault," Evan said.

"I'm not arguing. We did what we had to do." Kylee shuddered with a flashback of the rugged Sierras; a horrendous place to get stranded, an impossible place for a rescue. Then she stared at equally hostile terrain below.

Coming up was the southern end of Zion National Park; a vast landscape of hills, gullies, mountains and canyons. The Virgin River sliced through this sun-baked neighborhood; a dazzling blue green river walled by beautiful shades of red and brown sandstone. No doubt, it was a great place for a hike—but a bad place for a plane.

"It's eighty-five out there." Daz jabbed the window thermometer.

"And the river's forty-five," Kylee said. "They'll have hyperthermia if they're in the sun or hypothermia if they hit the water. Not a whole lot in-between."

"We have crossover!" Russell shouted.

"I don't see it," Evan said.

"It's somewhere below; I'm sure of it."

Daz swung the copter in a tight circle then hovered above the rocks and cottonwood trees. He searched for the target. "Likewise; I got nothing."

"Head upstream," Kylee said. "Like I said before, we can hike our way down. We'll find the plane for sure."

"Will do." Daz banked right then cruised by the river until he found level ground and a clear space for the rotor. After a last look around, he landed and set the engine to idle. "This is the best I can do. You're on your own."

Evan gave a thumbs-up then hopped to the ground. Once again, every second counted. In a scramble to save time, he slid the rear door to the stops and pulled out whatever he could. "We'll need a raft, paddles, radio—"

"Back boards, air splint, and blankets," Kylee said.

"Blankets?"

"Hypothermia or shock; it's routine."

"Got it." Evan leaned through the door and looked forward. "Don't hang around, Daz. Whatever happens, we do not want to draw attention."

"Understood. I'll be downstream when you call."

When Daz flew the helicopter to the next ridge, the surrounding sounds settled down to little more than the river below and wind gusts from above. Kylee wondered why she carried a backboard. Body bags would've made more sense. The hills and canyons seemed imposingly steep and unforgiving now that she stood on the ground. No granite in sight, but the sandstone and limestone boulders were still hard as a rock. A bad situation was sure to follow.

After a careful descent along a make-shift trail, Kylee stood at the river bank. She craned her neck to see the top of a fifteen-foot wall. Sure enough, the tail of the downed plane loomed overhead like a freeway sign in the middle of nowhere.

Evan and Russell clambered over rocks and shallow pools to get to her side. "First, find the four corners," Evan said, subdued.

"Four corners; what's that?" she asked.

"Two wings, the tail, and in this case, the engine."

"The tail's there," she said abruptly.

"Look to your left."

Kylee turned her gaze downstream and saw the remnants of a wing. Right or left; she couldn't tell. Not that it mattered; it had fallen far from the tail. The impact must have been horrendous.

"I don't see the cabin," she said, trying to sound optimistic.

Evan propped his foot on a rock and pointed. "My guess, most of the fuselage is on that ledge."

Russell grimaced. "With the scorch marks on the rocks above it; makes you wonder if it's a moot point."

"While we're on-site," Kylee said, "we are obliged to check it out."

"How do we get up there?" Evan asked. "You got this wall and no footholds, no handholds, no nothing. And someone forgot the ropes." He turned to Russell.

"Daz should have the ropes," Russell said. "Ask him to drop 'em off."

Evan turned his back on the wall, set down his pack, and rummaged for his radio. When he found it, he looked for Daz. "Hey, Kylee," he said, keeping his gaze downstream, "do you need that thing for the rocks?"

Before Evan got an answer, Russell tapped his shoulder and aimed him toward the wall. "I guess some of us don't need a staircase."

Kylee was already halfway up the wall. She stretched her legs in search of a toehold in the invisible cracks of the sandstone. White chalk covered her palms and fingertips. Her shoulders—normally smooth and firm—turned to muscle as she easily pushed her weight one arm length at a grasp.

Russell stood below her. "Should Daz bring the ropes?"

"Not yet."

Evan walked closer and yelled. "Don't touch anything—unless you find someone alive!" Then he turned to Russell and told him in a low voice, "Fat chance of that. Sorry, but this one's for the coroner."

"Keep your voice down," Kylee said as she reached for the ledge.

"What do you see?" Evan asked impatiently.

"I'll start with tail number," she said. "It's zero-nine something; probably an R—if that helps."

With a first glimpse of the wreckage, the reality of plane versus rock became clear. Hardly any section but the tail itself remained intact. The fuselage, remaining wing, the 1,000-horsepower engine were scattered in a smoky debris field about the size of a tennis court. The stench of burnt fuel and charred leather seats filled the air. Kylee's nausea was coming on fast.

She braced herself against a boulder and stared at another soot covered boulder. Then she fell to her knees, half in shock, half in pain from the overwhelming nausea. She realized that the form was not a sculpture of the desert but the remains of a victim. Which victim—she couldn't tell. Not that it mattered; it was a sad outcome by any account.

She pushed aside the urge to give up and retreat. Instead, she moved forward, carefully stepping. She found the remains of a second victim and a third—Bob Aukram. Bob had fared only slightly better than the crew members. His body remained strapped in his seat but thrown clear from the burning wreckage. When Kylee saw the deep laceration on his left temple and his open terrified eyes, she realized how horrible it must have been for all on board.

She touched Bob's hand and immediately felt overwhelmed as she pictured the last moments of the doomed flight. In full color and fragmented like the highlights of the evening news, she pictured the plane in a normal cruise from Las Vegas to St.

George, Nevada. Step by step, she saw the plane lose power. She saw the crew frantically scanning their instruments for the source of the problem. She saw the pilot—desperate for a place to land. She heard the terror in the co-pilot's voice as he tried in vain for radio contact. He told his one passenger, "Everything is fine." Finally, she felt their hearts race as they flew into the canyon and braced for impact.

"Kylee!" Russell yelled.

"I can hear you fine," she said.

"What did you say the tail number was?"

Kylee opened her eyes and staggered to the tail. "Zero nine R. Or maybe a P at the end."

"That's it!" Russell shouted.

"That's what?"

"This plane has a data recorder."

"Okay, so?" Kylee said.

"So, our mystery is solved; if you can find the black box."

"It's a mess up here," she said, "but tell me where to look."

"It should be near the tail," he said. "But it's orange, not black."

"Make up your mind."

"One more thing," Russell told Evan. "Get Daz to bring over my tablet."

"I'm on it."

While Kylee searched the debris field for any orange or black box, Daz guided his chopper overhead. At first, Kylee griped about the blowing sand and the speckles of fuel; tough on her eyes and a pain on her skin.

Then she squinted and saw it; definitely orange and now free of dust and gravel. She moved closer to the tail and confirmed the box. If it was good news, it sure didn't feel like it. The entire scene was much too gruesome for any sign of hope. Still, she had a job to do. Ignoring the victims for the moment, she went to the ledge and waved at Russell.

"Found it!" she shouted.

"Hang on!" Russell stood below the chopper as Daz dropped a bright green package. Russell cursed as the package hit the ground, and he grumbled until Daz flew off to the neighboring ridge. As the roar of the engine died down, Russell carefully unwrapped his tablet from the layers of the down filled sleeping bag. He powered it on, checked the display, and finally exhaled. He gave a thumbs-up to Kylee.

While he checked his custom app, Kylee took another look at the black box. "What's that beeping noise?" she asked Russell.

"That helps you to find it."

"What's the blinking light for?"

"What color is it?"

"Yellow," Kylee said.

"That's not good."

"Low battery," Evan said.

"We have to move fast." Russell hurried to the base of the wall and looked up. "Okay, Kylee. Catch!" With a smooth, easy motion, he lobbed his tablet into her waiting arms.

Evan shivered. "You're crazy."

"Kylee, I trust," Russell said. "She's got a grip like a ball player." He waited for her to check out the screen then he walked her through the application setup. When she gave a nod, he told her to head to the black box.

Meanwhile, Daz called on the radio. "Looks like we got company."

"Come again?" Evan said.

"The sheriff and the FAA, I'm guessing. They're flying in fast. They saw me, and I suspect they'll be looking for you."

"Copy that."

"Where do I plug it in?" Kylee called out when she stood by the black box.

"It's wireless," Russell said. "Hold it near the red wire and press Download."

"Got it!" Kylee followed the self-guiding prompts and hoped for the best. While she waited for the progress bar to turn green, the loud thumping of approaching helicopters became impossible to ignore. "What's happening?" she asked Russell.

"Never mind," Russell said. "What's happening with the box?"

"Battery; ten percent. Download; thirty percent."

"That's cuttin' it close."

Evan yanked at the self-inflate cord on the river raft and tossed in the remaining supplies. He dragged the raft to the water's edge. "I hear three, maybe four choppers," he said to Daz.

"Affirmative," Daz said. "They are tracking me, but when they pick up the locater—"

"They'll be heading for us."

"How are you doing?" Russell called up to Kylee.

"Five percent battery. Eighty percent download."

"You're doing fine."

"Download complete!" Kylee shouted. "Now what?"

"Toss me the tablet and let's get out!"

Kylee closed out the app and carefully dropped the tablet to Russell. Then, shifting her focus to the marked handholds on the sandstone wall, she retraced her steps and eased herself down to the flat ground. Pausing only long enough for a backward glance at the wreckage, she quickly joined Evan and Russell as they boarded the tiny raft. Then they pushed off to midstream.

She ducked low as helicopter rotors thumped the air overhead. But the fear of capture soon faded as the canyon walls narrowed and the shadows darkened. Surely, the small yellow raft would escape unnoticed.

Russell cushioned his laptop in a thick red blanket and cradled it like an only child. "Call me in the morning," he said. "I have a hunch that today's mess is only the start."

***

The next morning, after a good night's sleep, Kylee rushed to the Cottonwood Building to see if Russell's intuition was as good as her own. She found him at his workbench, buried among a bank of computer monitors and electronic displays. Evan stood at his side. From first appearances, it seemed that Russell had put in a very long session.

"You should've called me," Kylee said. "I would've stopped by your house. You know, to pick up some fresh clothes and a razor."

"Grab a seat." Russell ignored her offer. He pulled up a rolling chair for Kylee and motioned at another chair for Evan. "Boy, do I have a show for you."

He tapped at the keyboard and slid the mouse until the main screen displayed a large Time = 15:12:12.14.Z. He pressed Normal Speed to get the show started.

"I'm starting this about forty minutes into Bob's flight. Until then, it's pretty much routine. There's nothing to see, nothing to take notes on. Now however, we are ten minutes to impact."

A dozen graphs suddenly appeared, scrolling reams of data. Russell waved at the screens and spoke as if every sentence had a time limit. "A normal black box gives you this, this, and this. My link gives you this; cockpit voice recording and data from every module on board."

"Not bad." Evan said.

"Data overload," Kylee said, "from my angle."

"Forget the data and listen." Russell switched everything off except the monitor labeled; Voice Prints. He turned up the volume.

At first, the recording was little more than loud engine rumbling and faint—almost indistinguishable—voices.

Russell cancelled the noise, and suddenly the conversation seemed barely a room away. "First, the pilot," Russell said.

"Then she says 'courtside is nice, but now?' What with my schedule and her schedule, she said it didn't make sense."

"Now, the co-pilot," Russell said.

"But the Lakers. Come on, it's a season ticket. The schedule's only part of it."

"I know. It's the playoff that counts … Hey, what the—"

"Power drop," the co-pilot said. "What was that?"

"Pulling out the QRC."

"Quick Reference Checklist," Evan said.

Russell clicked another tab to remove noise. Without the loud roar of the engine, the voices seemed a cubicle away. Kylee heard pages flipping and assumed the co-pilot was looking for the emergency procedure.

"Glide speed, eighty-four," the pilot calmly said. "But we need power."

"Feathering the prop."

"Give Center a call."

"Mixture rich," the co-pilot said.

Kylee saw Transmitter On.

The co-pilot continued. "LA, Mojave-4; emergency."

"Fuel status?" the pilot asked.

"We have plenty of fuel, but the computer has shut it off."

"Override computer and go to manual."

"Unable," the co-pilot said. "The computer says, 'no.' "

"Turn to heading three-six-zero."

Evan put his finger on a Zion map. "They won't say it because of Bob, but they're looking for a place to land."

"But there is no place," Kylee said.

"LA center. Mojave-4. Mayday! Mayday!" The co-pilot raised his voice and then shut off his mic. "Could be, uh, vapor lock. What's the procedure? Airport's out of range."

Russell switched on his data display that showed Fuel Flow. The display showed 20%.

The pilot's voice came back. "No power. No fuel. Check breakers."

The co-pilot's voice, already a half-octave higher, squeaked even more when he leaned back to speak to his one passenger, "Bob, if you don't mind, could you, uh, put your briefcase below your seat?"

No reply from Bob.

The pilot called air traffic control. "LA center, Mojave-4. Going down over Zion."

No reply from the control center.

"Aim for the river," the pilot said. "Look for anything flat."

More clicking of knobs and levers, and then, "Shutting down fuel and power. Wheels down, uh, stand by."

Silence. Then, as the clock stopped on the monitors, the pilot whispered, "I love you, Daria."

The monitors flashed red or flatlined. The clock remained frozen. Kylee shuddered and felt weak all over. Without the chair, she would've dropped to her knees. After an awkward stillness, she finally spoke. She wondered if they had missed the obvious.

"Daria?" she asked. "Who's Daria? I only saw three at the site."

"This part of the recording the public never hears," Evan said. "The pilot knows there's a black box. His last words are to his wife. End of tape. Goodbye, I love you all."

"Oh."

"I know. I hate the voice recorder too." Evan swiveled his chair toward Russell then leaned back. "So far, we have the Gibraltar aircraft, a sudden loss of power, no recovery, and no radio contact."

"That's exactly what I pictured," Kylee said.

"Give me your take on this, Russell. You were on the team from the get-go."

"I spent half my life on the project. Engine power loss; yes, it happens. Not often, but I've seen it." Russell tapped on his keyboard. "Remember this? Service Bulletin 621."

"Vaguely."

"Here why they warn against cell phones. Once in a while, the altimeter would glitch." Russell jabbed his finger at the heading marked Safety Issue.

"Glitch?"

"It got confused. The altimeter's electric, of course—not like years ago. However, it is cheap."

"I agree."

"On Gibraltar, the altimeter wire is one big antenna. A cell phone would switch on and suddenly the altimeter reported fifty thousand feet. Yeah, I know—physically it can't happen. But the computer doesn't know that. It leans out the fuel to compensate. And if you're flying low, it's like shutting off the gas."

"The Mojave crew," Evan said. "They never knew."

"They didn't have to know. We fixed it long ago."

"So what happened?"

"Here's your problem." Russell pulled up another file and pointed at the screen. "The black box tells me that someone put in the old software—bugs and all."

"But why?"

"It doesn't matter," Kylee said. "No one used a cell phone. Go back and listen to the recording. There are no calls going out or coming in. That couldn't have been the cause."

"She has a point," Russell said.

Evan shook his head. "Unless Bob was using the data link on his phone. You know, like Fred. No voice, only pressing of keys."

"Like texting to Bullman Stock?" Russell asked.

"Exactly."

"No way!" Kylee said. "Bob was helping us. Inside trading—no. I'm sorry. No way."

"If he had a phone," Evan said, "he could do it."

"You're missing my point."

Russell wagged his finger. "Come on, you two. The real point is; who swapped the software?"

"And why?" Evan asked. "Why would anyone downgrade the software?"

"If it's intentional," Russell said, "you may be talking murder."

"How are you going to prove it?" Kylee asked. "You go to the NTSB and they'll know you were at the site. We're already in hot water. You want 'em to file charges?"

Evan threw up his hands. "Only a few of us know. Let's keep it that way while we check it out."

"A few?" she asked.

"Yeah; us, Daz, my father, and Mireille."

"Mireille?" Kylee laughed. "Why not tell the six o'clock news?"

"Mireille, I trust. Anyone else, I'm not so sure."

"Too bad we didn't get his phone," Russell mumbled as he shut down the main screen.

"Bob's phone?"

"Yeah, I'm getting pretty good at these." He opened a drawer and pulled out Fred Mott's phone. "I can tell who called who, when, and for how long."

"Probably burned to a cinder," Kylee said. "And I don't know if it's satellite or not."

"Still, it would be good to have."

"Forget it," Evan said. "We are not going back to the site. If you want a phone to check out, here you go." He slid his phone along Russell's bench. "I'm always charging it. Cheap battery or cheap phone; you tell me which."

"I'll get back to you." Russell set the phone aside.

Kylee grabbed her purse and headed for the door. "Sorry, guys, my gadget limit has just been exceeded." She looked at Evan. "Let's talk over lunch?"

"Not today." He faced away. "I have plans."

"Russell?" she quickly asked before her voice quavered.

"Yeah, sure, fine." Russell grinned. "Meanwhile, I'll see what else I can dig up."

***

Impatient for results, Kylee decided that lunch would be at eleven o'clock sharp at the quaint but secluded Joshua Cafe in Victorville. She also decided that she and Russell would take separate cars and park at separate corners. She apologized for the inconvenience.

At ten-fifty, she arrived at the café. She ordered creamy zucchini soup and waited for Russell. When he arrived, she quickly and quietly waved him over.

"You weren't followed, were you?" she asked as he sat across from her.

Russell grabbed a menu, ordered a tuna melt and Pepsi, and glanced at the cherry pie on the counter. "I'm still trying to figure out why we left the plant. A beef burrito at my desk was all I wanted."

"No, someone at the company is behind the crash. I'm sure of it."

"Maybe so, but this is a little extreme. I mean, no one knows we went to the site. No one cares if we're seen together or not."

"Except Mireille."

Russell raised an eyebrow. "What about her?"

"You know Pierre and Paul—they made a deal. It's complicated, but the bottom line is; if our stock goes down, Mireille takes over."

"That's kind of what I've heard."

"Ask yourself; if you wanted to drop the stock price, how would you do it?"

"Listen, Kylee. I like Mireille. And I like you. Don't ask me to get in the middle. I agree; there's something odd about Bob's crash. There's something odd about Fred's crash. But conspiracy and Mireille—that's a big stretch. We've got four thousand Gibraltar aircraft out there. One crash will never hurt the stock price."

"Then you tell me; who brought down the planes?"

"I cannot tell you *who* did it." Russell pulled his phone from his pocket and flipped through his notes. "But I can tell you *when*. It was two days before the crash. Two-fourteen a.m. to be exact. That's when the bad software was installed."

"Where?"

"At the Mojave Air hanger. And if they have security cameras—"

"Then we'll find our man." Kylee paused then said, "Or woman."

"Mireille again?" Russell shook his head. "I can't believe it."

"Believe what you want, but there's some connection." Kylee stirred her soup and sprinkled on the salt. "I don't know hardware, software, or anything about planes. But people—"

"Hold on." Russell glanced to his left. "We have company."

"Oh great. You said you weren't followed."

"I may have told some of the guys."

"Wonderful." She glared at the restaurant door.

Evan burst through alone. He carried a laptop and homed onto Kylee's booth. While she slowly crossed her arms, Evan slid next to Russell. Without a simple "hello" or "excuse me," he pushed aside the soup and bread plates. He set down the laptop and lifted the top.

"Here's your killers," he said, keeping his voice low. "And you can thank Mireille for the legwork."

"How's that?" Kylee asked.

"She spent half the morning at Mojave Air, collecting evidence." Evan waved a memory stick and grinned. "This here's a copy. The FBI, I'm sure, will want their own copy. Look close and learn."

He shoved the stick into the laptop and hit Play. As he swiveled the screen for a better view, a grainy, black and white image appeared. The corner flashed 02:10.

"Two-ten a.m.," Kylee said.

"Camera seven of twenty." Russell pointed.

"Bob Aukram's plane," Evan said. "At least it will be when he boards it in Vegas."

The security camera aimed at the aircraft, although the poor lighting made it tough to discern details. Russell adjusted his glasses as two fast-moving, blurry images approached the plane and stopped at the aircraft door.

"Whoever it is, they have a key," Kylee said when the shadowy figures swung open the cabin door and stepped inside.

"These planes are not Fort Knox," Russell said. "Give me a head start, and I'd be inside with or without a key."

"Don't tell the FBI that."

Evan continued, "No alarms and security that's half asleep. No wonder they don't catch 'em."

"Two-fourteen?" Russell turned to Kylee. "Sound familiar?"

Evan turned up the brightness. "Now, the two men come out. They close the door and disappear."

"How do you know they're men?" Kylee asked. "It's so dark; I can't tell if they're men, or boys, or women."

"Stay with me." Evan hit the fast-forward. "Now they're back. Same two. Inside again and messing around. Watch as they come out."

Headlights of a passing car lit up the scene for barely a flash. Evan hit Pause.

"My God," Kylee said.

"That's right. Our good friend; Madison Grier. We laid him off, but apparently, he's working the night shift."

Russell pressed his finger at the obscured face beside Grier's. "That's gotta be Markus Sullivan. Those guys are like twins."

"My guess," Evan said, "Len Harris is in the car."

"The safety manager," Kylee said.

"Former safety manager," Evan said. "We laid him off with the rest."

"There's your motive." Russell threw open his palms. "Basic revenge."

"Keep your voice down," Kylee whispered as customers walked by. "You accuse these guys of murder, you better be sure. One mistake and their lives are ruined."

"I thought you would say that." Evan dug into his pocket and pulled out another memory drive. "Playing my hunch, I had Mireille call them. She followed a script, and here's the good part … First is Mireille, then Grier." He pressed Play.

"I understand you're still looking for work," Mireille said.

"Me and others," Grier said.

"Well, a whole lot of people got restructured. That is the nature of business."

"Restructured? Call it what it was; a whole lot of people got laid off. My guess is you're calling me 'cause you went too far."

The audio went on for a few more lines, but Kylee never heard. Her face turned pale, and she began to shake. "That's it," she said. "That's the voice. 'A whole lot of people are going to die.' Madison Grier is our man."

Chapter *19*

RUSSELL WALKED backward as he left the Joshua Cafe. He held a take-out bag in one hand, waved his glasses with the other hand, and kept his eyes on Kylee and Evan. He spoke slowly, for once.

"He knows our planes. He knows each and every fault. If he wants to bring us down—bring our planes down—he can do it at any airport, at any moment. We have to find Grier or the killing won't stop."

"Unfortunately," Kylee said, "we can't go to the feds. They don't trust us. And I certainly don't trust them to investigate."

Russell raised his voice. "Well, *someone* has to stop him. I don't care who, but I do care when. The longer we wait; the more lives we risk. Oh, and by the way, find out what he did for Everest."

"What's that got to do with …?" Evan lowered his jaw.

"That's right," Russell said. "We lost six people on the Gibraltar aircraft. Everest carries six hundred."

"I'll look into it. But for now let's keep this between us. The last thing we need is publicity. If people think Everest has a problem, we'd have a media circus."

"We still need to find Grier," Russell said.

"I'll talk to Mireille; we'll work something out."

"Mireille," Kylee mumbled. "P-O-P."

"Pardon?"

"Part of the problem. You don't see it. But sooner or later, you will."

"Sooner or later, you're going to admit you're wrong. Like it or not, she's helped us. We'll find out what happened with the crash, resolve it, and move on without a fuss. No, there's no problem—not even close."

"We'll see. Meanwhile, Russell and me; we have our own plans for tonight."

"Come again?" Evan shifted his laptop for a better grip. He looked at Russell then back at Kylee.

"We were talking about it over lunch until you barged in. It's Bullman Stock. Like it or not, there's a problem there. And like it or not, Russell and I are going to resolve it; by ourselves and without a fuss."

Evan shook his head. He veered off toward the Jaguar, his voice fading as he turned the corner. "Great. You kids knock yourselves out. I've got real work to do."

"Kylee?" Russell squared his shoulders with her.

"Sorry. I hope I wasn't presumptuous, but I hate it when he treats us like, uh, like kids."

"So what you said; we *don't* have plans for tonight?"

"Actually, we do. Rather, I do. I'll tell you when we get there."

"Get where?"

"Mason Street. I want to go back to that rundown apartment. And don't give me that 'you're crazy' look. Evan has his connection to follow; I have mine. And the longer we wait; the more lives we put at risk—that's what I've heard. Between us, Russell, we can find the real connection, huh?"

"I don't know." Russell shuffled his feet and looked at the pavement. He shoved his glasses into his pocket and folded the top of his take-out bag. "Evan might have a point."

"Please, Russell." Kylee softly lifted his chin and widened her hazel eyes. "Please?"

***

At 9:00 p.m. on Mason Street in Hesperia, Russell sat with Kylee in his minivan. He nervously tapped the steering wheel and furtively darted his gaze. "They don't deliver pizza to this part of town," he said. "Why are we here?"

"Thank you for coming," Kylee said. "And I'm sorry we left the coffee at the office."

"That's not what I asked."

Kylee peeked at the floor behind the seat. "You brought the camera?"

Russell rolled his eyes then reached behind and retrieved a leather case. He unzipped the top flap, reached in, and handed Kylee his new, state-of-the-art, Japanese camera.

"What's this?" She held the camera in the street light. She gazed in horror at the switches and buttons on the back cover.

"Twenty-five mega-pixels. Optical zoom and ..." He pointed at a small button. "Automatic flash."

"I can't use this," Kylee cried. "All I wanted was a camera with one button. Small, easy, and *no* flash. I don't want to be seen. I don't want to lug around a toaster!"

"No, this is perfect; auto focus, auto exposure, memory stick, and wireless." He flipped open a latch and shoved in the stick.

"I have to aim it, right?"

"You're joking."

"Just set it up. Tell me what button to push."

Russell enthusiastically did.

Kylee paid attention and learned what she could during the short lesson in the minivan. She finally accepted the camera and slipped the strap around her neck. For practice, she took photos of Russell. When his close-up image filled the view screen, she called the training done.

"Are you sure about this?" Russell asked. "You didn't know Fred; not like the rest of us. You never worked with him. I don't think you even met him. Honestly, why do you care what happens?"

Kylee frowned. "You weren't there on the mountain. You didn't see his eyes. Fred was old. He was tired. But he was not ready to die. I could tell that by his face. What happened there was no accident. I'm sure of it. Someone killed him, Russell. I'm aiming to find out who and why."

"Fair enough," he said. "You know I've been with you from the start."

"I appreciate that." Kylee softly stroked the graying hairs on the back of his head. Then she dropped her hand and eased open her door. "Shall we?"

Before Russell replied, Kylee stepped out and stood in the dim yellow light. She gazed up at the second floor and pointed. "That one."

"How can you tell?"

"Second floor; end of the hall to the right. Positively, that's the one. You see—lights are out, and nobody's home."

She tied her hair back with an elastic band and pushed a wooden pallet against the wall. "Now, with a small boost," she whispered. She raised her foot to the middle slat and looked over her shoulder at Russell.

Russell froze, and Kylee didn't need to wonder what he was staring at. Her black, rock climbing shorts were cut mid-thigh and hugged comfortably to her hips. Her sports top—sleeveless and cut high above her midriff—displayed her well toned stomach and firm shoulders. She glared at him and swung her head up. "Let's go, let's go."

Russell quickly moved in, grabbed her hips from behind, and pushed up with a grunt.

Kylee nearly flew up the two stories. She easily grasped a handhold on the rainspout and used every ledge and crack for a toehold. She whispered down to Russell and motioned. "Go to the front door. If anyone comes, give it a rap."

Russell waved an okay and ran around the corner.

Kylee peeked into the apartment and gave thanks that no one around here could afford a window screen. She reached in and cranked the window fully open. Another push and she rolled herself into the darkened room. Her heart raced; and not because of her second-story climb. With someone at the front door, she would have barely a breath or two to react. Get in, take photos, take notes, get out. That was her mission, and she felt hard-pressed to get it done.

The dim lights from outside were useless. Kylee took her LED penlight and snapped it on, carefully avoiding the door and window. She listened for unfamiliar footsteps or voices and then gave herself an all-clear.

She quickly studied the room that, at first glance, seemed utterly disappointing. Here was the standard drifter apartment; scattered mail on the chairs and floor, beer cans—empty and full—on the kitchen counter, dirty socks a mile from any hamper—if they knew what a hamper was. Why take pictures, she wondered; Evan's room was undoubtedly the same.

She peeked into the bathroom to the same disgusting mess. She muttered a few words about raised lids and bad aims then backed out. The kitchenette—a two-burner stove and a can-opener—was no less a surprise.

"What a wasted trip." She slowly padded across the living room and fixed the camera strap on her shoulder for an embarrassing retreat to the ground. With a half-hearted, nothing to lose yank, she swung open the living room closet. "Sweet Jesus."

Kylee didn't know what she was looking at, but she did understand the meaning of strange. Stacked floor to ceiling was a bizarre array of amplifiers and meters, cables and switches. Flashing lights and a low humming sound meant a whole lot of power was crammed into that small space.

This is it. Definitely, we found it. Kylee fumbled with the camera, trying to remember which of the buttons gave the one-button operation. She pressed them all until the Recording message appeared on the back display.

She moved closer and snapped as fast as she could at everything she saw. Twenty photos later she heard a light knocking at the door. Her heart skipped a beat. Then came heavy knocking and a muffled, "Get out of there fast!"

Kylee clicked the closet door shut and scrambled for the window escape. She straddled the ledge and reached long for the downspout. Then she heard a heavy pounding from the front door, followed by a familiar voice crying out.

"Man, what was that for?" Russell raised his voice and pleaded with a stranger. "I already told ya, I'm with the city."

"Ain't this city, man." A loud thud and the stranger went on. "You knock on my door, you be dealing with me."

Kylee heard more thumping noises from the hallway. "That's not the plan," she told herself. "Why are you doing this, Russell?"

Another dull thud and Kylee knew that Russell was in for the fight of his life. She felt torn between a race down the window escape and a play-it-by-ear confrontation with a violent—possibly deadly—stranger. Then her instincts took hold.

She ducked inside and raced across the apartment, grabbing the one weapon she could find. She threw open the door and stood absolutely stunned when she saw a linebacker mountain of a man. He was bald, Hispanic, and teardrop tattooed. He was punching holes in the far wall with Russell's battered head. Russell's glasses were tossed onto the vinyl floor, and his eyes took on a blank, faraway stare. So far, the assaulting man did not seem to notice or seem to care that Kylee stood by his side. This was her one chance.

Like a rock in a sling, she swung the camera over her head and spun it until it whooshed. "You knock on my friend!" she yelled. "You be dealing with me!" She moved in and caught a solid blow across the stranger's forehead. The camera split apart, throwing odd pieces down the hall.

The bald man staggered to the wall and pressed his palm to the deep gash in his head.

"Let's move it, Russell." Kylee swept down to pick up his glasses. She put her arm across his shoulder and urged him forward.

Russell struggled to stay on his feet. He fumbled his crooked glasses to his head and staggered along the hall and down the stairs. They raced side by side out the lobby door and down the street to the minivan.

Kylee took a last look behind them and saw the assailant running hard to catch up. She grabbed the keys from Russell's hand and pressed the keyless unlock. She pushed him in and then raced to the driver's seat. She dropped the camera to the rear seat and jammed the keys into the ignition. Thankfully, the engine started and the door locks worked. As they sped down the street, she kept the accelerator pressed and didn't let up until I-15 was back in sight.

"That was close," she said when they merged into the fast lane.

"What close?" Russell whimpered and held his head. "A broken nail, a stubbed toe; that would've been close. This, uh, this really hurts."

"Don't worry; we'll get you cleaned up. You wouldn't believe what I saw in there."

"It better be good," Russell moaned.

"Oh, it is." She set the remains of the camera on his lap. "I got plenty of photos, and your one button actually worked."

"Well, the camera's trash. Where's the stick?"

"In the camera."

"Not this half. Try again."

"It has to be there," Kylee said.

"This is … this *used to be* a nine hundred dollar camera."

"And your life is worth how much?"

"At least I wanted something for the effort." Russell pulled down the visor mirror and poked at the gash in his forehead.

"Looks like we'll be back tomorrow," she said.

"Looks like you're out of your mind! You're not getting me within ten miles of that place. I don't care what you found!"

"You should've been there, Russell. With that closet full of electronics, we didn't have to take pictures."

"What electronics?"

"Lights, meters, gadgets. You wouldn't believe it."

"Can you be a little more specific?"

"That's your job, sweetie. All I can tell you; one box was called Marley. Like my aunt's maiden name."

"Marley?" Russell softened his tone as he studied his face in the mirror. "They make communication gear. You know, like repeaters and microwave transmitters."

"No, I didn't know."

"If they have stuff like that, they're not your typical transients."

"That's what I've been saying." She leaned over and turned on the radio to her jazz station. She leaned back and smiled. "Tomorrow, I want to take the sheriff there and show him what's going on."

"And what is going on? All you have is a closet full of stuff, and last I heard; that's not a crime. Trespassing, on the other hand, *is* a crime."

"You were assaulted there, Russell. That's reason enough to find the owner. And once we get the owner—"

"You want me back at the apartment?"

"I'll protect you," Kylee said. "Don't worry about that."

"Hey, I was doing fine. I don't need protection."

At the next stop light, Kylee turned to face Russell. She flipped up his mirror and told him, "Do me a favor; don't use a bandage. We'll need that for evidence." She poked at the two-inch gash above his brow until he winced.

***

Morning came too quickly, and Russell, despite his reluctance, agreed to meet Kylee at the apartment parking lot. All it took was the promise of a tri-tip dinner in LA, or San Bernardino, or any place far from the Victor Valley.

"I'm glad you came." Kylee grinned at Russell as she shut the door of her Jeep. She straightened her sunset orange top and smoothed a wrinkle on her white pants. "I called the sheriff—a Sheriff Penard. He said he'd meet us."

"What, like I got something better to do on a Tuesday morning? Do me a favor and let's keep a low profile till he comes." Russell locked his minivan door and tucked his shirt into his Dockers.

"Fine. Actually, all I want from Penard is the name of the renter. Of course, if I knew where they worked or what that equipment does; that would be better."

"All I want is an aspirin." Russell massaged his temples. He moved face to face with Kylee, smelling of garlic, bagels, and Pepsi. "You're a nurse. You must have some in your car."

Kylee dug into her purse to get the pills and went to her Jeep for the bottled water. "You know, a good woman would take care of you."

"I do fine by myself, thanks."

"Speaking of Claire …"

"What about her?" Russell said.

"You two would hit it off. I know you would."

"You said that before." He crammed the pills down his throat and chased them with big gulp of water.

"And?"

"Me and women don't 'hit it off.' 'Hit or miss' is more like it. Especially at work; women see me as an engineer and assume I have the personality of one. Which I don't."

"I know that." Kylee pulled a tissue from her purse and wiped the cheese spread from his shirt pocket. "And I'm telling you; give Claire a chance. It took me, what, two lunch dates to appreciate you. With her, you have to be patient."

"If I live that long." Russell poked at his swollen lip and frowned.

"Save it for Penard." She wrapped her arm around Russell's shoulder. She turned him to face the Crown Victoria that was pulling to a stop across the street.

Kylee hurried for a quick introduction with the nearly retired, gaunt, and tall Deputy Sheriff. As she led him and Russell to the lobby, she quickly told Penard the point of the meeting.

"What we would like, Sheriff, is the name of the renter in 2-H … You tell me, is this a felony or not?" She stopped by the stairwell, touched the nape of Russell's neck, and urged him to face Penard.

"It rather depends," Penard said.

"Depends on what?"

"The other guy's story and this guy's story." Penard glanced at Russell and slowly climbed the stairs. "Circumstances are key. Injuries, yeah, they're borderline. But if you catch the D.A. in a good mood, he might go for it."

"Might?"

"You got witnesses?"

"I'm the witness," Kylee said.

"Anyone else?" Penard replied, somewhat breathless. He pulled open the fire door at the top of the stairs.

"Who else do you need?" She frowned, suddenly unsure whose side Penard was on. At the end of the hallway, she ran her hand along the fresh dents in the wall then compared them to Russell's head. "You see; evidence."

Penard barely nodded as the door to apartment 2-H swung open.

A mid-twenties, medium build, blond haired man emerged and carefully adjusted the fit of his jogging suit. He widened his eyes at the three visitors. "You're not here for Billy, are ya?"

Kylee peeked beyond the jogger into the cluttered apartment. She tried to glimpse a familiar face or any new sign of criminal intent. "Billy? He's your roommate?"

"Next door neighbor." The jogger nodded toward the facing door. "I told him; don't mess with child support. Those new laws are going to do him in. He didn't listen, huh?"

Kylee lifted her hand over her head. "Big, Hispanic man. Three hundred pounds. Deep cut on his forehead?" She ran her finger above her right eyebrow.

"Well, *now* he has one," Russell said.

"How about white, thirty-three, big gut. Doesn't care what shape he has." The jogger slid his palm against his tight abs and gave Kylee a sly smile.

"Who are you?" she asked.

"Call me Tyler." He smiled wider.

"You rent this place, Tyler?"

"Who's asking?"

Penard glanced at his watch. "Listen, I don't want to keep you, sir. But if you know anything about a possible assault here last night, around …"

"Nine-ten," Kylee said. She pointed at the dents in the wall.

"I didn't get home till midnight. Sorry, looks like you're on your own."

Kylee focused on Tyler's eyes. "You didn't say; do you rent this place?"

"You didn't say; who's asking?"

"Name's Kylee."

"Very well, Kylee. If you must know, I'm a guest. Reggie Whitehead pays the rent on this palace."

"Mind if I come in?"

Russell popped open his eyes and scowled.

"We've been here long enough," Penard said to Tyler. "You have a good day, sir."

Tyler held up his palm and spread a wide smile. "Hey, for a last name, I'll give you a tour."

"McKenna. Kylee McKenna," she replied with no hesitation. She pushed her way in.

Tyler nearly danced behind her. "Fabulous. How about a phone number?"

"I'm listed. What's in the closet?"

By now, Penard was motioning from the hallway. "Mrs. McKenna; a word please."

"You're into shoes." Tyler pointed at his feet. "I can tell. By the way, these are size fourteen, if you know what I mean."

"Mind if I look?" Kylee placed her palm on the door knob.

Tyler turned to Penard. "Is she for real?"

"Mrs. McKenna. Now!"

Kylee kept her eyes on Tyler.

Tyler shrugged. "Hey, go for it."

Kylee twisted the knob and yanked the door open. She looked inside. "Dear God," she groaned.

"I know," Tyler said. "We're bachelors. What do you expect?"

"Where's the equipment?"

"Equipment?"

"You know what I mean," Kylee said. "The amplifiers and the cables. All the meters and stuff."

"I got a Jambox in the corner." Tyler pointed.

Kylee fished through a maze of jackets, pants, shirts, and shoes. There was no hint of high tech electronics except for the Jambox on the floor.

"I got a receipt for that, Sheriff. We're clean."

"I can see that," Penard said. "Sorry for the trouble."

Kylee dragged herself to the hall. She closed the apartment door behind her while tuning out Tyler's, "I'll give you a call."

Russell and Penard merely looked at each other with their 'what are we doing here' faces.

"I know it was there," Kylee said. "I did not make a mistake."

"That's well and good," Penard said. "But let me tell you why I'm here."

Kylee ignored him. "You believe me. Don't you, Russell?"

"I had a call," Penard said. "From the National Transportation and Safety Board. It seems they want to see you ASAP. They asked me to escort you to their office."

"They knew we were coming. That has to be it. They cleared it out."

"Mrs. McKenna, we can use my car, or you can follow me in yours."

"What?"

"The Safety Board; they're waiting."

"Yeah, fine, whatever," Kylee said. "I guess we're done here."

"So which will it be?" Penard asked.

"Pardon?"

"My car or yours?"

"Mine, I guess." She sauntered along the hallway, giving a last look at apartment 2-H. "I'm parked at the corner."

"Me too," Penard replied. "I'll wait for you."

Penard moved quickly down the stairs and out the lobby. Russell and Kylee followed at a slower pace. When they got to the street corner, they stopped and talked.

"I don't get it," Russell said. "Why'd you tell that guy your real name?"

"They already know who we are. They know our moves, what we say, probably what we think. I don't know how they know, but they do." She yanked at Russell's sleeve and nodded at the sheriff as he walked to his car. "Think about it; the feds didn't know we were in Hesperia. Why would they call the sheriff? How could anyone track us here? It's frustrating. I feel like we're two steps behind and not close to catching up. I have no idea what to do next."

Russell let his gaze wander, seeming as frustrated as Kylee. But when he looked at the window of apartment 2H, his eyes suddenly grew wide. "Wow. I saw it before, but it didn't click."

"What?"

He pointed up. "See that satellite dish? There was one more last night. Now that I think of it, it was definitely a transmitter. And this morning, it's gone." He faced Kylee. "I believe you. Something weird is going on. You don't put a microwave link at a place like this."

He spun and pointed at the San Bernardino Mountains. "The antenna was aimed that way."

"That's a thousand square miles of wilderness," Kylee said. "I know—because that's where my cabin is."

"I don't know what else is up there," Russell said. "But I'm guessing that's our next stop."

Chapter 20

WHATEVER they called it—discussion, interview, or interrogation—any meeting with the federal government invariably aggravated the knots in Kylee's back. Allegedly for her own convenience, the investigators had moved the meeting from their office in downtown Fresno to the Dove campus.

As she entered the conference room with Daz and Evan, she easily recognized the same setup and the same government players. She took her place on a plush leather chair, but no way did she feel comfortable. Her intuition took hold, and she sensed an impending doom. Now the voices of Investigators Chapp and Ward seemed harsher. The lights in the room seemed hotter and brighter. The air felt dry and tense. The chair wobbled. Everything else was a pain in the neck.

Investigator Chapp sipped from his 'World's Best Dad' coffee mug. He wiped the sides of his mouth and leaned forward on his seat. "Now, I believe in coincidence like anyone. But you have to admit we are pushing the envelope."

"How so?" Evan leaned back on his chair and folded his arms.

Daz and Kylee leaned forward.

"In March, we examined the Gibraltar crash. What we found was a Dove plane, a Dove passenger, and Dove employees on the rescue team. Most of the evidence burned. Okay? Now, we go to

Utah and what do we find; Mr. Donahue's helicopter within two miles of the site—the crash site of an identical Dove plane."

Evan kept his arms folded. "Of course, without us, you'd still be looking. It's no coincidence that you followed us from the airport. You were tipped off and had us tracked."

"No matter. If *your* helicopter is at the crash site, then *you* are at the crash site." Chapp looked at Evan, then Daz, then Kylee. "That is our assumption."

Investigator Ward cleared his throat, rose to his feet and rested his hands on the conference room table. "CFR 831.11—did you get the copy I sent?"

"Who can and cannot investigate," Daz replied. "Received, read, and well understood."

Evan turned up his palms and glared at Ward. "Our mission was to find survivors. Regretfully, we found none. If it helps your investigation, I'll swear on a stack of Bibles we weren't close to the wreckage. We didn't have to get close. From where we stood, we saw the crash was not survivable."

Ward turned to Kylee. "Mrs. McKenna, you seem like a reasonable woman. You understand the penalties for giving false or misleading statements. Can you tell us what happened on the river? Did you, let's say accidentally, disturb the site? I understand that you're a nurse. It's only natural—"

"Evan's right," she said. "We were there. And that makes sense. If there was a chance in a hundred of finding a survivor, we had to try. If I could save a life, I'd walk all over the site. That's how much it mattered. But, as it turned out; it didn't matter. All three died on impact; that was clear. And I want to make this clear; Evan, Daz, and me—we touched nothing. What you saw on the ridge was exactly how we found it. I'll swear to that just like Evan."

Ward shifted his tall, heavy frame next to Kylee. He loomed above like a grizzly over salmon. He narrowed his eyes and exhaled hot, Hazelnut coffee breath.

"I believe you," he finally said. He faced Evan and Daz. "However, that begs the question; what were Dove workers doing at the hanger? Specifically, Madison Grier and Markus Sullivan."

"*Ex* Dove workers," Evan said.

"We have the video, and we will prosecute. Trespassing will be the initial charge, which is nothing compared to murder."

"When we find them," Chapp said.

"They've skipped town?" Daz asked.

"Apparently, they were tipped off," Ward said. "Any idea by whom?"

Evan and Daz shrugged. When Ward looked at Kylee's eyes, she also shrugged.

Ward turned to Evan. "You weren't planning to leave town, were you?"

"I'm the president of Dove Air; worldwide Dove, that is. Sooner or later, I may leave the office."

"Very well," Ward said. "Nonetheless, if you have a contact number, we'd appreciate it."

Evan passed him a business card with his satellite phone number along with a half-dozen other contact methods. "It's nearly impossible *not* to find me."

As he closed his wallet, his phone abruptly chirped with a message. "Great; a 911 text from Russell. And 'Bring Kylee,' he says." Evan frowned then turned to Chapp. "Are we finished?"

Chapp closed his briefcase. "If there is more, we'll be in touch."

Kylee shuddered. She eased out of the conference room and followed Evan to the nearest exit. She hurried to keep pace as they put distance between themselves and the federal procedure experts.

"I keep wondering," she said, "if the government is here to help us or to get us."

"Welcome to my world. FAA, IRS, SEC—you name it; we're being squeezed from all sides. If the Wright brothers had ever had this hassle, we'd be assembling buses." Evan lifted his phone and double-checked the message. "That headache aside, I'm wondering if Russell is going to help us or get us."

"He hasn't missed yet."

"So far, yeah. '911 and bring Kylee.' What's that supposed to mean?"

Kylee smirked. "If I had a phone, he'd say, 'Oh, by the way, bring Evan.' "

"Of course he would."

They quickened their pace to the nearest golf cart. From there, she and Evan rode the back alleys to Russell's lab. By now, Kylee had memorized the route and the best shortcuts. After a few turns around the patches of Teddy Bear cholla and prickly pear, they were there. Evan opened the door to the lab, and they stepped inside.

Russell, already busy with his scopes and meters, barely looked up from his bench. He rolled his chair to a bank of monitors. "This has bothered me to no end, but I finally figured it out."

"Keep it simple," Kylee said.

"I don't know any other way." Russell lifted a satellite phone and set it next to a flight simulator. "For starters, recognize this?"

"That's Fred's," she said, brushing back her wind blown hair.

"Yes, it is. And do you remember what I said about the canyon crash?"

"You said the phone brought down the plane. A computer glitch."

"Close enough." Russell nodded. "I said you need two things to make the plane crash; bad software and bad hardware."

"We know about the bugs," Evan said, frowning. "Show us the hardware."

"Coming up."

Russell slid back his chair, pulled out his own phone, and casually made a call. He pressed a few more keys, stood up, and said, "Counting down; in three ... two ... one."

Then he grinned and pointed ahead like a magician on a stage. Almost on cue, the simulator in front of him panicked. Red lights flashed, horns sounded, and the fuel gauge went to zero. A crisis in the blink of an eye.

"That can't be good," Evan said.

"Here's the deal. Fred had a special phone. And so did Bob. Power like you wouldn't believe. When I trigger it—remotely—the aircraft radio gets jammed, the computer freezes, the engine quits, and there's no turning back. It's slam, bam, right into the mountain."

Kylee shivered as her mouth slowly gaped. "They never had a chance."

"A power surge from a phone," Evan said. "Okay, that's a concern. But who changed the phone? Who made the planes crash?"

"Oh, I think we know who." Kylee propped her hands on her hips.

"Mireille?" Evan said. "All she did was hand Bob and Fred the phone. Anyone could've rigged them."

"Major denial," Kylee mumbled.

"The surge did a couple things," Russell said. "It meant Fred couldn't call 911, and it drained the battery in nothing flat."

"Sounds familiar," Evan said. "I had the same phone and same problem—with the battery, that is."

"There's more." Russell took a sip from his Pepsi then beckoned them to a neighboring room. "Prepare to be amazed."

Kylee—already uncomfortable with the high-tech gear and flashing lights—felt more on edge when she stepped into the test chamber. "What kind of room is this?"

"My special cage." Russell beamed. "It shields signals from getting in ... or out. A cone of silence, so to speak."

"Cage is right." Kylee shuddered. The chamber spanned the width of a mobile home, but the shiny cones on the walls and ceiling made her feel like a chicken in a convection oven. There were no windows, no chairs, no shelves, books, pictures, carpets, or anything warm and comfortable. At least the CT scanner in the hospital had music playing. Russell's chamber was technology gone mad. She lingered by the door and urged him to get to his point.

Russell squeezed behind, pushed the door shut, and slid the latch.

"Do you have to close that?" Kylee asked.

Russell nudged her and Evan to a steel table in the center.

"Great," Evan said when he spotted his phone. "You fixed it."

"Kind of," Russell said, handing him the phone. "Place it in your pocket."

Evan shrugged but obeyed as Russell dashed to the far wall.

"What are we doing here?" Kylee asked.

"Pick a number between one and a hundred," Russell said as he covered his ears with his palms.

"What?" Evan asked.

"Go ahead, and whisper it to Kylee."

Evan did.

Immediately, Russell went to Evan's side. He extracted a small earpiece and asked for the phone. "It's two hundred twelve."

"Great, you guessed my number. You got my phone to work. Why the big show?"

"Check it out." Russell pointed at the phone display. "It's off, right? No display, no lights, power down. Guess again. All I got to do is call your number and type in a code. And *voilà*, I have a one-way sat' phone. I can hear you anytime, anywhere. And you don't have a clue I'm listening. It doesn't matter if your phone's on or off; it doesn't matter if you're using it or not. I can listen in."

Evan's jaw slowly dropped. Kylee's eyes widened as the realization sank in.

"You wouldn't believe the fidelity," Russell said. "With a room like this, you could whisper anywhere, I can hear it. At a restaurant, a meeting, wherever you go; it's like I'm there with you, hearing every word, every breath. Except for the battery that wears out fast, you'd never know." Russell smiled, leaned against the table, and placed his palms behind his head.

"Jesus," Evan muttered. "They heard every word in the board room."

"Forget that," Kylee said, raising her voice. "That phone was in our bedroom." She balled her fist and fought the urge to grab the phone and smash it against the wall. Instead, she broke for the chamber door, yanked it open, and let it slam against Russell's cone of silence.

Desperate for fresh air, she stomped to the outdoors. She slammed her eyes shut and let the sunlight fall on her face. Her head throbbed with anger.

She leaned against a railing and tried to clear her mind of the rage. Any thought was better than dwelling on tricks and deception. Any emotion—other than resentment—would be welcomed.

Kylee saw red and couldn't help but flash on the image of Mireille in prison orange. She imagined Mireille in jail, and for a moment, felt a token amount of solace. The thought of retaliation and retribution gave her a glimmer of hope. The remote prospect of justice helped her to move on.

She took shallow breaths, calmed herself, and slowly opened her eyes to a courtyard of lilacs and butterfly bushes. Blue flowers, fresh air, and a delicate scent of lilac blossoms; *that* she understood. Technology and double-dealing made her sick. Mireille made her mad.

She sat on a bench in the center of the garden. Slowly, with her hands clasped on her lap, her shaking subsided. Piece by piece, the puzzle came together. Clearly, it was not a pretty picture.

Kylee returned to the lab and found Evan and Russell outside the chamber. "Mireille's behind this, you know. She gave Fred a phone. She gave Bob a phone. And you, Evan, she gave you the exact same phone ... Finally, you have nothing to say. At least admit she was involved with the crashes."

"That's a bit of a stretch. But I will admit Mireille owes me an explanation."

"I wouldn't play our cards yet," Russell said. "With a little maneuvering, we can find out who's at the other end."

"We were talking," Evan said to Kylee, "about writing a script and setting a trap."

"It's a phone. Why can't we just listen to the other end? That would tell us who it is."

Evan chuckled. "Only in the movies."

"Wait," Russell said, digging into a drawer of parts. "She might have a point. With a bit of time—and talent—I can rig a bi-directional call. And if they use their own phone—"

"We have our man," Kylee finished. "I mean woman."

"Fair enough," Evan said. "Let's turn the tables. Let's find out who is behind the murders."

**

Kylee returned to her cubicle but gave up the notion of doing real work. She shuffled papers and waited for Russell's call. She snacked on cashews and pita chips. She tried to keep her mind off of Mireille, but she felt like a prosecutor waiting on a jury. Mireille Prudhomme; guilty or innocent. In her heart, she knew the truth, but waiting for confirmation made the minutes seem like hours. She kept on the edge of her seat, waiting and wondering. A short while later, Russell called. The verdict was about to be read.

Kylee hurried to his lab. She walked into the same room of scopes and monitors, feeling less apprehensive than earlier. If Russell had eavesdropping equipment, she couldn't see it. It all looked the same. She moved to his side as Evan entered the lab.

Russell swiveled his chair, raised his finger, and motioned for Evan and Kylee to sit. "We're not on the air yet, but I've traced the wiretap calls. A lot of them happen around seven thirty, eight o'clock."

"That's usually when I go home," Evan said.

"On an early night," Kylee said.

"By the way," Russell said, "these phones have GPS. Not only do they know what you say—"

"They know where you are." Evan shuddered.

"Yeah, so they know we're in the lab. Follow the script and let's see what we catch." Russell passed out index cards and watched the light on his transmitter. As the light changed from green to red, he whispered, "Showtime." He pointed at Evan.

Evan fumbled the cards but held up the one marked #1. "This better be good," he began with a faltering voice. "The cafeteria's closed and I'm starving."

"Don't worry, I'll make it worth your while," Russell read from his own card. "I'm running data on the canyon crash. I think I can line up the power loss with the bad software."

"Great, how long will that take?"

"Maybe five, maybe twenty minutes. Have a seat. I got the catering covered."

"What, a bag of chips and a root beer? Looks like we don't pay you enough." Evan shook his head as he read the card. He grabbed the chips and popped open the bag.

"Sit tight," Russell said. "I'll get back to you." He pressed his index finger to his lips and then pointed at a voice recorder. He clicked it to start a playback of him munching potato chips and sipping a root beer. Like the director of an action thriller, he motioned to his shielded room. He led Kylee and Evan inside and carefully latched the door. Then he turned up the volume on a tabletop speaker.

"If my stuff works," Russell said, "we should hear the other end."

"You're recording this?" Evan asked and Russell nodded.

"They can't hear us, right?" Kylee asked and Russell nodded.

While they waited, Evan passed around the bag of chips and snapped open the root beer.

Suddenly, Kylee's appetite was back. The reflective walls of the room didn't bother her as much. The cold table seemed warm and inviting. She leaned close to the speaker. "I hear something. What is it? A printer? Vending machine?"

Russell gave a thumbs-up.

"Sorry for the rush." A low-volume, drowning-in-noise voice belonged to none other than Mireille herself. "Let's get started," she said.

Evan closed his eyes and lowered his head. Kylee widened her eyes and bobbed her smiling head. She punched up the volume.

Russell sat back on his chair and took it for a spin. "No need for applause; I told you I could do it."

Mireille continued, apparently talking to some yet-to-be-identified person in the same room. "I prefer Evan's opinion," she said, "but please, speak your mind."

A man's voice, definitely Pierre's, spoke up. "Coffee?"

"Why aren't they speaking French?" Kylee asked. "Are you sure they can't hear us?"

"Positive," Russell said, leaning forward and double-checking his equipment.

"The federal agents have no confirmation on what brought down the plane," Mireille said. "Power loss is their one clue."

"We can wait and see on McKenna," Pierre said.

"Perhaps, yes," Mireille said. "However, we invited you because you know him well. You can tell us; will he make the connection or not?"

"Specifically, will he find the root cause?" a loud male voice asked.

"Yes," Pierre replied.

A long silence, then a chair slid across a tile floor, followed by a throat clearing. The new voice said, "That is true, I do know Evan. He's good. He's thorough. He knows what he's doing. But he's not perfect. Far from it."

"Waterman!" Evan grumbled. "He's supposed to be in Siberia."

"Apparently, that's not far enough," Kylee said. "What's he doing there?"

"Shh," Russell said as Waterman filled the room with his voice.

"Everyone knows that the Gibraltar aircraft has problems. Everyone but McKenna, that is. You crash two planes and lose both a founder and junior accountant. Not to mention the crew. And the best he comes up with is 'pilot fatigue.' I don't think so. McKenna's lost touch. He doesn't see the real world anymore. Perhaps it is best he stay a manager."

"You idiot!" Evan screamed at the loudspeaker. "You can't manage folding a paper plane. You never could. That's why we fired your butt."

"You're the president now," Kylee said. "Doesn't he know that?"

"Evan is also tracking a computer bug," Mireille said. "I believe that *eventually* he will find the root cause."

"What, and run the company at the same time?" Waterman chuckled. "You and I are well aware that the man is overloaded. He's got to delegate, or we will not see any progress."

Kylee swung her head in agreement.

"First rule of aviation," Waterman said. "If you don't have a safe plane, you don't stay in business. That's a given. Another Gibraltar crash would ground the entire fleet. Need I remind you; had the first crash been properly handled, you would not have had the second crash."

"You don't know what you're talking about!" Evan glared at the speaker.

"What is it you propose?" Pierre asked.

"I'll come on board as a safety VP, reporting directly to you or Mireille."

"Avoiding conflict of interest," Pierre said.

"Exactly. I'll put together a team. We'll investigate the crashes and manage the media. There's a reporter I know—"

"That's fine," Mireille said. "Before we reinstate you, I will discuss the matter with Evan."

"Might be a showstopper," Waterman said

"We will get you on board," Pierre shot back. "McKenna's approval or not."

"No," Mireille said. "It's only proper that I talk to him first."

"Not necessary. You already talk to him more than required."

"Pierre, do not say what you do not mean."

"Oh, I mean it. *Certainement.* Too much talk, too much time with that *garçon.*"

Mireille raised her voice. "*Je sais que tu vas dire. Mais Evan et moi, nous serons liés longtemps. C'est un vrai homme-orchèstre. Écoute bien …*"

Kylee had no clue what the words meant, but judging from Mireille's tone, she had a few opinions to share. Mireille and Pierre went on, but whatever she said put a final halt to Pierre and his ranting.

"Listen," Waterman said, calmly. "We'll meet again. Say the word, and I can start tomorrow."

"Place my number into your contact list," Mireille said. "Call me at noon."

"As you wish."

Kylee heard a loud beeping, together with Waterman's clear voice repeating the last four digits, "… seven seven two one. Got it."

She heard other noises—like closing doors and footsteps— then the line went silent. For a while, Evan, Kylee, and Russell remained silent themselves. They exchanged glances and squirmed in their seats.

"Now it makes sense," Evan said. "I should've seen it coming."

"She had all of us fooled." Kylee carefully avoided her 'I told you so' tone.

"What? Mireille?" Evan glared. "That's not who I was talking about." He turned to Russell. "You heard him punch the numbers."

"Loud and clear," Russell said.

"You know what that means."

"Waterman's the source."

"Exactly," Evan said. "His voice was the clearest. Those are *his* footsteps we heard at the end."

"Waterman?" Kylee asked. "Why would he bug your phone?"

"Don't you see it? It's the fireman arsonist."

"The what?"

"It's called job security. It's the rogue fireman who goes off and starts a fire. Then he wanders by, puts out the flames, and looks like a hero. Why? Because he's the first to figure out the cause."

"Waterman saw a layoff coming," Russell said, "and he was desperate for a job—any job. Of course, with a recall in the works, he's guaranteed a position for years."

"And with our phones being bugged," Evan said, "he gets to know us and our planes."

"That's scary," Kylee said.

"Finally, we're not two steps behind. Do you agree?" Russell asked Kylee.

"I'm still miles behind. I don't understand any of this airplane stuff."

"Disappointed about Mireille, are ya?" Evan asked.

"Surprised; for now. I do have an open mind, you know."

"At what point do we call the sheriff?" Russell asked.

Evan frowned. "We need someone to speak our language. We start throwing around words like satellite bugs and fuel starvation, the sheriff's going sit there like Jean-Petit looking at a watch. Even the feds—how can we get them to listen?"

"Then how about Mireille?"

"What? Not her!" Kylee said. "She might be part of this."

Evan took on a condescending tone. "You heard her speak. Does it sound like she's involved?"

"I only heard part of a mess that's been going on for months. And half the call was in French. I say, until we get real evidence, we keep it between us."

"Agreed," Russell said before Evan could open his mouth. "Let's see how things play out. Waterman's not going anywhere."

"Especially if he gets his old job," Evan said.

Russell shut down the equipment and left the shielded room. "We have a target now," he said. "Electronically, it's easier to track someone when you have a name."

"You mean like phone calls, or hotel bills or," Kylee tapped his elbow, "his connection to Bullman Stock."

"For example." Russell nodded. "And now that I know how these phones work, we can track him on GPS."

"And when Mireille gives him a phone," Kylee said, "we'll be right behind him."

Chapter *21*

"PACK YOUR BAGS, we are flying to France." Mireille stepped into Evan's office, wrapped her arm around his shoulder, and dropped an airline ticket on his desk.

"Pardon?" Evan turned his head and nearly came lip to lip with her.

"It is time to see how the other half lives." Mireille smiled. She slid his mouse and clicked through his emails. "And they are eager to see our American partner."

"What's this?" Evan looked at the screen.

"Trudeau reorganization. After our own layoff, we are operating with a, oh, what's the word—a skeleton crew."

"Eighteen thousand workers—that's your skeleton crew?"

"It's all relative. Like the workers at Dove, they are also afraid of turmoil. With you being an optimist, you can raise their spirits. Yes?"

"You're confusing me with someone else." Evan pulled up a spreadsheet and scrolled through his red-item safety list. "We've got problems, and the list is not getting shorter."

"Speaking of that." Mireille quietly closed the office door. "I talked to John Waterman."

"Really." Evan chuckled. "How's the old boy doing?"

"Eager to help us any way he can. I know you didn't care for him—"

"Like him or not, he got the job done. I say bring him back, give him a phone, and get these problems fixed."

"I can do that," Mireille said, "as soon as we find him."

"How's that?"

"I left him a voice mail. He never got back. I sent him an email. He never replied."

"Keep trying," Evan said. "He's got to be somewhere."

"Meanwhile," Mireille tapped his ticket, "get ready. Tuesday, we leave. Monday, we return."

"Six days for business?"

"Four for business. Two for pleasure. That's sufficient to see Trudeau, the Alps, and the family."

"Is that so?"

"They've seen your picture. I want to show them the real Evan."

"You mean your family or your company?"

Mireille nodded.

And Evan shuddered. Business or personal? Since the first day he met Mireille, he wasn't sure where he was headed. Should he leave it a four-day business trip or go for the full package? It was hard to say what Mireille was thinking, but it sure would help to get inside that head of hers.

After staying awake half the night and half-paying attention during his morning meetings, he made a few calls. He found the one man who could solve the dilemma; the one man who could help him make up his mind.

At four o'clock, Evan drove to the local high school. He lightly knocked on the door of room 112 and peeked inside. He saw the late fifties, gray haired, gray-bearded man sitting at the teacher's desk. "Mister DeRemer?"

"You got it?" DeRemer asked with a raspy voice.

Evan—brown paper bag in hand—approached the desk and spread open the top of the bag. He had never seen DeRemer before, but he came highly recommended. He was someone who was available, knowledgeable, and willing to do anything for a buck.

"Great," DeRemer said. "Let's walk."

He led Evan through a maze of empty corridors and toward the athletic field. They crossed mid-field and took a seat on the bleachers. Downfield, a football team scrimmaged. Evan discreetly set the paper bag beside him.

Immediately, DeRemer took the bag, reached inside, and fondled the cold six pack until he licked his lips. He pulled out a beer. "I'm working cheap." He snapped open a can and took a swig.

Evan casually glanced at the boys lining up for another play.

"Two quarters; then disability," DeRemer said. "Then retirement. Yeah, wake up from one nightmare; start another."

"I thought you enjoyed teaching French."

"After two decades of '*écoutez*, you brats,' I'm due for a change." DeRemer set the beer aside, reached into his shirt pocket, and pulled out a pack of cigarettes. He lit one up. "Okay, what have you got?"

Evan pulled out his phone and clicked a voice recording app. He tried not to stare at DeRemer's yellow-stained teeth and wrinkled face. "I hope you can hear this. It's a phone conversation, and the cell drops out here and there."

"Proceed."

Evan touched Play, and immediately Mireille's voice came through clear and strong. He had cued the audio to a few words before the French dialogue. "It's coming up."

"Nice voice," DeRemer said. "Parisian, I'm guessing. Trained in London."

Evan nodded.

"*Je sais que tu pense,*" Mireille said. "*J'ai besoin de son aide pour tout.*"

DeRemer said, "Pause it." He translated, "I know what you think. I need his help for everything."

Evan pressed Play, and Pierre spoke up.

"*Pas vrai,*" Pierre said. "*Je crois qu'il te lave le cerveau.*"

"Not true," DeRemer said. "I believe he is twisting your head."

Mireille went on, and DeRemer tried his best to keep up with her silky French voice. "My head has never been so clear," he translated. "It has been so long since I have felt this way. You do not understand. How could you understand? When Francois died, my heart was crushed. Back then, my head was twisted. I did not care if I lived or died. I thought the pain in my head would never end …"

DeRemer puffed his cigarette and tried to catch up, "You have seen me. You know how I have been these past years. I know you love me. But you and I will never be. I am sorry. And I have never lied to you. I understand that it is difficult. But please be happy for me. Evan brings me to life. I wish you could see that."

"I do see that," DeRemer said, translating Pierre's voice. "I cannot understand what I did wrong."

"Nothing. Nothing at all, my love. You were just being yourself. And Evan is being himself. I cannot explain why I feel this way. How can any woman explain why she loves one man and not another?"

Evan gulped as DeRemer went on.

"I have made no secret that I love Evan. I have for a long while now. I can see myself married to him and raising a family. If that is twisting my head, then that is exactly what I want. Evan and me, we are partners now. Please do not step in our way. I don't know how he feels. But at least give me the chance to find out. That is all I ask."

The recording became silent after that. Evan had carefully erased the non-French, non-critical section of the wiretap. Evan, himself, became silent. Mireille's words—her voice, even with the faltering translation—sent shivers up his back.

"I can have that transcribed," DeRemer said with a wink.

"No, that will do," Evan said. "I appreciate your help."

Later that night, he packed his bags for France.

Chapter 22

A FIRST CLASS flight to Paris, a glass of Pouilly-Fumé, the delicate scent of lavender drifting from Mireille. She sat there in her red silk blouse and black pants. She sipped wine and occasionally brushed strands of hair from her face. Jean-Petit lay asleep on her lap.

Evan was envious. His heart raced like a teenager's on a first date.

Mireille set aside her phone and glanced down the aisle. "If things work out, this will be our last flight to Paris. On this model aircraft, that is."

"Why is that?"

"Certification, sales, and then we fly Everest. This route is what the plane was designed for. Our dreams," she sighed, "are about to come true."

"In more ways than one." Evan grinned.

"We have our launch customers," Mireille said. "And if we demo the LA-to-Paris run, they'll sign the purchase order."

"I never thought we'd see it."

"I never had doubts." She checked her phone, clicked an email, and then set it down. "About the test flight—"

"To Paris."

"Exactly. I have an idea." She reached over and gently held Evan's hand. "Your father's been transferred to LA, yes?"

"Glendale Convalescent," Evan said. "Until December. Then we take him home. And, of course, he gets better."

"I wish Paul could be part of this. From the start, Everest was his dream, his vision. I'm sure he would like to share the spotlight."

"What do you have in mind?"

"Simple but dramatic. On the leg from Apple Valley to LAX, we'll do a low flight over the hospital. It's a small detour at most. I'll make sure he's near a window. When Everest flies over—"

"We salute." Evan nodded. "I love it."

"It's the least we can do."

"In less than a month," Evan said, "we'll be ready for the flight."

"Could be sooner," Mireille said as she reclined her seat. "When you see our operation, we'll make you a believer."

"You know I'm desperate for any sign of progress."

"Your father believed in us," Mireille said. "That's why he made us a partner."

"You throw a rope to a drowning man; does that make you a partner?"

"You should be smiling, Evan. We're on a comeback. These customers are just the beginning. I have many more willing to sign."

"Open the floodgates. Dove is back in business."

"Dove and Trudeau," Mireille said.

"You and me. It's up to us now to keep the show running."

"You and me." Mireille leaned over and kissed his cheek. "I like the sound of that."

From Paris, they boarded a company jet for the short hop to Grenoble. From there, they grabbed a limousine to the factory at the foothills of the Alps. Once there, Evan slowly settled in.

But despite his best intentions to be the perfect Dove ambassador, jet lag got the best of him. His first tour of the plant became a whirlwind of oddly pronounced names, French faces, and 'he does this' and 'she does that.'

All Evan remembered was that Trudeau was huge, and everyone seemed to stare at him. "I can't help it," he said to Mireille the next day as they walked to the Everest simulator. "It's like I'm being watched wherever I go."

"That makes sense. Dove is our largest partner; and you, Evan, are the man from Dove."

"It's more than that. I get the feeling I'm being followed. It could be the jet lag, but I swear I saw faces peeking around the corner."

"Hold onto that thought," Mireille said. "Saturday, with my family, I guarantee you'll be watched."

"That's comforting," Evan said.

"Don't worry; everyone there will wish us the best."

"Us?"

"You, me. Dove, Trudeau."

"I see."

Mireille slid her badge along a card reader and led Evan into a hanger.

"Of course, meanwhile, we'll be watching you." She pointed at the piston mounted, minivan sized, full-motion simulator that sat on the concrete floor. "We have cameras aimed at your hands, feet, and eyes. If you blink, we'll know it. If you twitch, we'll see it. If you sweat, well, that's something we can't see."

"Ergonomics, right?"

"Yes, another French word. The pilot must not hop around like a drunken sailor."

"Such as Ken Nakamura on that first flight."

"Check out his last flight," Mireille said. "You'll see; he's back in control."

"With Trudeau software, he's suddenly fine. That's what you're saying?"

"Try it yourself. It's like—how do you say—flying a bicycle."

"Close enough." Evan climbed the metal stairs to the hatch of the simulator. "I'm not an expert like Daz, but I'll take it around the block."

"Actually, we changed it to Everest style well before Dove came to us. Good to plan ahead, yes?"

"Just how far ahead do you plan?"

"Watch your knees." Mireille guided Evan through the hatch. She handed him a flash drive then sat beside him. "Here's your flight plan. It's a quick flight; Apple Valley to LAX. It's fifteen minutes to climb, cruise, and descend. If we have problems, we'll see it there."

"Agreed. And if I can fly Everest, then surely anyone can."

"Load the flight plan, sit back, and relax."

"Not quite," Evan said. "But I've seen your miracles. I suppose one more is not going to surprise me."

"We have a hundred engineers on the panel interface alone. Hard work is not a miracle."

"What I meant was—" Evan snapped on the master switch, and suddenly, his jaw dropped. The monitors lit up in a vivid display of yellow and red gauges. Quickly, the gauges turned green, and a Ready for Ignition came on.

"You've been busy; I can see."

"We took software from your flying car." Mireille pointed at the displays. "And soon, we will take out the yoke and install a joystick."

Evan grinned. "Great, let's see what you got."

He flipped the Ignition-Enable switch and spooled up the engines. One by one, the 100,000-horsepower engines whirred to life. The cockpit barely shook as the simulator vibrated to match the real engines. Evan ran through the computerized check list. Eager to fly, he taxied to the Apple Valley runway and got ready for takeoff.

"You have clearance for departure." Mireille pointed at a screen. "We can do autopilot if you like."

"You know the answer." Evan kept the autopilot disengaged. "It's me and Everest all the way."

"I thought you would say that." Mireille sat back as he gripped the throttles and yoke.

Evan sent the simulated Everest down the runway, taking off into the desert landscape with a near flawless performance. Any deviation was immediately reprimanded and corrected by the new and improved Everest software.

"Got to tell ya; even Jean-Petit could fly this plane." He landed Everest at the simulated LAX runway and taxied to the gate. "I can also tell you; it takes a lot to impress me. And Mireille, you're getting seriously close."

"Close, huh? What would it take to sway you … permanently?"

"If you can manage to keep the same pace," Evan said, "that would be impressive."

"It only gets better. After we finish—"

"I'll be a believer." He patted her hand. "Yes, I can see it now."

Evan's prediction of an accelerated pace quickly became true. The next couple days became a non-stop marathon of technical reviews, marketing reviews, budget and schedule reviews. According to Mireille and her staff, the entire Everest project had been one of the smoothest, best organized, and most ambitious endeavors they had ever seen. Only the small details remained; like the maiden voyage and the sales.

On Thursday, Mireille delivered a cup of ice for Evan's Coke as he ate lunch at the Trudeau cafeteria. "I'm leaving now," she said.

"Short day at the office?"

"My work in Grenoble is done. You'll stay and keep us on track."

"Where will you be?"

"Two days at Dove," she said. "Then back here with you. As I said, you must meet the family."

"As if I didn't have enough stress."

"You'll do fine. *Au revoir, mon cher.*"

***

A quick goodbye, and suddenly, Evan felt as though he was stranded in a French desert. With no Mireille and with no meetings, he wandered the alleys and pathways, trying to learn his way around. Ten thousand workers on this campus; but few spoke English and fewer still seemed comfortable around the president of a major American company. This was not like Dove, where he could wander anywhere, talk to anyone, and feel totally at home. Was it French culture or specifically Trudeau? Yet another question for Mireille.

His thoughts jumped from one matter to another; from the buildings around him, to his father in a convalescent home, to the Everest schedule, to Mireille. He tried to remember directions, and names, and numbers, and the phrase *Je t'aime*. He tried to prioritize. At the top of his list; when to say that he loved her.

Evan nervously laughed at himself. Then, as he turned a corner, his nerves gave way to goose bumps and a suddenly-dry mouth. That odd, being-watched feeling came back with a vengeance. Footsteps behind him, the fleeting movement of a shadow, whispering voices.

Whatever it was, it was not jet lag. He picked up his pace, trying to put distance between himself and paranoia. The feeling persisted; an echo here, invisible eyes watching, footsteps that didn't match his own. He started to jog. He dashed around a blind corner, and suddenly, his paranoia became real. He felt his body slam against the brick wall. A powerful hand covered his mouth.

"Don't say a word," the voice warned.

Evan struggled to see his captor. He freed one of his pinned hands. He pulled down the palm that covered his mouth, turned his head, and bumped into the ugly face of one elusive American. "Madison Grier," he groaned. "I should've known."

As he struggled to free the other hand, Markus Sullivan rushed to Grier's side. He placed a heavy hand on Evan's elbow.

"Quiet. Not a word."

"What do you want?" Evan grumbled. "You're miles from your turf."

"You don't get it, do ya?" Grier relaxed his grip but kept Evan between him and Sullivan. "And they made you the president? We're doomed."

Evan, for the life of him, couldn't remember where the nearest security was. He knew the path to the main gate, but he didn't know if he was faster than Grier or faster than Sullivan. He felt trapped, yet curious to what was happening. This was about the last place he expected to see those two. He got ready to curse a few pointed questions then he turned his head and saw one more familiar face.

"Len Harris, of course." Evan jerked his arm from Sullivan's grasp. "Not happy enough to stay at home; you had to follow me to France."

"Well, be that way," Harris said. "We could leave you alone and let you find out for yourself."

"He'll be too late and too dumb to figure it out," Sullivan said.

"We didn't fly here for nothing," Grier said.

Evan glanced at the alley, looking for a friendly face, looking for help. "They got security all over. How did you—"

"Break into this fort?" Harris laughed. He pulled out his inhaler and puffed. "You're not the only one with a French connection." He whistled, and three more men appeared.

Evan recognized the small, well built man as the French equivalent of Russell. The man's name; Alphonse somebody. He didn't recall his last name and didn't recognize the two tag-along men. But he did understand that he was clearly outnumbered. Perhaps it was best to go along for the ride.

"Is this about Mojave Air?" Evan said.

"What do you know about that?" Grier asked.

"We got video of you, Sullivan, and Harris hours before the crash. You were poking around the plane, up to no good."

"Then you don't know squat." Grier frowned then turned to Harris. "I told you; he's no good."

"Who else is going to do it?" Harris asked. "We gotta take a chance."

"You'll never get away with it," Evan said to Grier.

"We'll put the brakes on. I guarantee."

"Everest?"

"Of course, we're talking Everest. What'd you do, leave your brains in California?" Grier turned to his comrades. "Come on, let's go."

One of the tag-along Frenchmen peeked around a corner. He discreetly waved them forward. Grier poked at Evan's ribs.

"Mind telling me what's going on?" Evan said.

"Keep your eyes and ears forward."

They marched the deserted alleys and hidden paths to the rear of the simulator building. Alphonse swiped a badge along the security box. The box beeped, and he quietly cracked the door open. After a look inside, he signaled the men to follow.

Evan and the others slipped into the dark and vacant hanger. Alphonse went to a panel and flipped on the lights by the Everest simulator. Evan sensed a show coming on, and somehow, he or Everest would be center stage.

"We know you've been flying this," Harris said, sliding his inhaler into his pocket.

"Yeah."

"Think you're pretty good?"

"Good enough," Evan said.

"Get in and show us."

"First, tell me why."

Grier emphatically pointed at the captain's seat while Alphonse booted the simulation software. Quickly, the flight monitors sprung to life.

Evan, growing more curious, sat in the left-hand seat. "Fine, I'll play your game. What do you want; a flight to Switzerland?"

"Yeah, funny." Harris took the right seat. "We'll make it easy. Fly me from Apple Valley to LAX. I assume you've done it before."

"Plenty. It was Alphonse's flight plan. He should know it."

"It was Mireille's flight plan," Alphonse said over the speaker. "*Now* we have mine." His accent was heavy, but Evan understood the message.

"Whatever you say." He spooled up the engines and taxied to the Apple Valley runway. As he took off, the simulator showed Victor Valley with vivid colors of sunset orange and sandstone brown. "Trust me; if you want a real pilot, I'm nobody's choice."

"Okay," Harris said. "Now we add turbulence."

"With a million-pound jet," Evan said, "it's like blowing on a glacier."

"When you reach ten thousand feet, descend to nine and then climb."

"Are you kidding? No one gets that command."

"Just do it," Harris said.

"That's why you brought me here; to play traffic cop?"

"Evasive maneuver!" Harris shouted. "Descend immediately!"

Evan obliged by easing the control forward, then back again. The turbulence went from a light jostle to a lap grinding ride on a bumpy road. But it was nothing that Evan or Everest couldn't handle.

He shrugged and said, "So what?" Then he blinked. Suddenly, the landscape image spun upside-down and turned a solid red.

"What the—" Evan muttered as he twisted knobs and toggled switches. "What's your game, Alphonse?"

"No game," he said. "What you see is what you get."

"Doesn't that give you a warm feeling?" Harris reset the computer for the same flight. He reduced the turbulence but carefully timed the big bumps. "You are over the mountains, flying level with a routine flight. Now—take it down to nine."

Again, Evan eased forward on the control and reduced power. Again, the image flipped and went red. He turned his head to Alphonse. "You simulator stinks."

"Not the simulator."

"Alphonse is correct," Harris said. "With the right—or wrong—conditions, Everest flips over and dives for the ground."

Grier poked his head through the simulator door. "You got rate limit on the ailerons. And guess what—the computer gets confused. Left is right and right is left. Everything locks up."

"So, you found a bug. Write it up and get it fixed. We'll deal with it."

"So, you got a hundred bugs; and more coming."

Evan shut down the simulator. "As I said; I appreciate your input. But honestly, you were laid off months ago. Why do you care what happens?"

Sullivan shook his bearded head. "Where's Paul McKenna when you need him?"

"Or John Waterman," Evan said. "If I'm not mistaken, he's pushing to get his job restored. And yours, for that matter."

"Waterman?" Sullivan frowned and moved closer. "The guy's a fool. Laying him off was long overdue. No, sir, we are not doing this for Waterman; or you, for that matter. If you want to know why we care, talk to your father. He knows about jobs. He understands loyalty. He cares about family and friends. When times were tough; he still paid us and paid us good. From his own pocket if he had to. You tell me, who else would have done that?"

"Not Mireille," Grier said. "Not even close."

"But she came along," Harris said, "and Paul didn't have a choice. He had to downsize. We hold nothing against Paul. But you and Mireille are oblivious—totally blind to the problems. And I'll tell you straight out; if you let us go, safety drops and people die."

Evan finally recognized the significance of Kylee's so-called death threats. He shuddered. It was all said in the name of safety.

"Personally," Grier said, "we don't care what happens to you. But we don't want Paul or his company to fold. We owe him big, and we'll do what we can to repay him."

"What do you expect from me?"

"You're the president," Sullivan said. "You're about the only one who can stand up to Mireille."

"He said 'stand up.' " Harris sneered. "Not lie down next to her."

Grier dropped a flash drive onto Evan's lap. "Here's the file on Everest gigs. And here's one on the Trudeau jet … and helicopter and …" He tossed one drive after another.

"It's not only Dove?"

Alphonse nodded. "Trudeau has so many issues, you might be safer driving."

Evan frowned. With this last-minute revelation, dinner with Mireille's family was bound to be more tumultuous than, "Please pass the pâté."

Chapter *23*

"I HATE IT when they talk behind my back in front of my face." Kylee sat in Claire's cubicle and patted her new French-English dictionary. It was Monday morning, and for once, she was glad to be at work.

"Come again?" Russell leaned over her shoulder as she thumbed through the pages.

"Those guys from Trudeau; like Mireille and Pierre. They jabber in French, and they don't care if you understand them or not."

"That is annoying."

"Did you know that Claire speaks French?"

"Is that why you want to learn?"

"Don't you think it's odd—Mireille and Claire—so cozy. Especially the last few weeks; lunch together, shopping together, sharing files on their phones. Except for the phone thing, that's what Claire and I used to do. Something's going on. Let's say; I'm uncomfortable."

"Not too uncomfortable," Russell said. "You're sitting at her computer. Aren't you afraid she'll—"

"Find out and start screaming? Don't worry. Both Claire and her master are in LA. I figured it out myself." Kylee patted her dictionary.

"And her password?"

"I sit by Claire. Of course, I know her password." She pointed at the screen. "You should see the stuff I'm finding."

"Personal files?"

"I know what you're thinking. But look; my marriage is on the rocks, we got a murderer running loose, and my job, believe me— it's hanging by a thread. The way I see it; I got nothing to lose."

"That's one way to look at it," Russell said. "But didn't we agree that Waterman is the bad guy? Aren't we done?"

"Until we tie him to Bullman Stock and the money at the crash site, we're not finished."

"That's why you're fishing?" Russell leaned closer.

"Look at these files." She clicked a tab and scrolled down a long list. "Websites that she has links on; Day trader, Caller ID, Microwave transmitters, and Jetsons.com. Why does she care about that?"

"Strange." Russell took over the mouse. "I've been to the same sites, except for the Jetsons. And I can show you what I found."

He clicked on the Caller ID site and stood aside. "If you have patience and the right equipment, you can trace any call. That's kind of a given, these days. Of course, that's a problem if you use a sat' phone and you *don't* want to be traced."

Kylee watched the monitor as the logo of longhorn bull appeared. She waited for Russell's explanation.

"Here's what happened." Russell pulled Evan's phone from his pocket and set it onto Claire's desk. "All these wiretaps; yeah, sure, you can trace them. Up to a point."

"Which point?"

"Bullman Stock," Russell said. "Believe it or not, it's a dummy site for wiretaps."

"I don't understand."

"Bullman—they're not about stock or money. That's only a cover. When you call them, you actually link into a transmitter.

"A transmitter," Kylee said, "like at a rundown apartment in Hesperia."

"Very good." Russell gave her a pat on the hand. "Of course, that's the end of the line for traceability. It turns out they re-transmit over the air, then re-transmit and so on."

"You know you lost me ten minutes ago."

"It's all a game to throw us off. You know; hackers who can trace a wiretap to the middle of Alaska." He raised a finger and smiled. "However, there is only one thing that's important."

"And that is?"

"If you find the receiver," Russell said, "you will find the culprit behind the murders."

"The receiver in the hills by my cabin."

"Exactly." He nodded. "That's your surefire link to John Waterman."

"Or Pierre."

"Pierre? Why him?"

Kylee closed an app window and called up another. "Remember that jogger at the apartment? Remember who his roommate was?"

"Whiteman … Whitehead. Something like that?"

"Yeah, that's it—Whitehead." Kylee pointed at her book. "And the French equivalent is *Teteblanche*. That's a company near Toulouse … France. Pierre worked there before Trudeau. As it turned out, that's where we found Claire. I checked her résumé. She met Paul in New York, but she worked in France with Pierre."

"Coincidence?"

"Hardly," she said. "Forget Waterman. Claire and Pierre are the common thread. I mean, yeah, Mireille's still involved somehow. But Claire; she's the wild card I never saw."

"Makes you wonder; who else is part of it?"

Kylee stared at her screen. "And where is that recording of Mireille; you know, with John's phone? I got some translating to do."

"Tell you what. Give me an hour. I have my own plan."

"For the recording?"

"For the receiver. I know how to find it."

Kylee swiveled the chair. "Don't let me get in your way."

"I'm on it, ma'am." Russell grinned. He checked his watch and trotted to his lab. He seemed happiest next to a pretty woman or next to his radio gear. And as long as he stayed happy, there was progress to be made. Kylee's aim; keep him that way.

While Russell did his work, Kylee got busy on her own assignments. She poked her head above Claire's cubicle and gave herself an all-clear. Quickly and discreetly, she copied as many files as she could. "Evidence," she told herself. "Finally, I have something to show."

True to his word, Russell returned to her desk during the morning break. As Kylee spread cream cheese on her sesame seed bagel, Russell slid Evan's phone across the desk.

"You keep saying we're two steps behind," he said, brushing sesame seeds into the trash can.

"Yeah, because of that stupid phone."

"Worry not. I have a plan that will turn Pierre into a little *garçon*."

"That arrogant Frenchman," Kylee said. "Or is that redundant?"

"I modified my direction finder," Russell said. "Finally, we can locate the repeater."

"And the evidence. This time, we'll take the sheriff. Pierre won't have a chance to clear out the equipment."

"Exactly. How's two o'clock sound?"

"I like it." Kylee smiled and made a note on her calendar.

Russell held his finger up to the air. He held his breath and then said, "We're clear."

The light on Evan's phone turned from red to green. "You think he bought it?" she asked.

"Well, someone was listening."

"Claire and Mireille are in LA; it could be them."

"Or Pierre," Russell said. "Now, if he drives to the repeater, we'll follow him every mile."

"Your direction finder—does it really work?"

"I have no idea how to make one. But Pierre doesn't know that."

"Let me call some friends," Kylee said. "We can tail him as a group. Pierre will never know."

"Don't bother." Russell held up the phone and pointed. "As long as we have this, we're fine. I tapped into Pierre's GPS. Sweet, huh?"

Kylee nodded. "We can follow him without being seen?"

"Yep, we sure can." Russell stood close to Kylee. He exhaled, smelling of mint toothpaste. "And as a bonus, we can tell the sheriff about Fred."

"What about Fred?"

"I know about his last call on the mountaintop. My guess; he actually did dial 911. Or at least he tried to dial. Unfortunately, the wiretap jammed his call. So he walked up the hill for a better signal. Now, this will make you sick. Whoever was listening in;

they heard the plane crash, they heard him leave the plane, *and* they heard him fall off the cliff."

"That's horrible," Kylee said.

"That's the kind of people we're dealing with. Poor Fred didn't have a chance to fight." Russell shook his head. "It's up to us now; we have to get the sheriff to listen."

"We can do it, Russell. If we—"

"Hang on; I think we have our man." Russell pointed at the phone. "Pierre's on the move."

"That was fast."

"We'll use my van, okay? I'm good at tailing guys—as you know."

"Forget it." Kylee grabbed her purse. "We'll take my Jeep. I'm good at driving in the hills—as you will find out."

"Okay, fine," Russell said. "Oh, and by the way, we can listen in."

"You did a wiretap on Pierre's phone?" Kylee grinned, thinking like an engineer.

"If he uses the phone or not, we'll catch every word."

"That is so much better than sweet."

Kylee and Russell jogged to the Jeep. While he pulled up on his belt, she pulled keys from her purse. To keep her diamond heart necklace from bouncing, Kylee shoved it beneath her blue cotton blouse. No surprise, she easily outpaced Russell across the parking lot. By the time he caught up, she had the Jeep ready to move. She reached over and pushed open the passenger door. As Russell plopped in and lifted his foot from the pavement, the Jeep was rolling.

"I'm a little impatient these days," she apologized. Then she revved the engine and took the quickest route to I-15. No more apologies.

Russell pressed the map printout to his lap to keep it from blowing through the open top.

"He's not talking," Russell said, keeping one eye on traffic and the other on his tracking device. "He's probably alone."

"They cleaned out that Hesperia apartment in a couple hours. But you know, I think we'll catch him with his pants down."

"What a thought." Russell shielded the sun from his tracker and then pointed straight ahead. "No question though he is moving fast."

"Then hold on, so are we." Kylee tightened her seat belt against her jeans and slipped a hair band over her head.

"Turn left," Russell said, showing the GPS map.

"He's in my territory now. We got him, Russell. We finally got him."

"Great, but slow down. We don't have to ride in his back seat."

"Okay, fine."

As they raced from Apple Valley to the dry, golden foothills of the San Bernardino Forest, Kylee took a moment to regroup. She reached into her purse and pulled out a note. As she passed it to Russell, she said, "You had your plan; this is mine. Once we get there, I want answers. And we're not leaving without them."

Russell unfolded the note and held it close. He read aloud each question on her list; "Is there enough evidence to call Fred's death a murder? What was the link to Bob's death in the Utah canyon? Why was Fred carrying cash? Was Mireille involved in any of this, and how can we send her to prison for the rest of her life?"

Russell raised his eyebrows. "Sounds straightforward. No hidden agenda here."

Kylee shoved the note into her purse. She kept quiet and held the steering wheel loosely until they hit the switchbacks and narrow mountain roads. It was either the clean autumn air or her adrenaline, but she felt invigorated. She felt a surge of motivation. She gripped the wheel tighter and pressed harder on the accelerator. Strange; for Pierre to drive here—that had to be more than coincidence.

"If I didn't know better," she said, "I'd swear he was headed for my cabin."

"I don't know what he's up to," Russell said, "but he's talking to someone in French."

"And someone thinks I'm driving too slow." She jabbed Russell's arm and then touched the rear-view mirror.

"Use a turnout. There's no need to push it."

"The next turnout is two miles ahead, and this guy does not want to wait."

Behind the Jeep, a newer model, white SUV pulled to within inches of Kylee's bumper, swerving side to side, skidding around corners.

"There's no room to pull over," Kylee said. "But let's see what kind of horsepower he's got." She eased the accelerator forward and hugged the curves next to the cliffs. Hairpin turns and no guard rails, but, "I can do this in my sleep."

"That's fine if you stay in the lane. This guy has a death wish. He doesn't care how he drives."

"He's on a cell phone," Kylee said, glancing behind. "No wonder he's driving wild."

"Can't be. You've got no cell connection in these hills."

"That means Pierre is on the other end of a sat' phone. How on earth did he know?"

"Are you kidding? Pierre's too lazy to move equipment. He called in his muscle to help. This SUV—I bet they recognized your Jeep and called ahead to Pierre."

"Could be," Kylee said. "I think the driver's from the tail assembly group."

"There's one passenger from what I can see."

"We're ten miles from my cabin," Kylee said. "I'll bet he's going there."

"Not quite," Russell said. "Pierre's turned away from your cabin."

"Then I don't know where he's going."

"How about this guy behind us?"

"I have an idea." Kylee brushed back the hair from her face. "We'll take a shortcut." She reached up to adjust the rear-view mirror, but suddenly, it shattered and stung her fingertips. She snapped her hand to her lap.

"Wherever that shortcut is," Russell said, "take it now! They're shooting at us, so move it! Move it!"

Russell struggled to work the numbers on the phone. He canceled the GPS and got to the '9' of 911. Then Kylee stomped on her brakes and cranked the steering wheel a hard left. They careened off the road and sailed across a shallow ditch. Now they climbed a hill of dried weeds and timber.

"Access road!" Kylee shouted. Deep ruts slammed against the wheels of the Jeep, and Russell's glasses bounced off his nose.

The jarring climb tortured their spines and knocked the phone to the back seat floor. Russell tried to fetch it. But despite his contortionist efforts, he could not twist his frame to get anywhere close. Instead, he ducked his head from low-flying branches that smacked against the windshield and the roll bar.

"Well, it used to be an access road," Kylee said.

"What do we do when we get there?"

"I have another idea."

"Any better than the last one?"

"Yep. They're messing with the wrong girl. I'll stop them dead in their tracks."

"How about *we* stop in our tracks? We're safe now."

"If we stop now, Russell, we're bound to lose it all; Pierre, his equipment, every shred of evidence. I'm not going to chance it."

"How about I call the sheriff? The least I can do is that."

Kylee narrowed her eyes and glared at Russell. "Okay, you want me to stop? I'll let you out here. Take the phone if you want. I'm going up!"

"Forget it." Russell ducked another branch as Kylee set her sights on the hill. "I've come this far; what's a few minutes more?"

With her eyes straight ahead, Kylee reached across to Russell's chest and checked the seat harness; it was good and tight. She let off the gas as the Jeep reached the berm of the upper road and flew across the single lane.

Russell shielded his head from the dashboard as they landed hard and slid through the next curve.

"Sorry, no airbags." Kylee spun the steering wheel and slowed the Jeep to a crawl on the gravel shoulder. "That gave us about five minutes. Now ... if I can find the right barricade."

"Pierre's straight ahead. You want to catch up?"

Kylee ignored the question and carefully maneuvered the front bumper against the base of a massive pine. She placed the Jeep at right angle to the road. "Okay, that's step one."

"That's not going to help," Russell said. "They can still see us."

Kylee poked his shoulder and then pointed. "Run over there and keep your eye on the road. If you see 'em coming, give a yell. We'll get out of here fast."

Russell muttered a few complaints but quickly obliged. He brushed back the hair from his forehead, pulled up on his belt, and then disappeared around the bend.

Kylee raced to the rear of the Jeep and jammed a rock by the tire. Then she grabbed the hook from the winch and dragged the steel cable across the road. She stood by the dry remains of a tall Douglas fir.

"Perfect," she said, looking up. "This is going to work fine." Like an experienced mountaineer, she tossed the hook and looped the cable around a high and sturdy branch. She gave it a good tug.

"How's it looking, Russell?" she yelled out.

"Clear, so far. They might be looking for us back on Dart Canyon."

Kylee scrambled to the Jeep and flipped on the winch. In moments, the cable rose from the pavement and grew taut against the old tree. The motor whined and struggled against the load. The cable tightened as the front of the Jeep lifted. The tree skeleton at the other end began to creak.

"What's that noise?" Russell called as he rushed to her. "What on earth are you doing?"

"Beetle disease. Some of these trees are already tagged and dying to come down. I don't care if that SUV has two or four-wheel drive; there's no way they can drive around this."

Russell looked up at the tree, at Kylee, then back at the tree. "This is *not* a good idea."

"Don't worry." She lifted her hand. "The angle to the top is forty-five. That means when the tree falls, we'll stay clear—but the tree blocks the road. You see; Evan's not the only one who can do the math. Easy peasy, huh?"

With a loud crack, the huge fir toppled their way.

Russell stared up and moaned. "My God."

He shook his head then dove against Kylee. He desperately tried to push her out of the path of the falling tree. Whether it was the heavy trunk or Russell's own weight that forced them down, they both hit the ground hard with a bone crushing thud.

Dry dirt and pine needles flew up in a choking cloud of forest debris. Snapping wood and shattering glass made it seem like a tornado strike. Whatever happened, the damage seemed immense; probably total. No doubt about it; they were in a jam.

Slowly, unbearably slowly, the air became breathable. Kylee took shallow breaths and looked around. She lay next to Russell; his arm stuck by her shoulder, his face firmly planted in the dirt, his eyes facing away. The tree skeleton—now a massive log—pressed heavily on their spines.

Kylee spit dry needles from her mouth and gasped, "My God, what happened?" She painfully faced Russell. "I was so sure I had it."

She dug pine needles from his mouth and knocked away bugs and bark. She checked Russell the best she could, but by far, his big problem was the log that pressed on his back and twisted his spine.

"Talk to me, Russell. Talk to me." Kylee's heart stirred when she saw the glimmer of movement from his head.

He coughed then spit out dirt. "Can't move," he finally moaned.

"You have a tree on your back."

"Can't feel my legs."

"Where does it hurt?" she asked.

"I told you, I can't feel my legs."

"Does your back hurt?"

"Yes," he said.

"How about your head?"

"What about my legs?"

"I'll take care of you, Russell. Don't worry; I'm not going to leave you."

"You got the math wrong," Russell moaned. "If you're standing on a hill, that's not how it works."

"I'm sorry."

Kylee twisted her head to look around. The huge tree had split into two massive logs. The brunt of the force was absorbed by the Jeep itself, but heavy wood painfully pressed on their backs. Russell, being the wider of the two, accepted the greater weight. For what it was worth, Kylee was thankful. Less than an arm's length away, a splintered branch poked the ground like a deadly spear.

She closed her eyes and silently cried. Every inch of this disaster was her fault. This hunt for murderers and conspirators and home wreckers; what good was it if she got Russell paralyzed or killed? Was any of this worthwhile? She stared at the top of Russell's head and felt relieved that she couldn't see his face and that he couldn't see hers.

Here was the one man who trusted her and followed her on this wild obsession. He had asked for nothing in return. Even now, as he lay pinned on his stomach, Russell seemed less willing to blame and more eager to get out of the mess. But then, she couldn't see his eyes and couldn't read his mind.

Kylee took in the silence and tried to gather her senses, but her heart shot into overdrive when she heard the engine of a distant, but fast moving, vehicle. The white SUV was undoubtedly back on their trail. It would be a matter of minutes before they sped around the last corner. For sure, they would see the smashed Jeep and the captive victims beside it.

Kylee struggled to push herself free from the log that pressed on her hips and thighs. "I'm stuck." She pushed harder but got nowhere.

"What's going on?" Russell asked.

"If I can get out—"

"They're coming back, aren't they?"

"My pocket's snagged," she said. "Just give me a minute."

"What are we going to do? I don't want to die here, Kylee. Get me out!"

She clawed at the ground and tried in vain to push herself away from the tree that tugged at her jeans and dug into her hip. The roar of the SUV engine grew louder, and her heart pounded faster.

"Wait—I can do this." Kylee tugged at the top of her jeans. She pushed against the tree and pulled at her zipper. Finally, she wiggled her feet and kicked off her tennis shoes.

Russell painfully moved his head to see what Kylee was up to. His eyes widened as she finally broke free. She crawled on her hands and knees, showing her peach colored panties and beautifully tanned legs. Russell closed his eyes—at least partly.

"Try not to move," she warned him and patted his shoulder.

"What are you doing?"

Kylee glimpsed the SUV as it screamed up the road. She quickly arranged her jeans and shoes on the ground and grabbed the one weapon she could find. Then she ducked behind the nearest large pine and held her breath.

The driver slammed on the brakes and slid to a stop. Dust from the gravel shoulder drifted by Kylee's face, and she held back a cough. She stayed in place, hoping to stay invisible, hoping for an easy way out.

Then she heard a muffled voice as the driver shifted to Park. A moment later, the engine shut down, surrounding them with nothing but silence. The only noise came from her heart—beating louder than a drum. She listened for the engine to start again and for the gunmen to retreat to the ridge road. But to her dismay, she heard the door of the SUV slowly open, and then slam shut.

Chapter 24

SOFT FOOTSTEPS on the pavement, then crunching, sliding footsteps on the gravel shoulder. One man, Kylee surmised, with the passenger staying put. One man with a gun was trouble enough. She was afraid to peek beyond the bark of the tree that hid her. What if he turned and fired? What if he caught her and marched her deep into the woods? What if he killed her where no one could find her body? What if she had never started this painful obsession in the first place?

Her stomach churned with a hundred 'what ifs.' She forced herself to focus on the moment. *Timing is everything*, she thought. And this was no time for a 'what if.'

She gathered her nerves and peeked around the tree. She saw a tall, casually dressed man struggle to keep his footing as he slid to the front of the Jeep.

The man laughed and shook his head. "Looks like somebody stepped on his own trap." He kicked the soles of Russell's well-worn shoes.

"Hey!" Russell said. "Leave us alone."

The man faced the passenger in the SUV. "Which one first; the girl or guy?"

"You idiot!" the passenger yelled. "Get 'em to move the tree. Then shoot 'em."

"The girl's probably dead already." The man kicked the well placed shoes. "What the—" He jerked his head when the shoe bounced along the ground. He leaned closer to find the girl's foot. Slowly, with a look of confusion, he spun to the sound of light footsteps headed his way.

Too late for the man to protect himself, Kylee used the phone as a blunt wedge. With all her strength, she slammed the case against the man's skull like an axe to a watermelon.

The man jerked his hand to his head and knocked the phone to the ground. Kylee moved in for round two and shoved her knee far up his groin. As the man buckled to his knees, she wrestled the gun from his hand. She stumbled back, putting distance between her and the assailant.

Now she had momentum. Without missing a step, she raced up the embankment to confront the passenger. No doubt, he would come out shooting if he also had a weapon. But to her relief, the wide-eyed passenger ducked below the dash and slid to the driver's side. He flipped the key and jammed the SUV into reverse. With the tires spinning and SUV rocking, the driver sped down the hill and out of sight. The roar of the engine quickly faded.

Like the end of a sprint, Kylee felt her pulse gradually slow from panic speed to normal. She struggled to catch her breath, grateful for another day alive. And she gave thanks that she now held a weapon and the power to extract a few answers.

"What are you looking at?" she growled at the thug holding his head. "This ain't a peep show." She glanced at her panties and ankle socks. Then she tiptoed across the dirt and yanked her jeans from beneath the fallen tree.

Keeping her distance from the thug, she slid into her jeans and shoes. She squinted at him and waved the gun. "I've seen you before. You're Mathieu from the tail assembly group."

Mathieu was in obvious pain but apparently coherent enough to speak his mind. "All he said was keep you away. He told us you had a gun, and you weren't afraid to use it."

"Well, *now* I do. And you know what, he has a point; I wouldn't mind shooting you on the spot."

"Pierre said you were out to get him. If anything happened, '*cherchez la femme.*' "

"Look for the woman. Yeah, I've heard it. But God, you're a miserable liar. You're up to your neck in this; don't tell me otherwise. Murder-one and twenty years; if you keep lying, it only gets worse."

"I don't know what you want me to say." Mathieu lifted his eyes. "Pierre calls me a half-hour ago. He says we got some packing to do. I ask him where and he says Pilot Rock. I say fine. That's about it."

"You always pack with a gun?"

"Pierre knows I keep one in the car. He said there might be trouble."

"Trouble, yeah; and you're most of it. Aggravated assault; that's only the start. Wait until the sheriff gets here. We've got battery and conspiracy for murder."

Kylee carefully went to the Mathieu's side and picked up the phone. She shook off pine needles and dry clumps of dirt. She blew on it, and the face plate came loose. The antenna swung free, hanging by a thread.

She tried to punch on the power but got no response. She glared at Mathieu. "It's your hard head, you know. But don't worry; if it's manmade, it can be fixed. And if it can be fixed, Russell Torello can fix it."

She stepped over the fallen tree and passed the phone to Russell. "What do you think? Can you get it to work?"

With his face firmly pressed into the dirt, Russell struggled to grab the phone. "Jesus, what happened? You stripped half the chips."

"I improvised. Can we use it?"

"Yeah, sure. Get me back to my lab and give me a microscope, I'll give it a shot."

"You don't have to get sarcastic."

"I'm lying here, paralyzed in the woods, and you want me to fix the phone."

"We need the paramedics and the cops," Kylee said.

"Start by getting the log off. You and Mathieu; you can lift it."

Kylee crossed the log and gave Russell a hard pinch on his thigh.

He yelped like a stung puppy. "Hey, what was that for?"

"I thought so. If you can feel it, you're not paralyzed."

"Fine. Make sure it stays that way."

Kylee motioned for Mathieu to use some muscle and lift the dead wood. She moved a safe distance from him, crammed the pistol into her jeans, and pulled up on a branch. They both grunted, Mathieu mostly for show. Whether it was bad footing, lack of trying, or timber that was too heavy, Russell remained pinned tighter than an elephant in a shoe box.

Kylee scratched her head for a solution. "Well, my winch is dead, my engine's dead—"

"Please, don't use that word." Russell groaned.

"Pierre has a phone and I have a gun. I think we can work a deal."

"You're not going to leave me here, are you?"

"Mathieu will keep you company. Don't worry." She stepped to the crushed Jeep, pulled out a length of climbing rope, and carefully arranged two butterfly loops. She tossed it to Mathieu. She told him to tie his hands and drop face down into the dirt. When he did, Kylee cautiously pulled the knots tight and added more loops around his wrists, arms, and ankles. She secured him to the Jeep.

"You both stay put while I get some help." She went to Russell and kissed his dirty cheek. "I'll be back before you know it."

That small token seemed to pacify Russell. He closed his eyes, relaxed his shoulders, and settled down to wait for imminent reinforcement. Hopefully, it would be a short wait.

Meanwhile, Kylee put aside her apprehensions and tuned out Mathieu's whining about the tight ropes. She tightened her shoe laces and began the long walk to Pierre's mountain hideaway.

She didn't have a real plan beyond getting his phone and calling for help. However, since she had a weapon and restored motivation, some quality one on one with Pierre might set the stage for some long-overdue revelations.

Odd place for a transmitter, she thought as she looked around her. Sure, the land was isolated and a good place for a hideout, but why here; so close to her own cabin on the hill? Coincidence or not, Kylee believed she had the upper hand in this territory. She knew that the road behind was blocked and the road ahead was a dead-end. Pierre and his equipment were inexorably trapped.

She walked the final switchback and saw Pierre's Mercedes parked next to the two-room, wood shake cabin. It had been a year since she had been to her neighbor's place. But she easily recalled the layout of the property; heavily wooded with pines, a peek of the lake from the front, and a filtered view of the Victor Valley from the top of the ridge. If Kylee's memory served her correctly, the southwest side had no views and no windows. She decided to approach from that angle.

Quickly but quietly, she moved from the cover of one tree to another. She watched her footing and watched for movement around the cabin. She moved forward, cautious but confident. In no time, she stood at the porch. It was now or never. With a quick peek by the front door, she rushed in and raised the pistol with both hands. Pierre, predictably, was kneeling by a far wall and dismantling a stack of electronics.

"Okay, Pierre!" she shouted. "Step away from the radio and drop the wrench!"

Pierre, only half-startled, placed the wrench by his feet. "Kylee McKenna; I rather expected you. They said you were stalking me, but I refused to believe it."

"Save your breath. I didn't come for your lies."

"And you didn't come to shoot me." He grinned unsteadily and carefully stood. "Why don't you lower the gun and we'll talk. If that's what you want."

Kylee twitched her finger. With a loud bang, the pistol sent a bullet whizzing by Pierre's ear and into the stack of electronics. Sparks flew, and the pungent odor of gun smoke and ozone filled the tiny cabin.

"I hate repeating myself," she calmly said, suppressing her own astonishment. "So sit down, shut up, and don't move till I tell you."

Pierre dropped to the floor like a wet gym towel. He spoke as if he still had some semblance of control. "What is it that you want? Cash? I have it. But you won't find it in the cabin."

"That's probably what you told Fred Mott. But you made him look for it in the middle of the Sierras."

"Pardon?"

Kylee allowed her gaze to wander around. She stepped to the rear window and looked up. "A microwave tower aimed straight for Hesperia; I wonder what that's for. Solar panel on the roof. Tank of propane in back. And inside ... what's this—recording equipment? I'm guessing it's not for Katy Perry downloads."

"Nothing illegal."

She stepped to another window but kept the gun on Pierre. "And this?" She placed her hand against a telescope, similar to the robotic ones at Dove. She sighted down the scope and popped open her eyes when she got a clear view of her cabin. Then she looked up and caught the familiar shape of an audio dish, also aimed at her cabin.

"You filthy, lying scum! You've been spying on me. That's what it's for." She banged her fist on the telescope. "You got Claire to watch me at work and this robot to watch me at the cabin. That's sick. We can't get a minute's privacy—me or Evan. A phone for him; this telescope for me. What are you afraid of? I'm meeting with the cops up here? We're plotting to bring you down? Yeah, well, you should be paranoid. But this; you had no right, no right at all."

Kylee's stomach churned. At her wilderness cabin, she rarely shut her window blinds—except at night. She rarely locked her doors—except at night. After all, there was no one around for miles; no one but squirrels and deer and friendly neighbors. Or so she believed.

She fired another round into the telescope lens, sending the shattered glass to the floor of the cabin. She fired two rounds through the open window to the dish antenna. She turned to Pierre and aimed at his head. "You should die on the spot!" she screamed at him. "For what you did to me, for what you did to Fred."

"Think about what you're doing," Pierre said.

Kylee fingered the trigger, her hand shaking. It scared her when she realized how easy it was to fire the gun. A slight pull and bullets went flying. She never imagined it would be like that. She never imagined firing a gun at all. But now she aimed at a living creature; a human being, or Pierre as it were. One nervous twitch and his life would be gone.

She slowly lowered her aim to his heavily breathing chest. "You're right. I didn't come here to shoot you … But if you give me any trouble." She raised her aim again.

"What is it you want?"

"For starters; your phone."

Pierre shrugged. He slowly reached into his pocket and pulled out the phone.

Kylee motioned for him to slide it across the floor. "Let's see what the sheriff says." She switched on the phone and glared at Pierre. "Okay, *monsieur*, what's the password?"

"Yes, I have the password. But it does have a price."

"Remember? I'm the one with the gun."

"You would not shoot me in cold blood."

"Are you sure?" She fingered the trigger and took steady aim.

Pierre nodded at the door. "Let me go, then call anyone you want. You know these hills. You'll probably catch me anyway." He nervously laughed.

"Save your bargains for the DA. I don't need your stinking password. Russell's smart. He'll figure it out." Kylee waved the gun toward the Mercedes. "Let's ride."

Pierre opened his palms and opened his mouth as if to plead, but Kylee spoke the next words.

"*Fermez votre bouche*," she said, prompting Pierre to raise his eyebrows. "And keep it shut. I don't want to hear another word." She smirked. "Yeah, I know that and a whole lot more."

Pierre dragged his feet to the Mercedes-Benz.

Because Kylee played it extra safe on the ride back to Russell and Mathieu, Pierre didn't get the chance to overpower her. Of course, considering the shape that she was in and the shape Pierre was in, Kylee would've held control, loaded gun or not.

When they pulled up to the barricade, Russell, regrettably, was still pinned beneath the log. Mathieu, thankfully, was still tied.

"You remember Mathieu," Kylee said to Pierre. "Have a seat next to your friend."

Pierre refused to acknowledge him. The two men remained stubbornly silent while Kylee passed the phone to Russell. Russell winced as he moved his hands.

"It's got password-protect," she told him. "I told Pierre you'd get around it."

Russell played with the keys, spun the phone front to back, and then said, "Back at the lab, no problem. Out here, forget it."

"You mean; you can't do it?"

"That's exactly what I mean. Without the password, all you have is a box of silicon."

Kylee grumbled then glared at Pierre. Her patience had come to an end. "Stand up and get by the branch."

While Pierre obeyed, Kylee untied Mathieu from the Jeep. Then she prodded both of them to the log. "Put your backs into it," she sternly said.

Despite the grunts and groans, the log remained in place.

"Forget it!" Russell screamed. "You're breaking my back!"

"Then how about this," Kylee said. "We can use the car to slide it off. It shouldn't be that hard."

"No way! You move it wrong; I'm paralyzed for life."

"What do you want me to do, Russell? We can't drive around it. We can't get it off."

"Give Pierre whatever he wants. Just get the password and call for help."

"He has a point," Pierre said. "With one car, speeding around the corner ..." He gestured to show the impact on the tree and Russell's body.

"Nobody but you travels this road. He can spend all day under that log and never see a car."

"What do you mean, all day?" Russell yelped. "Get me out."

"I have an idea," Kylee said, looking beyond the trees. "My cabin is a three-mile ride. I've got an axe there and a shovel."

"I don't like the sound of that."

"It's pretty safe, Russell. Don't worry."

"You're not giving me a lot of confidence."

"This has gone on long enough," Pierre said. "Pass me the phone."

"Now you're talking sense." Kylee carefully passed him the phone. "If you help us out, I *may* put in a good word."

Pierre worked the keypad. He casually and silently passed the phone to Kylee.

She glanced at the display then snarled, "What's this? Enter password? Come on, Pierre, this is *not* a game."

Pierre shrugged. Almost immediately, a huge boom echoed across the mountain ridges. Kylee stared across the hill, terrified to see a towering column of flames reaching high into the clear blue sky.

"That's the cabin!" she yelled.

"Whose cabin?" Russell yelled. He strained his neck toward the sound of the explosion.

"Pierre's cabin. He just blew it up, I'm sure. What was it, Pierre? The propane tank?" She jabbed him with the phone.

"Whatever it was; you now have a dilemma." Pierre nodded at Russell. "You have had no rain since April. Between us and the cabin, you have nothing but timber—extremely dry timber. If you call the firemen now, they *might* arrive before the flames."

Kylee raised the gun. She slid her finger on the trigger. "I am so tempted."

"As you said, Madame McKenna; I know you well. Vengeance is not your style. If you would be so kind to offer me a small head start, I will offer you the password."

Kylee narrowed her eyes. She paced between the road and the crumpled Jeep. There was no such thing as a small head start. Pierre was slippery. If he disappeared for a minute, he would be gone for a lifetime; back to France and the land of nearly impossible extradition. If that happened, there would be no answers to the questions of Fred Mott, Bob Aukram, and the others. There would be no punishment and no justice for the horrendous murders.

She returned to Pierre and passed him the phone. "Yes, Pierre. I may have qualms against violence. Justice, however, is a separate matter."

"What are you saying?"

"There are consequences for what you did. It is my intent to see it through; regardless of your diversion."

"Be sensible, Kylee." Pierre waved at the distant—but approaching—flames. "Considering the circumstances, you have little margin for negotiation."

"Again, Pierre, you are not speaking to Fred. This is not a business deal. And considering my situation, I honestly believe that my, uh, my margin is improved. I think we can walk to my cabin, get the axe, return to Russell, and chop through the log. Really, there's no rush. I know a shortcut."

She stepped to Pierre and studied his face. "Actually, we can swim across the lake. It's freezing cold. You might drown. Or go face to face with the Silver Pike."

"Silver what?"

"We call them high mountain piranha. There aren't too many this season, but you can never tell. If we make it through, we'll save a half-hour."

Pierre shrugged. "If that's what you want."

"Or there's a tunnel through the East Ridge. It's a little tight, with a few bats and rats. But it's dry and makes for a good shortcut."

"Very well; that's fine."

"Then there's the forest trail. If you don't mind a few snakes and loose gravel by the cliff."

Pierre blinked once, but that was enough. Kylee chose their path then waved the gun. "Yes, Russell, we'll be back before you know it."

Mathieu yanked at the ropes that held him tight. He screamed, "You can't leave me here! Look at the smoke!"

"Leave her alone!" Russell yelled. "I'm tired of you guys. Whatever she wants; do it!"

"Thanks," Kylee said. "I won't let you down."

She grabbed a pack from her Jeep and marched Pierre to the alleged shortcut through the rugged mountain terrain.

For a while, the trail stayed level and wide. The smoke blew the other way, and no one sweated a single step. As long as Kylee prodded him forward, Pierre kept a steady pace. They stayed on-plan.

Kylee pointed at the phone. "Whenever you want, Pierre, punch in the code. Pass the phone to me, and we'll call it square. I'll make one call, and we'll sit tight in your air conditioned car—if it's not disabled. Nice deal, huh?"

"No, thank you," he said.

"Then I guess we keep moving." She kept her voice calm. She kept the weapon in her hand. She pointed ahead.

Slowly, as the path became more rugged, Kylee stopped using the word 'shortcut.' She stopped apologizing for taking a wrong turn. And now, as the trail zigzagged through massive slabs of granite and crumbling shale, she stopped for nothing. She ignored the steep ravines and the slick gravel. Even though their pace had slowed to a crawl, she had one thing on her mind; "Keep moving."

Pierre—with what had to be the first real hike of his life—seemed to hold up under the stress, so far.

"Don't worry, Pierre. This is part of the tour if you want to see my cabin; up close and personal. That was your plan, *oui?*"

"Well, it's almost noon. We should be there by, uh, would you say twenty after?"

"Maybe."

"Very, well, Kylee. You have made your point. You have a gun with several bullets. Mathieu and Russell are tied up on the road. You certainly have the advantage. What would it take—"

"Sorry, no deals. I didn't trust you before, and I don't trust you now. Keep walking." She ignored his attempts at small talk and distraction. She didn't care if his ankle hurt or the sun bothered his eyes. If she was right, the view up ahead would make him forget any trivial aches and pains. If she was right, the trail ahead would lead her to some easy truths.

As the path narrowed to a shoe-wide ledge, Pierre's eyes grew wide. He began to sweat a whole lot more than justified in the mid-seventies temperature and ultra low humidity.

"I wouldn't look down," Kylee said as she jabbed him. "That's a fifty foot drop and I believe granite at the bottom. I knew a climber once; he fell on his spine and never walked again. Granite looks great in a kitchen but *not* on your face."

"You said the path was safe."

"I said short. *Safe* is a judgment call."

"This can't be the easiest path. There must be another."

"I'm pretty sure it gets wider. Until then, keep moving." She tested the loose rocks for secure footing then sent part of the ledge to the rock-strewn floor. "Oh, I might agree with you, Pierre. This ledge seems a bit unstable."

"You want the password; I will give it to you. But please, do not push."

"Well, look at that, Pierre. The fire's not moving like you thought it would. You may proceed at your leisure."

"Take the phone anyway. The password is Matterhorn."

"Keep it. You'll need it, I'm sure."

Pierre's gray hair blew across his temples. His eyes darted. His hands trembled while his unsteady feet pressed him against the canyon wall.

Kylee reached into her pack for a bag of chalk. She dusted her hands and studied the rocks by her feet and by her face. "That's the one."

She jumped and landed hard a rock that seemed ready for flight. As the ledge crumbled beneath her, she grabbed for the sliver of stone above and swung to safe side of the path. Like billiard balls across a granite slab, the ledge tumbled into an eye-stinging cloud of dust and debris.

"You lost your mind!" Pierre shouted. "I'll never get out." His words seemed distorted by his accent and agitation, but his message stayed clear.

"Apologies to you, Pierre. I didn't think that would happen."

Pierre shuddered.

"Oh, and double apologies," Kylee said. "The fire—actually, *your* fire—might be coming our way after all. Wow. And with that brush below; if the flames don't get ya, the smoke sure will."

"*Mon Dieu*, I'll do anything; just get me across." He reached for Kylee but came nowhere close. He flailed his arms for a better grip on the wall, but the rocks crumbled in his hand. He stood in place with nothing but a fistful of gravel and a face overwhelmed with fear.

"Motivation, Pierre. Give me some incentive. I *might* give you a hand."

"Tell me what you want!"

"Okay, then we'll start with the easy questions." Kylee leaned against a boulder and tried to coax Pierre into a meaningful dialogue. She realized that the questions might be easy, but the answers might be intolerable. Nevertheless, she began the interview.

"First, tell me about your remote control phone. I already know you brought down the Mojave flights. I want to know how."

Pierre shivered. He shuffled his feet. He jerked his head but kept his mouth closed.

Kylee carefully stepped around a bend and disappeared from sight. She watched him discreetly from above.

Pierre's eyes grew wide, and suddenly his lips began to move. "Your planes; it's a wonder more of them don't crash. All we did was push on a small defect. The plane crashed by itself."

"How do you mean?" Kylee asked as she poked her head into view.

"That's what happens when the computer flies the plane. A small problem becomes a big nightmare."

"A small problem—compounded by a cell phone."

"Especially by a cell phone."

"Especially one with high power and in a plane with bad software."

"Yes," Pierre said, faltering. "Like Fred Mott's phone. Like Bob Aukram's phone. Is that what you want to hear?"

"But why Fred? What'd he ever do to you?"

Pierre stopped to catch his breath and wipe the sweat from his brow. He glanced at Kylee then stared at the sky. "Nothing at first. He was in favor of the merger. It was a smart move, he thought. Then he did what you call 'due diligence.' That was a mistake. If you look for trouble, sure enough, you will find it. Yes, Trudeau does have problems; many more than Dove. And *Monsieur* Mott, he found them all."

"The hard way, I bet. You didn't volunteer a word."

"Some workers are loyal," Pierre said. "Some are not."

"Fred wanted to cancel the merger, right? But you and Mireille thought that Dove was a pretty good deal; so you sweetened the pot for Fred."

"A signing bonus," Pierre said.

"A half-million-dollar bribe."

"We almost had him."

"I doubt it," Kylee said. "He was probably flying back to return the cash."

"Yes," Pierre said, "No merger, he told us. The deal was off."

"Then you brought him down in the middle of nowhere. Except he lived; at least long enough to get rid of the cash. My guess; he didn't want to be caught with it—dead or alive. Real bribe or not; he couldn't take the chance. So he threw it away; suitcase and all. Only problem was; he slipped and died."

Pierre lowered his head.

"Now, tell me this." Kylee pushed a strand of hair from her face. "Where's the money?"

"You mean from the mountain?"

"You know what I mean. A half-million dollars all over the snow. You know I saw it."

"We had hoped to be the first on site," Pierre said. "But apparently, you were faster. Either way, that was too much money to lose. We went later and picked up what we could."

"And spread around some worthless notes."

"We had no choice."

Kylee kicked a loose rock off the cliff. As it bounced down the ravine, she leaned closer to Pierre. "And what about Bob Aukram? What was your choice there?"

"Fred saw our technical problems. Bob—the financial ones."

"Trudeau was not the superstar everyone thought."

"We could not hide our losses forever," Pierre said. "Ultimately, the numbers catch up. That's why we needed control of Dove. You had the product; we needed the sales. It was our last chance for a turnaround."

"And with Mireille in control, the American money flows directly to Trudeau."

"We hoped to get fifty-one-percent."

"Then you fire the Dove accountants and VPs. Ultimately, your secret remains safe."

"That's business."

"Not in my world," Kylee said. "Especially when you wrap it up by framing Grier and Sullivan. You did frame them, yes?"

"Frame?"

"*Un truc*," she said. "Or trick, as we would say. They take the blame for your sabotage."

"They were suspicious long before you," Pierre said, subdued. "So they followed us to the Mojave Air hanger. I installed a defect, but they couldn't find it."

"And when they left the hanger?"

"Mireille flashed the headlights of her car. Her timing was excellent, as always. The police saw them and never saw us."

"And Waterman. Let me guess; he's nothing more than a stooge. You used him like you used us."

"Apparently, you know everything. *Now* will you help me across, *s'il vous plait?*"

"One more question."

"What?" Pierre said.

"Paul's heart attack; was that Mireille trying to kill the old man or what?"

"Sorry to disappoint. She actually did save his life. She is not as evil as you say."

"I imagine a crocodile can miss once in a while." Kylee disappeared around the bend.

Again, Pierre began to scream. "I gave you what you asked! Don't leave me! Please!" His panicked eyes darted until he was hit in the face with a rope from above.

"Wrap it around your chest and tie a good knot," she told him. She wrapped the other end around a sturdy tree above. "Now jump!" she yelled. "Jump!"

Pierre did. He faltered as the rescue rope stretched to accommodate his full girth. Clumsy and on the verge of panic, he scrambled back to the wider path and solid ground.

"Remove the rope," she told him. "And take small steps."

Pierre fumbled with his shaking hands and sweating palms to undo the knots. He baby stepped his way to less intimidating ground. Once there, he begged for a respite, but Kylee would have no part of it. She impatiently coaxed him along the path that led to the real short cut. Time was running short.

As expected, the new trail was flat and wide. Kylee prodded Pierre forward until she got a view of the smoke-filtered sky that was away from trees. For sure, the satellite signal would come in strong.

"All right, Pierre," she said, motioning at his phone. "Here's the payoff. You pass me the phone, I'll make one call; 911. Then we both walk to the cabin. We still need tools, and we still need to help Russell."

"Uphill?" Pierre groaned, looking that way. He breathed heavily and leaned against a rock. No doubt, he was sorry to be away from the office. No doubt, he would've preferred a nap. "We had a deal," he said. "The phone for my freedom."

She laughed. "That deal has long expired. All I want now is a shovel, an axe, and a saw. You and me; we'll give Russell *his* freedom—with the paramedics and without your whining. So if you don't mind, Pierre; hand it over. And if I see 'Enter Password,' I'm not going to like it."

Pierre brushed the gray hairs from his forehead. He gazed down to his feet then up to the phone in his hand. He panted like a French bulldog and seemed on the verge of collapse. He lifted the phone, stared at it, and slowly entered a code.

"No password," he said, showing Kylee. "As you can see; I gave you what you wanted."

He flipped his hand then, with his usual condescension and disrespect, he flipped the phone to the grass behind Kylee. She expected a trap—a grab for the gun—or worse; another sad attempt at a bargain. She didn't expect him to take off like a scared rabbit. But he did.

Like a sprinter with a second wind, he dashed for the nearest trees. Any leftover energy went straight to his feet. He stumbled, got up, and kept running. He didn't bother to dodge her aim.

Kylee was amazed that anything that old could move that fast. She raised her sight to the middle of his back, eager to shoot. Then she became distracted by a beeping at her feet. She looked down and let out a sigh; better to make a call than waste a bullet.

"Coward! I don't need you anyway." She picked up the phone. To her relief, the display did not ask for a password. But her relief turned to anger when she saw Low Battery flash on the screen.

In a flash of insight, Kylee had figured out his ploy. All this while, he had kept the phone on. GPS tracking, making a call, or playing a game; at this point, it didn't matter. He had drained the battery. No doubt, that was part of his ultimate plan.

Kylee figured she had enough charge for one call, perhaps two at the most. She punched in 911. When she hit Send, the phone beeped then went blank. She tried again, but the screen stayed blank. At this point, one call would have been a luxury.

Now, she had a choice. She could take the phone to Russell— dead battery and all—and hope that somehow he could recharge it. More likely, he would yell at her again for handing over a useless device. Or; she could shove the phone into her pocket and carry on with her original plan—get an axe from her shed and chop through the tree. Or; she could toss the phone far into the woods and sit down and cry.

Kylee settled on a compromise; she cursed at herself and cursed at Pierre. Then she dropped the phone to the dirt; now that device was about as useful as most of her ideas. She cried as she trudged to the shed on her property. At this point, it was a short walk up a gentle hill. At this point, she wondered why she didn't go there first. Why did she ever bother with Pierre? Why couldn't she get her priorities straight?

Despite the headaches and pounding self-regret, she marched ahead, slowly but steadily. Soon enough, she got to her property and felt a little better—at least for a moment. She went to her shed and got her shovel, saw, and axe. Heavy tools, but thankfully, the return trip was downhill all the way. She cradled the tools the best she could and began the walk. Then she sniffed the air. Unavoidably, she frowned.

She went to her porch for the best view of the terrain around her. Suddenly, her optimism dropped faster than a fir tree with beetle disease. With a clear view, she got a good look at the fire. As a bluff, she had told Pierre that the fire was coming fast. Now, as she studied the smoke and flames, she realized that it was no bluff. She was truly surrounded by a conflagration; a scary sight like she had never seen before.

The wind shifted, and thick fingers of gray and black smoke drifted her way. Her heart sank when she looked at her cabin of twelve years; her sanctuary, her dream home in the wilderness. How much longer before the fire took it away and destroyed all of her dreams?

She stared across the hill toward Pierre's burning hideaway. Now it was obvious; the glint of metal from the eavesdropping antenna, the outline of a microwave tower disguised as a Ponderosa pine. She felt stupid, violated, and totally enraged. She dropped her tools and raised the gun skyward. She squeezed off the last rounds. The shots echoed like sobbing cries.

Then she felt like a fool for being thoughtless. She sat on the ground and lowered her head. *Russell must've heard those shots. He was worried before and now this. How can it get any worse?*

She looked up and realized that it could easily get worse. She knew that the spread of fires in southern California was often measured in acres per minute. And she knew that the fire could easily cut off access to Russell—from all directions, from all help. And she knew that it would be a miracle if the smoke stayed away from Russell—or her.

Her heart ached when the realization sunk in. How could she get to Russell before the fire swept through the valley? How could she hike a mile through heavy brush or walk three miles of open road? How could she carry heavy tools, chop through a stubborn tree, and get Russell to the hospital? There had to be a better way; Russell's life depended on it. Forget Pierre. Forget Fred and Bob. Forget everyone else. Saving Russell became her sole mission.

Her head hurt from the lack of choices. This direction or that, inside her cabin or out; no matter where she looked, she found no hint of what to do. She felt as though her feet were glued in place.

Then she trudged along the driveway, glanced to the side, and stared for the longest while. Her heart raced, and her throat went dry as the Santa Ana wind. She gazed curiously at the tarp covered outline of Evan's fan-jet. Somehow, Daz had neglected to retrieve it. Somehow, Evan had neglected to mention it. It sat there exactly as he had left it. Kylee suddenly had the power to get things done.

"I might kill myself trying." She shivered. "But today, I'm going to fly."

Chapter *25*

KYLEE HAD proudly finished one flying lesson in her life, but unfortunately, during the lesson, she had never left the ground. According to Evan, his fan-jet was "so simple, a child could fly it."

Kylee was not a child, but she did understand the concept of simple. And with the fast spreading fire, hiking to Russell was simply not an option. She put her faith in flying.

She yanked off the tarp and thanked Evan for setting the lock to her birth date. Next step; she lifted the gull wing door and stared inside. With the engines off and lights out, nothing seemed intimidating. It seemed inviting, much like the inside of an old Jeep.

With a growing confidence, she moved ahead with her plan. She dropped the shovel, saw, and axe onto the back seat. Then she took the pilot's position. When she settled in and closed the door, she took a deep breath, then another. The new-plane scent had long-ago vanished.

So far, so good. When she switched on the power, the monitors jumped to life. The red screens and warning lights seemed overwhelming, but soon enough, everything turned green. The main display lit up with a large Welcome Aboard.

Just like I remember. Kylee scanned left and right then hesitantly pressed Engine Start. She regretted that she never asked Evan for Lesson 2. But as the engines began to whir, she realized that Evan didn't lie; nothing seemed confusing, nothing seemed intimidating … yet.

Almost immediately, the noise settled down, and the monitor displayed a large green Ready for Liftoff.

"Great. So am I."

She felt secure as the aircraft rested patiently on the firm ground. The engines barely whispered, and the plush leather seat cradled her with a welcomed coolness on this warm October day. She moved her hand to the control stick. The labels seemed intuitive; left, right, forward, reverse. The thumb lever on the stick; up, down. What could be easier than that?

She looked across the hill as the flames on the far ridge reached high into the noon sky. The wind was picking up, and the fire was pushing downslope—toward Russell and Mathieu. She didn't try to guess the speed and direction of the blaze. Between the wind and the rugged hills, all directions seemed equally at risk.

The interim safety of the cabin was only an illusion. Smoke and flames had already cut off the main access road. Firefighters couldn't get in, and Kylee could not drive out. The isolation was complete. The danger was real.

"Sorry, Russell. This contraption is our only hope."

With lingering trepidation, she pushed her thumb up on the Up lever. A slight increase in the fan speed and noise, but still, she remained on the ground. She pushed more, and suddenly she floated like a hummingbird. A sense of joy swept through her as she easily mastered the sophisticated flying machine. Barely knee-high off the ground, but she felt like an eagle soaring across the canyons and through the clouds.

"I got it!" she yelped. She eased the control stick forward and twisted it to aim away from her cabin. Her exhilaration was short-lived as the fan-jet picked up a gust of wind and drifted to the stack of firewood.

"Where's the steering wheel?" She grumbled as the fan-jet knocked over logs. She twisted the control a bit too far. The machine lurched back and spun, cracking a wood post on the deck.

"Not a problem," she told herself as dust swirled and blocked her view. "But Evan better fix his machine."

She pushed the joystick and drifted forward—toward Russell and the fire. She broke out of the dust cloud and flew higher; almost above her cabin. Now she felt certain; she had a clear path to the lake and Russell. Help was on the way.

"I can do this," she kept repeating.

She flew above the gravel driveway then blinked when she saw a totally welcome sight. She had to squint to be sure, but that was definitely Daz riding up on his Harley. She sighed in relief and pushed down on the control. More help was always welcomed.

Daz skidded to a halt, jumped off the motorcycle, and threw down his helmet. He raced—waving his arms—and put himself in front of the fan-jet.

Kylee pulled back on the lever to avoid hitting him in the chest. But the fan-jet became sluggish. Daz dodged to the side, and Kylee finally stopped; but not before she eased into the bike and knocked it flat to the ground. She pushed more, and mercifully, the aircraft came to a gentle rest on the dry grass. As Daz ran closer, she shut down the engine and pushed open the door.

"Daz, thank God. I need your help."

"What, to fly this thing?" He leaned his head into the cockpit and scanned the instrument panel.

"No," she said, stepping from the cockpit. She hugged Daz and then pointed at the advancing fire. "Russell is trapped. He's stuck under a tree. I got an axe. I got a shovel. We can dig him out."

"Understood." Daz peeked at the back seat then swung his gaze toward the blazing ridge.

"You must've passed him," Kylee said. "He's right by the road."

"Sorry, I took a detour." Daz waved his hand at the downwind smoke and to the ridge he had just climbed.

From his raspy voice and red eyes, Kylee guessed that he had passed through plenty of that smoke.

"And let me tell ya, this Harley is not a dirt bike." He struggled to upright his touring machine. "How about we team up? I'll fly and you tell us where."

"Have you had lessons?" Kylee asked, but she already knew the answer.

"You forget; I taught your husband how to fly." Daz tapped the door handle. "And if I would've had the combination, this fan-jet would not be here."

"Okay. Then let's go."

Kylee yanked on the right door and hopped in. She buckled up and slammed the door closed.

"To the lake," she waved, "then left at the point."

Daz obeyed and flew the aircraft high, straight, and fast as if he had written the flight manual himself; which, of course, he did.

"I understand you had some problems," Daz said as lowered the fan-jet at the lake's edge. A light spray layered the windshield. He found and activated the wiper.

"Who told you?" she asked.

"Paul called. He said you might need some backup."

"Paul? What's he know about this?"

"I'll explain later," Daz said. "With Russell when we free him."

"Paul's right about the trouble. You wouldn't believe the story I got from Pierre."

Kylee searched between the trees along the road, and soon enough, she pointed and said, "There's Russell! Oh, and by the way, I got Mathieu tied up."

Daz slowed the fan-jet to a hover then lowered it to the road, all the while staring at Russell and the tree. "Sweet Jesus, what happened?" He climbed out and slid his way down to Russell.

"A small accident," Kylee said, grabbing the axe from the back seat. "Russell is fine, but the tree is a little stubborn. He's pinned on a rock. I can dig around it, if you can—"

"Chop off his legs," Daz said. "I got it."

"What, no!" Kylee screamed. "This is for the tree."

"What's going on?" Russell bellowed.

While Kylee hustled her tools to the tree, Daz stood like a statue by the fan-jet. He kept his hands on his hips and stared ahead, apparently dumbfounded. Kylee didn't have time to explain.

"Come on, Daz, the fire's not going to wait; and neither should we."

"Too slow." He held her back by the sleeve. "Let's try another approach."

He circled the log then made his way to the front of the Jeep. After giving Russell a comforting pat on the shoulder, he yanked at the winch cable. He studied it and then borrowed the axe. He whacked at the winch end of the cable, severing it. He kept the other end looped around the tree. Finally—as if he knew what he was doing—he tied the free end to the landing gear of the fan-jet.

Now Kylee understood. She put the shovel aside and cleared a path for the winch cable. She agreed that Daz had a pretty good idea.

"Now you pull the boy while I lift." Daz went to the pilot's seat and spun up the engines. With the door open and Daz leaning out, he gained altitude until the cable was taut.

Both the tree and Russell moaned with an odd noise. Dust and debris flew in odd spirals. Mathieu shielded his eyes but stayed curious.

Kylee spun her hand in the air, and Daz increased power. When she saw daylight between Russell and the tree, she pulled on his shoulders. With a renewed strength, Russell dug his foot into the earth and pushed himself clear of the log. Kylee gave a thumbs-up to Daz.

He acknowledged, and as he cut power, the log settled to the ground.

"Finally I can see the sky!" Russell nearly cried. He propped himself up on his elbows.

"Are you all right?" Kylee asked.

"My right leg's asleep, but otherwise, I'm fine." He looked up at Daz.

"Lucky you still have it. If Daz had his way—"

"No luck about Daz." Russell nodded. "My plan actually worked."

"What plan?"

"Playing the same game. Remember the wiretap on Pierre's phone? All I did was route his calls to Paul's phone. Since we left, he's heard everything. If there was one man who could help us; that would have to be Paul."

"That explains the dead battery on Pierre's phone. But I'm sure Paul's heard enough ... probably more than enough."

"So where is he?"

"Pierre? Don't worry about him. He might be faster than the fire, but there's no way he's going to outrun me. I'll be back, and

I'll get him. That's a promise ... Hey, Mathieu, if it works out, you and Pierre may get the same cell. And I don't mean phone."

"He's not our problem now," Daz said. "We've got the fire to worry about. I called Forest Service while I still had a signal. I told them about the buildings over there." He pointed toward the cabin.

"Thank you."

"We've got enough fuel to get home." Daz nodded at the fan-jet. "So what do you say; let's load up and take off. Time on the ground is time wasted."

"We'll get Russell to the hospital," Kylee said. "I'll check him in myself."

"Like I said—I'm fine." Russell ran his palm behind his back. "All I need is a hot pack and massage."

"A cold pack and X-ray is what you need."

"How about this guy?" Daz nodded at Mathieu. "You want to leave him here?"

"What? No way!" Mathieu screamed. "Pierre's the one you want. I swear; he lied to us. We didn't want no part of this."

Kylee stood face to face with Mathieu. "Hey, Russell, did you record that call between Mathieu and Pierre?"

"You mean, when they spoke French? When they shot at us and ran us off the road?"

"That's the one." Kylee grinned. "What do you say we have it translated?"

"Not a problem."

"I want a lawyer." Mathieu moaned.

"Yeah, we'll get you all right." Kylee wagged her finger at him. "Just like Pierre, Mireille, and Claire. We'll get them all."

"Claire?" Daz asked. "What about her?"

"The French mole; that's what she is. Mireille's personal gopher. I should've known."

"You're off base, hon. Claire's one of us. I guarantee it."

"We'll see about that. I have a hunch we're about to find who our real friends are."

"But not around here." Daz urged them to the fan-jet. "Once we clear the hills and smoke, I'll call the sheriff."

"Sounds fine by me." Kylee kept the ropes on Mathicu but freed him from the Jeep bumper. She helped him and Russell into the fan-jet as Daz struggled with the cable beneath.

"Jammed," he said. "Stuck tight around the landing gear."

"Just wrap it tight and let's fly," Kylee said. "You want me to take us up?"

"Save it for Sunday. For now, sit back and take notes. We'll be at Dove before you know it." Daz unhooked the log end of the cable then, as Kylee suggested, wrapped it around the landing gear. He returned to the pilot's seat.

Kylee settled into the right seat. She stared outside as they climbed above the trees and smoke. With an overall view of the fire, she felt more confident that her cabin was safe, but her Jeep, already crushed beyond repair, seemed to be in a direct path of the flames. It was a small sacrifice for a job well done.

Finally, she began to relax. Her bad day had quickly turned around. She found a Taylor Swift CD in a side pocket and pushed it into the player. She slipped on a headset as the first track began to play. Her Fred and Bob nightmares would soon vanish, and now with the case closed—or nearly closed—she could coast home, floating on a cloud of pure adrenaline. She closed her eyes and figured on keeping them closed until they landed at Dove. A short flight, but First Class all the way. She felt great.

But as the third track of the CD faded, she slid her eyes open. Slowly, her long-overdue contentment dissolved into waves of apprehension. She expected to see the long Dove runway and a gradual descent to the hangers. But when she looked below, it was obvious they were still above the foothills, circling at the same altitude. She looked at Daz.

Daz punched numbers into the GPS. He called air traffic control and shook his head. He seemed more confused than ever. He dialed in one radio frequency after another, checked his charts, checked his numbers, and then scratched his head.

"I thought you knew how to fly this," Kylee said. "At a hundred miles an hour, we're going nowhere fast."

"Bedlam," Daz muttered into his headset. "Absolute chaos."

"What is?"

"All frequencies are totally jammed. I can't get a word in. We've got a flight restriction and a whole lot of panic. Something's going on."

"It's got to be the fire," Kylee said. "It's spreading fast. You've got Forestry planes, rescue planes—"

"Listen to this." Daz switched on the speaker. Suddenly, strange voices spoke incredibly fast with jargon only Daz could understand.

"American Seven-forty-two, clearance amended. Vectors to San Diego. Stand by."

"American Seven-forty-two, Roger."

"Qantas Seventeen Heavy, destination amended. Turn left, heading three-four-zero. Vectors to Dove Field."

"Left, three-four-zero. Qantas Seventeen Heavy."

Daz let go of the control stick and raised his palms. "Why are they sending planes to Dove?"

Russell leaned forward. "Evan's coming in today, right? Paris to LA. That flight arrives about now."

"I haven't talked to Evan for almost a week," Kylee said. "Call Mireille. I bet she knows the flight."

"It doesn't make sense," Daz said. "No flights to LA?" He pulled out his phone and tried to make a call. "All circuits busy? Now, I'm worried."

"All we need is the sheriff to pick up Mathieu." Kylee glanced behind. "That can wait till we land."

Daz eased forward on the control lever and pushed the speed another forty knots. "I just got clearance to land at Dove, but I still don't know what's going on."

"Clearance?" Russell laughed. "You don't need a clearance to land at Dove."

"Apparently, now we do. All flights around LA—LAX, Long Beach, Van Nuys—there's not a single landing. They're all diverted. The only open fields are Palmdale and San Diego. And Dove too, it seems."

"We're not a terminal," Kylee said. "What are we going to do with the passengers?"

"And where's Everest?" Daz wondered as the Dove field came into view. "It was there when I left. I spend two hours in Riverside and now this."

"Call my lawyer," Mathieu said. "I want him there when we land."

"A fabricator with a lawyer." Kylee laughed. "Just how connected are you?"

"Forget him," Daz said. "What happened to LA?"

Russell grabbed Daz's phone and confirmed, "Still no service."

"What are those—747s?" Kylee pointed at a row of wide-body jets parked next to the Dove runway.

"City buses, too, from the looks of it." Russell squinted at the line of buses that rolled up next to the airliners.

"I don't like the looks of this." Daz lowered the fan-jet for a vertical landing near the fuel station.

As he shut down the engines and filled the fuel tank, Kylee helped Mathieu from the rear seat.

Russell scanned the parking ramp for a familiar face but saw none. "It's a zoo," he said. "A freakin' zoo."

From a distance, a faint voice called, "Torello!"

Russell spun around and stared at a man waving from between the city buses.

Kylee looked close. It was Evan all right, dressed in his traveling khaki slacks and a light-blue shirt, briefcase in hand. He picked up his pace and jogged. In moments, he joined the group.

"I looked up and I couldn't believe it." Evan panted, trying to catch his breath. "I thought you said it was stuck at the cabin." He turned to Daz.

"Don't look at me," Daz said. "Your wife is the one who got us airborne."

"What?"

Kylee flipped off the fuel pump and hung up the nozzle. "It's not that hard," she told him. "The hover control drifts to the left. But I'm sure that's a small fix."

Evan shook his head. "I've been out of the country way too long."

"What's the deal with LA?" Daz asked.

"Don't know," Evan said. "I couldn't speak to the captain. I'm sure I heard the same as you; no flights to LA."

"That's weird." Daz closed and locked the fan-jet door. "Flight service should know. Let's get them on the line." He turned toward the Cottonwood building and urged the others to follow.

Evan looked at Mathieu's hands. "What's with the handcuffs?"

"Long story," Kylee said. "By the way, where is Mireille?"

"Another long story—that she needs to finish." Evan rapped on his briefcase.

"I'm sure she does."

As they made their way to the Cottonwood lobby, another 747 flew overhead.

"Strangest thing I ever saw," Daz said, shielding his eyes from the sun.

Evan agreed. "You got no storms, no fog; LAX should be open."

"Could be fires," Kylee said. "Smoke covers a lot of ground."

"Maybe," Evan said. He motioned to an airline pilot. "What's the deal with LAX?"

"All I got was 'airport emergency' and vectors to Dove."

"I'm the president of Dove. What kind of emergency?"

"Airport emergency." The pilot turned his head and quickly walked to a waiting bus.

Evan turned to Daz. "As usual, no one tells me anything." He picked up the pace and looked around, but other Dove workers were nowhere near.

Their confusion quickly dissolved as they passed through the Cottonwood entrance. No wonder the Dove workers were missing. A large crowd—including maintenance men, sales reps, assembly workers, and gardeners—had gathered around a small-screen TV.

Kylee studied the shocked and silent faces of the group. She knew this would be a moment-in-time memory. She, Evan, and Daz pushed their way forward and became one of the stunned faces. They stared at the unfolding scene on the TV monitor.

"We understand there is only a pilot and co-pilot," a woman's voice blared from the TV. Kylee recognized her as a Los Angeles news anchor, Sharon Nguyen. Sharon spoke from her desk at the newsroom.

"No passengers," a male reporter said as they cut to a view of him at an LAX ticket counter. "But we're still trying to confirm."

"Where were they headed, Gene?"

"Again, this was not a scheduled airline. But I understand the flight was for Paris."

"LA to Paris. That's a jumbo jet route."

Gene adjusted his earpiece. "I'm told the flight is not from Los Angeles. But so far, we don't know the origin."

"What can you tell us about the crew? I understand one is a foreign national."

"Again, no confirmation. And no one, as of now, has ruled out terrorism."

The TV showed a close-up of Sharon. "Joe Paramis in Chopper Five is back in range. We'll switch to him now."

The TV kept on Sharon as she called to the helicopter. "Joe, can you tell us where the jet is?" No response. She looked to her left. "Okay, we're still trying to get video. Chopper Five, can you hear us?"

Suddenly, the static cleared. Joe's voice came through clear and strong. "We're above Glendale. You can see—"

"Hold on, Joe. The video's coming through."

Almost in unison, everyone in the Dove lobby let out a gasp. They stared at the shaky, grainy image of Everest filling the screen and zooming over the suburbs of LA.

"We're at three thousand feet," Joe said. "But I'll tell ya, this jumbo is huge. It looks a whole lot lower than it really is."

"Can you see the crew?" Sharon asked.

"We're trying to move in. Look at the size of that. The pilot's window is barely a dot."

"How about a close-up?"

The helicopter camera zoomed in, but the image shook violently and disappeared from the screen.

"Too close," Sharon said.

"We're flying ninety knots. We can only keep up for a short time."

"How about radio contact? Can you talk to the crew?"

"We can listen in," Joe said, "but they're not saying much. Traffic control; that's where the action is. They're clearing a path for the Dove plane."

"I understand the following airports have been cleared of air traffic; Van Nuys, Long Beach, Burbank, Ontario. And LAX, of course. Even the smaller airports; Santa Monica and Compton— closed until otherwise told."

"A lot of those planes are going to the Dove field itself."

"We are trying to contact Dove Air," Sharon said. "What we do have is this clip from LAX."

The TV switched to another image of a Trudeau helicopter parked somewhere on the tarmac. As a crowd of reporters parted, Mireille's face appeared on screen. She seemed totally cool and professional, dressed in her black, Chanel pantsuit and delicate white blouse. It seemed as though this was simply another day on the job. No doubt, she had flown the helicopter herself and arranged a press conference by the Trudeau logo.

"What we have is a change of plan," Mireille said to the camera. "The FAA agrees to it. And with their blessing, we are moving ahead."

"What was your plan?" a reporter called out.

"Style," she said. "And lots of it. We want to show Los Angeles the first jet of a new generation. A front row seat as it were."

"What went wrong?"

"Nothing's wrong. We disagree with the FAA on how long the demo should last."

"You're saying this is part of your show?"

"Keep watching. The Trudeau 2100 is one incredible flying machine."

After that last remark, Claire walked on-screen and tugged at Mireille's elbow. The camera followed them both until they disappeared into an LAX shuttle van.

"Trudeau 2100?" Evan muttered. "How did she come up with that name?"

"Don't argue," Daz said. "You want the name of Dove linked to this?"

"Good point." Evan faced the lobby exit. "And the longer we sit here, the more we can lose. Daz, do me a favor; get us a priority flight to LA. Russell; grab your files and a laptop. Kylee—"

"I'm going with you," she said.

"Pardon?"

"Claire and I have some unfinished business."

"I was going to have you call the sheriff for Mathieu and *then* come along."

"I can do both," she said.

"I imagine you can," Evan said. "And then some."

After a few calls and a quick ride in a borrowed golf cart, they arrived again at the fan-jet. Russell took the back seat, placing his files and paperwork on the rear ledge. Daz grabbed the pilot's seat and buckled up.

As Evan flipped open the right door for Kylee, he said, "So, Daz said you know how to fly this aircraft."

"I had a choice of walking or flying. I had the combination, and I thought; what's the worst that could happen? Actually, it was easier than you said. Up, down, left, right. Yeah, nothing to it." She tapped the cowling. "You call this the Mac-1?"

"It's on the paperwork."

"I like it."

Evan smiled as Kylee took a seat next to Russell.

Russell patted his thick binder of files and folders. "Every knob and every switch on Everest is described in this book or on these drives." He showed titles like; Diagnostics, Navigation, Communication.

Daz glanced back. "How about disasters; you got a binder for that?"

Russell lowered his eyes.

"I've got clearance for LA," Daz said to Evan. "After that, it's up to you."

"And I've got circuits busy." Evan pounded the keys on his phone. "I can't get one bureaucrat on the line. No text, no voice. Nothing."

"Keep trying," Kylee said.

Daz switched on the engines then took off to the southwest. He eased the fan-jet into a cruise above the mountains. Moments later, Los Angeles came into view, and his frustration grew. "The controllers told me nothing except; 'God help us all.' "

Evan gave up on using the phone. He spun the radio knobs on the console and tried to contact Flight Service for a hint of what was happening.

"Gridlock," Daz said. "We have too many planes and not enough channels."

Evan jabbed his finger on the airspeed display. "Let's juice up the speed, huh, Daz? Raise the gear and get us moving."

"Sorry, bud. We got a cable wrapped around it."

"Cable? What cable?"

"We'll discuss it later," Daz said.

Evan looked over his shoulder at Kylee.

"Yes, later," she said. She swung her head left. "How are you feeling, Russell?"

He looked at her over the top of his glasses. "Much better." He went back to his books.

After a few more calls, Daz received a priority clearance to land at LAX. He set the fan-jet down by a side gate. "Expect more chaos," he said. "And a lot of yelling."

"No doubt," Evan replied.

As Kylee and the others stepped onto the tarmac, a security agent tugged at Evan's elbow. He aimed him toward a glass door and a mob of people behind it.

"I've told them who you are," the agent said. "But there will be no press conference until we sort this out."

Kylee cringed. With a crush of reporters and camera crews pressed against the door, she desperately hoped for another way in. Apparently, they had no choice. The agent moved forward, yanked open the door, and motioned for the others to follow. The crowd barely parted. Evan wrapped his arm around Kylee's shoulder and burrowed his way through as quickly and politely as possible. Daz and Russell followed.

"What's your next step, Mr. McKenna?" a reporter called out.

"What?" Evan said.

"Are you in touch with the Air Force?" another asked.

"How many crew on board?"

"Is the pilot armed?"

Evan's eyes darted from one interrogator to the next. "Please, no questions until we get some answers ourselves."

"You're the president of Dove," a man said. "If you don't have the answers; who does?"

Evan lowered his head but charged forward. He led Russell, Daz, and Kylee into an improvised briefing room.

Immediately, Kylee saw the catalyst of those nagging media questions. Mireille stood in the center of a circle of city, county, state, and federal officials. She was outwardly calm as ever, seemingly more eager to make a fashion statement than a real, conciliatory explanation. In her low cut heels, her striking black and white pant suit, and her diamond studded earrings, she seemed more the spokesmodel than the vice-president of a major corporation.

Evan raised his voice. "If there's a problem with Everest, how come we're not in the tower?"

"I wouldn't call it a problem," Mireille said. "At least not yet. But I won't argue the point. If we overreact, let's do it for safety. That's why we're here. We have a minor situation. Let's not make it worse."

"Exactly what is the situation?" Evan asked.

"There appears to be a small lapse in the heading control."

A white-haired man with a 'Manager' tag eased forward. "I'm Ferris," he said without offering a handshake. He turned toward an east facing window. "That small lapse has had your plane circling Los Angeles for the past hour. From Glendale; to Inglewood; to East LA; and back to Glendale. The pilot's no help. We asked him what happened, and he said that the computer froze. He's stuck in a left hand turn."

"It figures," Evan grumbled. "Mireille, if you don't mind; a few words." He gestured at a neighboring room.

"Very well." Mireille leaned close to Claire. "Claire, you know what we talked about."

"I'll take care of it," Claire said. Then she disappeared to the corridor.

"This won't take long," Evan said to the assembled officials. He led Mireille, Kylee, Russell, and Daz to the private office.

As soon as Kylee latched the door, Mireille turned to Evan. "Where have you been? I've been calling you since Saturday. Nobody's seen you. Nobody's heard from you."

"You know where I've been; in France, doing your job."

"I don't know what you're talking about. My job is to get orders. And I got them. Three customers; each for a dozen planes if we make the LA to Paris run before the seventh."

"That's tomorrow."

"Yes, and if you had read your email, you would've stayed in Paris."

"Why is that?"

"*Mon Dieu*, Evan. I send the plane off in LA. You receive it in Paris. That was the plan. The media knows it. Everyone knows it. Except you, it seems."

"I'll tell you what I know; Everest should be grounded. We have so many problems, I don't know if we can fly it a year from now. What were you thinking? A test flight over LA; how'd they ever approve that? Let me guess. You went to the FAA in person. A little smile and lots of leg; they couldn't resist."

"I agree that it is not a perfect flight. Nevertheless, we are ready."

"Ready for what? You've got two minor league pilots, a busted computer, and a wide-body jet circling LA. That's a plan for disaster and you know it."

"Ken is the pilot," she said. "He's taken responsibility."

"What are you talking about?"

"He'll say he's been despondent, distracted. He pushed the wrong button and made a bad choice."

"You're serious," Evan said.

"Don't worry, he'll be compensated."

"Pay him off for taking a fall? What kind of answer is that?"

"It'll work," Mireille said, "if we stay calm."

"Fine, you do that." Evan placed his hand on the office door. "But for me, I got a plane to fly straight."

He pushed the door open. Immediately, Ferris rushed closer. "What are we doing here?" Evan asked him. "The tower is where we ought to be."

Ferris—phone in hand—ordered a shuttle bus on the double. Again, Kylee and the others made their way through a mob of reporters. They scrambled to a nearby exit and impatiently waited for the shuttle. Mireille remained behind, saying she could work the issues better from where she stood. Evan refused to argue.

As the bus drew close, Kylee saw Claire in the shadows of a catering truck. Claire quickly slid her phone into her purse and quietly made her way to an employee entrance to the terminal.

Kylee caught up. "I thought we were friends," she told Claire. "But I guess I was wrong."

"Kylee, why would you say that? We *are* friends."

"We have lunch together, we shop together, and we talk about men. But lie to me or stab me in the back; that's where I draw the line."

"I've never lied to you. I swear!"

"Give it up, Claire. I know your game. I know exactly what you and Mireille did. You're not going to get away with it."

"Get away with what, Kylee? You're not making sense."

"You never told me you worked at Teteblanche."

"You never asked."

"Well, I'm not going to ask *how* you got that job or *how* you got this job. You've been loyal to Pierre from the start. Mireille and him are two of a kind; I know that. But you—you are a disappointment."

"I spent three summers in France. I saw Pierre once in a while; that's it. He liked my work so he got me that job. And he got me this job. What difference does it make?"

"It makes a big difference; especially if we talk about murder."

"You're scaring me, Kylee. I know how you feel about Fred, but keep me out of this. If you think you got a murder, go to the cops." Claire lowered her voice. "You've been on this since we met. Look at yourself; you're over the edge."

"You know, Pierre's already confessed."

"To what, trying to take over Dove? That's hardly news. Why do you think they're flying today?"

Kylee was taken aback. This was one piece of the puzzle she had overlooked. "Okay, tell me. Why are they flying today?"

"The report was leaked."

"What report?"

"The Gibraltar memo from five years ago. John Waterman got hold of it and gave it to the press. He said that the crew was fine, and there was no pilot error. He said the engine failed; both in Fred's plane and Bob's plane."

"I can tell you right now; the planes were fine."

"It doesn't matter," Claire said. "Dove stock dropped to the cellar. If we have to recall a thousand planes, that'll cost a fortune."

"And if Mireille gets an Everest order now—"

"Her stock goes up. And sure enough, her next step; take over Dove. That was Paul's agreement. That was Paul's mistake. What can I say; Mireille finds the desperate men."

"Well, Evan is *not* a desperate man. If I have my way, she is not going to take my husband. She is not going to take over Dove."

"I just work for the woman," Claire said. "But you and me; we're supposed to be friends."

"Truth is; I don't trust anybody. Except Russell, and Daz, and Evan—when I tell him about Mireille. That's where I should be— with my real friends."

Chapter 26

EVAN ENTERED the elevator and held the door for Kylee, Russell, and Ferris. Daz popped in at the last second. They rode up to the deck of the LAX control tower, but with every foot they climbed, Evan's heart sank to an ever-decreasing low. The Dove Air jet of the century—the newly named Trudeau 2100—floundered like a wounded shark in the clear skies above Los Angeles.

"I'll hand you over to Sanchez," Ferris said as the elevator slowed to a stop. "Ten years on the job; this day has got to be her worst."

The door opened, and a woman in her mid-fifties confronted them. Sanchez stood there as if her hint-of-gray hair would turn white by day's end. Her brow creased as she gave the Dove group the once-over.

"God help us if you're the Dove PR team. That woman downstairs—what a spin master."

"So I've seen." Evan introduced himself and the others. He set his briefcase onto a console then quickly found the appropriate radar screen. He gave the screen a glance and gave a long look at the north-eastern sky. "Tell me what you got."

Sanchez slipped on a pair of glasses and urged him to an aviation chart that was taped on a wall. She slapped her palm on

Wilshire Boulevard. "Here's the aircraft now. This is where he's headed."

She waved counterclockwise over Culver City, South Gate, East LA, and Glendale. She finally stopped on Hollywood. "Speed is a hundred twenty. Turning left at twenty-four degrees a minute. Wind is zero-seven-zero at four." She looked over the rim of her glasses, directly at Evan. "Basically, you have a heavy jet in a holding pattern over LA."

"At three thousand feet," Evan said.

"Correct."

"That's not far above ground," Daz said.

"Glendale is the tallest." Sanchez jabbed her finger on the map.

"I'll need a headset," Evan said, "and a couple words with Ken." He scanned the sky through binoculars. At this range, he could not see Everest, but he knew it was approaching fast. At this range, he could see the city's freeways and side streets. Every car was barely moving; if they were moving at all.

He got the headset and clicked on the mic. "Okay, Ken. This is Evan. Whatever you need, I'm here to get it."

"Thank you, sir."

"Can you tell me what happened?"

"I'm not sure," Ken stuttered. "I was distracted. I may have extended the flaps. Then I fixed it."

Daz lowered a tower phone from his ear and told Evan in a low voice, "I've got Tom Hernandez on the line. He talked to First Officer Jee as soon as it happened. Seems Ken couldn't find his white gloves, so he left his seat for his carry-on. Ken said, 'Flaps up ten.' Jee heard 'Flaps down.' And with increasing power for a climb—"

"Starting a climb over Glendale, right? Dad's hospital."

Daz nodded. "I know; flaps down didn't make sense, but Jee didn't argue. And with flaps down, the plane goes down."

"Let me talk to Tom." Evan took the tower phone. "Tom, this is Evan. So what's going on?"

"We think the hydraulics blew out the right flap and stuck all the way down."

"And power?" Evan asked.

"You can't have full power with the flaps down. The computer won't allow it."

"Manual override?"

"None," Hernandez replied.

"How about wings level?"

"What they have now is the best they got. If they lower the left flap, they descend fast. If they bank more, they descend fast. If they—"

"I got it. Stay on the line, and we'll pass along updates." He handed the phone to Daz and balled his fist. "Their software, our plane; I must've been mad." He clicked on his mic. "Hey, Ken, how are you and Sang-Ki holding out?"

"Been better, sir. Trying to hold three thousand. Hydraulics unresponsive."

"They're losing altitude," Sanchez said.

"How much?"

Daz held up his calculator. "A hundred feet a minute."

"Pull up!" Evan raised his voice.

"Trying!" Ken replied.

"The reset didn't work," Jee said.

"What reset?" Evan asked. "Ken, what are you doing up there?"

"Power drop, ten percent."

"That woman," Daz grumbled.

"What woman?"

"Mireille told them to do a partial reset. Good idea if you're six miles high. They're skimming the trees now. That's a bad place to lose power."

"We can reset again," Ken said.

"Don't touch it!" Evan yelled then clicked off his mic. "And where is Mireille?"

No one answered. Sanchez ignored Evan and set up a TV on a vacant console. As she turned the TV on, Evan's stomach instantly churned into a hundred knots. He lost his focus and couldn't help but stare at the small screen.

"It's on all channels," Kylee said. She pointed at the fly-like dots buzzing around the Everest fuselage. "You have three news choppers and a sheriff trying to keep up."

"You didn't ban those guys?" Evan glared at Sanchez.

"It's the only close-up we have."

"That's true," Russell said. "You can see the flaps; right extended, left one straight. Software was supposed to limit it. Maintenance was supposed to change the valve. Looks like they never did." He put away his book and pushed a flash drive into the laptop.

The TV—with Sharon Nguyen—continued the report. "As of this moment, the mayor has not ordered an evacuation."

"It wouldn't help," Joe Paramis said from the news chopper. "We have gridlock on the 405 and the, uh, the 110. Same on the side streets; they're all packed, and no one's going anywhere."

"Terrorism has not been ruled out. Do we have any word on military action?"

"From News Five, we can see the sheriff's helicopter. He's flying hard to keep up. There is no sign of the, uh, the Air Force or any military."

"Once they arrive, what would you expect?"

"Hard to say, Sharon; probably get us to back away."

"We have a great feed, Joe. Stay with it."

Evan pounded his fist on the map. He spun to face his team. "This circus is about to close. Russell, tell me what we can do without resetting the computer. Daz, talk to Ken. Find out what controls they *do* have. Kylee, find Mireille. Get her butt up here."

Russell grabbed more of his drives and went back to his computer. Daz walked off with Sanchez to search for another headset.

Kylee quietly inched closer to Evan. With a low voice, she told him, "You know, your father's directly in the path."

"I know." Evan grimaced. "And so does he."

"Do you want me to call?"

"We have a million people to worry about. We can't afford a single delay."

Kylee lowered her eyes.

Evan softened his voice and gently held her elbow. "Call him. Make sure he's safe."

Kylee acknowledged with her eyes. She moved to a quiet part of the room to use the one functional phone.

Evan pulled out a calculator and studied the chart. He grabbed a pad and pen. At first, he wrote nothing. Then, in spurts, he jotted numbers and city names. With every calculation, he wrote notes, shook his head, and crumpled another sheet of paper. No college exam was ever like this.

Five sheets later, Daz came with an update. "Everest has a few controls. But unfortunately, each one sends the plane down."

"I don't believe it." Evan faced Russell. "Come on, Russell. You're saying we don't have a single knob to get the power up?"

"Trudeau software," he said. "Fly-by-wire, talk-by-wire. You can't flush a toilet without the computer's nod."

"What you have is a six hundred ton flying computer," Daz said.

Evan stared out to the window as Everest slowly came into view. "What we have is two hundred tons of jet fuel and a fireball if it hits the ground."

"First priority," Daz said. "Get that plane away from the city."

"Agreed. But how do we level the wings?"

"The Air Force," Russell said. "An F-16 could do it."

"What, and lift the wing?" Daz scowled. "Forget it. Why do you think we call it Everest? You're pushing a mountain. Believe me; it's not going to budge."

Russell crossed his arms. "Not if they shoot holes in the left wing. The fuel drains out, and suddenly we're balanced."

"You're serious," Daz moaned.

"Sure, why not?"

Evan shuddered. "One stray bullet and Everest blows up. Ken, Mr. Jee; they won't have a chance. Not to mention the people below."

"Trying to climb," Ken's voice crackled over the loudspeaker.

Kylee stood between Evan and Daz. "I don't think his arms can take it. He's pulling so hard he can barely breathe."

"The control's frozen," Daz said. "If he lets go of the yoke, he ain't gonna fall."

"He's not going to chance it," Evan said. "If you're wrong, they drop a thousand feet."

"Gentlemen," Sanchez tapped her watch, "we have twenty minutes."

"We got the math," Daz said. "And we know; Inglewood is the most probable site."

The room suddenly went silent. Evan set down his pad when he heard the elevator door open. With a gnawing feeling, he turned around. He glared at Mireille as she eased herself into the background. "Any ideas?" he shouted.

Mireille turned on her heels. She defiantly moved to a window and stared out.

"No, I didn't think so." Evan ignored Mireille and slid his arm across Daz's shoulder. "Let's do what we can to get this plane home."

Daz waved his hand toward Everest. "I'll tell ya, boss; if I was up there, I'd find some way, somehow to level those wings."

"That wouldn't help. You can fly straight, but so what. They're still dropping, they're still gonna crash."

"At least get them away from LA. At two thousand they can bail."

Kylee widened her eyes and looked at Daz. "You mean parachute?"

"The side window is removable," Evan said. "If they grab a chute and crawl out—"

"They float down like a feather," Daz said.

"Not quite. But they stay alive."

"And we lose a billion-dollar aircraft," Daz said.

"It's only money," Kylee said.

"And the jobs of, what, ten thousand workers," Evan said.

"So, what's your plan?"

"Impact, eighteen minutes," Sanchez said.

Evan shuddered. Two men aboard Everest. Over ten million men, women, and children below. It seemed a sickening prospect, no matter the perspective. He raised his binoculars. The small dot on the horizon grew larger, and Evan quickly recognized the

Everest silhouette. He stared as the aircraft zoomed across the bumper to bumper 110 freeway.

The twenty foot, frost white image of a dove emblazoned the blue tail. The gold stripes on a white fuselage looked stunning in the afternoon sun. Impressive and dazzling—for a minute. Then Everest zoomed off again to the populated flatlands of LA County.

What were the odds, Evan wondered, of saving such a beautiful aircraft? Of saving Dove Air and thousands of jobs? What were the odds of saving the city? He gazed at Kylee as she drew Everest flight circles on the map. No matter where she drew, her red lines fell over some population. No lakes, parks, or open areas. And the ocean was miles away. What kind of city was this?

Options were few, and time was running out. He looked at Daz, Russell, then back at Kylee. Was this the miracle team? Were these people his only hope? LA's only hope? He looked at Mireille, standing silently in the background. What did she have to offer, and how could she possibly help?

He looked northeast and wondered what his father would say, what he would do. There seemed only one logical choice—one desperate chance. Evan clicked on his mic. "Time to punch out, Ken. We're coming to get you."

He grabbed Kylee's marker, circled a section of the LA map, and said to Sanchez, "Evacuate this area, and get Daz a clearance!"

Evan patted Daz on the shoulder and walked him to the elevator. "You know the rules of roulette; let's see if we can beat the house."

"Are you sure?" Daz asked after he got Evan's briefing.

"I'm already sick. Let's not repeat it."

"Roger." Daz ducked inside the elevator and headed off to obey orders.

Sanchez lifted the crash phone. She worked with city officials to evacuate a five-block stretch of suburban LA.

Kylee clamped onto Evan's elbow. "You're saying Everest is going to crash?"

"The flap is locked. The computer is trash. There's not a single override. Ken and Mr. Jee are passengers now. There's no doubt; Everest is coming down. The only question is where."

"All those people on the ground?"

"We have one chance." Evan jammed his finger onto the map. "Griffith Park. It's big enough to take an impact."

"You cannot let it crash," Mireille finally spoke up. She kept her voice subdued. "We can recover and go to Paris. In a manner of speaking, we can reset and start the plan over."

"Plan? There's no plan. Everything we worked for is coming down in a ball of flames. Don't you get it, Mireille? It's over. There's not a thing we can do."

"You can't give up, Evan. We're so close."

"I'll tell you this; we're close to killing a thousand people unless you back off. Let me do my job!"

"Evan, please. You're talking about *our* lives too."

Evan scowled. He moved to a radar screen and clicked on his mic. "Listen up, Ken; help is on the way."

"Roger, sir. Tell us how to respond."

Evan studied the LA map as Kylee drew more circles. As Everest crossed the 101, he set his plan into motion.

"How do you read, Daz?"

"Loud and clear," he called from the fan-jet. "I have crossed Inglewood at seven hundred and climbing. Cable is extended. Belly-cam is operational."

"We have radar contact," Evan said. "Everest at two o'clock and two miles."

"Aircraft in sight. Big as a whale."

"Level off now."

"We're cuttin' it close," Daz said. "Cal State is now the high point."

"Glendale is coming up; another high point. Watch for towers." Evan turned to Sanchez. "How's that evac coming?"

"Police and fire are on the roll. With this traffic, it'll be tough."

"Do what you can."

"Your father's been moved," Kylee whispered.

"Thank God. I hope he doesn't see this."

"Approaching Everest," Daz said. "How about getting the news hounds to back off?"

Sanchez passed along the order.

"How's it look?" Evan asked.

"Not a scratch on the whole aircraft. Not a single dent. She is beautiful, no doubt. It's a crying shame."

Evan spoke slowly and clearly. "Okay, Ken, Sang-Ki. Listen up. We have one chance to get it right. No pressure, but you will have a split-second tolerance. Set your watch. The target is approaching."

"Target?" Ken asked.

"You're bailing out, my friend."

"Too low!" Ken yelled. "The chute is not going to work!"

"Look up," Daz said.

Kylee swung the TV for a better view as a news chopper zoomed in on the makeshift harness. Evan cringed when he saw the cable slam against the Everest cockpit window. He turned away from the TV screen and went back to the radar image.

"We understand," Jee replied.

"I see you," Daz said. "Image tracking on the fan-jet is locked on your window. Thankfully, *this* computer works."

Evan flashed the hint of a smile at Mireille. That was her software that made the difference. "Next step," Evan said, "blow out the window."

A moment later, the cockpit window sailed off and behind. The blast of air from the open window sucked out loose papers and charts. Ken faced the open window, and even with the shaky image, his face appeared terrified.

"That window and the bottled water," Russell said, "are the only two parts with a manual control."

"Now, we start the countdown," Evan said. "We have three steps. Jee leaves first. Then Ken; you lower the left flap and climb out. Got it?"

"When do we start?"

"Mr. Jee, you climb out now."

Silence, followed by jerky motions on the TV screen. Then, like a gopher in a hurricane, Jee poked his head out of the escape hatch and into the high speed wind. He madly waved his arms at Daz's harness.

Someone in the tower had set up another TV to show the fan-jet in perfect lockstep with Everest. The news helicopters kept their distance but kept the images crisp and clear.

Jee grabbed the harness and eased himself out. His chest, then his legs, then his entire body left the aircraft. He seemed a small dot against the huge fuselage. With a push, he became a human pendulum; swinging in the wind like a helpless sack of rags. He banged his chest on the aircraft skin and smashed his face against the cockpit window.

"You want me to do what?" Ken yelled into his mic.

Evan kept his eyes on the radar screen. "When I tell you, hit the flaps and get out. Grab onto Jee, and hold on tight."

"He's too far away!" Ken shouted as Jee swung out with the wind.

"Closer, Daz. Get Jee to hold on to the window."

Daz obeyed, and once again, Jee smashed the window. But on this collision, he found a grip and held on tight.

"Coming up on ten seconds," Evan said, staring at the radar. "Nine, eight, seven. Get ready to switch. Two, one, and deploy! Get out of there, Ken!"

Ken switched the flaps to full down. Suddenly, Everest lurched downward and straightened the wings. Evan watched the radar to ensure they stayed on track.

"Jee let go!" Kylee shouted as she stared at the TV.

"What do you mean?"

"Ken's still on the plane. He never got out."

"You're too high," Evan yelled to Daz. "Get lower for the pick up!"

"How far?" Daz shouted.

"How far?" Evan asked Kylee.

"Ten feet down, five back!"

"Ten down, five back!" Evan said to Daz as Everest accelerated downwards. "Stay with it, Daz!"

Everest flew low and skimmed the tall trees near Cypress Park on the approach to the target. People in the flight path were undoubtedly racing to the streets. The people in the streets were racing to their cars; but those in their cars were going nowhere. With rush hour gridlock everywhere, duck and cover seemed futile.

"He's got him!" Kylee shouted when Ken and Jee linked arms.

"You got 'em!" Evan shouted to Daz. "Pull up and get out!"

Daz veered off at the last second. Then, like a slow-motion bad dream, Everest began its torturous, traumatic demise at the border of Griffith Park. First impact came with the high-tension wires and towers that cut through the park. High voltage, heavy-gauge cables sliced through the wings and ignited a fireball that burst forward and skyward. Instantly, the beautiful, gold and white fuselage became swallowed up by flames. The airframe tumbled earthward to the oak trees and Manzanita brush.

"As far as we know," Sanchez said, "the area's clear, and no one is on the ground."

East of the impact lay the hiking trails and picnic spots. The torrent of flaming jet fuel flowed like a raging river through the area to the interstate, but mercifully stopped short of a total conflagration. An ominous mushroom cloud of red flames and black smoke rose to the clear LA skies. As Evan watched the event unfold on the TV screen, a deep, stabbing pain struck to the middle of his heart.

The image of Daz flying Ken and Jee safely away from the flames could not assuage the total sense of loss. Years of work, the dream of a revolutionary jet; gone in a heartbeat. Evan turned from the TV screens as Kylee turned down the volume on a tragic death that was televised nationwide; live and in high-def.

"You did it, Evan," Daz radioed in a soft, consoling voice. "A land-based arresting cable. No one else could've done it."

Evan clicked his mic to acknowledge what was really a coincidence, but the words never came. All he could do was hang his head low and stare at the radar screen at the point where they lost contact. He ran his fingers through the long strands of his reddish blond hair, wondering if by tomorrow, the hairs would turn gray; if by tomorrow, he would have his first heart attack.

"My father," he said. "This is bound to kill him."

He sought out Kylee for some long-overdue comfort and consoling. He wasn't sure what he would say, but he thought he would start off with a sincere apology. Then, if that worked, he would call his father with the same apology. Obviously, this would be the start of a thousand more.

He found Kylee in a corner, phone to her ear, finger raised for Evan to remain silent.

"It's Claire," she said. "Mireille's taking off."

Chapter *27*

"I BELIEVE YOU," Claire said. Her words were soft, but her message came through. "Mireille and Pierre; both of them killed Fred Mott."

"And Bob Aukram," Kylee said. "And the others."

"Yes, all of them. It makes me sick I trusted her. Don't let her get away with it."

"Wait, can you say that again?" Kylee held the phone so Evan could hear. "You know the part about Mireille and Fred."

"Well, I don't know how she killed him or why. But I do know she records her calls. That's evidence, if you can get to it before she does."

"You mean at her cabin in the hills?"

"No, her office in Grenoble. Hundreds of recordings; most of it French, most of it private. Mireille's been good to me. But I draw the line at murder." Claire sighed at the understatement. "She can fire me if she wants. I am not going to help her again."

"Unfortunately," Kylee said, "after today, none of us has a job. You don't have to worry about that."

"If she leaves the country, we won't have a chance."

"I know," Kylee said.

"I tried to stop her. I took her keys, and I called security, but …"

"But what?"

"Pierre's back," Claire said, faltering, "with his own helicopter and pilot. He picked up Mireille, and they're heading south."

"Not if I can help it. They're both guilty if you ask me. I should've shot him when I had the chance." Kylee cringed when she realized where she was and what she had said.

The nearby controller looked at her and raised an eyebrow. Then he shrugged and went back to work.

Evan took the phone. "We'll take it from here," he said to Claire. He hung up the phone, took in a deep breath, and avoided Kylee's gaze. "I don't know what's going on, but Claire has a point; if they leave the country, we got nothing. Everest went down and I want to know why. If I have to strangle Mireille to get answers, I'll do it."

He plugged in the headset, looked out the tower window, and clicked on his radio mic. "Give me your status, Daz."

"I dropped off Ken and Jee. I've got six—maybe eight— victims to pluck from the bushes. This fire is not contained."

"Roger."

"You've got Mireille's helicopter," Kylee said. "Remember; that's what she arrived in."

"Of course. How else would she do it?" Evan unplugged his headset, yanked it from his ear, and passed it to Sanchez. He dug deep into his briefcase and came up with a flash drive labeled Trudeau Anomalies; Helicopters. He patted Russell on the shoulder. "Find me a way to bring them down."

Russell took the drive and shoved it into his laptop.

Sanchez grabbed a phone and made a call. She quickly arranged for a security car and driver. Then she pointed out Mireille's helicopter. "She's flashy, and she's a pain in the neck, but at least she flew in legally and safe. This other guy though—Pierre Simon. That's his name?"

"Correct," Evan said.

"I've got ten violations on him and his pilot. Five minutes ago, he flew in with no clearance. He picked up the woman and took off. No calls at all. I got a problem with that."

"You and me both," Evan said, raising his binoculars. "But hey, if you want his pilot, there he is." He pointed at the fueling pump. He recognized the man in a Trudeau shirt as one of Pierre's trusted pilots. "Looks like Mireille took over the flying. No witnesses, I guess."

"More violations," Sanchez said. "If you catch her—"

"I know. Get in line." Evan turned to Kylee. "Coming?"

"You bet; at least to keep her honest." She walked to the elevator and held the door for Evan. "Sooner or later, the lies catch up; and so will we."

They rode the security car across the airport and pulled to a stop next to Mireille's helicopter. Evan jumped out and grabbed the keys from Claire.

"I'm so sorry," Claire said.

"You and me both." Evan stared at the southern sky as he yanked at the pilot's door. "Mireille too, when I catch her. Boy, is she going to be sorry."

Kylee settled into the co-pilot's seat and buckled up. "They already have a head start in the same helicopter and with Mireille as the pilot."

"Not a problem," Evan said. "I can out-fly that girl; any day, any aircraft."

"*Now* do we call the sheriff?"

Evan held up his finger as he switched on the radio and called the tower.

"Trudeau helicopter is five miles," Sanchez said, "heading one-five-zero."

"Roger," Evan said. "Then we'll take the same heading."

"Mexico?" Kylee asked.

"Not if I can help it."

"How about calling Homeland Security?"

"Do me a favor; forget the sheriff, forget Homeland. Use my phone and call Russell. Ask *him*, how do we catch her?"

"Roger that," she said.

Evan leaned left and made sure that Kylee's seatbelt was snug. He passed her a headset and found one for himself. Then he cranked up the engine and apologized for the noise. Even with the headset, the whine of the engine seemed immense. Kylee nodded that she was fine.

Almost immediately, he got a clearance from Sanchez. He said, "Thank you" to Sanchez and, "Hold on" to Kylee.

Kylee felt her stomach sink as the helicopter sprung into the air. She stared out as Evan swung the chopper around and flew straight for the Santa Ana Mountains. The landscape below passed by in a blur.

"Watch the horizon," Evan said. He squinted at the fast-approaching hills. "They should be a small dot, flying low."

Kylee looked ahead then moved her attention to the phone. She dialed Russell, finally got through, and said, "Evan wants us to move faster, and he wants you to tell us how." She listened and then relayed the message. "If you want to catch them, Evan, go to full torque. You might burn out the engine, but—"

"By then we should have them on the ground." He pushed the speed forward. "This is Mireille's chopper. She can afford a new engine."

"Radar contact lost," Sanchez said. "You are on your own."

"That's what I would do," Evan told Kylee. "Get under the radar. Nap of the earth."

"If they're heading south," she hung up the phone and slid her finger along the aviation chart, "that's got to be San Mateo Canyon."

"Then likewise; that's where we're headed."

At full power, the engine roar was deafening. Without air conditioning, the heat was stifling. Evan pushed the RPM beyond red-line as they dove toward the twisting canyons and dry river beds of the Cleveland National Forest. Huge stands of chaparral beckoned the helicopter rotor as they squirmed their way through the winding valleys and impossibly narrow chasms.

"Tell me you've done this before." Kylee dug her nails into the upholstery.

"Let's see; if I climb and fly straight, I can head 'em off." Evan passed over a ridge and skimmed a tall pine.

"If you kill us, Evan, I swear ..."

"Close your eyes if you want, but we're not giving up." He banked the helicopter sharply. He quickly descended and gained speed. "Watch out! We should be close!"

"There they are!" Kylee said as they rounded a bend of the dry river.

"Good eyes. Now call Russell again."

Kylee lifted the phone, although she didn't understand exactly how Russell could help. "Should I ask him for a radar report?"

"No. Ask him what he has on the Trudeau Falcon. Tail rotor maybe. This thing's squirrelly."

She pressed Redial then watched the helicopter in front of them. "Any lower they'd be scraping the trees."

"They're also beyond the red-line. That's got to be Mireille driving."

"White top, brown hair, mean look; that's her, for sure."

"Like I said; we're in for a ride." Evan kept the controls smooth and light but easily matched Mireille turn for turn as they sped through the Manzanita canyons.

Kylee sniffed the air. "What's that smell?"

"Burning oil. They're smoking; we're probably worse."

A couple more blind turns, then Kylee screamed and closed her eyes.

"That was close. See, I told you we're faster." Evan twisted the radio knob and clicked on the mic. "Let's see if they're listening ... Mireille; let's talk. You and me; one on one. We can do it here or back at the plant. Your choice."

He adjusted the volume to max but heard no reply. "Okay, ignore me. Be that way."

Kylee set the phone aside. "We lost the signal, but Russell said, 'downdraft the tail.' Something about LTE."

"Loss of tail effectiveness; good call, Russell. That's one bug they never fixed. Yeah, once in a while, that little French tail spins like mad but doesn't work. And I don't mean Mireille. Their choppers have so many problems, you wouldn't believe."

"Like the one we're in."

"Yep." Evan zoomed closer. He carefully put the rotor above the tail assembly of Mireille's helicopter. "This may get bumpy. It's formation flying the hard way."

They turned into a shallow valley, keeping tight as a pair of shoes. Suddenly, Mireille's helicopter rotated sharply to the left.

"They've lost control," Evan said. "They're going down."

"They're crashing?"

"Nope, but they can't fly for long." He backed off and watched as Mireille struggled her way to a forced landing. The helicopter shook like a wet dog and billowed gray white smoke from the engine. They headed for a rock-free space of dry sage and chamise.

"My mistake," Evan said. "Looks like they *are* crashing."

Mireille's helicopter went down hard. The rotor dug deep to the forest floor, sending dirt and debris in a tall arc above the nearby trees.

Evan circled to assess the damage. "It's a walk-away, but she's going to be mad."

"Finally, we get answers. And believe me, Pierre's got the story."

"Likewise Mireille."

Evan found a small clearing uphill of the downed helicopter. He eased between swaying branches of chaparral and landed on the loose dirt.

As he shut down the engine, Kylee thanked him for stopping the noise. Her head felt clear again, and she was grateful for the silence. She passed him the phone and said, "Sorry, no bars."

"Maybe I should've kept the sat' phone." Evan frowned then pointed at a thicket of chamise. "Anyway, they're below that brush ... Shall we?" He climbed out, dropped the keys to his pocket, and slammed the door behind.

Kylee scouted a path through the low hanging branches of Manzanita and chamise. As they eased down the slope, she pointed at her feet. "You see, Evan; practical shoes. Mireille won't get far in this wilderness."

"If she's smart, she won't leave the chopper. She may be hurt, and this is not a place to get stranded."

Shortly, they came across sliced branches and the glint of a broken rotor. As they stumbled around a thicket of sage, the crumpled tail and wrinkled cabin came into view.

"No sign of them," Kylee said.

"Mireille!" Evan called out. He scanned the hills. "Time to go home! Hide-and-seek is a game for kids!"

Kylee moved to the shattered cockpit and peered inside. "She left her jacket but took the old man. No blood, but no doubt; they're shook up bad."

Evan studied the dry acres around him. There was nothing but silence and dense brush with a million places to hide. He placed his hand on Kylee's shoulder. "If you had to escape, which way would you head?"

She scanned the same area. "I used to hike these hills. There are only two ways out. Down there, you get most of your trails." She pointed across the shallow valley.

"The other way?"

"Your helicopter. Any other path is a dead-end."

"Yeah, that makes sense." Evan stood on a boulder and searched the valley and the dry river bed. Then he looked upslope to the good chopper. Then he turned right. "That's where she's gone," he said, gesturing that direction.

"No way," Kylee said. "She'd have to be mad."

"And your point?"

Kylee climbed a taller boulder and gazed across the hill. She shielded the sun from her eyes and shook her head. "Yeah, there they are; Mireille and Pierre. How pathetic. Looks like they're trying to circle us and come in above the chopper."

"They won't get far. Believe me; they've got no stamina and no sense of direction."

"What a day." Kylee set her hands on her hips. "At least now, we have the chance of satisfaction."

Any hint of a trail had long-ago vanished. Nevertheless, they made short work of catching up. Loud, crackling footsteps and a slow pace made Mireille and Pierre much too easy prey. A short scramble up a brush-covered hill, and suddenly all four were face to face. Mireille and Pierre defiantly stood in place, seemingly exhausted or struck with the realization that they had nowhere to go.

Mireille stared at the ground. She wore an oil smudge on her forehead, a dark swelling on her chin, a tear on her blouse, and the hint of wrinkles by her green eyes. The fashion icon was nowhere near.

Evan lifted her chin with his finger, but she kept her eyes lowered.

It's finished," he told her. "You, me, Dove, Trudeau. Everything's gone. When Everest crashed, that sealed the deal. We close the doors and shut down the plant. What happens now; who knows? But you don't see me running away, you don't see me hiding. I thought you were better than that. I thought you had some pride, some dignity. I guess I thought wrong."

"You can't say that." She finally looked up. "It's not fair to me or our customers. They saw what happened. They saw the pilot. He snapped and tried to kill himself. You can't blame that on Everest."

"Customers?" Evan laughed.

"The plane is solid. We can sell it regardless of what happened today."

Kylee threw up her palms. "I can't believe what I'm hearing. How can you talk about work? Mireille, you're going to jail. Forget Everest. Cigarettes and a young body; that's what you'll be selling."

"What are you talking about?"

"We got the evidence on Fred, and Bob, and the crews of the Mojave flights. You pulled the trigger. You brought them down. That's murder, and there's no way out. You're going back and you're getting charged."

"Are you referring to Pierre's story? I don't blame him for what he said."

"Story? What story?"

"You held a gun," Mireille said. "He knew what you wanted to hear, so he told you. He was scared; scared for his life. He would say anything to stay alive."

Pierre shrugged. "What could I do?"

"The gun was my own protection," Kylee said. She glared at Pierre. "And what he confessed; he volunteered. All of it true. The eyes don't lie."

"Pierre is not afraid of heights," Mireille said, "but he is afraid of guns. He felt duress."

"Not buying it, Mireille. Pierre was shaking like a baby on that cliff. If you don't believe me, we can hike over there." She motioned at a ridge. "There's a cliff twice the size."

Pierre blinked and swallowed hard.

Mireille stood firm. "Pierre owns a helicopter, and he knows how to fly. How can he be afraid of heights?"

"That's enough." Evan held up his hand. "I don't know what's going on, but between here and France, we have plenty of witnesses. Pierre, I appreciate your honesty, and so will the sheriff. Now, if you don't mind." Evan motioned downhill toward the good helicopter.

Mireille grumbled but straightened her blouse and steadied her feet. She began a slow, unsteady downhill walk. She kept quiet and well behaved for at least a few yards. Then she stepped on a branch and grumbled again. Ankle twist or not, she came to a standstill. One more delay of many.

Evan was not fazed. "Go ahead and take it slow, Mireille. From this point on, we've got nothing but time."

Mireille said nothing as though words—finally—had failed her. Instead, she braced herself against a tree. Casually, as if to recover her footing, she took off her shoe and dropped out the spec of a twig. She slipped on the shoe and then fixed her hair and top. So predictable.

Then, with a less than casual move, she reached behind the tree and snagged her hidden purse. She pulled out a small black revolver. That was not expected.

Evan's eyes widened. "Okay, maybe you do mind. We'll talk some more, if that's what you want."

"I'm sorry, Evan. We are not returning to Los Angeles or to the sheriff. We did nothing wrong. I can prove it. In France, that is. Why won't you listen?"

"Leaving the country is not going to help." Evan lifted his palms. "Deal with it in California. Do not make it worse."

"You give me no choice. The authorities in America will not listen. I honestly must leave; for the truth, you see."

"Mireille, please." Evan carefully raised his hand to accept the gun. "We'll take you home to France if you want. But not this way. Give me the gun, and I assure you; I will listen."

"You were the one man I believed in; the only man who understood. Please understand me. I cannot return to LA. Not now. Maybe not ever."

"Whatever you want; it's yours—*if* you hand over the gun. I'll give you a trade; the chopper keys for Mexico." He pointed at his pocket.

Hard to say if Mireille was listening or not. Her faraway gaze held no clue. Slowly, she lowered the gun, halfway to the ground. She faltered and shook her head. She muttered something, possibly French, and twitched her finger.

With an ear popping bang, the gun went off. Evan staggered back. He clutched his thigh and winced. "You shot me?" He stumbled to his knees next to Pierre.

Pierre stared wide-eyed.

"I'm so sorry, my love," Mireille said. "I never meant to hurt you. I never thought it would come to this."

"Oh my God!" Kylee cried and dropped to Evan's side. She cradled his head and pointed an accusing finger at Mireille. "What have you done? He gave you everything, and this is what you do?"

"You're wrong. I offered him the chance of a lifetime. I did all the giving. I took all the risks. Evan—all he had to do was come along for the ride."

"It's always you, isn't it? You call the shots. You make the rules. Well, not anymore. I don't care if you have a gun. Evan is my husband, and you'll never change that. Never!"

Mireille sneered at Kylee then waved the revolver. "What, this? You ignorant woman. I don't need this to get what I want. Evan, Pierre, or any man; with a simple smile I can lead them to bed. What do you expect? They will do anything for sex. What kind of wife are you anyway? You have no idea how men behave."

Evan scowled. "Don't talk to her like that. She's more of a wife than you could ever be." He pinched his eyes closed with the burning pain. Then he glared at Mireille. "Kylee had you pegged from the start. You're nothing but a user. You lie, steal, and murder to get what you want. And now we can prove it."

"Doesn't matter," Mireille said. "Soon enough, I'll be in France. Prove whatever you want; you can't touch me there."

Kylee went face to face with Mireille. "You're in America now, and I'll give you a piece of my mind."

"Don't be crazy!" Evan shouted. "She has a gun, for God's sake."

"One minute; allow me that, and I'm done." Kylee nodded toward Pierre. "Give him the gun. I promise I won't touch you; I won't raise a hand. But I got something to say, and I don't want *that* in my face." She carefully pointed.

Mireille remained silent.

"Exit interview, Mireille; I deserve it. It's the last day on the job. You can look at me, or if you're too afraid, go hide in the shadows. But you're going to hear me no matter where you stand."

Mireille grinned, patronizing in a way, but she eased over to Pierre. She told him as she passed him the gun, "Watch him and her. She's been nothing but trouble, but what's one minute more?"

She moved a safe distance and faced Kylee. "Very well, speak your mind. But fair warning; I've heard it before. With American women, it's always the same; blame the company or the boss. Blame the man or woman in charge. Blame anyone but yourself. But please proceed; tell me who's at fault for your problems?"

"What can I say, Mireille; it's true. Without a doubt, you are the biggest pain I have. From the moment I met you—from the moment I heard about you—I knew sooner or later; we'd get to this point. Face to face, with me telling you exactly what a fraud you are. No surprise, I'm sure. All that eavesdropping; you knew how I felt months ago. What did I call you? Liar, cheater, murderer? That was behind your back, or so I thought. You were good, Mireille, I'll grant you that. You knew what I thought, and you didn't blink. We worked side by side like nothing was happening."

Kylee glanced at Pierre, who was still holding the gun on Evan and standing close. She turned to Mireille and gave her a slight grin. "Of course, what you didn't know is how—or when—I'd catch you. You didn't know that I never quit. Yeah, despite what you did, I never gave up on Fred—or Evan. You really thought I'd quit my marriage. Ironic, isn't it? Turns out, you actually helped us—helped me, that is.

"Until you came along, I had no clue what Evan did at work. For the most part, I didn't care. All I knew was I didn't see him that much, and that was a problem. But now, I see him at work. I see how important his work is—to the company, the community, his family, whatever. I was selfish back then. But not anymore. Thanks to you, Mireille, I'll be with Evan no matter what." She glanced at Evan and saw him smile back, or trying to smile though clenched teeth.

"At least you still have Pierre," she told Mireille. "He'll be with you no matter what. What is it you said; a little sex, or the promise of it, and men follow you anywhere? That's probably true. For some men, I agree. Take Pierre, for instance. If I gave him the hint of sex, he'd do anything I want. Even now; all I have to do is take my shirt off." She unfastened the top button. "And Pierre would ignore you or anything you say. A few more buttons," she undid the next one, "and I'd have him exactly where I want. I mean, that's what you implied, yes? You're not the only one with a good body." She spread her shirt and popped the third button.

Mireille popped open her eyes; undoubtedly perplexed and no doubt, expecting a trap. She opened her mouth as if to speak, but before she stammered the first word, a shot rang out.

Kylee jumped at the noise. She quickly calmed herself when she looked at Evan. Thankfully, he held the gun, barrel pointed skyward. He pushed Pierre away and narrowed his eyes as if to signal the end of the turnabout.

Kylee smiled. "Thanks, Mireille. There's one thing you taught me; some men—like some French women—are predictable. Evan, though; you were a little slow. I had one more button. After that, I didn't know what I would do."

Evan grimaced his apology as Kylee buttoned her shirt.

"Now what?" Mireille muttered.

"Same as before. We fly home, talk to the sheriff, and take it from there. I know what you did to Bob and Fred. I know you killed the flight crews. You'll pay for what you did; no question about it. So look around you, Mireille. This is your last taste of freedom."

Kylee knelt by Evan. She gently lifted his pants at the bullet hole. "I've seen worse," she told him. "The exit wound's clean, and it missed the femoral by an inch. That's got to hurt though."

"I've felt worse."

"With an hour at the hospital, you'll be fine."

"There's a small problem," Pierre grumbled.

"Sorry, Pierre," Kylee said. "Where you're going, expect some *big* problems."

Pierre stared at the sky.

Evan looked up and sniffed the air. "You did shut off the fuel?"

"It did not enter my mind," Mireille said.

"No, I suppose it wouldn't."

Kylee gazed at the thin fingers of smoke overhead. "Their chopper's on fire." She grabbed the gun from Evan and faced Pierre. "I knew it; I should've shot you the first chance."

"It is not a trick," Pierre said. "I did *not* start the fire."

Kylee raised the barrel and took aim at his head.

Pierre trembled and raised his hand to protect his face. "It's not me. I didn't do it."

"Sorry, Pierre. I don't believe you." She squeezed the trigger and the hammer moved.

"It's true," he stammered. He widened his eyes and looked at Mireille. "Ask her. She'll tell you. We didn't do it."

Kylee aimed the gun at Mireille. "If you're pulling another stunt—"

"I swear," Pierre said. "It is not our fault."

Kylee aimed at Pierre and narrowed her eyes.

He turned away. "*Mon Dieu, s'il vous plait.*"

Kylee relaxed her grip and raised the barrel skyward. She knelt by Mireille's purse and searched it. "No more guns and no phone. So where is it?"

"My phone?" Mireille said. "Regretfully, I left it in the helicopter."

"Regretfully, we're in a bind. Now we're stuck." Kylee sneered. She passed the gun to Evan. "If he blinks, shoot 'em both."

Evan held the gun tightly as Kylee climbed the ridge for a better view.

"We can work this out," Mireille said, almost inaudibly.

Kylee shouted through the chaparral, "Oh, and if *she* opens her mouth, shoot 'em both!"

After a quick scan of the heavy brush above and below, she returned to Evan. She tried to remain calm. "Here's what we got; the fire's spreading along the canyon—about a quarter-mile from us and moving fast. I'd say that the good chopper is in the path, and I'd say that *we're* in the path. Yeah, Pierre, we do have a slight problem."

"Can we make the chopper?" Evan looked through the trees but couldn't see much beyond the smoke. "I can still fly if—" He was suddenly cut off by a huge, rumbling boom.

"I was afraid of that," Kylee said, looking at Evan. "You parked way too close to them. That was our ride that just blew up. Now there's only one way out."

She studied the brush-covered hill and frowned. She took the gun from Evan and waved it at Pierre. "You, Pierre; grab his left arm. Mireille; grab his right. We have one chance. And that's straight up the mountain."

"Then what?" Pierre asked. "It's kilometers to the road."

"We reach the top, and it's downhill to the trails. It's not that far."

"Let's get moving," Evan said.

Kylee poked Pierre in the ribs with the barrel of the gun. "This is what, our third fire today? That's a bad habit, Pierre."

"Accidents happen."

"How about this for an accident; gun misfires, Frenchman dies."

Pierre quickly wrapped Evan's arm around his shoulder. Mireille grudgingly helped as they climbed the ever-steepening terrain. She was less than useful in her French Louboutin heels.

After a few slips and slides, they reached the halfway point. Mireille slowed her pace and said, "This is not working. The fire is too close. The hill is too steep."

Kylee already knew where the fire was. Gray plumes streamed overhead, drifting to ground level and filling the air with choking smoke. From the back of her neck, she felt the heat of approaching flames and the sting of dropping embers. That diversion was bad enough, but the crackling of burning brush shifted to a dull roar. Conversation became a chore. Staying understood became a challenge.

Despite the pain, despite the distraction, she had one thought; "Keep moving!"

"What's the point?" Mireille said. "Even if we come out alive, I have nothing left."

"Quit whining. We're almost there."

"Lock me up, and I might as well be dead." Mireille relaxed her grip on Evan's arm and lowered her head.

"Save it for later, Mireille."

"I can't live like that. You take away my friends, my family, my company; what do I have? What do *we* have?"

Mireille slowly turned from Evan. She let her arms go limp as she ignored the tears that fell down her cheek. She seemed tired and weak. The heat rash and spots on her face had aged her five years on their short hike. She seemed dazed and confused. Then she seemed irrational. Like a sleepwalking child, she walked straight down the hill toward the approaching fire.

Kylee raised her aim and shouted, "Get back here, Mireille! I'll shoot! So help me!"

"Let her go." Evan put his hand on the barrel. "She can't help us now. And you know we can't stop her."

Kylee let her arms go limp. She watched Mireille slowly and unsteadily disappear into the smoke and trees. "Useless woman. What good did she ever do?"

She latched onto Evan's elbow and watched him stare at the hill long after Mireille had walked out of view. She blamed the smoke for the watering of his eyes.

Evan took a deep breath then coughed a deep, hacking cough. He seemed to snap back to reality. He steadied his feet on the loose gravel, looked up at the steepening terrain, and beckoned for Pierre to help.

Pierre reluctantly placed Evan's arm across his shoulder. "We can use some help." He looked at Kylee.

"What, so you can grab the gun? I don't think so."

"We'll die if you don't help."

Evan motioned at a stand of Manzanita. "Get rid of the gun. He can't grab it if you don't have it."

"Without this, he'll run. I know he will." She waved the gun at Pierre to prod him forward.

"I won't run. I promise." Pierre gawked at the approaching wall of flames. He raised his voice. "Look behind you. What choice do you have?"

Kylee didn't have to look to be reminded. The noxious smoke and the dull roar overwhelmed her senses and robbed her of a clear and focused mind. "Okay," she finally said. "Just keep your hands where I can see 'em."

She slipped out the five bullets and two empty shells. She stuffed the bullets into her pocket then shoved the gun to the small of her back. Then she helped Evan. "How are you doing?"

"I've had better days."

"Same here."

Pierre struggled to grip branches with one hand while supporting Evan with the other. The loose, dry gravel made secure footing nearly impossible. Pierre slipped to his knee and moaned. He quietly said, *"Tout le monde son fou. Je regret, je dois partir."*

With an awkward duck and twirl, Pierre slid from under Evan's arm and pushed away. With no support, Evan fell to the ground. Pierre flailed his arms like a sprinter on ice. He scrambled on the loose stones. He grabbed branches and boulders and dug his French shoes for any hint of a foothold. Despite his age and despite his constant groaning, he found a foothold and scurried up the hill. He easily outpaced the flames and Kylee.

"Oh, no, you don't!" Kylee frantically reached to her hip and yanked out the gun. By the time she loaded a single round and fired, Pierre was long gone. She loaded the four remaining rounds, but with no target, all she could do was kneel beside Evan and cry.

"I love you," Evan softly said.

"Don't say that!" Kylee angrily replied.

"Listen to me, Kylee."

"I am not going to listen to you!" She stood and yanked at Evan's arm. "Get up! We're almost there!"

"Let me say this, please." He didn't try to stand.

Kylee violently shook her head and refused to look at him. Tears fell from her cheek, and she fell to her knees. She let go of his arm and buried her face in her palms. She took shallow breaths; only partly because of the surrounding smoke.

"This whole mess," Evan said, setting his hand on her shoulder. "It was my fault from the start."

"No," Kylee said. The roar of the fire made each word nearly inaudible.

"Everest is gone, the company's gone, everyone's gone; except you. That is so like you. No matter how I mess up, you stay beside me."

"Where would I go?" She brushed away a tear but kept her eyes low.

"I should've listened to you. From the start, I should've listened. I brushed off your visions of Fred and Bob, and that was wrong. I'm sorry. And I'm sorry that my apology is a bit late. For what it's worth; you were right about Mireille."

Evan paused as more timber exploded in the heat of the downslope fire, throwing sparks and more smoke overhead. "And right about me—the typical man. She fed me a line and I fell for it. I'm a sucker; that's for sure. I should've backed off when I had the chance. I followed her and look where it got us." He winced.

"And I'm sorry, Evan. I know how you feel, but honestly, I don't want to talk about her. I don't want to *think* about her. Please don't mention her name. You and me; we're in a bind. Let's talk about us."

"I know what you're thinking." Evan squinted as he lifted his chin. "But you can't stay."

"I'm not leaving."

"I refuse to argue," he said, raising his voice. "If you can walk, you can leave. And if you can leave, you have to do it. That's the one thing I'm counting on. You've seen it all, Kylee; from the crash in the Sierras to Mireille's bungling today. That's why you have to walk. Go home and tell them what happened; start to finish."

"Tell who? Paul? He already knows about Pierre. He probably knows about her."

"It doesn't matter. He's too weak to follow up."

"You're just saying that."

"You're strong, Kylee; don't assume everyone else is. We need you—*I* need you—to see this through. No one else can do it. No one else can pull it together; not Dad, not Daz, Russell, not even the police. No one cares as much as you do. Mireille was smart, but she can't get the better of us. Don't let it happen. Don't let her keep control."

"Smart women don't kill themselves," Kylee said. "Or others. She made plenty of mistakes. So did Pierre. If he gets out of this, he goes straight to jail. There's plenty of evidence. They don't need me."

"Wait. What'd you just say?" Evan tugged at her shoulder.

"I said they don't need me or you to put him away. I'm staying; that's what I'm saying. I'm not going to argue."

"Of course, now it makes sense." Evan dropped his hand to his lap.

"None of this makes sense." Kylee slowly turned his way and saw him staring downhill. She moved her gaze from his eyes to his knees. "We're together; that's all that matters."

"No, you don't understand. What you said about Mireille; that was totally true. I know her; she would never kill herself. She wouldn't walk off, not without a fight."

"What do you mean?"

"She's too smart for that. Don't you see it? She's playing us again. It's another trick to throw us off. Suicide nothing. She has a phone, a radio, or something. It's hidden on herself, in the woods, or somewhere."

"No tricks, Evan. Please don't push me away."

"I mean it; she's out there, laughing at us, calling for a ride. If I've learned anything; it's that Mireille's a magician. She's fooling us again."

Kylee shook her head. "I checked her purse, remember? She said she left it at the chopper."

Evan squeezed her shoulder and begged. "I don't care what she said. Please, Kylee, don't argue. Just find her! Get her phone and get us out! We can still do it."

"I want to believe you, but—"

"Listen, even if we have one chance in ten, we have to try. Any odds are better than sitting on the dirt."

Kylee's heart raced, if just for a moment. One chance would be welcomed, but the odds seemed impossibly long. "Where?" she asked. "Where do I find her? She could be anywhere."

"You don't have to guess," he said. "She disappeared down there, so—" The loud crackle of burning chaparral muffled Evan's last words. He struggled to his feet. He tugged at Kylee, encouraging her to stand on her own shaky legs. He brushed back tangled strands of hair from her tear stained face. He kissed her cheek then aimed his finger uphill. "We can do this. Let's finish what we came for. That's where she's gone."

Kylee stood in place, torn between staying with Evan or running away as fast as she could. Her mind raced with a hundred thoughts, but she took tenuous steps away from Evan and up the hill. "I'll find her," she said, half crying. "If that'll help, I'll do it."

She forced her hand to grab at a branch. The rough bark dug into her palm, but she held on and pulled herself up. She slipped and nearly fell. She recovered, then stumbled and clawed her way up the makeshift path. The upper ridge seemed impossibly far. Even so, Mireille would find her way there and wait for a pickup. Kylee would be right behind—or die trying.

The increasing smoke stung her eyes and blurred her vision. She climbed faster to put distance between her and the fire; and between her and Evan.

Where would Mireille go? If she was smart, she wouldn't be here in the first place. Kylee saw miles of brush ahead, acres of fire behind; she didn't know which way to turn. Should she follow her instincts or think like Mireille? Or should she trust herself and rush back to Evan? Either way, she feared nothing but trouble. She pushed forward until she climbed to a small clearing. Then her nightmare took a turn for the worse.

There, cowering like a wounded dog in the shadow of a granite boulder, Pierre sat silent but shaking. He seemed disoriented by the blinding smoke and the chaos of the surrounding fire. He recoiled and raised his hand to his face.

Kylee pulled the gun from her jeans and took careful aim. "At this range, I can't miss."

Pierre lowered his hand and pushed himself to his feet. He pushed his chin to his chest. As he stood, Kylee understood his dilemma. He had torn his pants at the knee and ripped his flesh to the bone. A long stream of blood flowed to his shoe. Apparently, he had slipped on the sharp, uneven rocks, and now his situation was no better than Evan's.

"I can still walk," he said. "With some help."

Kylee stared at his pant leg and snarled, "You're no use at all. You can't walk. You can't help Evan. What good are you?"

"In court," he said. "I can help you there. You need evidence. I can get it. Others are involved. Not just Mireille."

"I don't need anything. I can shoot you right now. Not one person would blame me."

"Please."

Kylee shuddered. The choking smoke, the hot stinging wind, and the steady roar of the advancing flames overpowered every sense in her pushed to the limit body. She squinted at Pierre, as he trembled in front of her. She shouted, "You know, I don't have to shoot. The fire will do it for me!"

"*Mon Dieu*, don't leave me."

She studied the upper ridge and figured Pierre was right; they could both make it to safety if she set aside her gut-level emotions. She asked herself; what would Evan expect in a case like this? She answered herself by slowly lowering the gun and pushing out the cylinder.

Then she wondered why she had a gun at all. She felt totally out of control; with the weapon or not. Help Pierre then find Mireille; that seemed her only choice.

She paused before dropping out the bullets. While searching her mind for the next step, she felt a push from behind—a hard push that knocked her off balance. She recovered her footing then spun around. She snapped the cylinder closed and fired two rounds at the sage and brush. There was too much wind and noise to hear footsteps. There was too much smoke in her eyes to see clearly. She squinted, trying to find a target.

"Mireille, you don't have a chance! I'll shoot you on the spot." Again she was hit from behind. She spun to face Pierre. "Pierre, that was your last mistake."

She raised the barrel level with his face and watched him squirm like a trapped animal. He meekly and desperately pointed to the sky as if to tell her that God was watching. Against her judgment, Kylee glanced up. But in a moment of revelation, she did not see the face of God but something equally endearing, equally inviting.

Hovering just above the treetops and avoiding the gray fingers of smoke was the godsend image of Daz in Evan's fan-jet. The near-silent machine swung side to side over the small hillside clearing, dangling a thirty-foot cable and a life saving harness. Kylee blinked, and when the harness hit her from the front, she assured herself that the image was real.

A wave of pure joy spread throughout her body when she realized that there was still a chance to save Evan—a good chance at that. She stared downslope to the fast approaching flames and vowed to walk over burning coals to reach him and get him out. When she looked up to wave at Daz, she saw him drop a handie talkie to her open arms. The high-speed catch stung her palms, but she couldn't help but laugh with joy.

"Daz, what a beautiful sight you are," she called on the radio. "How on earth did you find us?"

"I figure, where there's smoke, Kylee is close behind. Was I right or what?"

Kylee grinned. "Do me a favor; take this guy and drop him on the ridge." She pointed as Daz watched her with the fuselage camera.

"How far up do you want me to drop him; broken legs or smashed head?"

Pierre grimaced, and Kylee clarified. "You know what I mean. We've got him, Evan, and me."

"And Mireille?"

"Gone."

"Understood."

Kylee heaved the gun as far as she could into the chaparral thicket. She quickly swung the harness to Pierre then took off down the hill to save Evan. She stumbled and tripped more than once on her headlong dash through the brush, but she retraced her steps without a single error. Soon enough, she found him huddled by a granite slab. He breathed uncomfortably through an improvised mask torn from his undershirt.

"Are you out of your mind, Kylee? You're supposed to be on the ridge." He ripped off his mask and waved his arms.

"Listen to this!" Kylee shoved the radio near his face and shouted up to Daz. "Look south. Tell me if you see the rock tower."

"Affirmative," Daz said. "I got one to drop off, two for pickup. On my way."

"We're going home!" Kylee cried and hugged Evan. "We're going home!"

She gazed upwards and gave a silent prayer of thanks for the man above—and to the Lord above.

Evan wrapped his arms around her, kissed her, and let a tear fall from his eye.

The smoke obscured much of the sky, but within moments, they dangled and spun at the end of a three-story, life-saving cable. They held tightly to each other, grateful for another breath on earth. They landed on the ridge, released the harness, and embraced for the longest time. Right now, nothing else mattered.

***

The sun had just dipped below the horizon when Evan was released from Good Samaritan hospital. Kylee had helped to patch up the bullet wound, that—away from the fire—was not life threatening and not much more than a burning, throbbing nuisance.

Afterward, she drove Evan and Russell to a small hill that overlooked Griffith Park. Daz and Claire, with Jean-Petit, followed on a borrowed Harley.

They knew that the reporters would quickly swarm for a story, and this seemed the right time and place to figure one out—if any story was possible. Kylee said it might take years to understand a fraction of what really happened.

Claire set Jean-Petit onto the ground. He circled once around Evan's ankles then stood firm. Daz wrapped his arms around Claire's waist while she leaned her head on his shoulder. They both gazed to the west. Kylee stood by Evan's bad leg and held him tightly for mutual support.

Russell stood by himself, offering little more than a shake of the head and the aimless shuffling of feet. When his cell phone rang, he excused himself, walked off, and answered it.

Kylee was sure that Evan's phone would ring nonstop for days. But for now, he had switched it off, appreciating a few moments of quiet reflection.

Evan took a deep breath, exhaled, and gazed at the news helicopters that hovered over the Everest wreckage. "No one said it would be easy. What did I say about one mistake?"

"End of an era," Daz said. "Never thought I'd see it."

"I have no idea what I'm going to tell the media." Evan shook his head. "An accident, yeah. But who, what, and how; that's what they want to know. That's what we all want to know. I hate this game. And Dove; what am I going to tell the guys? Do we shut down or start over? Or, like Mireille said; pretend it never happened? Who knows? To be honest, right now I have only one thing on my mind." He shifted his weight, and Kylee helped to steady him.

He faced Kylee. "After all this—I hate to say it—but you know; I feel pretty good. Delirious maybe. I'll blame the smoke. But my head has never been clearer. Priorities; that's what it comes down to. That's what matters the most. For me, it's this; I still have a wife, a home, and a cabin for the weekends." He looked at his feet. "And a dog. After that, then I worry about work. Yeah, as long as I don't look over there, I'd say I'm doing fine."

Kylee smiled.

Claire softly said, "Mireille—what a shame."

"They found her," Daz said. "Alive but in shock. Another minute or two, it would've been too late. You can thank Russell for finding her. She actually did have a phone and a GPS. And you can thank Pierre for giving us the code."

"Shock or not, at least they arrested her," Kylee said. "Like Pierre and those guys at the apartment; they're all getting charged—just like I said. We got the sheriff on board now. With him and the FBI, we'll get 'em all. Unfortunately, a little late. "

She scanned the remains of the Everest jet. "Excuse me; way late. But still, I have to tell you; Evan's not the only one who feels good. Hey, I'm sorry—but right now, there's no other place I'd rather be." She turned and gave Evan a kiss on the cheek.

Evan squeezed Kylee's waist then looked at the wreckage. "Mireille—I still can't believe it. She had enough talent; she didn't have to—"

"Hey, Evan. Your father's on the phone." Russell stepped beside them, switched on the speaker, and handed the phone to Evan. "He's been calling for the last hour. He says; all of you—listen close."

"Like I said; this is going to kill him," Evan whispered to Kylee. He shook his head then spoke softly to Paul. "We were hit hard, Dad. But we've seen trouble before. Bottom line; we start over. We have good ideas, good workers—loyal workers. Believe me, I've seen it. It's not as bad as it looks."

"You bet we start over," Paul said. "That demo flight was just what we needed."

"I understand; you've got a right to be angry."

"Angry? Are you crazy? The orders are flooding in."

"Sarcasm then. *That*, I can deal with."

"You don't get it." Paul cleared his throat and carefully spoke. "It's not Everest they want. It's your flying car; the Mac-1 fan-jet."

"What?"

"Close to a hundred orders now. Easily a thousand coming. They don't care what it costs; they just want it now." Paul laughed. "I knew it, Evan; one way or another, you'd have a hit."

Kylee, Russell, Claire, and Daz huddled close to the phone and kept quiet to hear every word.

"The Mac-1?" Paul asked. "That's what you call it?"

"That's the family name," Evan said.

"The flying machine of the twenty-first century; that's what I call it."

"With your help, Dad," Evan said as he hugged Kylee, "I know we can do it."

"Start of an era, son. Start of a new era."

THE END